STRAY CAT STRUT

STRAY CAT STRUT

— BOOK 2 —

RAVENSDAGGER

Podium

Podium

STRAY CAT STRUT

CHAPTER ONE

HEARTWARMING

I shifted.

Something poked at my back, above my ribs. Had Lucy snuck into my bed again? I loved the girl, but sometimes she was all elbows and knees and a real pain to sleep next to.

Twisting a little, I found myself rolling onto my stumpy side, only to run into a problem.

I had an arm.

Or rather, a second arm.

Some of the sleep-addled grogginess faded as I turned onto my back and blinked up at an entirely unfamiliar ceiling. There wasn't any cracked drywall above me. Instead, I could see a ceiling with recessed LEDs through the gauzy curtains of a four-poster bed.

There was no way in fuck I was back at the orphanage.

"What time's it?" I mumbled as I looked around. I was still dressed. At least I had pants on, plus a jacket that left my stomach bare. My uncovered feet felt just shy of chilly.

It's six forty in the morning. Your daily allotment of points has come in. Your total is sitting at 9,283 points.

I started a little at the voice that . . . had come from somewhere in my head. Memories came back. The museum, the sky tearing open, and aliens raining down around us. Getting impaled and becoming a samurai. Myalis guiding and trolling me. The kittens flying off to safety. A few interminable and stressful hours spent trying to save people.

"Crap," I said as I sat up on the edge of the bed. I'd made a mess of the topmost blankets. My invisibility jacket was covered in alien blood and nonalien blood and a lot of dust and crap. It's a miracle Lucy even let me into the room with it on.

Another memory returned.

"Did I sleep through sex?" I asked with mounting horror.

You didn't get far enough to make your statement even remotely true.

"Fuck me."

That is, in fact, what didn't happen.

I groaned as I got up. Whisper, my stealth crossbow, rested against the wall next to the door. None of the kittens had grabbed it, at least. I still had my back-mounted guns and tail on, and a hand cannon tucked under my new cybernetic arm.

"I'm a mess," I said.

I'd offer you a self-cleaning system, but the washrooms in this place are . . . adequate.

I took off my jacket and flung it onto a sofa. Someone would need to clean the sofa—someone who wasn't me. "Yeah," I said. "Let's see if we can get some food first. And check on the kittens."

The penthouse we had was divided into little rooms. Lucy had dumped me in the big suite the night before, but from the open doors I passed on the way to the kitchen area, the other suites seemed pretty damned luxurious too. The wide-open living area, with its sofas and curved television, took up a space longer than a bus.

Everything was done in marble and wood, with a pinch of gilding here and there. I would have called it ostentatious, but somehow it wasn't. Obviously, they'd hired some decorators to make the place look like an old-money palace.

Nose and little Tim were knocked out on the couch, the TV playing some samurai cartoon on mute.

I elected not to bother them as I moved around an island bigger than my room back at the orphanage and yanked open the fridge. The damned thing was stocked. I grabbed some cereal of the colorful sort from one of the cupboards and an expensive glass bottle of genuine cow milk from the fridge door.

I poured myself a bowl of Longb'O's for irony's sake, then watched as all the little rings glowed on contact with the milk. "Neat," I said.

This food provides literally negative nutrition.

I munched through a mouthful of sugary goodness. "Tastes great, though." We could never afford the cool junk food back at the orphanage. I set the box on its side and watched the ads for neat toys scroll under a grinning image of a familiar samurai.

The bastard had been airbrushed—I just knew it.

"Cat?"

I looked up to see Bargain standing next to the island. He was a bit short, only his head visible above the benchtop.

"Hey," I said.

He looked at me, shrewd little eyes taking me in. "What would you give me not to wake everyone up?" he asked.

Some things never changed. I smiled big and wide at him, pulled my Trench Maker from under my arm, and let the heavy handgun clunk onto the top of the island. "This gun can be loaded with any kind of bullet," I said. "Samurai magic shit, you know? How much do you wanna bet there are some specifically made to deal with annoying little shits?"

"That's a good deal," he said before running off.

I think we're going to have a weapons safety lesson in the near future.

"The safety's on," I muttered before returning to my cereal. I had the enviable problem of running out of glowing rings before running out of milk, which meant I was obligated to refill the bowl.

The next ones to show up were the Twins, and while I was pretty cool with Alpha and Omega, the two of them took one look at me before squealing, "Cat's awake!"

Before I could eat any more of my cereal, they were joined by bleary-eyed kittens spawned from all over. Spark and Tim came over, then Nemo and Nose and Bargain, who still seemed cowed. It was too bad the others weren't.

I listened to their babbled questions for all of a minute before I felt a stress headache coming on. "Would you all shut up?!" I shouted.

That worked about as well as it usually did, which was not at all.

"Kittens, be quiet," a soft voice said from behind the lot of them.

They clamped shut like mousetraps going off.

"How about everyone pull up a chair and we can get some breakfast?" Lucy said as she pushed Tim toward one of the seats around the island. It was a little awkward, what with her still holding on to her crutches under one arm.

"You're going to cook?" I asked.

"Hell no. They have room service here," she said. "I bet it's better than those."

"These," I said, raising my spoon, "are great."

She scrunched her nose at me.

"I actually met Longbow, you know," I said, gesturing my spoon toward the box art. "He's . . . kinda insane. Nice, though."

"Showing off?" she asked.

I grinned back at her. "Just you wait," I said with a purr.

She smiled right back. "I waited plenty last night, but someone decided to fall asleep."

Much to my annoyance, a few of the kittens caught on and laughed at my reddening cheeks. "Oh, shut up, you guys. I had a long day."

"Is that your excuse now?" Junior asked as she came around and took a seat on my side. She slid the box of cereal over, then huffed and got up to fetch a bowl. "You still owe me a knife," she said as she fished for a spoon.

"Might as well," I sighed. "Lucy, you wanna order that breakfast? Also, where's Dumbass?"

"Sure," Lucy said as she clacked her way over to an old-school phone on a pedestal nearby.

Nemo ran off, returning a minute later with one of my little drones clutched between both hands. It was Dumbass the First, sans gun mount.

I had the drones disarm when the children started playing with them.

"How responsible," I said before clearing my throat. "All right, you little shits. This is Dumbass. It's got some fancy medical scanner doodad in it. You let it scan you, and then Myalis, my wonderful brain worm AI buddy, will tell me how to cure the stupid out of you."

If that were possible, wouldn't you think I'd have tried to talk you into curing yourself a long time ago?

I saw Lucy pausing by the phone, and a few of the kittens were looking at the drone with wide, hopeful eyes.

"Th-thank you," Bargain said.

"Oh, shut up," I said. "You know I'm just doing it to impress Lucy." Lucy snorted before picking up the phone.

Junior barked out a laugh next to me. "You're a shitty liar," she said. "And don't think curing some incurable sickness will let you off the hook."

I rolled my eyes while Dumbass got to work. "For . . . fine. Myalis, we got any knives available?"

You do. In your Sun Watcher Technologies catalog. The cheapest is a survivalist knife with an extendable monofilament blade. It will cost you five points.

"Perfect."

A cheap plastic box appeared on the table before me, and I slid it over to Junior. Her eyes lit up as she tore the package open and pulled out a long knife.

"Monofilament blade," I said. "Don't kill yourself."

"Awesome," she said, and then her smile froze and she turned the knife around. "Wait, why's it got a cat on the handle?"

I blinked and leaned over. There was, in fact, a feline on the handle. But it wasn't a cat, it was a kitten. "I think it's the button to retract the blade."

"Why's it shaped like a cat?"

"A kitten," I said. "Just like you!"

She glared, which warmed my heart.

"All right! Time to pull a Jesus."

CHAPTER TWO

A SLICE OF HAPPINESS

Times of peace aren't uncommon. But they never really last.

—Deus Ex, June 2057

"What've you got for me?" I asked Myalis while looking over at Dumbass the First.

I suppose I could start with the youngest and work my way up.

"Sure," I said. "So we'll start with Nose, or is Spark younger?"

I believe that Nose is the youngest, judging by the scans Dumbass has taken.

The kittens were all gathered around the kitchen island—even Lucy, who'd returned from ordering breakfast with a sly smile on her face. Daniel had spun around on his chair and waved me hello before deep-diving into his phone.

Nose and Spark were both standing near the edge of the table and looking at me without blinking.

Nose—and that is an awful name I've no doubt you had something to do with—seems to suffer from chronic obstructive pulmonary disease. It's at the third stage. It's rather surprising that he can still function moderately well. He has a few other conditions, mostly centered around his nasal cavity and esophagus.

"Nose is a tough little shit," I said.

Nose nodded seriously. "Yeah."

"Got a cure?"

Obviously. A Nano-Regenerative Suite should be sufficient to cure the ailment.

I grinned. "Don't keep us waiting, Myalis. And tab it all up for me in one go at the end."

A box appeared on the island, small and cheap. Inside was an inhaler with a tank the size of a soda can and a red button on the top. Its front was shaped like a rather basic oxygen mask.

Spread out the use over the course of the day. Tell Nose to drink a lot of water and have a big, varied meal later. He's got a few nutritional deficiencies. In fact, all of them, you included, do. There are also traces of heavy metals in your blood and in some of your organs, and some nitrates, plastics, and a few other chemicals that I suspect were used as fertilizer and pesticides. It's fortunate humans are so resilient, or you'd all be tumorous masses by now.

I slid the inhaler over to Nose. "Take a puff every hour or so. And then eat a lot tonight. Oh, and down a couple of glasses of water, all right?" I'd need to get some sort of detox thing for all the kittens later, but that could probably wait a day.

"Yeah!" he said before taking the inhaler. Everyone watched as he took a deep breath from it, then coughed a few times. "Tickles."

"It'll get better," I said. "Spark, you're up next."

"All right!" Spark said. "Hit me up, Doc Cat."

Spark has an interesting one. It seems like a sort of prion disease. I suspect he came into contact with something while very young. It has mostly kept to his parietal lobe, reducing his ability to feel touch.

"Right," I said. "It's why he's called Spark: he likes licking power outlets."

"I don't!" Spark protested. "It just feels weird."

A simple Neuro-Regenerative should do.

Another box, this one with a red plastic nib and drawn instructions on the side to place it against the crook of the arm. "Can you figure it out?" I asked.

"I'm not an idiot," he said before fumbling with the injector. He didn't even wince as he pulled back his sleeve and jabbed it in. "When's this going to work?"

It will take approximately an hour for the first signs of regression to show. Six for a complete cure. Also, he's far too thin. I suspect that he can't feel hunger pangs at all.

"Give it until this afternoon," I said. "And eat more. You're too damned thin. Tim, you're too thin too."

Tim here is missing a leg. That much is obvious. Otherwise, he's in decent health.

"Tim's new to the kittens," I explained. It was kind of shitty that being new meant he hadn't collected a bunch of problems yet.

"Will you regrow my leg?" he asked.

"Do you want a new leg or a prosthetic?" I asked, wiggling my metal fingers around.

"Can I have one like yours?"

"Only if you want to lose an arm," I snarked back. It earned a few laughs, which was nice. The mood with the kittens was about as high as I'd ever seen it. "But nah, just a normal samurai-grade prosthetic. Mine can fire rockets. Yours . . . won't."

"Aww," he said.

His current prosthetic is rather pitiful. I'd suggest a Sun Watcher replacement. There are some that are inexpensive, require little to no maintenance, and are far superior to what he has without needing complex neural links. They can also expand over time so that they won't require replacing for some years. I'd also suggest a skin irritation cream.

I tapped the table. "Come on, Myalis, don't keep us waiting."

Tim's new leg came in a little case, and next to it came a small jar of some sort of cream with instructions printed on the side. "Spark, Nose, wanna help him put it on?"

The three rushed off with the couches in the living room, with Tim demanding they be careful with his new leg.

"Bargain," I said.

"Cat," he replied.

Bargain has a few smaller issues. Chemical burns on the lower half of his body, a slight defect in his heart, and a minor case of cerebral palsy as well. The skin issues can be relieved with a cream. I'd advise the same for your own burns if you ever want to repair them, actually. The lung issue will require a Nano-Regenerative Suite. The cerebral palsy will require a Neuro-Regenerative. It won't disappear instantly. He will need to exercise, stretch, and straighten his posture over the course of several months.

"All right," I said. "Lay it on the table."

The boxes appeared. Bargain looked at them, then up at me. I could see the gears turning behind his eyes.

"No more wheeling and dealing," I said. "Not with me or Lucy."

He nodded slowly. "And the others?"

"Do as you want with them, but be fair to the other kittens," I said. "Oh, and you'll need to stand taller and exercise to fix yourself up properly. And probably eat something other than the shit we usually have."

"All right, deal," he said.

"Nemo?" I asked.

Nemo popped her head up and blinked at me.

Very mild autism, some selective mutism, and a terrible diet. A Neuro-Regenerative would aid with the issues with her brain, but most of Nemo's problems are due to a poor diet and some psychological issues.

I nodded and flicked the next box that appeared her way. "You need to eat better too," I said.

Nemo nodded, smiled, then ran off to see Tim and Spark and the others.

You are aware that the Twins aren't genetically twins at all, right?

"Yeah, they're just missing the same bits," I said.

The Twins—who did look like each other, with the same shitty haircut, brown hair and eyes, and too-pale skin—leaned forward at the same time. "We want rocket launcher arms," they said as one.

"No," I vetoed.

Two new, non-rocket-equipped arms later, and they were off helping each other install their new prosthetics and playing around with the features on their new arms over in the living room.

"Okay, so, for my final acts . . . Daniel, you've got some sort of muscular fucked-up-ness, right?"

"That's the medical term, yeah," he agreed with a grin.

Muscular dystrophy. Chemically induced at that. A simple fix.

I flung the next box over to him, and he saluted me back. "Thanks, love."

"Don't try."

"How long until I can start dancing?"

Two to three days.

I snorted. "Your pasty white ass will never be able to dance," I said. "But in a few days, you'll be able to traumatize the kids by trying."

He flipped me the bird, but he was still smiling. "We'll see."

And finally, we have Junior. She . . . is merely malnourished, with traces of contaminants in her blood that will pass eventually.

"Junior," I said.

"Yeah?" she asked as she looked up from her bowl.

"You're too fucking skinny."

"Fuck you," she said.

I felt a shy, tentative hand touching my shoulder. "What about me?" Lucy asked.

Lucy has multiple sclerosis. An easy thing to cure.

A fresh box appeared on the table.

Give her those. Then allow for a few hours to restore all of her cognitive functions. It might be mildly unpleasant. Afterward, she'll need to practice walking and running once more.

"You'll need to take these," I said. "But they'll make you feel all tingly."

She smiled up at me. "Tingly, huh?" she asked. "Will you help me get rid of all my tingles?"

I leaned down and our lips met while I fiddled with the box with my free hand. I had the tablets out soon enough and was carefully pressing the single pill between her lips.

"For fuck's sake, get a room," Junior said. "Don't do that in front of my cereal."

Lucy and I happily complied, though it was a bit hard to make it back to the room with our faces practically glued together.

"Oh, oh man, it really is tingly," Lucy said as she sat on the edge of the bed. "My feet are all . . . You know when your arms go to sleep and then they come awake?" She wiggled her legs, then wiggled them some more as she slid off the pajama pants she was wearing to expose two beautiful dark legs.

I got to my knees to capture one of her feet. Carefully, I massaged it, just a bit of pressure in the way she always liked. The pleased little noise she made said a lot.

I leaned down and pressed a kiss onto the top of her foot.

And then, before I could lean back, a pair of panties dropped down and came to rest around her ankles.

I looked up to meet Lucy's bright eyes. "You said you'd take care of *all* the parts that tingled."

"So I did," I agreed.

INTERLEWD

I trailed kisses up Lucy's leg while my hands fumbled with the zipper of my auto-loader jacket. Her hands fell onto my head and scratched into my scalp in a most delicious way, and by the time I'd reached her thigh, I was tearing the coat off.

"Cat," Lucy said.

Her voice was breathy and husky and sent shivers down my spine. "Yeah?" I asked.

"When's the last time you took a shower?"

"Uh."

"You smell like . . . rubber and smoke," she added.

"Yeah, I was a bit busy yesterday with that kind of thing," I admitted. I leaned down and gave myself a sniff and . . . yeah, I needed a shower. That splashed some cold water onto my libido.

"You know, the showers here are really big," Lucy said. "And I'm already dressed for a shower."

I looked up to see her casually slip out of her top.

"Oh," I said. I got up a little awkwardly, then extended my hands to Lucy to help her onto her feet. She was so light I barely felt the strain of lifting her, and the little two-step she did to slip her panties off her feet made the blood rushing to my ears sound like a pulsing waterfall.

"Let's go?" she asked.

I nodded, bent down, then scooped her up into a bridal carry while she squeaked. "Always wanted to do that," I said.

"Give a girl two arms and all of a sudden she's all gallant," she said before bending forward to kiss.

For a moment I forgot we were supposed to be going anywhere.

But Lucy reminded me by trailing a hand behind me and pinching my rear. "Get moving," she said. "Your new arm is cold." She wiggled her legs, both currently draped over my new forearm, for emphasis.

The en suite bathroom was huge, with two sinks—why?—and a shower that was bigger than the entire bathroom back at the orphanage, with glass walls and a tiled backdrop covered in little carved flowers.

I set Lucy down only for her to push against me and seal her lips against mine. Her hands fumbled at my belt while mine slid down her back and pulled her closer.

She pulled back, then gestured at my shoulders. "You're wearing that into the shower?" she asked.

I swallowed. "Oh, right. Uh." I couldn't recall how to remove the back-mounted guns, not through the haze in my mind. "Myalis, how do I get this off?"

You only had to ask.

The mounting running along my spine undid itself with faint little pops, and it fell to the floor, tail and all.

Lucy looked up to me. "Is, um, Myalis . . . watching?"

If it reassures her, I have performed full-body scans of her already. There's very little to hide.

"That really doesn't help, Myalis," I muttered.

"It's okay," Lucy said. "It'll be my first threesome."

"I really don't think it counts," I said.

Please inform Lucy that I'm very much not interested in procreating with a human.

"What's that even mean?" I asked.

"What?"

I feel like a third wheel here.

"She's being a pain," I said. With my hands now a bit more free, I tossed my pants down and bent my legs up one by one to tear my socks off. "So, uh, I don't think I can shut her out? Is that . . . a problem?"

Lucy shrugged. "I guess not."

I felt my shoulders relax. I was worked up enough that Lucy calling it off would have been disappointing, to say the least. "So, how good is this shower?" I asked.

She grabbed onto my hand and pulled me toward it. "Alone? It's all right," she said. "Shower, on. Hot."

The shower came on behind her, its door silently sliding open. "Fancy," I said before ducking down for another kiss. We stumbled into a dozen jets of water so hot it almost hurt. My hair plastered down around me and I had to move it out of the way.

That allowed me to take in Lucy in all her splendor, dark hair against dark skin, her eyelashes fluttering as water collected on them, her lips wet and curved up in a genuinely happy smile. "Look at this," she said. "Shower, soap!"

The water turned into a stream of warm bubbles that fell down around us and turned the world white. I laughed. "Does it do shampoo too?" I asked. The amount in the water alone . . . that was such a waste. A decadent luxury I couldn't imagine getting used to.

"That's for later," Lucy said before she pressed herself against me, all wet and smooth and soft. "You need to scrub up first." Her hands, cooler than the soapy water around us, pressed against my ribs, then slid around to my back while moving in little circles.

I reciprocated, my flesh-and-blood hand touching her almost timidly at first before I recalled doing this kind of thing with her. I reached up a little and gently grabbed at her breasts.

"Cat! I'm not the dirty one here," she admonished. Then because she liked down there, she pinched my rear again before pulling me so close I had to let my hand drop. Her arms wrapped themselves around my chest and she tucked her head in against me. "I was afraid, you know?"

The sudden turn left my mind spinning for traction. "Oh?" I asked.

"You left and . . . I guess it doesn't matter now." Her lips pressed down on my clavicle, then my neck while she kept rubbing little soapy circles across my back.

When her hand came around and squeezed my breast I had to hold back a little moan. "Am I clean enough yet?" I asked.

"Hrm?" she asked, turning the purr into a question. "I don't know."

I was about to ask something, but the question was lost when Lucy pushed me back and I encountered the cold tiles of the shower wall. I gasped at the sensation and pushed forward, only for Lucy to meet me with another kiss.

Her hands wandered down, grabbing at my hips.

"Lucy," I said.

"Cat?" she asked as she pulled back a bit. She was still close, very close.

"I love you."

She grinned, big and happy and a bit silly. "I love you too," she said.

Then her hand reached down between my legs and carefully ran down my thighs.

"So dirty," she said.

"Lucy!" I squeaked as she pressed her thumb in small circles around me. I forgot all about the cold seeping into my back and the warm water running between us where our skin didn't meet.

Lucy knew me, from well-earned experience and a few too many hours spent in closets, in showers much smaller than this one, and just cuddling in bed. She knew which buttons to press, how to play with me with just a few strokes, and when to push in so that I ended up on the tips of my toes, breath coming in raspy and hard.

Climbing to my toes was a mistake; it brought her face closer to my chest. She pressed kisses down my clavicle and to my breasts, then latched on and did something with her tongue.

I bit my lip until it hurt to stop from making any noise. Junior had once informed me, after a rather pleasant evening, that I was very loud, and since then I'd always tried to keep a lid on it.

Then Lucy's hand sped up and I lost that battle with a throaty noise that set her to giggling. She stopped, bending almost double as she tried to keep the laughter in.

"Lucy," I pleaded.

"Sorry," she said, but her smile suggested she was anything but.

I fell back onto my feet and reached for her, intending to return the favor, when she pushed me back.

"I wasn't done," she said. "Shower, a bit warmer."

The water turned a notch hotter, enough that it started to hurt just a little, but then she did something with her thumb and fingers and I forgot all about that.

"I really do love you," she said before a wave of heat shot through me and I felt myself shivering. "Oh, getting close?"

I made a noise that I think sounded like a yes, or something akin to that. She laid kisses around my neck and cheeks, then captured my mouth in hers while her hands kept on doing frankly magical things.

A minute passed while our tongues slid around each other, and Lucy's concentration around my core slipped a little as she focused on the kiss. I moved my hands around her, pulling her closer and bringing my real hand down to grab her ass.

She gasped into my mouth, a sensation that stole my breath in the best way, and then she returned the favor by tweaking something below that had me making another embarrassing noise.

"Faster?" she asked.

I hadn't said anything remotely like that, but she didn't seem to care. Her fingers moved faster, a lot faster, and I felt another wave of heat pass through me, making my abdominal muscles contract and my back want to bend.

Lucy took that as a challenge and pushed into me, stretching and rubbing while she peppered kisses across my upper chest.

And then the dam burst, my legs wobbling and my abs contracting. I felt Lucy's fingers squeezing together in me before she slid them out and left me feeling empty even as my head spun.

I might have fallen if she hadn't held me up and kissed me to within an inch of my life.

"Was it good?" she asked with a knowing grin.

"You're the best," I said between pants. The warmth was sinking away now, leaving in little shuddering waves. I might have been sweating, but there was no way to know with the water coming down around us. "I'll have to return the favor," I said.

"I doubt you could manage," she said. "I'm the best, after all."

I kissed her again and wondered how long it would take for the water to run cold here.

"H-hey, Myalis?" I asked. "You remember mentioning that catalog, with the toys?"

CHAPTER THREE

POSTCOITAL INTERRUPTIONS

Do you know what kind of opportunity the average person has?

Fuck-all. If you're not born in the right family, have the right connections, and go to the right schools, you're pretty much stuck kissing the ass of anyone one rung above you on the ladder while hoping they'll slip up badly enough you can take their spot.

Worse, your fortunes can turn in a blink. Spent ten years working your way up to middle management in your department? Too fucking bad, some shareholders decided your entire division needs to be pruned to meet some elusive goal or to make the curve on their graphs look smoother.

Good luck starting from the bottom again. There's no one to blame but yourself for failing to read the room.

—Anonymous Reddit user, June 2029

I couldn't decide *how* I was feeling.

Parts of me that I didn't know could tingle were tingling, and I had sore muscles across my everything. Not a bad sore, but the sort from exercising a lot, which was probably fair.

I decided, after a moment's reflection, that what I was feeling could best be described as "good." I was feeling really good.

A giggle escaped, one that was soon echoed by the person lying down next to me.

Lucy shifted, then brought her head to rest on my stomach. "That was . . ."

"Yeah," I agreed as I continued to stare at the ceiling. Eventually, I got enough energy to bring a hand down and brush it through Lucy's hair, her very sweaty hair.

"I didn't know I could do that so many times," Lucy said.

"Yeah."

"I'm sore."

"Yeah," I agreed.

We weren't alone on the bed. There was also a very rumpled and probably unsanitary pile of blankets and pillows spread around here and there, and more importantly, there was a machine.

It was a horrifying machine, like something out of some madwoman's worst nightmares. It was eldritch and tentacled, and it looked wet and almost alive.

It was the best hundred points I have ever spent, even if it had made me question my own sanity a few times. I wasn't even sure what time it was anymore. For all I knew, a day could have passed. The details were certainly hazy enough.

Shifting my hips, I got into a slightly more comfortable position where Lucy's head didn't dig into my stomach quite so much. "That was something," I said.

"It was," Lucy said. "Think we can go at it again?"

I considered that. "The mind is willing, but the flesh is . . . not."

She snorted, the motion bouncing her head up atop me. "Yeah."

I smiled and continued to run my hands through Lucy's hair, content to do nothing but that for the rest of my life if need be.

And then some jerk knocked on the door. "Hey, are you two done fucking?" Junior asked.

"Urgh" was the most coherent response I could manage.

"I sure hope so, because there are people here for Cat. Like, lots of them. And some androids too. Shit's annoying."

"Tell them to go away," I called back.

"Yeah, I tried that, you moron," Junior said. "They're real insistent. Some of them look important-like and they won't fucking leave."

I sighed. I didn't want to leave. This place was a happy place and the world outside wasn't. "Tell Dumbass to shoo them away."

"Yeah, no," Junior said. "Look, I'm coming in. Some of the kittens are getting scared and it's annoying."

"Oh shit," Lucy said as she scrambled up and off me with a sudden burst of energy. I did the same, looking for my clothes, only to find that I'd left everything on the floor in a trail leading into the en suite bathroom.

The door clicked open just as Lucy and I bumped into each other by the base of the bed.

Our friendly eldritch tentacle machine seemed to notice the excitation because it started wiggling around too, especially when the door handle wobbled.

Three very confusing minutes later, I was slipping out into the corridor outside our room while doing up my belt. I didn't actually have a shirt, just the autoloader jacket, and despite having taken a very thorough and long shower with Lucy, I knew that I smelled a little.

I'd have to take another once things were dealt with.

The tentacle machine could join too.

"Where're these assholes?" I asked Junior, who looked exceptionally unimpressed by me and my antics. Her nose wrinkled up and she gestured down the corridor a ways.

"They're by the entrance. The kittens are all off in their rooms. I knocked earlier, but you didn't reply, just made these weird-ass donkey noises."

I felt some warmth gathering in my cheeks and looked past her and toward the entrance. "Right," I said. "I'll go see what they want, I guess."

I left Whisper in the bedroom with Lucy, which was probably for the best. That meant that all the armament I had was my Trench Maker, a shoulder-mounted railgun, and a plasma-firing gun on the other shoulder. And a tail with a thagomizer.

That . . . was probably enough to convince some less-than-wholesome people to vacate the area.

I tugged my jacket on straighter and stomped toward the living room and kitchen area. What I found there were three groups of people.

The first were a pair of serious-looking men in black suits, standing ramrod straight and wearing sunglasses indoors. The second were also wearing suits, but these were patterned and more colorful. They were smiling as if their cheeks were tacked in place that way. And the third were a pair of soldiers in dress uniforms with little maple leaves on their shoulders.

The three groups all elected to talk at the same time, a cacophony of noise that I couldn't make heads or tails of.

They seemed to catch on that if they all talked at once, they wouldn't make much sense, but instead of taking their time, they turned on each other and bickered.

It was like something out of a particularly unfunny comedy sketch.

"Okay, everyone shut up," I said.

I was still getting used to the idea that people respected me, adults especially, but it was incredibly amusing to see adults snapping their mouths closed just because I'd told them to. "You, with the shades. Who are you?" I pointed to the guy in between the pair in black suits, the one that looked in charge.

"Miss Leblanc, we are an organization charged with the protection of American assets. Upon seeing that you became a samurai we thought it appropriate to inform you that, were you so willing, our organization could assist you in coming to your own an—"

I stopped him with a raised hand. "Just send me a fucking email. Now, who are you guys?" I asked the next bunch.

They all started talking over each other, and I could feel my postcoital bliss draining away as they prattled on.

"One at a time, you fuckwits," I said.

As it turned out, all of them were representatives of one corporation or another, every one of them eager and excited to sign me on and use my likeness to promote . . . everything from cereals to soft drugs, and one sleazy guy said that they mostly dealt in deepfake pornography.

"Right, right, I've heard enough, please kindly fuck off. If I want something I'll contact you, not the other way around."

Some of them protested, but Myalis, being the best, had my railgun slide out over my shoulder, and it made a deep, ominous hum.

"And who're you guys?" I asked the soldiers.

"We're representatives of the Canadian Armed Forces, ma'am," the one with the more elaborate medals said.

"Aren't you guys a joke?" I asked.

"No, ma'am," he said without so much as twitching.

Well, at least they were polite. "And you want me to join up? Become Private Leblanc?"

He shook his head. "Nothing of the sort. We merely wished to both thank you for your efforts yesterday and extend an offer to you. If you ever wish to join the forces, there's a place for you. We will send a recruitment package to your email address, if you wish."

Real polite—I liked it. "You know what, sure," I said.

I didn't intend to join, but their uniforms looked nice, and I bet I could find a use for one. Lucy did always say that she liked women in tight uniforms. They saluted my way and made for the exit, only to be blocked as someone shoved past them.

I stared at the newcomer, initially pissed at the gall, then I recognized them, or rather, her. Deus Ex looked on the wrong side of tired, but her armor was impeccable and so clean it could have come fresh off the alien presses. She didn't have her whole hover system with her, probably because it wouldn't fit inside any normal building, but she did have a few things strapped to her hips that looked like they might be dangerous.

"Stray Cat," she said. "We need to talk."

CHAPTER FOUR

MEAN MINION MODE

To say that samurai are dangerous would be a wild understatement. They aren't truly beholden to any laws, corporate or governmental, they can act as they see fit, and they can do so with technology and tools that no normal force can match.

They are only held accountable by their fellows.

But most samurai are at least somewhat mature. They're adults, with the responsibility and maturity that entails.

Not all of them are so old. Many of them are young. What do you do with a teenager given unlimited power? Someone who has never been tempered by life and experience?

Come, my flock, and let us pray for these lost souls!

—John Johnathan Johns, Twitch priest, June 2034

Deus Ex was a meter-and-a-half-tall stack of contradictions.

She stood with her back straight and her brow set in a glare; her hands rested on her hips and her lips formed a little line. She was trying very hard to be intimidating, but she looked more like a mildly annoyed puppy.

I kind of wanted to pat her on the head to see what would happen.

"You two, go away," she said to the guys in black suits. She hadn't even looked at them.

"Ma'am, we are here on official business," one of them said.

She slowly turned her head his way, then reached for the small of her back and pulled out a rounded, curved device that unmistakably had a handle and trigger mechanism on it. "Will your life insurance cover damages to the building?" she asked.

"Pardon?"

"Because this weapon will go right through you, and then through the rest of this building. Will your life insurance cover the damages, or will I need to find out who you work for and empty their accounts directly? I use this hotel sometimes—I don't want them thinking I'm a bad client that won't pay for damages and corpse removal."

"Um," the guy said. His whole stoic attitude was really getting tested. "We can return later."

"Please don't," I said. "Send me an email or something instead. I don't do cryptic much."

A few seconds later, Deus Ex and I were the only ones left in the living room. I gestured with a nod toward the inside and walked over to the couches before the television.

"Were you injured?" Deus Ex asked as she followed. "You're walking crooked."

"I'm fine," I said before sitting down and leaning back. I was surprisingly tired. Maybe a nap would feel good once everything was done. "So what brings you here? Wanted to bask in my presence some more?"

"No," she said. "The incursion is pretty much done with. All that's left is the sewer crawling, and I'm not going to participate in any of that."

"All right," I said. Couldn't blame her.

"I'm actually here to give you some work."

I blinked and paid more attention to her. "Some work?" I repeated. "I don't recall being on your payroll."

"I'm paying for these rooms. And you owe me a favor," she said.

"Uh. Usually there's a bit more communication than this," I said.

She pouted again. Or maybe she was trying to glare? Either way, I wanted to pinch her cheeks. "Don't be an ass. You're still a newbie, and you have a bunch of normies to take care of." She gestured in the vague direction of the kittens. "I don't mind paying for this place for a bit longer, but that means you'll have to be my minion."

"Your minion?" I asked.

"Yes. There are things I need to do that I don't feel like doing. You'll do them for me."

"Do I get a say in this?" I asked.

"You're too weak to get a say," she said.

I glared at the little extortionist pain in the ass. "You're not as cute as I thought you were," I said.

The little bitch actually seemed proud of it! "Good. I don't have time to babysit you or anything, and your profile says that you're too stubborn and stupid to join up with a proper group, so you get to be my minion."

I laughed. The situation was . . . well, it was funny, in a weird absurdist way. "Okay, great boss-girl, what do you want your humble minion to do?" I played along. I did kind of owe her a favor or two.

Deus Ex didn't answer me right away. Instead she glanced over to the television. The screen came on, and an image of a young woman appeared on it. She looked bored, with her shoulders set and her eyes looking into the camera. An ID photo, probably.

Brown hair, with a purple streak in it. No piercings or tattoos. Blue eyes, though one was a lot lighter than the other. Probably some eyegear or an aug.

"Who's the girl?" I asked.

"Katallina McCarthy," Deus Ex said. The image shifted to only take up part of the screen, the rest filling up with school records, hospital records, and a moving social media feed that looked like it was going through years of stuff in a hurry.

"She your girlfriend?" I asked.

Deus Ex huffed, but her cheeks reddened. "I don't have a girlfriend."

"Look, if you want me to stalk someone for you, then . . . Well, then that's a bit creepy. I bet I can help you get in her pants, though. I could coach you. Give you a bit of advice. How to talk to other girls, how to hint that you're interested. I can do this thing with my tongue, it's really impr—"

"Sh-shut up!" Deus Ex said.

I giggled, especially on seeing how red she was going.

"You're disgusting."

I grinned. "So, what's up with Katallina here? Also, where did you get all of her files?"

Deus Ex shook her head. "We're samurai, they're not exactly hard to get. And what's up with her is that she might be one of us."

"You don't know?" I asked.

She shook her head. "No. It's . . . Okay, so the Family are the group that pretty much take care of North America. We're pretty big and we do a lot of stuff. Most members just join and don't do too much, but that's all right. One of our core tenets is helping out new samurai. That means making sure they survive and don't get in too much trouble with the corps. You don't want to accidentally sell your rights to anyone."

"All right," I said. "So . . . like Longbow helping me?"

She nodded. "Like big brother Longbow asking me to save your sorry ass, yeah."

I snorted. "All right, but why?"

She actually seemed confused. "Because otherwise idiots like you would die a lot more. We need every samurai we can get."

That sounded way too optimistic to be real, but she seemed to believe it. "All right. And this girl's a samurai?"

"Maybe," Deus Ex said. "Look."

The screen filled with footage of a corridor. It was poorly lit, and the camera was fixed. No doubt some security system tucked away in a corner. A girl came around a bend, trailed by a dog, a big German shepherd.

She looked nervous and sweaty, her brown and purple hair plastered to her face.

The girl and the dog ran halfway down the corridor before a pair of Model Threes came around. They were as I remembered them: big, doglike, with bony bodies in matte black, and triple-hinged jaws opened wide.

The girl stopped and raised a rifle. She called something out to her dog, who had stopped too and placed itself between her and the Model Threes.

She fired off a burst of strange red beams that tore the aliens apart, and then she continued running with her dog by her heels.

"A fresh samurai?" I asked. The scene was pretty damned similar to my own initiation to the world of samurai.

"We think so," Deus Ex said, "but we don't know for sure. She was in a building on the very edge of the orange zone. Not too many Antithesis around there. She might just be a civilian that found an old samurai gun."

"Can't you ask your AI?"

I'm afraid that we can't divulge information about other Vanguards.

"Ah," I said. "Never mind." I rubbed at my chin. "So what happened to her and her dog?"

Deus Ex shrugged. "Don't know. Honestly, I have better things to do."

"Uh. Why bring this all up, then?"

"Because someone needs to check up on her," she said. "And you're not doing anything important."

"I'm sorry, but what? I was doing plenty of very important things. Most of them are in bed with my girlfriend."

Her nose scrunched up, and then realization sparked in her eyes. "Oh, eww. That's gross." She bounced off the couch as if it had been contaminated or something. We hadn't even made it out of the room yet. I didn't see what had her so freaked out, but it was cute. Probably a good thing that Lucy wasn't around. She would be hugging Deus Ex by now.

"Can't you just track her electronically?" I asked.

"We tried that, obviously," Deus Ex said. She was eyeing the furniture with suspicion. "But it didn't work. She went dark. So we need to find her, or her corpse. Make sure no corporation gets to her."

"Why?" I asked. "The corpse bit, mostly."

"Because she's one of us," Deus Ex said, as if that would explain everything.

I guessed that to her, it did.

CHAPTER FIVE

PROFESSIONALISM

The importance of samurai in our modern society cannot be overstated. In the 1900s there was a surge of popularity centered on celebrities, especially in the West. Movie stars, musicians, sports stars. They became the idols of their generations, faces and names known to all.

After the initial incursions, some attention turned to the samurai who had, seemingly, saved us all.

That attention turned to idolization as the full scope of what they could do became known.

That is why it is imperative that Nimbletainment continue to be the predominant holder of the image rights of samurai across North America.

—Nimbletainment Inc. CEO during a company-wide brief, 2037

"So," I said. "How?"

"What?" Deus Ex asked.

I gestured to the television where Katallina's face was still displayed. "You want me to find that girl, right? How?"

Deus Ex shrugged. "I don't know. You figure it out. It'll be like a test or something."

"Or something," I repeated, deadpan. I gave her my flattest look. "You're real professional, aren't you?"

The girl bristled at that, sitting straighter in her seat and glaring right back at me before her face twisted to neutrality. "Fine," she said. "If you need someone to baby you, I can take some of my precious time to help you."

I snorted. Maybe that would have tweaked the pride of someone who hadn't had my stellar upbringing, but it did nothing for me. The kittens regularly came up with better insults. "So how do you expect me to find her? Better yet, how would you do it?"

She rolled her eyes. "I'll give you a packet with her info." The moment she said that, I got a ping in my vision, an email.

I blinked a few times to open it, then noticed that I had five digits' worth of unread emails. "Damn, how come my email hasn't blown up yet?" It was a good thing I was using one of the free email services. Some charged a fee for every email. Those usually had all sorts of encryptions and stuff, and they claimed not to sell your messages to advertisers, but I never got anything important enough to warrant that.

I might have had something to do with that. You receive a lot of spam. And viruses. Also, images of genitals. The news that you've become a Vanguard isn't widely circulated yet, but some people have connected the dots.

I winced. "Just delete all the nasty ones . . . Well, keep the nudes if they're tasteful."

No.

The afternoon was turning really sour, especially compared to the morning. I opened Deus Ex's email, then stared at an image of Deus Ex giving me the finger before a plain background. "Uh."

Oh. The information is all in the image. It's stored in the image's pixelation, with different color values representing different bits in hex. The sequence to read these is randomized, with the code to decipher the randomization written as a multiplication of the image's resolution. Once the actual code is parsed, you need only de-encrypt it. It's a bit simple, and I've no doubt that even some humans could figure it out given a few hours, but for nonsensitive information, it will do.

"Uh," I said.

"You know, talking to your AI out loud is generally a sign that you're really new," Deus Ex said.

"That might be because I am new," I said. "Besides, it's impossible to snark through text."

Deus Ex placed her hands on her knees and got to her feet. "Right. Well, that package has everything we could trawl on Katallina in a few minutes. It's got her last known location too. I'd start there. Ask your AI for help. It's definitely smarter than you are."

I wasn't going to argue with that.

"Cat?"

Both of us turned toward the kitchen to see Lucy walking over. She was a bit bowlegged and had a hand trailing against the wall to keep her balance. She was wearing a nice set of silken pajamas, no doubt stolen from a drawer somewhere.

"Hey, Lucy," I said. "Wanna come over and sit?"

"Ah, yeah, sure," she said. "My legs are still wobbly."

"Disgusting," Deus Ex muttered.

I wanted to give her shit for being rude, but with Lucy's MS being cured and all, there were only so many possible reasons for her to feel wobbly, and Deus Ex was probably thinking the right thing.

"Who's this cute little girl?" Lucy asked as she came closer.

Deus Ex's face registered her disdain for the comment clear as day. "I'm Deus Ex."

"That's a very cute name," Lucy said. "Did you pick it out yourself?"

If I hadn't known Lucy for as long as I did, I'd probably have assumed she was being genuine, but I knew that slight shift in her voice too well. She was messing with Deus Ex.

"Right, I'm done here," Deus Ex said. "Stray Cat, try to find the girl. She might be dead, or she might be in trouble with some corp or the government. If she's fine, then . . . just don't be yourself around her. Maybe give her my number? And if she's in trouble . . ."

"Get her out?" I asked. "Or call for help?"

"Nah, just kill anyone causing issues. If it's to protect a new samurai, then it's justified."

I had to wonder what kind of headspace someone like Deus Ex was in if she thought killing people to get things done was just business as usual. "Right," I said. "And when do you want me to start this . . . Wait, I didn't agree to start this at all."

"I'm paying for the rent for this floor," Deus Ex said. "Unless you want to pay for it yourself, and that probably includes some decontamination for wherever you . . . urgh, you start right away. Have your AI text me if you need anything."

"Bye-bye!" Lucy said with a little wave as Deus Ex walked past.

The girl just marched her way on out of the room without so much as a second glance. "Call me when you find her!" she said before leaving.

"She's a weird one," I said.

Lucy hummed as she made her way around the couch. She took a moment to look at all the available seats, then picked the one she liked most.

I exhaled hard as she plopped herself down onto my lap. "Are you comfy?"

She wiggled, then leaned back and tucked her head against mine. "Yup."

Grinning, I pulled her in with a hug, luxuriating in the warmth and the softness of her stolen pajamas. "I need to ask Myalis a couple of things."

"Oh, I'll only get to hear half the conversation then."

"I guess so."

That is easily remedied. One moment.

I wondered what she was up to, and then Dumbass the First skittered its way into the living room and hopped onto one of the sofas. It wiggled around to face us, then lowered itself down. "Greetings," the drone said in Myalis's voice. It was a little strange hearing her out loud.

"Hi, Myalis!" Lucy said with a wave.

"I'm still physically within Catherine's skull—I'm merely using the drone as a mouthpiece," Myalis explained. "Nonetheless, it's a pleasure to speak with you through a more reliable method than Catherine's abysmal communication skills."

"Hey!"

"She is really bad sometimes," Lucy agreed. "It's all threats and cute little grunts."

"H-hey!" This time my ire was directed at the girl on my lap.

Myalis bobbed up and down.

"You're both awful," I said. Then Lucy gave me a conciliatory peck on the cheek, and I settled in to pout until they stopped teasing me.

"This mission, if we can call it that, is rather simple in its objective, but I suspect that carrying it out will be a great deal more complicated," Myalis said. "Evidence of Katallina's disappearance will be time-sensitive. Tracking her down might also be difficult."

"So you're saying we should head out sooner rather than later?" I asked.

"Essentially, yes."

I really didn't want to leave. I was comfortable, with Lucy's bony behind digging into my thighs and my arms wrapped around her waist. Leaving was the last thing I wanted to do.

"Who's Katallina?"

"She's a girl that went missing. She might be a samurai, maybe. Deus Ex wants me to track her down, make sure she's all right," I explained.

"Oh. That does sound kind of important."

"Mmm, I guess." I sank my face into the crook of Lucy's neck. "I should probably take off. The faster I find this girl, the sooner I can return."

Lucy pressed a kiss on my cheek. "I'll be waiting here."

I smiled. "I know. I'll leave the dumbasses here to keep an eye on the kittens."

"That would be nice. I bet Myalis is a great babysitter."

"I regret informing you of my ability to communicate," Myalis said.

CHAPTER SIX

ARMOR UP

We spend a lot of time romanticizing the samurai as people of action and power, but this image is almost always framed with an incursion as the backdrop.

The samurai are saving civilians and killing aliens, averting, sometimes single-handedly, disasters no government or corporation could tackle on their own without massive losses.

When there isn't an active incursion, we see the samurai as laid-back celebrities or pioneers pushing radical new ideas.

But what about those other times? The times when they're not in the limelight?

The *International Enquirer* is there for you at those times!

24/7 coverage of all of your favorite samurai, delivered in a twice-daily format for the low, low subscription price of 350 credits a month!

—*International Enquirer* ad, June 2031

I looked at the image on the television one last time before sighing and poking Lucy in the sides. "Lucy, I need to get up," I said.

"Aww, but I'm comfy," she complained.

I chuckled. "You're not the one with a bony butt digging into your lap."

She gasped and half turned to face me. "My ass is not bony."

"It's practically nothing but bone."

Lucy jabbed an elbow into my gut, not hard enough to hurt, but enough to send a message. "Keep talking about it like that, and we'll see if you get to play with it anytime soon," she said as she hopped to her feet.

Laughing, I accepted the hand she extended to help me up. "Maybe I won't let you touch mine, then."

She shook her head. "Nope. That ass is mine."

I pulled her into a hug. Not a sexy hug, just a comforting press of two bodies together, holding her close so I could feel the tickle of breath against my neck and the hummingbird beat of her heart.

"You'll be back?" she asked.

"Always," I said. "I just need to go out and act the hero for a bit."

She nodded. "All right. Can you be safe?"

"I can try," I said. That was the best I could do. I'd never been out on samurai business before, or whatever they'd call going out to track some girl, but I had the impression that it wasn't exactly the safest thing to do.

"You're going to get changed?" Lucy asked.

I looked down at myself, at my very dirty pants and lack of a proper shirt. "I should. I've been thinking of buying some sort of armor too. Might as well do that now, before heading out. Maybe a few other things."

"Can I see?"

I couldn't help but grin. "Sure."

She would probably be disappointed. The movies and games made the whole process where a samurai got new gear out to be this big thing. In reality, it was much simpler.

Lucy and I headed over to the bedroom again, with only a few pauses along the way for a bit of kissing and groping. When we stumbled our way into the room, though, we separated. Lucy bounced on the edge of the bed a few times, then brought her knees up to her chin. "Do the thing!" she said.

"I'm afraid," Myalis said as Dumbass scurried into the room before I closed the door, "that the process isn't nearly as amusing as you might think."

I shrugged. "That's pretty accurate," I said as I undressed. "Myalis, I need some sort of armor. Nothing bulky, though."

"Of course! I have many millions of options for you, though I believe I can narrow it down to a few choices that would suit you best."

"Was that a pun?" Lucy asked.

Dumbass bobbed up and down but didn't answer the question. "I see three avenues you could take. Your Sun Watcher Technologies catalog has a few decent armors at tier one that could be very useful. They tend to be slim and form-fitting, with kinetic redistribution gels and nearly uncuttable materials. The better options have inbuilt systems for regulating temperature."

"All right," I said. That sounded neat enough. "And the other two options?"

"Your stealth specialty has some suits that allow for audio-ocular camouflage of the entire body. They can also serve as armor, though these wouldn't do much beyond stopping some very low-caliber weaponry. It would be more useful as a method to avoid getting hit than as one to prevent the damage from being hit, so to speak."

"Ooh, invisible BDSM Cat," Lucy said. "That could be kind of hot."

I decided to ignore that, even if it was hard to keep my mind on track. There was no way I was still hot and bothered after our morning, but all signs pointed to that being wrong.

"And the third option?" I asked.

"Purchase an armor catalog and buy something piecemeal, or a full set of proper armor. This is the option with the widest range in prices." Myalis, or maybe Dumbass, moved over to the side of the bed, then hopped on and nestled next to Lucy.

"Right," I said. "Okay, let's start with the Sun Watcher stuff."

"Might I suggest improving the catalog up one tier?" Myalis asked. "You have three tokens and an ample supply of points. The improvement in the level of technology cannot be overstated."

I thought about it for a bit. "How many points will I have left after that?"

"Eight thousand, seven hundred and twelve."

Still a lot of points. But those were limited. I wasn't going to get any more for a while. "You know what, sure."

Class II Sun Watcher Technologies unlocked!

Points Reduced from . . . 8,812 to . . . 8,712

"Good, now the armor. What price are we talking here?"

"That would depend on what exactly you're looking for. A simple gel suit with some protective capabilities and not much else would cost you ten points. A full suit, with self-repair, integrated medical load-outs, automatic adjustments, a deployable mask, Class II armor and weaves, temperature control, and minor reflex enhancers would cost two hundred points."

"You should take the more protective one," Lucy said. "Your new arm is cool and all, but I'd rather keep the rest of you all flesh. It's a lot more squishy."

I hesitated, but that was practically just for show. I'd already made up my mind. "What color does it come in?" I asked.

"Any color. Even those that can't be properly perceived by human eyes."

"Neat. Can you make it black?"

"Not black!" Lucy said. "That's so boring!"

I huffed. "Black is always in fashion," I said. "Plus I'm supposed to be stealthy. You'd probably want it to be pink or something. Black, or maybe that dark blue, like some of my other gear."

"A mix of both, perhaps. There are some complex parts to the suit," Myalis said.

"As long as by both you mean black and blue, then yeah, sure. Let's go with that."

New Purchase: Mark IV TIGER-B armor

Points Reduced from . . . 8,712 to . . . 8,512

A box appeared next to Lucy on the bed.

I stepped out of my pants, leaving me in not much at all except for my underthings, and moved over to the case.

Inside, I found a large belt and a few weird bracelets and something that looked like a very large necklace. All of them were big and bulky, and rather heavy when lifted. "Uh?"

"Put them on. The suit will assemble itself over your body."

"Cool!" Lucy said.

I had to agree—the belt was little more than a series of linked boxes with a clasp on the front. The bracelets went over my arms in a similar way, as did the sections over my ankles. The necklace, quite a bit heavier, sat awkwardly around my neck.

With the last piece on, the whole set buzzed. In the time it took to blink, plates of some bluish metal unfolded across my body, and a clothlike weave raced across my skin, then pulled taut.

"Nice!" Lucy said, clapping. "You look awesome!"

I stared down at myself and kinda had to agree. The armor clung, tight and formfitting, with plates following my ribs and covering my chest and upper arms. Armored sections covered my elbows and knees too, which would probably come in handy. The cloth had a few sharp lines done up in dark blue, giving it some contrast over the darker material.

"Oh man, that's tight," Lucy said as she reached out and ran a hand over my stomach. The material was pretty tight there—I could actually make out the dip of my belly button through the material.

"Is this actually bulletproof?" I asked.

"We could test it," Myalis said. "Give Lucy a gun."

"Oh," Lucy said.

I shut that down quickly enough. "Yeah, no, I'll take your word for it."

"I like the way it makes your butt look," Lucy said with a thumbs-up.

I snorted and made a mental note to look into a mirror later. "It already looked good."

Lucy nodded. "Your best asset," she said before breaking off into peals of giggles.

I shook my head and reached down to pick up my autoloader jacket. It would be that much more cover. As cool as the armor looked, it was a bit . . . skintight. I was far from self-conscious, but still.

"You should perhaps invest in a few other things before heading out," Myalis said. "Your armament seems appropriate for the likely level of threat you're going to face, but you're lacking in other areas. Your sensor packages are visual only so far, and not that terribly advanced."

"And you need to look even cooler," Lucy said. "And a bit more colorful. Like . . . a scarf or something."

I sighed. "All right, we can do a tiny bit more shopping."

CHAPTER SEVEN

LENDING AN EAR

Each samurai's personal appearance is, technically, owned by the samurai in question.

That is why it is strongly advised, when you sell clothes that imitate their look, you do so through the intermediary of at least three shell companies.

This will inevitably mean a large loss in profits, but it also serves as a method to keep your company safe. Even with the losses, copying samurai fashion is wildly profitable.

The moment a samurai comes out in public, their looks, their color scheme, their style and mannerisms become iconic. Some change their appearance on a near-weekly basis; others keep to a certain look and style for months or years until their equipment changes.

As long as the samurai never decides to question you, you can expect to make a tidy profit.

—Brian Ludlum, CFO of the Coco–Gucci–Vuitton Fashion
Consortium, 2051

I picked up my invisibility jacket, shook it once or twice to get the gunk off it, then sighed. "One sec," I said before heading over to the bathroom.

The shower, a place that had recently climbed to my personal top ten, became host to my jacket, which I flopped to the floor.

"Shower, on," I said.

When I returned to the bedroom, the shower still running behind me, it was to find Lucy cradling Dumbass the First on her lap and patting its head. The robot had turned on its hologram projector again, making it look like a rather smug tabby cat, though the illusion did break where Lucy's hand touched it.

"Okay, so things to buy," I said.

The cat nodded. "Indeed. As I mentioned, I believe your next investment should be a sensor suite."

"And what would that entail?" I asked.

"Oh, 'entail,'" Lucy repeated. "Big words, Cat."

I stuck my tongue out at her. "I can use more complicated words too, you know."

"Really? This morning you seemed to have a hard time articulating anything more complicated than baby seal noises."

I felt my cheeks warming and turned my focus back to Dumbass the First. "Sensor suites," I said.

"I would suggest a Sun Watcher Twin Ear system. It's a bit intrusive, connecting to your auditory cortex, but its uses are quite interesting. The Twin Ear comes equipped with ultrasound, laser microphones for hearing at long distances, a Geiger counter, thermal sensor, radial sonar and motion sensors, selective sound filters, and spatial recognizers. It even has a balance-assist system and long-range wireless communications."

"All right, that sounds pretty cool," I said. "How much?"

"Seventy-five points. The installation requires that your head be uncovered," Myalis said. "You may feel a slight tingle atop your skull."

I weighed the options back and forth. I didn't feel that more sensory stuff was pressing, exactly, but on the other hand, it was probably something similar to armor. I didn't need it until I did, and then it might be too late to ask for it.

"All right, let's do it."

New Purchase: Mark III Twin Ears

Points Reduced from . . . 8,512 to . . . 8,437

My head did tingle, and I felt my . . . hair moving?

I was reaching up to investigate when the world exploded into sound. Not overwhelming noise as I might have expected. No, it wasn't that. The world just became incredibly . . . clear.

I'd once switched from shitty in-ear buds to a proper headset, one that another orphan outside of the kittens had splurged on, and the difference in the sound had been wild.

This put that to shame. I could hear everything. The kittens fighting a ways away, the thumping of feet below us, air vents shifting above. The elevator was a low rumble, and Lucy's heart was a steady twin beat in the background.

"Whoa," I said.

My voice sounded . . . Well, it was still my voice, but it sounded more, somehow.

Lucy made a little squeaking sound, one that I heard loud and clear.

I looked over her way, only to see her grinning like mad and pointing at me . . . and something above me.

I reached up. My questing fingers bumped into something, something that seemed quite firmly attached to my skull. Something that *moved*.

Turning, I rushed over to the bathroom, every step sounding very loud.

I didn't *need* to, of course, I had a sort of sense of the world around me that I'd never had before, but I still had to see.

"Myalis, what the fuck?!"

Standing nice and proud above my head was a pair of metallic cat ears in a familiar dark blue. The interior was black, with a pink dot in the center of each ear surrounded by a faint pinkish glow.

"It's a very advanced sensor suite," Myalis said.

"You gave me weeb ears!"

Lucy clapped. "They fold back when you're mad!" she cheered.

I looked over to the mirror to see that they did, indeed, fold back. "What the hell, Myalis?"

"Cat," Lucy said, "you shouldn't talk to Myalis like that—she's trying to help you."

"I am," Myalis agreed.

Lucy hugged the faux-cat closer. "Plus, I think they look cute." She smiled. "I wouldn't mind something to nibble on, sometimes."

I felt myself flushing again, then stalked off into the bathroom to pick my jacket out of the shower. The water had been enough to soak most of the dried-up alien blood and soot from it. "Shower, dry," I said, and then I waited a few minutes, ears peeled to the sound of Lucy talking in the next room over.

"You really should have shown her what they looked like," Lucy said.

"Perhaps. But then she would have likely refused them. And I'm afraid that without additional systems like these, she might hurt herself," Myalis returned.

"And there wasn't a single system that didn't look like cat ears?"

". . . Perhaps. But these are the most amusing."

"Myalis," Lucy said with the same warning tone I'd heard her use so often on the kittens. "Cat is a very sensitive soul. You need to be careful with her. She's all soft and gooey under that hard shell."

I glared at the shower. I wasn't sensitive.

"I am aware," Myalis said. "Perhaps I can tone it down a little. Though it is still greatly amusing to embarrass her."

"It really is," Lucy agreed. "Oh, speaking of, do you have scarves?"

"Yes."

I grabbed my jacket from the shower, waved it around a bit to push off some of the last drops still clinging to it, then barged back into the bedroom. "What's this about scarves?" I asked.

There were about two dozen of them hovering around Dumbass the First. Holograms, obviously. Lucy smiled at me, then gestured to all of the cloth around her. "This makes buying clothes a lot easier," she said.

"We could never afford clothes," I pointed out.

"You can now," she said with a shit-eating grin.

I crossed my arms. "What makes you think I'd buy clothes for you?"

"I bet Myalis can get some really comfortable lingerie," Lucy mused.

Internally, I cursed Deus Ex for giving me a stupid mission that would drag me away for so much as an hour. "M-maybe later," I said.

"I think this one, but in pink, like the color around her arm," Lucy said as she gestured to one of the scarves.

"Really?" I asked.

"It's one point," Lucy defended herself.

I rolled my eyes. "Fine."

New Purchase: Plain Cloth Scarf

Points Reduced from . . . 8,437 to . . . 8,436

The packet with the scarf appeared next to Lucy, and she was quick to open it. "Ohh, silky," she said as she got to her feet, Dumbass scurrying off her lap in a hurry.

She placed the scarf around my neck, then used it to pull me into a kiss.

"Come back safe, all right?"

I leaned into a second kiss. "I will," I said. "The dumbasses will stay here, just in case."

She nodded, then turned me toward the door before giving my rear a smack I barely felt. "Go be a hero."

CHAPTER EIGHT

HOVER

The great selling point of hovercraft was the lowered traffic.

That was until someone realized that a complete lack of oversight was an absolute disaster. So the bureaucrats came in. They set height and speed limits, created avenues and aerial roads. They formed new departments specifically to regulate traffic in the air, then commissioned new companies to act as police forces.

New permissions had to be handed out to EMTs and police and paramilitaries so that they could use the roads too.

Soon, the air roads became just as clogged and congested as those on the ground.

New roads were added atop them, ones that required special permits, or that were policed by private corporations that purchased the airspace and sold traffic rights for exorbitant prices.

Now an executive can get across the city in mere minutes, while the middle class wait in traffic, and the poor have to contend with the ultraviolence of the ground and what few public transit systems are still in place.

Our stratified society became far more literal.

—Alex Begler, *The New Air Race*, 2034

I stepped out of the penthouse while adjusting my new scarf.

A scarf shouldn't have worked to tie together my rather eclectic outfit, but somehow it did. It probably helped that just about everything was a mix of the same three or so colors. It made matching things easy.

I moved past a cleaning android and toward the elevators while adjusting Whisper over my back. I wasn't expecting to find two guys in the hotel's livery standing by the elevator doors.

"What're you guys doing here?" I asked.

They looked at each other, and then one cleared his throat. "We're with the hotel's security, ma'am. Just making sure there are no more intrusions like this morning."

"Huh," I said. "Well, that's nice."

People doing nice things for me just because? That was going to take some getting used to.

I've called the elevator up. We'll have to find a way to get to Katallina's last known location. It's not within walking distance, and I suspect that there will be some barriers along the way.

I nodded, not wanting to make a fool of myself before the guards. The elevator rose, clearly audible thanks to my new ears, and I stepped into it before turning around to face the exit.

A moment or two after the doors closed, I heard one of the hotel guys muttering to his friend. "She's scary."

"Scary but kinda hot," the other said.

I rolled my eyes as we descended. "Where was she last seen?" I asked Myalis.

Her last known location was in the orange zone of yesterday's incursion. That area has returned to being a green zone as of this morning.

"Am I likely to run into some aliens?" I asked. I could probably use a few more points.

Statistically unlikely.

"Well, that's no fun," I said as the elevator slowed to a smooth stop and its doors opened to the hotel's lobby.

I hadn't really taken much time to look around the night before. It was a bit hazy. I remembered getting out of a car that Speedy the Clenze soldier drove over, and then a minute later I was falling asleep on a comfortable bed.

Now I could take in the big marble pillars and the holographic modern art sculptures and even the people moving about. There was *something* about the rich that made them stand out. Not just the expensive-as-hell clothes, but their demeanor and way of moving.

The women all wore impractical gowns and looked like they could be on a catwalk. They were showing off body mods that probably cost more than what most people made in a lifetime. The men were no better. Some in suits and ties, but the really rich wore clothes meant to look casual at first glance.

They didn't need to wear a suit, because they were so important that tradition would bend over backward for them, not the other way around.

By contrast, the hotel staff all looked like they had twice-daily applications of sticks up their asses. They were uptight and servile and looked like they were dead inside.

I stepped out and felt a few eyes turning my way. The pretty women took in my half-burnt features and lanky hair, then realized that my looks didn't matter because I was carrying a fuck-huge crossbow.

Really, all those shows Lucy and I had watched as little girls telling us we had to be pretty never mentioned that you would get just as much positive attention from carrying half your body's weight in guns around.

It was with a smug little grin that I cut past a line at the front of the lobby and stationed myself right in front of the only human behind the counter. The other rows had androids, and far fewer people waiting.

The young woman behind the counter blinked, then smiled through the transparent mask over her mouth. "How may I help you, ma'am?"

"I need a taxi," I said.

She nodded. "Of course. We have an in-house taxi service available right outside the main entrance. You need only flag down one of our valets . . . I'll call ahead for you, if you want."

That was handy. "I'd appreciate that," I said. "Thanks!"

I crossed back to the middle of the room, then looked around.

You're lost, aren't you?

"Just a bit," I said. A large red arrow appeared in my vision, and then because Myalis was being a pain in the ass, a dozen more arrows appeared around that one, all pointing toward a doorway across the room. I . . . could probably have found it just by listening to the traffic, I realized as I moved closer.

Stepping through the airlocked entranceway, I found myself next to a tunnel built into the side of the building. There was a car dispenser—basically a lift where you could park a car and it would be stored somewhere deeper in the hotel—and a few more impressive cars were parked out front, where they were plugged in to recharge.

"Miss Samurai?" An acne-faced valet asked as he moved over. "Um, you need a taxi, miss?"

"Yeah," I said. "Got anything?"

"Yes, of course," he said. "Could you wait here for just a moment?"

I nodded as he pulled up a tablet and pressed a few buttons.

One of the dispensers rumbled up, cars flashing by as they rotated past, and then a small yellow hovercar drove off the system and floated its way over to us.

The valet and I both stared at the little yellow clown car. "I . . . can order up something, um, better," he said.

"It's self-driving?" I asked as I looked inside. It had two pairs of two seats, both facing the middle where a little table sat. No controls that I could see. "It'll do," I said. I wasn't looking for anything fancy anyway.

The boy—who was probably older than me but had a spine like a wet towel—opened the back door for me. I tossed Whisper in, then contorted myself into the seat.

"Thanks," I said before he shut the door. I had to shift to accommodate my tail a bit, but it wasn't so bad. "Now . . . how does this work?"

You have no public record of using one of these that I can find. It's meant to connect to your augmentations, then drive safely and securely to a destination you specify. The cost is extracted from your credit account based on mileage, plus service fees, membership fees, special fees, local taxes, and a few other price-gouging techniques.

"Uh-huh," I said. "I spent most of my credits on a sandwich yesterday."

Your purchase was reimbursed, actually. Your current total would . . . not cover the reparking fee.

"That's . . . annoying."

I've hacked into the vehicle's controls. Or rather, I did so before you stepped out of the hotel.

My eyes narrowed. "Are you the reason I'm in this tiny thing?"

We're taking off now.

"You didn't answer the question, Myalis!" Any further conversation was curbed when the hovercar took off with a lurch, cut off some fancy car, then shot into the sky.

There were roads, with plenty of midday traffic flitting through the smoke let out by smokestacks, and low-hanging smog clouds, which drizzled down a haze of rain that smacked into the car's windows. Myalis didn't seem to care about such trivialities.

We didn't merge into the traffic flows or slide into one of the far more expensive express routes. Instead, Myalis flew across the city on a diagonal.

"This can't be legal," I said.

It isn't.

"Uh."

It's not as though traffic laws apply to us. Most traffic enforcement vehicles ping off any law-breaking hovercar's onboard computer to make it come to a stop. I can merely tell them that this vehicle has been commandeered by a Vanguard.

"And what's stopping anyone else from doing the same thing?" I asked.

Superior coding. That, and on occasion traffic police will nonetheless chase down a Vanguard's vehicle. It usually ends in disaster. In this case, though, our flight plan is bringing us directly into a semiactive incursion zone. There's nothing for them to worry about.

I settled into my seat, one foot pressing against the table in the middle to keep me in place. "Nothing to worry about," I repeated as I worried.

CHAPTER NINE

TWITCHY

In this three-part summary, we will explain the historical precedent for the fall of global powers after the first incursion.

There were three, arguably four, major economic and military power-house nations on Earth. The United States of America, the Russian Federation, the People's Republic of China, and, by some reckonings, the Federal Republic of Germany.

By 2030, the three most powerful of these nations no longer existed in a form that people prior to 2020 would recognize.

The fall of the United States was rather abrupt for some, though others had predicted it for some time. The nation, after years of turmoil, broke apart and might have fallen into civil war if not for the intervention of some key players.

The reversal of *Roe v. Wade*, the increased power of increasingly religious authorities in some regions, the crash of the federal economy, increased tensions between growing minorities and the police, and the rise of a third "corporate" party all hastened the demise of a once-powerful nation into a mess of nation-states with their own laws, regulations, and animosities.

—A History after the Drop, online lecture by Professor Sterne

The amount of traffic on the immediate edge of the incursion zone was surprising. I expected people to keep away but might have been giving them too much credit.

Not that it truly mattered. We shot right past an aerial barricade manned by a few police chasers and deeper into the city without so much as twitching. I saw a cop's head snap around, but no one followed us, so I figured we were safe.

It was eerie flying through a city with no cars moving around at a snail's pace, the lights in most towers completely off, and the smog layer above broken in a few places to reveal the sky above. I found myself taking things in through the rainbow-wet sheen of the windshield.

We weren't moving toward the center of the incursion zone but rather skirting along the edge.

Right over here.

The little taxi started to slow down while rising. Floors flashed past, accompanied by huge unlit billboards for health insurance and the newest shoes, until we leveled off and turned into an open parking garage.

The place was only lit by a few dozen red emergency lights, enough to make out a lack of parked cars and a whole lot of empty space.

Myalis parked in the middle of the lot, coming down with a faint lurch before the hovercar's engines whined to a stop.

"This is it?" I asked.

The door next to me opened with a hiss.

Yes. This is the place. Our subject was last seen two floors down.

I stepped out, pulled Whisper along behind me, then looked about for anything interesting. I could hear all sorts of things: metal ticking, the patter of the rain outside, the humming of some ventilation systems and old neon lights. Nothing that sounded alien or alive.

I tucked Whisper up against my shoulder, then thought better of it and slung the crossbow over my back. "Let's head out, then," I said as I pulled out my Trench Maker, still loaded with some highly flammable high-explosive .45 rounds. Probably more handy in the tight confines of a building than my crossbow.

Elevator access is to your right.

Following Myalis's instructions brought me to an elevator that opened as soon as I got close to it. "So, do you have a plan? Because I know fuck-all about finding lost people. I've seen a couple of police procedurals, but I don't think those count."

The building's camera and security network is on a closed circuit. Part of it is stored online, hence why the other Vanguards found what they did, but the rest is better secured. I could break in, but there might be physical shutoffs. I think the best solution is to search around the area where Miss McCarthy was last seen, then find out where the security system is actually stored to verify what we can.

I stepped into the elevator and hummed along to the shitty autogenerated music. "Sounds good," I said.

The doors opened again when I was a couple of floors down, and I stepped out into a long corridor lined with doors that had little numbers on them.

Most of them were torn open already, lying on the floor off to one side, or just left open.

All the junk on the floor hinted at why they'd been opened, as did the noise of people moving deeper in the floor.

"What the hell?" I muttered as I brought my Trench Maker up and walked down the passage. A glimpse into one of the apartments showed a tiny little home. There was a kitchen–living room combo, with a little office space at the back missing any computer hardware. Another smashed-open door inside showed a bedroom hardly bigger than the queen-size bed within, with a cramped en suite bathroom.

The entire thing didn't take up half the space of the bedroom Lucy and I had shared the night before.

A picture on the wall showed off a family of five: three kids and their parents. It was a bit small for that many people but seemed pretty standard for a middle-class home.

I kept moving, passing more and more apartments with doors torn off hinges and interiors ransacked and emptied of anything valuable. Printed pictures and the like were left behind, but it was obvious TVs had been torn off walls, and computers were missing from desks.

Some of the apartments had little two-by-two windows looking out onto the smog. Those were probably a bit pricier.

I increased my pace, ignoring some of the apartments in favor of making better time toward the end of the corridor where I could still hear someone . . . multiple someones . . . moving around and grunting.

The moment I came around a corner I found myself facing a group of men in overalls and bulletproof vests manhandling a battering ram into a door.

Behind them was a long cart, stacked full of computers and screens.

One of them, an obvious lookout, screamed something incoherent on seeing me, raised a compact SMG, and pulled the trigger.

I dove back around the corner just as a wild spray of bullets tore holes into the wall across the corner.

"What the hell!" I shouted.

"Th-this area is under the, uh, control of the NMS and R group!" one of them called back.

I pressed my back against the wall while my heart calmed down. I hadn't been hit, and my hearing was fine. That was a start. I could hear six distinct heartbeats around the corner, and more idiots moving farther away.

"Who the fuck are you?" I asked.

"You're trespassing on corporate territory!" someone else called out. "Come out with your hands in the air and all weapons dropped. All goods on your person are forfeit. Prepare yourself for fines and imprisonment!"

From what I can tell, the NMSR is a group of postincursion scavengers. They are here legally.

"Wonderful," I said. "They've been emptying people's houses?"

That is what they do.

"All right," I said. "I'm coming out. If I see any of you with a gun point-ing my way, you're dead. I've got some new weapons I haven't tested out yet. You don't want to play guinea pig."

Myalis got the hint, because my shoulder-mounted guns unfolded and came to a rest beside my head. The railgun to one side, plasma caster on the other.

"Threatening us won't do anything. Come on out right now!"

I could hear them moving around, placing the cart between us and bringing guns to bear. "Myalis, can you send them a nice warning?"

With pleasure.

There was a long moment of silence, only faster heartbeats filling it, then a soft "Oh, fuck."

I turned around and waved out the side with my mechanical arm. "Hey, guys, how about you lower those and we won't have ourselves a mess?" I asked. "I'm sure your insurance premiums would be much lower if you didn't add suicide by samurai to them."

"It could be fake," one of them whispered.

"It isn't," I said.

I could tell most of them had lowered their guns thanks to my weird-ass echo-vision, so I carefully moved out of cover, arms lowering so both hands wrapped around the handle of my Trench Maker.

Six pairs of eyes locked onto me. They didn't seem all that enthused about the guns on my shoulders. "So, which one of you just tried to shoot me?" I asked.

Five of them glanced at the weediest guy of the lot, who was shaking his head like a kitten caught with his hand in the cookie jar.

"Yeah, next time maybe, you know, don't shoot random people?" I asked.

"Are . . . are you a samurai?" one asked.

"Yeah. I'm here investigating something, and now," I said with a growing smile, "I have all of you to help me!"

CHAPTER TEN

MORE QUESTIONS THAN ANSWERS

By 2020, China was well on its way to becoming the world's second superpower.

By 2025, the country was in turmoil, plagued by economic instability (much of it caused by a global recession where many countries simply stopped importing goods), social unrest, and a growing feud between the ruling party and the few samurai in the country.

Most major shifts in global affairs past 2020 can be linked in one way or another to a samurai, or a group of them, but China's near-collapse is the most obvious of these.

In 2022, an incursion appeared over Fujian. The reaction of the government was, surprisingly, positive. By then, many other global powers had their own samurai, and China was looking forward to obtaining its own.

The incursion went poorly, as it was the first mass appearance of Model Sevens. Someone, and it is still unknown who was responsible, authorized the use of low-yield nuclear weapons over the province.

It secured a victory, but at the cost of nearly all local samurai.

In the following year, another pair of incursions appeared over the area: in Taiwan, and near Hong Kong. The samurai born from these did not share an enthusiastic relationship with the Chinese government. By 2030, the area was governed by three countries, two of which were, and still are, under the protection of local samurai warlords. The Democratic Republic of Hong Kong, the Independent Republic of Taiwan, and the People's Republic of China.

—*A History after the Drop*,
online lecture by Professor Sterne

I grinned at all the workers. "Where's your manager?" I asked.

It took all of a minute for some sweaty middle-aged woman to jog over to meet me in the same corridor I'd almost been shot in. "H-hello," she said as she caught her breath. "How can I help?"

"Well, first, you can explain what's going on here," I said with a gesture to the workers behind her. They'd stopped breaking into apartments and emptying them to stare at our little spectacle.

"We're checking the area for xenos, ma'am," the manager said.

I stared at her, then at the cart laden with computers and televisions and tablets. "Have the aliens been disguising themselves as PCs while I wasn't paying attention?" I asked.

The woman straightened. "It's within our charter to recover any valuables left in the area."

"Uh-huh," I said. "You're not even tagging them or anything. There's no way that someone who lives here will be able to tell their stuff apart from anyone else's."

"There are ways to recoup any lost belongings," the woman said. She didn't look comfortable saying it, and it only took a second of meeting her eyes to communicate that we both knew how full of shit she was.

"You guys can leave the rest of the stuff where it is," I said. "And leave the cart too."

She hesitated. I could almost see the math working itself out behind her eyes. She was no doubt going to be losing a lot of credits, but I found myself with few fucks to give. "I— Of course, we'll clear out right away."

"Good. Now, I'm looking for someone. Myalis, can you send her a photo?"

Of course. Consider it sent.

The manager shook her head. "Never seen her. One moment." She had me nervous as she reached into a big pocket, but it was only to retrieve a tablet. Soon she was clicking through images: faces, some bloody, others not. Most with their eyes closed, and all obviously dead.

"What's that?" I asked.

"One of our duties here is clearing out the dead. There aren't usually that many, but some xenos did make it over here."

I nodded. I'd seen as much with what little footage of Katallina I'd seen. "You keep a catalog of the dead?" I asked.

She nodded absently while still scrolling past pictures. "The dead, and their IDs if we can find them. I can't find anyone fitting the bill. The only person that looks about the right age is this boy."

She turned the tablet over so that I could take in an image of a boy, maybe Junior's age, with a nice set of augs and a face covered in dried blood. "Right," I said. "Did you guys see anything suspicious?"

"No," she said.

One of the guys shuffled, and I turned over to stare at him.

He froze. "I-I might have, uh, seen something?" he said.

"Spill," I said.

The man swallowed. "We found bullet casings on this floor. Um, lots of them, near some dead Antithesis. No guns, though, and no bodies."

It could be anything. Someone with a fancy gun or two that came out to help when the aliens came around. Or it could be Katallina. She had a gun on her in that little bit of footage I'd seen.

"Got any pictures or video of the casings and bodies?" I asked.

He nodded and looked over to his manager.

"We'll send it to you as soon as it's processed," the woman said.

"Good," I said. "We can all wait here while that happens."

She looked like someone that had just swallowed something sour. "I'll . . . see what I can do," she said before returning to tap at her device. "It's a lot of data to sift through."

"I'm pretty sure my AI can manage."

I'd say that your faith in me is reassuring, but really, there are only a few terabytes. It's child's play.

The woman reluctantly sent the file at me through an aug-code that my fancy new gear picked off her screen and parsed through.

This is interesting. Look at these.

A screen opened before me, then a few more. One had video of a camera panning across a couple of Model Threes, all very dead, and down to a small pile of casings on the floor.

The photos of the casings weren't all that helpful at first glance. They were a metallic white, with no serial numbers that I could make out on them.

I took a step back from the manager and frowned at the empty air. "Could they be from the gun the girl was using?"

They're not. Nor are these.

A different set of images, this one of more dead aliens. The image zoomed in on a few casings left on the ground, all small and coppery.

Standard ten-millimeter armor-piercing rounds. Not too common among human weaponry.

"That doesn't leave us with that many clues," I muttered.

No, but it is a start. I could perhaps trace these other rounds.

I shook my head. "It could be nothing. Let's find the security room first. We might be able to find something there."

I asked the very relieved manager for directions, then waved the scavengers off as I headed toward the security rooms near the center of the building. I could hear them arguing over whether to take the stuff they'd been "securing." The consensus seemed to be that the few credits they'd make after it was all sold weren't worth annoying me, which was nice.

The security room, as it turned out, was little more than a closet tucked into a maintenance passage. The door was heavy and had a pretty nice security system linked to it. It took Myalis more time to say something witty than it did for her to bypass it.

I found myself before a shitty old desk with a pair of dusty screens. There was a mini-fridge in the corner and an ashtray overflowing with used filters.

Sitting down, I turned to the screens, then, realizing I knew nothing about what had to be done, turned to the fridge instead. There was a small bounty of energy drinks in there.

You're really working hard on this mission, aren't you?

I kicked back, legs crossing atop the desk as I examined two cans. One was Hyper Sucrose Extreme!, a special-edition can with some anime figure on it. It had to be an import, because the can didn't have any nutritional information other than "fuckloads of sugah!" written in small text on the bottom.

The other choice was Boomerade. It had some silver-haired samurai on its side giving me a thumbs-up and occasionally winking.

I stuck to the can with the anime girl on it. She was less creepy. A sip and a full-body shiver later, I gestured to the screens. "Have you found anything?" I asked.

Myalis's response was a long-suffering sigh.

The screens came on, and I got to see the same video of Katallina running, though now from two angles.

"Do we have anything earlier?"

All the cameras in the other areas of the building are defective and have been for some time. Maintenance logs claim that they were taken care of, but the evidence suggests otherwise. There's more.

The footage sped ahead, changing angles every so often as Myalis changed cameras. I got to see the girl running, tears streaming from her eyes. The gun she had was definitely high-tech, more so than the raggedy clothes she had on.

Her dog barked on camera and jumped at a Model Three that was charging at her.

I was worried until she gunned the alien down and called her dog back to her side.

She seemed to be making good time across the building, no doubt racking up a few points as she went down one staircase, then another, meeting more aliens as she went.

No stopping for new gear, not even when she paused to replace the magazine in her gun with one from a back pocket.

Too nervous? In too much of a hurry? Maybe the adrenaline was in the way.

This one is from this floor.

The next bit was very familiar. Katallina running with her dog at her heels, Model Threes coming out behind her in chase.

And then she ran into a group of three men in black uniforms. Full-face masks, armored padding, all in pitch-black.

They gunned the aliens down, then approached Katallina, who looked surprised. I couldn't blame her.

She smiled, hope breaking through the tears at last, and pointed to something behind her.

Then one of the men grabbed her and tossed her to the floor.

The dog was kicked aside. Something was sprayed in her face, and she fought before going limp.

They tied her up, then did the same to her dog, knocking it out and tying its paws together with straps.

My feet dropped from the desk. "What the fuck," I said.

That is certainly the right question to ask.

CHAPTER ELEVEN

NOBODIES

Pre-2020 Russia was a military powerhouse with some economic issues and a growing sense of discontent in its lower classes.

Russia post-2030 is a military powerhouse with some economic issues and a growing sense of discontent in its lower classes.

Interestingly enough, despite being hit with the most incursions of any single country, Russia has changed few of its policies, and its methodology has remained mostly the same over the years. Its samurai are generally worshiped and idolized as national heroes and are given a fair amount of leniency and power in the nation as long as they don't cross certain lines.

Its government is as corrupt and bribable as it has ever been, and a host of narcotics have joined alcohol in poisoning the downtrodden.

It can't be said that the nation has prospered, but it has grown far more populous and, despite some repeated disasters, has managed to cling onto its power through turbulent times. Its borders are the same, but the population has become hyperconcentrated around a few massive cities. Its military still uses machinery and equipment dating back to the last century, but they outnumber any other nation's man-for-man.

—*A History after the Drop*, online lecture by Professor Sterne

Myalis, being the awesome AI that she was, tracked the movement of our men in black through the entire building. They had a pair of hover-vans parked up on the same level I had parked at. Just a couple of small, unmarked vehicles that slid in and waited while the other hovercar owners rushed out of the building in a hurry.

We were able to spot them moving down a few floors, always using the stairs, always ducking out of people's way without ever actually saying anything.

They had arrived within forty-five minutes of the incursion starting, and had reached Katallina by the one-hour mark.

Five minutes later they were back in their vans and taking off to parts unknown.

I looked at the images Myalis had picked out on the screens, one of each of the guys in black. There were two teams of four. Katalina had run into one of them; the other had retreated right after. I could tell that some of them were women under the armor, but that was it. They wore darkened visors that hid their eyes, masks over their lower faces, no skin or hair was visible, and each camera they passed fizzed out and died soon after they appeared.

Both teams had one member that wasn't as well armed as the others, a person with a large backpack with an antenna sticking out the top, along with obvious vents cut into the fabric. Judging by the glow behind their visors and the stuttery way they moved, they were jacked into something. Tech specialists, maybe?

"I can't see any logos," I said after eyeing the still.

None are present. I'm running their equipment through a list of manufactured goods. Most of it is standard issue for a few different paramilitary organizations, but none have their entire setup.

I shook my head. "Can you go over that again?"

Their boots, for example, are used by six paramilitary organizations in North America. Their guns are used by eight. Their helmets by four. None of them are all used by the same group. Their equipment borrows pieces from many companies, but not from one single organization.

Were they doing like the orphanage and raising some secondhand mercenary store? "What about their vans?"

Rentals, from what I can tell. From a local distributor, under a false name. All tags were removed, but one of the cameras by the entrance was able to see the serial code printed on the corner of a windshield.

Images moved around until I could make out a zoomed-in image of a window reflecting a finger-width serial code. "Nice," I said. "Does it point us in any useful direction?"

Unfortunately, no. I can't trace the credit information used. The bank they used to pay is secure enough that it would require more than a mere internet connection for me to slip past.

I put "calling the bank to ask nice-like" on my list of things to do. I leaned back into my seat, eyes idly following the motions of the group caught from odd angles as they made their way up while carrying a knocked-out girl and a dog with them.

"Why'd they save the dog?"

It was too much to imagine that they just didn't like the idea of hurting a dog. Not that people going around armed to the teeth during a crisis, with no doubt legally dubious intentions, couldn't have a conscience.

But something told me I probably shouldn't assume they were saints under those masks.

Maybe they're not cat people.

"Was that a joke?" I waved it off. "No, never mind, I don't want to know. We . . . Fuck, I don't know what to do from here."

Following them would be difficult. We don't have the resources on hand to see from every camera across this part of the city.

I hummed as I thought. I didn't have that kind of power. Myalis was pretty good at tracking things, obviously, but she had her limits.

My open palm smacked the desk. "Longbow!"

The Vanguard?

"Remember? He had control of the cameras across the street from where we were yesterday. He said something about hacking into them."

I could likely do the same. Though it would be a rather big investment of points to obtain the equipment to crack every security system in the area. Perhaps drones to physically connect to each closed network?

"Can you call him?"

One moment.

I spun on the chair, letting it squeak left and right while I sipped my drink and let the sugar do horrible things to me.

My augs displayed a video feed of Longbow . . . wearing some sort of medieval archer cosplay? "The fuck are you wearing?"

The man grinned. "Hey! It's my newest little sis! How are you doing, Stray Cat?"

I snorted. "I'm fine, big bro Longbow," I said. "But seriously, what's with the getup, and is that a codpiece?"

"Might be," he said with far too much confidence for a guy wearing tights. "I was in a game. What's up?"

"Like . . . LARPing?" I asked.

"What? No, I'm in a game now. This is an avatar." As if to prove the point, he poked his own finger through his opposite hand. "Just setting up for a raid."

"Right," I said. Longbow was a nerd. Duly noted. "I was wondering if you could help me out. I'm tracking down this girl, she's probably a samurai. Really new. As in, like 'me' new. And she got kidnapped by some mercs."

Longbow frowned. "That's fucky. What have you got on them?"

"Myalis?"

Sending.

I saw Longbow looking off to the side, little screens opening in the air before him, then winking out. "Nope, don't recognize them. Which is probably what they're going for."

"Yeah. I need help tracking them down."

"Using the city's cameras?" he asked. "I could probably do that, but there might be a faster way. You ever hear of Dial-Up?"

"You mean, like, before fiber internet?" I asked. "The one with the noises?"

Longbow barked a laugh. "Your age is showing. Right, so Dial-Up and Lag are this pair of samurai that basically live online. They're jacked in at all times. No sleeping, nothing."

"That sounds healthy."

"They invested a load of points into getting their brains jarred."

I imagined that for a second. "Why? And how would they fight off an incursion while in a jar?"

"They have tanks," Longbow said. "The jars are in them. It's pretty cool."

"If . . . you say so."

"They're pretty much the be-all and end-all of information brokerage online. Go give them a visit. They probably won't charge you if it's for helping another little sister. Probably won't help you IRL, but what can you do? I'm sending your Myalis the links to get to their place in MeshSpace. If you need, like, a drone strike later, give me a call. I've got a dragon to kill."

He waved me off, and I found myself staring at a wall with a poster of some woman wearing very little slapped over a server rack. "O-kay."

I've received the coordinates to Dial-Up and Lag.

"Can you call them?"

One moment . . . No.

"Uh, no?"

From what I can tell at a glance, there aren't any direct traces of them online. All links end with a packet entering your cyber warfare system that politely informs you to stop looking. This includes Google searches. It's actually impressive.

"That doesn't sound subtle."

I don't think it's meant to be.

"So we need to go see them in MeshSpace. This is starting to feel like a shitty fetch quest."

You might have to get off your no doubt comfortable seat and actually do some work. How unfortunate.

I let out a sigh, chugged the last of my energy drink, then left it on the desk. Someone could cash it in for a chit they'd be able to exchange for another drink . . . if they collected a hundred. "Let's go back to the hotel," I said. "If we're going to dive online, it'll be at home. Maybe I can use Lucy as a body pillow while I dive."

Your mind is a bizarre and terrifying place.

CHAPTER TWELVE

DOORFRAME

The internet has existed in one form or another since the 1980s. Though that far back, it's practically unrecognizable when compared to what people now think of as the internet.

MeshSpace, a creation started by a small group of samurai with the backing of IBM and Microsoft, was meant to be the next step in the evolution of the internet. A place where people who were "jacked in" (that is, connected directly into the mesh via neural augmentations) could communicate, play, create, and express themselves.

Within a month, it was a hive of advertisements and pornography.

There have been major steps taken to police and regulate MeshSpace, but, as with the original (and still extant) internet, these have been met with ridicule or outright ignored.

Truly an improvement.

—Extract from *A History of the Mesh*, 2048

Myalis parked our little taxi right in the middle of the driveway of the hotel and opened the door with a whoosh of expelled air. I stepped out and stretched while glancing around.

I'd left the last place in a hurry, only pausing long enough to make sure the scavengers had left all the shit that wasn't theirs behind. It would probably make the few people on that one floor happy.

The only other thing I did was place a digital warning at the door to Katallina McCarthy's little apartment. She shared a one-room apartment with her mother, apparently, a mother whom Myalis was able to confirm as dead.

Anyone stopping by her place would get a prerecorded message politely asking them to contact me, and then a prerecorded threat that if they fucked with the place, I'd be contacting them.

Making threats was turning out to be a whole lot of fun. It was kind of cathartic. At the same time I was a tiny bit worried I might become an asshole . . . *more* of an asshole.

I walked past a group of valets by the door, only acknowledging them with a wave before I was in the hotel.

The moment I stepped in, about six people from all over the lobby perked up and turned my way. Had it been only the one, I might not have noticed, but out of the fifty-odd people going about their business, six was just too many.

"Myalis, trouble."

I felt the guns on my back shifting. Not deploying yet, but certainly getting ready to.

I started toward the elevators, taking a circuitous route around part of the building where I'd pass some partial cover behind glass-walled terrariums with some no doubt exotic weeds within.

The first of them cornered me just past that. His opening salvo came in the form of a bright, startlingly fake smile. "Hello, miss! I'm a representative of Nimbletainment Inc., and I think I have just the deal for you!"

It took half a second for that to register. "Are you suicidal?" I asked, dumbfounded.

His smile never so much as twitched. "I'm a retail salesman, ma'am. The answer to that question is a resounding yes. And I hope that your answer will be a yes too, but to an entirely different question! Did you know that Nimbletainment has a sponsorship program, exclusively for samurai?"

"Uh, no." I said. "I'm leaving now, and . . . get help? Elsewhere. Please?"

I circled around him, then jogged to make it to the elevator. I think a few of them had the clever idea of joining me in a small, enclosed space for an indeterminate amount of time, because they started jogging too.

One of the elevator doors opened, and a businesswoman stepped out. "Myalis, door!" I said before I ducked down and scooped the lady off her feet instead of either shoving her back in or tossing her out of the way.

She squeaked, and wiggled in my arms while the door clicked shut behind me.

"Sorry," I said as I set her back down onto her heels. "Didn't mean to pick you up like that."

She smacked me with her purse. "I—I ought to sue you!" she said.

Then she took a good look at me and the color drained from her face. "You're not a samurai, right?"

"I am. A real sorry samurai who'd rather you didn't sue her," I said.

She huffed, then straightened her outfit. "Why were you in such a hurry?"

I shrugged. "Very aggressive, possibly mentally unhealthy salesmen?"

Her eyes closed and she let out a sigh. "That's fair. You're making me late to an appointment, you know?"

"Aw, well, shit," I said. The doors opened again, and I recognized the floor the kittens were staying on. "Sorry again," I said as I slipped out and jogged past two new valet-guards.

"What a bitch," I heard the woman mutter before she poked at the button to close the doors.

I sighed and slowed to a walk before stopping at the door to the penthouse. I knocked, just in case, then tried the handle.

The door opened about an inch, then stopped on a chain. I hadn't known they had that kind of low-tech security on top of everything else.

"Coming!" I heard Lucy claim. She walked over, her gait hesitant, like she wanted to run but wasn't sure.

The door closed, the chain rattled, and then I was face-to-face with Lucy again.

This time, when I swept a woman off her feet, it was to giggles and an intense kiss that only stopped when my back started to hurt. "You're heavy," I complained as I set her down.

She jammed a real hard finger in my ribs. "Close the door. And maybe go stand on the other side of it if you're going to be calling me fat."

I rubbed the flat of my hand against her not-at-all-fat stomach. "So chubby," I teased. It earned me another poke in the side.

"Why're you here already? Did it go well?" Lucy asked.

"Yeah!" Nose asked. "Did you kill anyone?"

"Can we see?" Nemo added.

I looked over and noticed our audience for the first time. About half the kittens were in the living room, and paying attention let me suss out the location of the rest in various rooms in the penthouse. "No, I didn't, and if I did you couldn't see it," I said.

Lucy grinned and pulled me after her toward the kitchen island. "So?" she asked.

"Went well enough. I have a lead to follow, so I'm not quite done. Where's Daniel?"

"Daniel?" she asked. Then Lucy gasped dramatically. "Did you misplace all your gayness and now you need a man in your life?"

I rolled my eyes. "You're an idiot," I said. "I need to do a thing online. Figured he could help."

"He's in the second living room," she said. "Want anything to drink?"

I shrugged, accepted a can of some low-calorie crap that was no doubt subtle revenge for that fat joke, and then followed Lucy. "Why does this place have two living rooms?"

"I don't know, and I never want to leave," Lucy said. "Oh, look, no crutches." She skipped ahead for all of two bounces, then slowed down with a huff so that I could catch up. She then used me as a two-legged crutch, confirming once and for all that all those times she hung off me before really were just disguised cuddling.

"You need to work on that some more."

"I'm going to learn how to strut," she said. "And wear heels. Sexy heels that you'll buy for me, then take off."

"Uh-huh," I said. I was more than willing to hear all about the heels I'd apparently be buying her.

We stepped into a smaller but still stupidly lavish living room to find Daniel on his back on one sofa, a bloody pile of toilet paper next to him and a cloth pressed to his face. He groaned as he strained his neck to look my way. "Oh. Hey."

"Hey," I said. "So what happened to you?"

"Walking's hard," he said. "It's not fair. You see the kittens running all over the damned place. Never stopping. Little shits making it look easy."

"Daniel's been rediscovering his long-lost relationship with gravity," Lucy said.

Daniel made a noise that could have meant anything.

"Right," I said. "And all the blood?"

"Doorframe."

I nodded. "I need your help with a thing."

"Does it involve walking?"

"No."

"I'm your man," he said. "What do you need?"

"I need to get into the Mesh to visit some folk."

"You couldn't have come to a better place. Now go get my shit from my room because there's no way I'm getting off this couch."

CHAPTER THIRTEEN

I HAVE PAWS

The Mesh is love. The Mesh is life.

You don't need a real body, you don't need to feel pain, you don't need to worry, not when you're in the Mesh. It's the perfect world, where everything is, at its base, truly fair.

Everything you could possibly want is a twitch away.

Is it any wonder those of us who live by this oasis don't want to leave our little matrix of friends and foes?

—Anonymous Meshizen, 2049

"So, there are two ways to dive into the Mesh," Daniel said as he sat up and bunched his legs beneath him awkwardly.

"Yeah, I know," I said.

"No, you don't," he countered. "Now shut up and listen to Daddy Daniel."

I blinked from my spot on one of the fancy reclining couches across from him. It was a big seat, made for one person to lounge back in, and with a load of controls for positioning and such in the arm.

Lucy, of course, was currently crushing me with her bony behind while playing with my mechanical arm's fingers. My other arm was wrapped snugly around her waist.

"Daniel, the day I call you 'Daddy' is the day you die."

"Of, like, pleasure?" he asked.

"I could buy a Taser," I mused. "Maybe some sort of automatic whip that hears people talking shit and just slaps them for it?"

"Oh, fuck off," Daniel said. "Fine, no need to call me Daddy. Maybe Big D?"

"I've seen you naked," I pointed out. "It's horrific, and anything but big."

"You wound me."

"I could find someone else to show me this shit, you know?"

Daniel grinned back. "Fine. So like I was saying before you threw a snit over my nicknaming choices, there are two kinds of dives in the Mesh. This shit's not the internet where you're just skimming the surface. There's mid-diving, which is slipping into the Mesh with normal aug-gear. You see stuff, and you can manipulate objects in-Mesh using whatever controls you have installed."

I nodded. "Yeah, it's the internet as an MMO, I know."

He nodded. "Yeah, it's normie shit. A full dive, a deep dive, that's something else. You need much better mods for that, and it locks your body up. Moving shit in your head moves things in-Mesh. I think you've tried that at school, yeah?"

"I remember that," Lucy said. "We had to wear that hat with the little nubs. You could still move around, though."

"A shower cap, yeah," Daniel said. "That's low-level, though. Real pros, real divers, they have some crazy-ass gear that lets them go deep. It turns off your body, kinda like when you're asleep. Try not to wake up before your brain realizes it. Sleep paralysis is freaky as shit. Had to replace one of my augs 'cause I kept getting stuck in between for a few minutes at a time."

"Wait," Lucy said. "Was that when you paid Nose to slap you every morning?"

Daniel frowned. "Little shit kept slapping me for weeks even after I replaced the faulty aug."

Lucy and I chuckled. "All right, all right. So I'm just going in to meet some people. I don't need to go deep dive, right?"

Daniel's expression shifted a few times. "I mean, no, but yeah. Mid-dives are cheap. You need to do it sometimes because you don't have the time and place for a full dive, but to people who are always jacked into the Mesh, that's like, I don't know, showing up to a wedding in jeans and a tank top instead of a suit. It's lazy normie mode."

I rolled my eyes. "Myalis, you've got some cheap full-dive gear?"

Cheap? No. Inexpensive? Yes. A ten-point Full-Dive Module augmentation should be all you need, especially since it would connect to your Mark II Cyberwarfare augmentation.

"That sounds good enough," I said. "Lucy, are you coming with?"

"Hmm? No, I need to keep an eye on the kittens. You know how they get when they think no one's watching them."

They're currently attempting to capture your Dumbass drone with a laundry basket.

"O-kay," I said. "Just don't do anything too kinky while I'm out of it."

Lucy pouted. "But what if I really want to?"

I pulled her close and pecked a kiss on her cheek. "Just a little, then," I said. "Daniel, how do we meet up in the Mesh?"

"Uh, I'll send you an address. Shouldn't be hard to meet—we're diving from the same local net. That'll place us in the same area."

New Purchase: Full-Dive System
Points Reduced from . . . 8,436 to . . . 8,426
This might feel like you're sneezing backward.

"Huh?" I asked. And then it hit and my head bounced back and I felt my nose scrunching up. "Oh—oh fuck, that's weird," I said before the weird tingling in my head shifted.

I sneezed.

"Oh, ew, Cat, what the fuck!" Lucy said as she jumped off my lap and touched the back of her head. "That's disgusting."

"Sorry," I said. "It's Myalis's fault." I rubbed at my nose and pretended not to see the look Lucy was giving me.

It really isn't.

"Disgusting," Lucy repeated. "I'm going to find some towels and look at the kids. You two stay safe."

I waved her off, then turned to Daniel with a sigh.

"Was that how you usually flirt?" he asked.

"Fuck off," I said as I leaned back. "Let's just dive, all right?" I poked at the controls on the seat and tried to settle in comfortably. My back-mounted guns made it awkward, but I was way too lazy to get up and remove them.

Daniel kicked his legs out to lie flat on the couch, shifted until he looked comfortable, then yawned. "All right. I'm the metal tentacle squid."

"Wha—?" I began.

Initiating dive.

The world flickered and faded away.

I batted my eyes open and found myself in a familiar lobby. Large marble pillars, a few terrariums, a wall with a revolving glass door at one end.

The big difference was the signs floating above the lobby entrance and the front desk. The employees I could see were all standing unnaturally stiff in pristine hotel uniforms, and the other people in the lobby . . .

Some were human, but they ran the gamut from supernaturally beautiful Barbie dolls to huge muscular monsters. Half of the people standing around were anime-esque figures, with large eyes and intricate clothes.

Some of those moving around weren't human at all. Monsters, familiar characters from a dozen TV shows I'd glanced at before, a few video game characters. Their appearances ranged from almost normal to downright impossible.

The biggest issue was, of course, that all of them were way taller than I was.

I looked around for some sort of point of reference and found a bench nearby. I couldn't even see past the top of it.

My arms were . . . not arms. I had paws. One was a cybernetic thing, all blue steel and glowing pink lights; the other was raven black and covered in fine fur.

"Myalis, you absolute bitch, did you turn me into a cat?"

I thought it was thematically appropriate.

I stared at my paws, then looked around until I caught myself in one of the chrome surfaces by the bench. I was a cat. A cyborg cat.

It was kinda cool.

"When did you even make this?" I asked as I spun around. It felt natural to move on all fours, which was so wrong that I couldn't even begin to express why I found it wrong.

I think you're severely underestimating my processing power if you think it took more than a second to create your current avatar.

"And you made it a cat?"

Yes.

"Because you thought it was on theme?"

And amusing. Your tail actually reacts to your brain's chemistry when you're irate. From what I know of human culture, you would be considered quite cute.

"I hate you," I said as I pawed at the scarf around my neck. Had she copied my entire damned look?

I could make it better. Maybe a bow in your hair? By the way, Daniel is approaching you.

I spun around—something made difficult by suddenly being built lengthwise as opposed to vertically—and took in the terrifying sight of a many-eyed mechanical squid thing floating its way toward me.

If that was Daniel, then he was probably one of the biggest avatars in the room. Not in terms of mass, but because of his many tentacles, each ending in a claw that grabbed onto the ground around us as he came to a stop.

"Nice model," he said. The voice was Daniel's, but with a distinct electronic twang to it, like a sort of flanging.

"I hate it," I replied. "What in the fuck are you?"

"I'm a Sentinel," he said. "From . . . Oh, never mind. It's classy, cheap, and has a lot of arms to grab stuff with. It comes in handy."

"I wouldn't know. I have paws."

CHAPTER FOURTEEN

MESH

The Mesh is a world unto itself, with communities and markets and entire micro-civilizations all packed into one somewhat-united world running on code so complex and convoluted that no one human could do more than scratch the surface of it.

It's not just "the internet, but more"; it's a whole new world, where with enough dedication, effort, and creativity, you can become someone entirely new.

—Anonymous, 2045

"All right," Daniel said. "What's the address you need to head over to?"

I spun around a few times, doing figure eights beneath Daniel's huge squid body to get used to the motions of my strange cat body . . . avatar thing. I was pretty sure I was completely messing up the terminology, and I was also pretty sure I didn't care.

"Myalis has it," I said. "Myalis?"

Sending. You know, I do believe I could set a waypoint and guide you there myself.

"And would you be able to guide me without stopping by every virtual veterinarian shop along the way?" I asked. "Nope, I don't trust you."

Oh, how awful it is that a Vanguard can no longer trust her AI. Would petting you restore your confidence? Perhaps some digital catnip?

"Now you're just fucking with me," I said, glaring ahead.

Daniel spun around, legs twisting about behind him like, well, like a squid. "You know, talking to yourself like that? Not all that great when it comes to making you look sane."

"I'm talking to my dumb AI," I said. "Did you get the address?"

"Yeah, I got an email for it," he said. "It's in nyan-speak, though."

My eyes narrowed. "What's nyan-speak?"

The squid wiggled, and Daniel laughed. "Nah, just fucking with you."

That was a good one. Do compliment Daniel for the joke, and thank him for the idea.

I sighed a kitty sigh and sat down. For all that I was complaining about the avatar, it was still pretty neat, in an existential-crisis sort of way. I imagined that Lucy would very much approve of me being in this form.

"All right," I said. I could endure being a cat for a bit. It would maybe help if people underestimated me. And I was a cat person. "So how do we get to Dial-Up and Lag?"

Daniel spun around so that he was facing me with his many, many red eyes. "That depends on a few things, but I think the fastest way to get to their district will be via the subway. There should be a station around here. If you have a few bucks, we could use a wayport to the nearest station."

"You know, I might be a samurai and all, but I'm still broke as fuck," I said.

Daniel's tentacles moved up and down in a gesture that I guessed was a shrug. "Fair enough. Want to follow me or should I carry you?"

"That doesn't sound safe," I said. All of his limbs were made of serrated bits of metal, and they ended in sharply tipped grasper hand things. He even had a few weapons tucked away.

"This is a non-PVP zone. So's the subway. I literally could not hurt you if I tried. Weapons are off too." He moved closer, some of his limbs reaching out for me. "Do you have 'ride' on?"

"Do I what?"

Daniel sighed, a strange flanging note that still conveyed a lack of patience. I felt a bit like . . . well, like one of those older caretakers at the orphanage being shown how to use some tablet or app by the kittens and just not getting it.

I was about ten years too young to be feeling that way.

"In your main menu— Ah, it depends which company programmed your OS, but there should be a permissions menu to allow you to interact with other avatars. One of the options is 'ride.' It means someone can physically take and move your avatar. It's off by default most of the time because otherwise some clever bastards can basically kidnap you."

"You can virtually kidnap someone?"

Again with the tentacle shrug. "Sorta. There was a whole thing where scripted NPCs would grab players off the street and stick them in ad mazes. It was pretty annoying. Also, there were a bunch of scams, but that hasn't changed."

I reached up to scratch at my nose, then reconsidered when I took in my lack of hands. "Right, sounds fucky. Let me find my menu."

A glance around showed me a lack of prompts or buttons or even a hub. I probably should have noticed that earlier. I'd grown up with some sort of screen over my vision nearly my entire life, though since I'd gone samurai my hub had gotten a bit less obvious and yet a lot more complicated.

I can bring it up for you, if you want. Or I could just control things for you. You won't have to worry about scams or viruses either way.

"Can I see it anyway?" I asked.

Myalis obliged, and a moment later, a pretty standard menu appeared before me. It had tabs for the usual things: graphics, interface, audio, and so on. The difference from any other menu I'd ever seen was the number of options available. Some of them were garbled messes of acronyms; others had nested sections that went four or five options deep. The scroll bar on the side (which looked like a cat's paw, because Myalis) was so small it was almost impossible to see.

"Okay, so maybe not," I admitted. Playing around in the Mesh seemed far too complicated. "Set 'ride' on."

It's on.

"You can't believe how jealous I am," Daniel said. "They have these little personal AIs that will do voice commands like that, but they cost an arm and a leg. Or you need to sign up for these really shit payment plans."

"Right," I said. "Float a bit lower. I need to get on you."

Daniel dipped down, his . . . head part coming closer to the ground.

I bunched my legs under me, then jumped majestically about half a foot off the ground before flopping onto my stomach.

Could you do that again? It was amusing.

I got back onto all fours, then bounced on the spot a few times. "Okay, I can do that, but why can't I jump? I'm a damned cat."

You can, actually. You're just really bad at controlling yourself.

Daniel was shaking, and I suspected the bastard was laughing at me. My second attempt at jumping was far better. I made it to Daniel's head before finding no purchase on his metal skin and falling backward and landing on my ass.

He was outright laughing aloud by the time I tried a third time and made it on top of him. "Stop laughing and tell me how to hang on."

"Just hang on as best you can," Daniel said.

Your feet can stick to things. Physics don't matter entirely in a digital world.

I tried to raise an eyebrow at that, but all that happened was that the whiskery things above one eye wiggled. "Right," I said. A bit of fiddling with my feet did have them sticking to the top of Daniel's body, so that was nice. "That works. Okay, Daniel, you're my valiant tentacle-robot steed for the evening."

"I might have to tell Lucy that," he said. "And please don't call me by my name. It's bad netiquette to use real names."

"You have a stupid name, don't you?"

"Better than Stray Cat."

I shrugged. "All right, fair enough. What is it?"

"404_Legs_Not_Found."

I looked down at Daniel, then snorted. "You idiot."

He chuckled, tentacles wiggling. "I thought it was clever. You know, apropos."

"Get moving, Legs. We've wasted enough time here."

CHAPTER FIFTEEN

SURFING

You'd think that in a purely digital world, where the constraints of the real world don't matter, the power of someone like a samurai would be diminished.

But no, just like the real world, there are some people with an unfair advantage.

We need to put a stop to the tendency of these people to overload our servers and shut down all of our ad revenue.

—A. Pai, CFO of Adcorp, December 14, 2039, six minutes before his Mesh connection malfunctioned, leading to his untimely demise

I rode atop my giant metal squid monster and enjoyed being carried. Not that I would admit it, but it was kind of neat to be so far above everyone else.

Daniel, that is, 404_Legs_Not_Found, swam around a gathering of rather plain avatars—that all still managed to be gorgeous people—and I waved a paw at them when they tracked us with their eyes.

"They're not actually looking at you," Daniel said as he moved toward the hotel's doors. "Those are Barbies."

"And what's that?"

"They're standard avatars? You can get them in a cash shop for fairly cheap. They come with some customization and all that, like a character creator, but their programming's shit. Their eyes will follow anyone looking at them, but their user doesn't need to be looking that way." He flicked a metallic tentacle to where a few other avatars were walking by, some with their own entourage of very plain people following them. "You can tell the fully custom jobs apart. Shit costs an arm and a leg, though."

"Neat," I said. "So, what, it's a status thing?"

"Yeah," he said. "A real Meshizen wouldn't be caught dead in a prefab."

"Isn't your avatar a prefab?"

He wiggled from side to side. "Sorta? It's based on an actual squid model from, like, ten years back? I got a friend who does modeling to set this model over the original squid skeleton."

I nodded. I almost understood that.

The entrance had a set of sliding doors, not too dissimilar to the actual doors of the actual hotel we were still in. I was having a bit of trouble remembering that I wasn't where I was in the real world. It was just too immersive, feeling wind against my skin . . . fur, and hearing things from all around. I had to remind myself that I was lying back on a couch in real life.

The doors opened, and we slid through a thin blue transparent screen and out onto a huge balcony overlooking a city, of sorts.

The problem with the Mesh—or one of them—was that it was such a surreal environment that it made my eyes want to cross. There were skyscrapers as far as I could see, some of them rising from the ground, others dropping from the ceiling. Some, the largest and most intimidating, connected the two.

There were walls off to the sides, solid barriers with images and words scrolling by them barely slow enough for someone to read them in passing.

"Have you been out in the Möbius a lot?"

"The what?" I asked.

"You know, outside of a structure?" Daniel said. "If you keep traveling down the tunnel, you'll eventually flip back over to the other side. It's a Möbius strip."

"Yeah, I've been out here before. Never spent much time in the open, though," I said. A glance around showed carlike things shooting by. Half of them were plain, boring cubes or spheres, sometimes with scrolling ads on their sides, but a good chunk were shaped like spaceships and modern cars.

I held myself back from flinching when a pair of X-wings cut around the corner.

"We're in the NA phase and it's midday, so it'll be busy as fuck," Daniel said. "We're taking the subway to, uh, lemme check . . ."

I vaguely remembered phases being a sort of unsynced copy of the world we were in, so that the millions of people around could all be in the same space without having to render or interact with each other.

A glance over at the YouTube building a block or two down showed a sea of people slipping in and out of the thousand-odd entrances all around the stark-white building. I couldn't imagine what it would be like if everyone everywhere were in the same instance.

"Right," Daniel said. "They're on the . . . nice, the ISS phase."

"The what?"

"The ISS phase, from when they converted that old space station into an oversized server rack? It's real classy," Daniel said. "Right, hang on."

Daniel moved ahead, his dozens of reddish eyes clicking and staring around us. The hotel's balcony wasn't empty. There were a couple of kiosks and a bunch of people just kind of . . . standing around. The weird part was how quiet everyone was being. I guessed that we weren't sharing the same audio, because I saw some lips moving with no noise coming from them.

Daniel juked around a person that tried to smack him with a rectangular screen. "Fucking ad bots."

And then we were off the edge of the balcony and I felt something almost like gravity tugging us down. I held back a scream. This wasn't real, and even if we hit the ground, we were in a non-PVP zone—we couldn't be hurt or anything.

Daniel's tentacles wiggled and he aimed us toward the streets below. We shot past bridges and connections that were slung out between some of the smaller skyscrapers at speeds that turned them into little more than passing blurs.

And then the ground reached out and met us with a dull thump.

I braced, expecting to bounce, or maybe get flattened, but all that happened was the ends of Daniel's tentacles pressing harmlessly against the ground before we started to float up again.

"Was that a shortcut?" I asked.

"Yeah, but it only works one way," he said as we took off again.

The lower streets, surprisingly, had a lot more people moving by. Most were moving at a steady jog, sometimes clipping through others as they passed.

Strange people with vacant looks in their eyes were flicking out flyers that some people batted away and others just allowed to smack them before disappearing.

Two of Daniel's tentacles extended ahead of his main body, and soon a pair of semitransparent shields were floating ahead of us. "Adblocks," he explained.

Daniel's avatar could float a decent ways off the road, so I had a good view of all the people we were moving past. There were a lot of the Barbies that Daniel had mentioned. In fact, it felt like three quarters of the avatars we were passing were female, which was saying something when a good number of them weren't in any way biological. From robots, to weird geometric shapes, to monsters from different shows and games. I even saw a few Antithesis models moving about. The models didn't quite match up to the real thing.

The sides of the street were lined with nothing but shops. Some were tiny, others much larger, and all of them were fake. Not fake in the sense that they were fake stores, but the entrances, I knew, would just lead into a fresh instance that belonged to that store. They didn't need to take up any actual space on the street.

The bigger the storefront, the more the owners were spending for ad space.

"There," Daniel said as he beelined across the foot traffic and toward a large, stately building done up in a Gothic style. It was surprisingly clean for what turned out to be a subway station. Maybe that was owing to the gargoyles on the roof that occasionally took off to tackle avatars away.

X

Welcome to Uganda Sonic's Portal Palace, Stray Cat!

I eyed the screen floating before me for a moment, then pressed a paw to the X in its corner. "What's that?" I asked.

Unlike every other ad I've been blocking, this one was sent by a fellow AI. This area is under the control of a Class III AI, which is, in turn, owned by a Vanguard. There was no spyware or any other malicious content, just a greeting.

"Huh," I said. "Are we supposed to . . . reply?"

That would be polite.

I nodded. "Send something nice back?" I said before turning my focus back onto the world around me.

The Portal Palace lived up to its name. It was a huge open area, like the ballroom of some fantastical castle. There were huge mirrorlike surfaces against every wall, and through them I could see shifting scenes from different places, all of them moving as we moved, as if those places were just one room over. None of that made any real sense, though—the rooms I saw would all be overlapping, and some seemed to be operating on different scales.

There were lines of avatars waiting before the mirrors, each one waiting their turn to interact with a panel that changed the image in the mirror. Once someone pressed on their panel a few times, they'd jump into the mirror and be off to who-knows-where.

The number of rooms I saw that had vaguely pornographic images in them said lots.

"Let's find a place to port from, and then we'll be real close to your samurai buddies," Daniel said.

CHAPTER SIXTEEN

IT

You would be right to think that the Mesh is a full-immersion world, that being in the Mesh can trigger every human sense, from smell to balance, and even the perception of time.

The Mesh can do all of these things.

If you have the right gear.

The issue comes with the steep price of that gear. Most normal Mesh users are simple people, usually in first-world countries and at middling incomes. That is to say, even the midtier Mesh gear is above their standard pay grade, and most need to purchase their equipment on credit or with payments.

High-end gear, the equipment really needed to fully experience the Mesh? That can run for prices in the tens of millions of credits.

Unfortunately, despite improvements in manufacturing and processing power, these setups cost more than a lower-class person would make in a lifetime. Mostly because the few companies making them want to keep the prices artificially inflated.

That must end!

—Meshizen for a Better Tomorrow, public address, 2050

"That's it," Daniel said as he floated down a dimly lit street.

There was no reason for the street to be poorly lit. It had just as many "lights" along its sides as any of the other streets we'd passed.

That had to be deliberate. It certainly gave a sinister cast to all the people walking along the sidewalks. I had to keep reminding myself that, in one sense, none of this was real. Being a cat certainly helped with the unreality of it all.

At the end of the street was the thing Daniel was talking about, the "it."

It was a huge bulky building. Or maybe calling it a building was off. I wasn't all that knowledgeable about architecture, but a huge black cube without so much as a window on it didn't ping me as a building.

The closer we came, the bigger it felt like the building was. It certainly towered above the street, just kind of there. The strangest thing was the absolute blackness of it. None of the buildings around it, all of them festooned in ads and neon highlights, reflected the building. It was just not showing up in any glass or anything, and its surface was pitch black, without so much as a hint of light splashing against it.

It certainly left a mark. And yet it was smaller than a lot of the skyscrapers around it.

Glancing up, I could see its opposite in the cityscape way above, just hanging off the ceiling like so many other buildings.

"So, is there an entrance?" I asked.

"Not really," Daniel said. He started to slow down, and the reason was obvious. The road leading up to the building (because it was right in the middle of an intersection) veered off to the left and right, but never reached out to the building proper. Instead, there was a railing at about waist height and then half a dozen meters of pavement before a sheer drop.

From my vantage above Daniel's head, I could make out the lack of a bottom to the building. It was just floating there, without even the common courtesy of throwing a shadow.

"Freaky," I said.

Daniel stopped right next to the rails, and I realized that we had something of a berth around us. The other avatars were keeping their distances. "Right past this," he said, bringing a tentacle around to smack the rail, "is a PVP zone."

"I thought you couldn't have those out in the open like this. I mean, outside of, like, game areas."

"You can't," he said.

I looked down, then smacked his head with a paw. "And? How come there's one here?"

"Because the people in that said so?" he said, pointing to the building. "This is, like, *the* place for all the cool hackers and crackers to hang out. Breaking the Mesh's code to have an illegal PVP zone on their doorstep was probably child's play for them."

I eyed the building up and down, then bunched my legs up under me. "Right, give me a minute."

"Seriously?"

I answered by jumping off him, over the rail, and landing on the pavement beyond with a bounce. I shook a little, the scarf around my neck fluttering. With a wag of my new tail, I set off toward the building until a prompt appeared in the corner of my vision.

YOU HAVE ENTERED A PVP AREA.

How daring.

"Yup, that's me," I said. "So, uh, think we can send a message to the people in there?"

I could. But you should maybe focus on dodging in the meantime.

"Dodg— Oh shit!" I bounced straight up and narrowly avoided a searing red beam about the width of a thumb that passed right where I'd been.

Stay close to the building. I'm sending a message over.

"Stay close?" I asked before leaping to the side. The beams—because they couldn't be satisfied with only one laser emplacement—were coming at me fairly slowly. Fastballs instead of lasers, basically.

I jumped, then spun in midair to avoid a beam that tried to pin me at the apex of my leap.

"Myalis, are you sending anything?"

I am. This place actually has some pretty decent cybersecurity. Though I suppose that's normal, all things considered. Nothing I can't bypass, of course, but it is taking me some time.

Time that I was spending trying not to get fried. The moment there was a pause in the rate of fire from the lasers, I started sprinting as fast as my cat body could, beams spearing out and hitting the ground behind me as I went. They weren't even marking the ground or anything, but that didn't mean I wanted to be hit.

Ah, there we go.

And just like that, the lasers stopped.

I slowed down and eyed the building, noticing for the first time the black-on-black turrets that were even then sinking back into the surface of the structure. I panted, then realized that I wasn't actually out of breath. "Okay. Okay, no more lasers. I like that. What did they say?"

They should be extending a bridge.

As Myalis spoke, a small door opened in the side of the building and a glowing bridge flickered into existence leading up to the pavement not too far from where I was. I looked over to Daniel, who was quick to jump the fence. Quite a few avatars behind him stopped to look, and there were suddenly a bunch of emotes floating in the air around them.

"You going in?" Daniel asked. "Didn't know if they'd lower the loser's door for you."

"Loser's door?" I asked. A glance back at the opening revealed a little neon sign right above it with the word "LOSER" on it. "Ah, never mind."

I shook myself one more time, resettling the weird clothes I was wearing, then started strutting over to the bridge. It felt cold-but-not under my paws, which was a bit strange. The moment Daniel and I slipped into the room at the top, the walls closed in behind us and we found ourselves in a small room. The walls were the same black as the exterior, but the floors and ceilings were gray, and recessed lights in the corners lit up the room from within.

In the far end of the room was a Barbie. It was a bog-standard avatar dressed in an off-white leotard. Even I recognized it as the default outfit, the thing that came with the plain model. "Welcome to the Black Cube," the avatar said in a feminine voice that sounded just a little bit off. A synth voice?

"Hey," I said as I looked up at the Barbie. "Are you the greeter here?"

"I am," the avatar said. "It is uncommon for the Black Cube to accept the undeserving into its hallowed halls. Why have you come?"

"Undeserving?" I asked.

Daniel shifted lower. "That's because we didn't break in, or crack past their security. We basically cheated."

"Exactly," the Barbie said.

"Yeah, well, I'm not here to show off any hacking skills," I said. "Not that I have any. I'm here to talk to Dial-Up and Lag. I've got some things to ask them."

"Merely being a samurai won't get you as far here as it would IRL." The Barbie looked over its shoulder, then back to us. "The Black Lords are busy. Can you state your business?"

I considered telling the avatar off, but I was on their turf, and this wasn't a situation I could explode my way out of. "There's a girl. Katallina McCarthy. She went missing during yesterday's incursion. She's a new samurai. She was kidnapped by some corpo goon types. I'm trying to track them down. Longbow said you could help."

The Barbie locked up, no emotions showing on her too-perfect face for a long, long time. Then she blinked. "Come with me. I'll lead you to them."

CHAPTER SEVENTEEN

DIAL-UP AND LAG

Pop Culture *is* Mesh Culture.

Memes are the currency of the digital world, where being a sweet-talker can get you further than having any amount of money. When everyone is divided into cliques and little in-groups, a bunch of them with huge crossover to other groups, knowing the right meme at the right time is like passing the right code phrase along to make sure you're the right kind of person.

It's chaotic, it's messy, and it's fucking beautiful.

—Anonymous Meshizen, 2031

The Barbie led us through a paper-thin portal in a wall that opened up onto a catwalk. Below were dozens of cubes, each one with plenty of space to walk around them. And each face of the cubes led into a different space occupying the entire cube.

"What?"

"Oh, neat," Daniel said as he spun his upper body around to see better. "They've gone full non-Euclidean here."

"Please walk in the center of the catwalk. It's the shortest path to the far end of the room," the Barbie said.

I looked at the back of her head, then stepped to the edge of the catwalk. Suddenly, the other two were shooting ahead of me. Returning to the middle made the space between us shorter in a way that had my head twingeing in pain. "What?"

"Space doesn't need to obey normal rules in the Mesh. Gravity and inertia are the rules that we usually break. You know, like how I'm floating right now," Daniel said. "But things like linear space can be messed with too."

"Yeah, but why?" I asked.

Daniel wiggled in a sort of shrug. "Because it means having more space in less space if two things can be in the same space at the same time?"

I shook my head, whiskers wiggling, and looked down again toward the cubes. There were people in them, a few in very strange avatars. Some were lounging around, others were typing on floating keyboards, and no two cubes were the same. "Are those cubicles?"

"Not quite," the Barbie said. "If you can prove that you're worthy of being here, you get some cube space. What you do with it is up to you. Most just carve out a little space for themselves. Some turn it into an exhibit, others into an access port to some other place in the Mesh. We attract some very creative people here."

"I can imagine," I said. "Gotta be creative to be a proper criminal, right?"

The Barbie slowed to a stop, turned, and looked down at me without her expression so much as twitching. "Is there a problem?"

"Uh, no? I'm cool with criminals. I crime all the time," I said. "But seriously, I'm just here to find some clues to save some girl. That's it."

"The people here, the real hackers and crackers, do more good for society than you could imagine. We act as a counter to some of the most corrupt assholes IRL. We make medical bills disappear, send the wrong information to the right people, make R&D projects for some nasty shit fall through."

"And yet the world's still a shithole," I said. "Doing your part's nice, but that's not what I'm here for."

"You're here for a single person. How narrow."

I shrugged. "I'm here because I'm being . . . I don't know if it's blackmail, a bribe, or some sort of really fucked-up favor, actually. Doesn't matter. I'm here for my own reasons. Now are you going to bring me to Dial-Up and Lag or not?"

The Barbie looked at me with her pretty, vacant baby blues before turning around and moving on.

"You're a real people person," Daniel said.

"I was raised in a barn."

He slowed down a little more. "Did someone piss in your cereal?"

I huffed. I was in a bit of a poor mood. "I'd rather be home with Lucy than out here. Also, I'm a cat. Also-also, this place just feels so wrong. I don't like it."

"It's not a reason to be . . . Okay, so it is a reason to be prissy, but it's not a real good one. Maybe don't piss off the nice hackers when they're being nice," Daniel said.

I tried to hum, but it came out as a meow. "When did you get so diplomatic?"

"Yesterday I was a shit-talking cripple whose entire family was made up of idiots like you. I learned how to be real diplomatic. Keeps my head on straight." He wiggled. "Plus, I kinda respect these guys. Some of their stunts are famous."

We reached the end of the catwalk, the Barbie stepping aside to open a large door that looked like something out of a bank vault.

The room we entered was a huge, expansive space with no floor. In the middle of it all, glowing a bright yellow, was a ball the size of a minivan, and a dozen steps past that were two guys staring at a red ball the size of their fist.

The Barbie stepped in first. There was no floor, but she didn't seem to have trouble just standing on nothing and letting a few asteroids the size of grains of dust flick through her. "Sirs, Stray Cat for you."

The guy turned our way, revealing a shock of white hair held back by some weird silver goggles. He had a stained lab coat on, and a strange thing over one arm with the words "Power Glove" written in electric blue over the knuckles.

Next to him was a golden robot with one leg that was red from foot to knee. His avatar was shiny and all, but it moved clunkily. "Oh my, we have a guest!" he said before raising his arms up. Not very high, they looked like something out of a failed science fair project.

The doctor-looking one brought his arm up and tapped at the controls on his glove.

The solar system around us, including all the little screens hovering around Mars, disappeared in a blink and we were suddenly in a garage. A really messy garage. One wall was covered in clocks of all sorts, and at the back of the room was an old-school speaker taller than I was . . . as a human, that is.

"Hey," I said before taking a chance and jumping up onto one of the counters so that I wasn't looking up at everyone.

"You must be Stray Cat," the doctor said. "I'm Dial-Up, the tin can next to me is Lag."

"Greetings!" the robot said.

"I will leave you to it. I'll be waiting by the exit," the Barbie said. She left, the vault door now replaced by a pretty typical wooden door straight out of the set from a really old movie.

I finished looking around and settled down a bit. "So, uh, hey," I said. "Nice avatars?"

"Thanks," Dial-Up said. "I'm a huge *Back to the Future* fan. A sci-fi classic, you know? This idiot got that piece-of-trash avatar from a fucking bootleg Disney merch stall."

"Hey, this thing works well enough," Lag said. It really didn't look like it was working well at all.

"So, what was with the solar system?" I asked.

The doctor shrugged. "We tapped into SpaceX's sensor suite and were snooping around. Just keeping an eye on things." He reached under a desk, pulled out a seat, and plopped himself down on it. "So, you were sent by Longbow, right?"

"Yeah," I confirmed. "I'm looking for a girl. A Katallina McCarthy. I got some video from the security system around her place. She was taken by a bunch of assholes."

"Send the footage over," Dial-Up asked. "We'll see what we can do."

"Just like that?" I asked. "No payment or anything?"

"If you're actually looking for your lost girlfriend or something we'll donate all your assets to the Eastern Russian Sewage Reconstruction fund, then make your digital life a digital nightmare," Lag said. "But yeah, you're looking for a kid samurai, right? We don't charge for that."

"Taking some of our time, though," Dial-Up said.

"Time better spent snooping on Mars?" I asked.

"Yes, actually."

Sending now!

"Nice avatar, by the way. Most folks stick to humanoids, but the both of you went off script. Good detail work on the fur. Bet some folks would pay top dollar for such an accurate model," Dial-Up said.

"Got the files," Lag said.

A moment later the robot's eyes went red, and suddenly we were no longer in a garage, but in a familiar corridor. The one McCarthy had been kidnapped from. I fell a few feet to the carpeted floor when the counter I was on disappeared.

"This is a reconstruction. It's not accurate," Dial-Up said. He gestured to some parts of the room that were just colorless holes in reality. "Blind spots. Now, let's see what's what."

I got to watch the mercenaries kidnap Katalina all over again, though this time in full three dimensions.

"Well, well," Dial-Up said. "Isn't that interesting."

CHAPTER EIGHTEEN

GOTCHA

Every niche has its celebrities. Every community has a few charismatic, or at the very least talented, individuals that everyone gets to know.

They're the name everyone mentions, the standard others try to meet.

This is true both on the micro and macro levels. Nations have popular leaders, and clubs and friend groups have the one person all the others look up to.

More often than not, when you introduce a samurai into that equation, they take that role, and quite comfortably at that.

There's just something about the people chosen to be samurai that makes them stand apart.

—Extract from a post on the PsychologyForever forums, 2036

"All right, so what can you tell me?" I asked.

Stepping forward, I started to weave my way through the scene, passing between the legs of the mercenaries and looking up at them from new angles. There wasn't that much more to see, really.

"This and that," Dial-Up said. "First, your girl here is using a cheap weapon. Twenty-five points, it's a rifle that fires guided micro-missiles."

"Like the Hummingbird?" I asked.

"That's an example, yes," he said. "Though this one's reloadable and a bit more reliable. Bit more expensive. You know how that works."

"All right," I said. "What else?"

Lag was the one to step up, his feet clunking on the floor in contrast to my cat's paws' silent tread. "I've got nothing on these guys. Their gear is just about all aftermarket stuff. Sold to SWAT and some police units. You know the sort."

I nodded. "And?"

"And this guy stands out." Lag pointed to the one member of the group with the big backpack covered in high-tech gear. "That kind of equipment doesn't come cheap, and it isn't exactly mass-produced. I'm getting . . . about a thousand pings for sales in North America in the last half decade."

I eyed the guy's little antenna and heavy backpack; most of the details were covered in black cloth. "Can you pinpoint the guy, then?"

"Not from that alone," Lag said. He gestured again and a screen appeared next to him. Lists and information scrolled by faster than I could read. "See, these things aren't meant for nice commercial uses. It's the kind of equipment you'd give to an IRL hacker on a squad just like this."

"Any samurai with similar stuff?" I asked.

"Yes. Us," Lag said. "The point is, as distinct as this thing is, it's not going to be easy to trace. The people who buy this stuff make a point of that. But this little guy was cheap."

"Cheap how?"

Dial-Up chimed up. "Software. He used some custom software to shut down the CCTV systems they crossed. Nice stuff. Well coded. A bit overkill for the level of tech this building has. Still, it left its mark. Purchased right over here, in the Cube."

"So you can track it? Point me to who wrote the code?"

Lag and Dial-Up looked at each other.

"Oh, for fuck's sake," I said. "Please tell me you're not going to have me go on a fetch quest just for you to tell me who made it?"

"No, nothing like that. It's just that there are rules. Unwritten rules, but rules nonetheless," Lag said.

"Giving up a member of the Cube to someone else, at least when it's not a referral, is a bit taboo," Dial-Up added.

"Aren't you two the bosses here?" I asked.

They both shook their heads. "No bosses here," Dial-Up said. "We're heavy hitters, popular in our own way, and we have good reps."

I bristled, then pointed with a paw—which was pretty damned difficult—to the wide-eyed still image of a girl. "And you're not willing to risk that? Not even for her?"

The two stared at me. "Of course we are," Dial-Up said. "Look at her. She's a kid, she's probably terrified. No one here should be selling anything to people that would kidnap a kid, regardless of if they're a samurai or not."

"I'm PMing the coder now. He's a kid by the name of Zoobreaker. Fourth circle," Lag said.

"Think he'll be able to point us in the right direction?" I asked.

"We can hope," Lag said. "Most of the people here say that they don't keep records of their sales, but that's bull. You wouldn't believe how many backdoors people fail to notice. It's why this place is left alone."

"I thought it'd be because of you two."

Dial-Up shook his head. "We're just two samurai. Nothing too impressive in the grand scheme of things. The number of corporations we've extorted from here, or information that we leaked over the years, that would make all the protection of even two vet samurai moot."

"So why aren't you being hassled, then?"

"Oh, we get hassled all the time. You wouldn't believe the amount of crap the media talks about us when they get the chance. But then we remind them that we can shut down just about all of their infrastructure. Even the biggest, most powerful corp needs to be able to meet payroll."

I grinned. "Nice. I like that. Probably better than my idea of a solution."

"Walk in and shoot everyone?" Dial-Up asked. "That's a lot of folks' go-to, at least in our line of work. It's nice and cathartic, but it doesn't work as often as you'd think."

"Really?" I asked. "I've seen plenty of news feeds and stories about samurai just kicking ass and taking names."

Lag nodded. "We make sure that normal folk hear all the stories. That they know that we're violent, but fair. The threat of violence is often a lot more useful than violence itself."

Dial-Up nodded. "It helps when some of that respect we get is actually earned. Stopping incursions is nice, but those only happen once every month or two, and not often in the same time zone, let alone the same country."

"I'll keep that in mind," I said.

"Good," Lag said. He raised an arm and tapped the side of his head, making a hollow clunking noise. "Just got a PM back from Zoobreaker. I think we have our suspects."

The room shifted again, turning from the corridor where McCarthy was kidnapped into the interior of a spaceship. "Damn. Warn a girl before you do that, would you?" I asked as I looked up and around. There were a bunch of consoles with weird chairs by them, and a lot of old-timey computer screens and big archaic buttons.

"Is this the *Enterprise*?" Daniel asked.

Dial-Up nodded. "It is. Lag, on the screen?"

Lag nodded and soon the front of the bridge, which had a nice view into outer space, flickered and was filled with a website's front page.

The Hour Men
Your Target Dead in an Hour or Less!

"Is that really their tagline?" I asked. The sidebar had a bunch of generic images, and some boring links above, like "Products" and "Locations" in bold.

"Looks like it," Lag said. "They're pretty open about what they do, but that's normal on the dark web these days. You need to be loud."

"They have a testimonials section," I pointed out.

Dial-Up shrugged. His eyes were flicking this way and that as he replied. "They have great reviews on Yelp."

I jumped to the captain's seat and spun around to sit while facing the front. The better view allowed me to see more of their screen. "So are they the ones?"

"Can't tell," Lag said. "The server their site's on has nothing else on it. The owner of the server . . . has been dead for twelve years. I can't find anything in the site's code. It's all prepurchased stuff, bought on credit that was later reported missing. They've covered their tracks well."

"So how do I get to them and find McCarthy?"

"Oh, they won't have her," Dial-Up said. "Not these guys. They probably brought her and her dog somewhere else."

"For fuck's sake," I muttered. "Can you tell me where?"

Lag hummed, then shook his head. "Nope. Tracing their vehicles leads to a parking garage, and then the trail goes cold. I could get you a list of employees, but none of them had phones or augs that tracked their motions across the city yesterday. At least, none of those I suspect were on that mission."

"Then . . . what should I do?"

Dial-Up grinned. "You were looking forward to using a bit of violence to solve things, right? Because we have an address IRL."

"So, I can ask them in person?" I asked. "Yeah, yeah, I think I can do that."

"We'll try to give you a hand," Lag said. "You're a stealth specialist, right? We can probably cut the power to the entire block."

"Wouldn't that just alert them all?" I asked.

Lag shrugged. "My body is a one-hundred-and-eighty-ton tank. I don't do stealth."

Fair enough. "Okay. Okay, yeah, I can do that."

CHAPTER NINETEEN

LOG OFF

If you don't know your Mesh etiquette, then you'll end up being the one caught walking around with your fly down. The one others shy away from because you're too loud at the wrong time.

That's why, in collaboration with Nimbletainment, we're presenting this five-part series on the etiquette of the Mesh!

Strap yourselves in, kids, because we're going to be learning a bunch today!

—Meshy the Manatee,
a Nimbletainment Education Mascot/Vtuber, June 2036

"Thanks, you two," I said. "You've been surprisingly helpful."

Dial-Up scoffed, shaking his head enough that his wild mane of white hair wiggled around. "Think nothing of it. You could do with learning a bit more about the Mesh, though."

I shrugged my kitty shoulders, and when the room turned into a grand library without so much as a twitch, I didn't startle. "I'm getting used to it, I think. But I have something waiting for me in the real world."

Lag shook his head with a rusty squeak. "This *is* the real world," he said. "It's perceptible, and follows its own set rules. It's even, technically, physically present. It's just different enough that some of us like it better here than in the IRL."

"But you still call it the IRL?"

He moved his arms in a sort of "what can you do" gesture. "We need to call it something."

I looked around the library, at the dusty shelves and old books. Daniel looked entirely out of place hovering there. "Well, I'm off to go scare the truth out of some mercs. Thanks again. I'll get the girl to send you some digital flowers or something once I get her ass out of the fire."

Dial-Up barked a laugh. "Sure. I think I'd like that. You know where the exit is," he said with a gesture behind me.

A glance back showed a heavy double door at the end of the library. "Can't I just log out from here?"

Daniel sighed. "She's real clueless, sorry," he said.

"What?" I asked.

"You can't just . . . that's like walking into someone's house and not taking your boots off, you know."

"I'm not taking my boots off for anyone," I said.

Daniel slumped in midair, like a squid that had just been stepped on. "Dammit. It's like, uh, someone opening your fridge without permission, or someone not leaving the room when you want some alone time with Lucy."

"Right, right, it's impolite, I get it. I'm not entirely daft."

Surprising!

"Shush, you." I turned and strutted over to the door. "See you two geeks around," I said.

"Good luck, Stray," Lag said.

"Don't die!" Dial-Up added.

Daniel flew past me and opened the door. A good thing, since I couldn't actually reach the handle at all. Though it wasn't a real door, so maybe there was a way to open it without actually interacting with the handle? There had to be something in place for the nonhuman avatars out there. Or maybe the digital world was just as ableist as the real world.

We didn't end up on the same catwalk as before. Instead the door led into a sort of bazaar, or at least a spot behind a stall set in a row of them. The stalls were wildly different, some looking like authentic wooden things from back when wood was a thing people could afford, and others looked like the sort I'd seen in pictures of conventions.

Some decided to raise their middle fingers to gravity and were just floating there, or weren't actually stalls, instead being geometric things hovering around.

"What's this place?" I asked.

"An NPC marketplace," Daniel said. "The people behind the stalls are programs. They sell stuff."

"People can't navigate a shopping site here?" I asked.

There were a few dozen avatars walking past the kiosks and staring, but for the most part the room felt way too big for the number of people present.

"It's more of a personalization thing," Daniel said. "You know, meeting someone, bartering, having a face to match the item."

"But that face is a program with no one behind it?" I asked. "Right, internet weirdness."

"You're way too young to be shitting on Mesh culture."

I snorted and sat down. "So, where's the logout button on this thing?"

"You can't log out here," Daniel said. "Come on, let's step out of the building first."

"Are you serious?"

I grumbled to myself as I followed after Daniel. I wasn't expecting a hand to grab me by the scruff of the neck and lift me off the ground. "Oh, aren't you a cutie!"

I was turned around to come face-to-face with a young woman, a young woman with a man's voice. "Put me down or I swear to fuck I will end you," I said. I swung my arms around, but I couldn't reach the idiot's arm.

"This model is top. The fur isn't even a texture, it's all modeled. The poly count has to be insane," he said. I assumed it was a he, there was no way what looked like a Japanese schoolgirl had a voice that bassy.

"Myalis," I said.

Deploying weaponry!

I felt something on my back shift, and suddenly I had a pair of guns poking over my shoulder.

"Oh, wow, it's some sort of mecha-shift too."

"Um, yo, dude," Daniel said. "Put her down, would you?"

"How much for the model? Or at least tell me where you got it."

A pair of reticules appeared in my vision, handy little circles with a plus in their middle. I centered both over the idiot's face, then with a mental command pulled the trigger.

The idiot didn't explode or burst apart; there weren't even any particle effects or anything. His avatar froze, twitched once, then disappeared.

I landed on all fours, my guns already folding back into my back. "Right, that's enough internet for today," I said. "Myalis, let's log off."

Understood.

The world turned the comforting blue of a BIOS screen fritzing out, then black for just a moment before I opened my eyes to see an unfamiliar ceiling.

A glance around confirmed that I was back in the real world, in the living room I'd left. Though I had a few more pillows around my head and my lips were wet. Had I been drooling?

Daniel was still knocked out on the sofa, legs over the edge and arms splayed out above him. He was twitching a little, his eyes moving under the skin of his eyelids. Nice and creepy.

With a sigh, I pushed myself up and got to my feet, only to find myself pausing as I wobbled. Everything felt just a little bit off. I bounced on the spot a few times, stretched my arm out, then bent my knees close to my chest to get everything back in order. It seemed to work.

"Cat?" Lucy asked from the corridor. She stepped in, her face lighting up with a smile the moment she saw me standing. "How did it go?"

"Eh," I said.

She pulled me into a hug, then planted a wet kiss on my mouth. "So, I experimented with a bit of somnophilia."

"You did?"

She nodded. "Yup. I kissed you real good. But it's just no fun when you're not reacting to it."

I snorted and returned the kiss. "Pervert."

"Come on, you'd have tried the same thing."

"No. But I might have copped a feel," I said before giving her an example of what I meant.

Daniel sighed. "Can you guys at least let me set up something to record this before you start?"

I rolled my eyes and pulled back from Lucy. The moment was kinda ruined. "Dammit, Daniel," I said. "You're lucky that you're useful enough to keep around."

The boy laughed and shifted on the sofa until he was sitting up, legs over the side and toes squeezing and letting go restlessly. "That's my goal in life, to be moderately useful."

"Keep trying," I said. "But, yeah, thanks for acting the guide."

"No problem. Oh, and I got lots of screencaps for Lucy. I bet you could talk her into petting you."

"What?" Lucy asked.

"Never mind that," I said. "Come on, we have some things to plan out. Like how to hit up a mercenary base."

"You're doing what?"

CHAPTER TWENTY

WARPATH

There are few things more terrifying than a samurai on a warpath.

These things include showing symptoms of whatever plague is currently in vogue, noticing a mushroom cloud in your vicinity, and seeing more than one samurai on a warpath.

It's real easy to die out there these days.

So remember. Wash your hands, don't live in an impoverished neighborhood, always shut the fuck up, and you'll get to live a long and . . . pleasant life.

—Jeremy Rotter, life coach, 2044

Lucy and I navigated over to the kitchen as I explained things to her. "So, the mercs that got Katallina were real, uh, discreet, right?"

"Yup," Lucy agreed.

"So Lag and Dial-Up, who are real weirdos, but they're all right. Anyway, they tracked them down. Or at least figured out which group they're from based on the software they used. I probably wouldn't have been able to track them myself. Now I know who they are, more or less, and where to go knocking to find them."

"So, you're going to go knocking at the door of a really dangerous, very competent group of mercenaries, all on your own?"

"That's the plan?" I tried.

Lucy smiled at me. It was a very dangerous smile. "You know, I do like you alive, right? You're nice and soft. You make for a good bed warmer. I would be very disappointed if you ran off to fight some mercs and got dead because you lack common sense."

I rolled my eyes. "All right, yeah. I get it," I said as I sat down. "Is there anything to eat?"

Lucy moved over to the fridge and popped it open. "There're leftovers, if you want something fast. Or we could order something?"

"Leftovers are fine," I said. "Probably better than anything from the orphanage."

"Aww, you don't miss the sugar and corn syrup with the occasional bit of protein juice pressed into . . . some weird shapes?" Lucy asked. "Oh, with that yellow cheese stuff!"

"Don't diss the yellow cheese stuff."

"Well, this one has real cheese," Lucy said as she pulled a plate out of the fridge. I only caught sight of something beige before she shoved it in the microwave and turned it on. I flinched with every beep.

Why were microwaves so damned loud? New ears aside.

"So," Lucy said as she leaned against the counter. "What are you going to do about the mercs?"

"I could call the police on them?"

We both giggled.

"No, but really, I'll ping Deus Ex. Maybe she'll get off her lazy little ass and give me a hand. Maybe I can ask my nun friend too."

"Marie?"

I blinked, then recalled the nun the kittens had escaped the museum from what felt like ages ago. "No, not her. Gomorrah."

"Oh, the flamethrower nun," Lucy said.

"Yeah. She's pretty cool. I bet lots of fire would work on some mercs." I could imagine the scene already. And the smell.

"Doesn't sound very nunlike," Lucy said. The microwave beeped and she pushed off the counter, then hissed a moment later as she touched the too-hot plate. A moment later she placed it before me, the corners pinched between some paper towels. There were two forks on the plate, next to some sort of pasta things filled with cheese and some green stuff.

There was a slab of meat too, covered in spices and big grains of pinkish salt, and next to that a puddle of some sauce that had suffered a bit in the microwave.

"I can't tell what half of this is," I said.

"It's all delicious is what it is," Lucy said. "The meat's actual meat. Like, from a cow or a pig or something."

I shrugged and sliced a piece off the steak, dipped it in the sauce, and tucked in. "Holy shit," I said, breathing hard to cool my mouth down.

Lucy took a nibble too. "I know, right? I'm going to get so fat living here."

"Nice and plump."

She bumped her shoulder against mine. "Try the cheese thing. It's real cheese too, I think."

"I could get used to this."

Lucy nodded. "We'll be real fancy folk soon. Hey, do samurai go to school?"

I shrugged. "I don't know. Could ask Deus Ex, but something tells me she doesn't do school all that well." I scratched the side of my nose with my metallic hand. "Why're you asking? Planning to get me enrolled in some sort of boarding school?"

"Ooh, one of those fancy ones filled with repressed girls that you can awaken with your masculine charms?" Lucy asked.

I bumped my shoulder against hers. "Weirdo," I said.

She shook her head. "I was actually thinking about the kittens. They'll need to go to school or something one day, you know? I think there's an education center in the hotel. You know, for fancy folk to offload their brats for the afternoon."

"Good luck selling them on the idea."

"You could help. Threaten them a bit to soften them up. Then I can come in and ask really nicely, and offer sweets or something."

I glared. "You're too damned devious, you know that," I said. It was very much like Lucy to pull that kind of thing on the kittens. Or on me. But she was always enjoyably apologetic when I caught her trying to pull a fast one.

"So, Gomorrah," Lucy said. "Should I be worried? Flamethrower nuns sound pretty awesome."

"She is kinda hot," I admitted.

Lucy snorted. "That was awful."

I nodded and poked my fork into some sort of teeny-tiny potato. "Hey, Myalis? Can you call Gomorrah or is that off-limits too?"

Dumbass clicked over, then jumped onto the far end of the table. The little robot shifted before depositing itself down. "I can call her, if you wish. Do you want it to be out loud?"

I waved her on. "Sure."

The robot spun around and soon the kitchen filled with the tri-tone beeping of a phone going off. Something clicked and a familiar voice came out from Dumbass. "Stray Cat?"

"Oh, they actually call you that?" Lucy whispered.

"You're not Stray Cat," Gomorrah said.

I cleared my throat. "Yeah, yeah, it's me. Well, no, that was Lucy, but I'm here. Anyway, yeah, how're you doing?"

"Smooth," Lucy muttered.

"I'm well," Gomorrah said. "Is this a courtesy call or something?"

"I don't actually know what that is," I said. "Nah, I'm calling you to know if you'd be willing to help me bust some mercs later? They kidnapped this samurai kid. So I'm going to be paying them the fun sort of visit." I gestured to Dumbass the First. "Myalis, can you send her the stuff?"

"Sending the . . . stuff now," Myalis said.

"Give me a minute," Gomorrah said. I hummed something agreeable-sounding and cut my meat up with the side of my fork. I was pretty sure that meat wasn't meant to be that tender. I wondered what it tasted like when it was fresher. "Ah, that's not good."

"I know, right," I said. I wiggled my fork through the air. "You want in? I'd go in alone, but my girlfriend would get all worried and annoying about me handling things on my own."

"We're pretty much done in the incursion zone," Gomorrah said. "The only parts left are right around the center of the hive, and that's being cared for by some higher-tier samurai. I suppose I have the time . . . that I'll *make* the time to save a sister."

"That's great," I said. "Wanna meet up . . . uh, where are you, and Myalis, where're the mercs?"

"If you're looking for a place to meet Vanguard Gomorrah, then this hotel is more or less between her and your objective," Myalis said.

"That works for me."

"Likewise. I'll see you in about half an hour. I'll send Myalis a ping when I get there," Gomorrah said. "See you later, Stray Cat. And good day, Lucy."

"Bye!" Lucy called out.

Dumbass shifted a little. "Call over. Shall I requisition a car?"

"Wait until Gomorrah arrives. She might have a car already." And squeezing into a clown car on my own was fine, but it would be a bit embarrassing with someone else. I sighed. "I guess that means I need to keep moving," I said.

Lucy patted my thigh. "It's all right. Just be safe, okay?"

"Yeah, no worries," I said. "I'll be back before you know it."

Lucy grinned. "I hope you won't be so tired that you'll just fall asleep this time."

I flushed. "I'll be sure not to."

CHAPTER TWENTY-ONE

GOD'S RIGHTEOUS FURY

Car culture was a multibillion-dollar industry before samurai came about and introduced technologies that changed the way driving worked for everyone.

Now, car culture is a multitrillion-dollar industry, with everyone from the super-rich who want their Rolls-Royce to be made to their exacting specifications, to street punks who cover their beaters with wraps of their favorite waifus. Anyone can mod their rides to be just a little faster. Everyone dreams of drift-flying around the smokestacks in the factory districts of various megacities.

—J. P. Kafka on the evolution of car culture, January 2038

I wasn't feeling my best as I rode the elevator down to the lobby. My clothes were in a bit of a state after Lucy's very enthusiastic goodbye, and if it hadn't been for the guilt of knowing that some kid needed help, I might have called off the whole thing to take another long shower.

As entertaining as your distress is, it might be best if you focused a little.

"You think?" I muttered. I tugged my coat back on straight, then made sure all of my gear was in place. I had my Trench Maker tucked under one arm and my Whisper slung over my back. My back-mounted guns were tucked away, and my tail was casually whipping from side to side.

It was a lot of weaponry, and yet I still felt like I could have a bit more.

Still, it wasn't worth losing points just yet, not if I could spare them.

The elevator slowed to a gentle stop and its doors opened. My freaky new ears almost immediately gave me an image of the room before I stepped out into it, and of the salesman in the corner whispering, "There she is."

I walked fast. I wanted to duck my head down and try to be unnoticeable, but there was no way that would work. My jacket, untransparent as it was, looked a bit like the acid-rain-proof long coats worn by some of the folk around, but my armor beneath sure didn't.

Lucy had once told me that one of the best ways to get around was to look like you knew what you wanted and to move ahead with your head held tall and your back straight. It was good advice for an orphan on the streets.

"Myalis, can you send a warning to the idiots coming over?"

Certainly. Do you wish to see it first?

"Will you send something embarrassing if I don't ask?"

Definitely.

I rolled my eyes, then blinked a few times to get over the still-strange sensation of having two eyes to blink. "Show me."

Dear unintelligent salesperson,

Be aware that the Vanguard you are approaching is currently on an important, uninterruptible mission to safeguard the life of someone more important than you.

Attempts to stall or interrupt this vital mission will result in one of the following:

- *The leaking of embarrassing personal information*

- *Dismemberment*

- *Defenestration*

- *Public humiliation*

- *The sudden and irreversible erasure of all personal information (including images, digital paperwork, identity files, records, video, and digitized memories) from any source connected to an open network, including banks, social media, schools, and the internet as a whole.*

Please assess whether the risks are worth the potential loss of the Vanguard's time.

Thank you <3

I nodded after reading it. That was suitably terrifying. "Why's it superimposed over a gif of kittens chasing a ball of yarn?"

That's a live feed from the internet, actually. And I enjoy the juxtaposition. I think it makes it just a little bit more intimidating.

"Send it," I said.

I enjoyed the way the morons coming at me paused. A few of them looked to each other, and one even seemed to be considering it, but then one scoffed and turned away, and soon I was across the room and the peer pressure had them looking elsewhere for other people to bother.

Pushing through the exit found me once more on the landing just outside the hotel. This time, there wasn't a shitty taxi waiting for me. Instead, with a familiar nun leaning against its side, was a boxy muscle car.

"God damn," I said as I moved closer and took the ride in.

Flat black paint so dark it almost hurt to look at, a shell of thick steel with a sort of cage around the front and back. The car was resting flush against the ground, its turbines off and clicking as they cooled, and yet it looked like it was ready to pounce ahead at a moment's notice.

No windows, because those were apparently for lesser cars, and if I wasn't mistaken, there was a turret emplacement on the hood. "God *damn*," I repeated.

"Using the Lord's name in vain is usually a sin," Gomorrah said. "But that is the appropriate reaction in this case."

"What is it?" I asked as I carefully reached out to run a hand over the hood. It was rough, coarse like sandpaper.

"This is what you can get for four thousand points and a tech tree specced into hovercars," Gomorrah said.

"It's gorgeous," I said. "I'm not a car girl, but still, damn."

I noticed that she had built up a bit of a crowd, a dozen or so people blinking at us with the telltale look of someone using their augs to take screencaps.

"She goes from zero to sixty in point nil one seconds. So fast that anything organic inside is turned to mush. Max speed in-atmosphere is just shy of Mach one. Point defense lasers, guided rockets, and a flamethrower under the hood. Fully airtight, of course. Oh, and there's a fridge between the seats. It keeps my soda cold."

"Christ."

Gomorrah huffed and shook her head. I looked up to her, but her face was covered in that same emotionless white mask as before. Not much seemed to have changed with my favorite nun other than the car.

"Does she have a name?" I asked.

"God's Righteous Fury," Gomorrah said with a hint of pride.

I stared at her, then shook my head. "O-kay. That's certainly a name. Can we get in?"

"Clean off your shoes," Gomorrah said as she pushed herself off the side. "Fury, doors."

The car's sides split, revealing two seamless doors that pushed out, then slid back to reveal a plush interior covered in white leather and golden trim. I tapped my boots together after running over to the other side, then slid onto the passenger seat.

The moment my ass was down, the seat shifted, the backrest moved, and I found myself leaning back into a sort of gel-like pad that seemed purpose-built to accommodate my gear. There was even a slot for my tail.

"That's a bit much," I said as I untensed and sank in. "No belts?"

"This car doesn't do accidents," Gomorrah said as she reached toward the dash. A pair of joysticks unfolded from the console and soon the front, sides, ceiling, and floor lit up with a crystal-clear view of our surroundings.

"You're not using autopilot?" I asked.

Gomorrah turned toward me and just stared with that expressionless mask for a few long seconds.

"All right, all right," I said. "So, we plan on the way?"

"Sure," she said as she reached out and flicked a pair of very old-school switches.

"Identify," a disembodied voice demanded.

"Fury: Roar," Gomorrah said.

I snorted, but the sound was drowned out by a low, primal rumble and a few bursts of blue flames burping out of the raised scoop on the hood.

The car lifted, and then I wasn't able to tell what happened because I was thrown into my seat, and breathing became a thing of the past. I did notice that the darkened landing pad became open sky through the canopy. For a few good seconds I was too busy trying to not die to observe anything.

"Oh, sorry," Gomorrah said as she loosened on the acceleration.

I gasped for air and pressed a hand against my chest. "What the hell?" I asked.

"Traffic in the upper levels is set at three hundred KPH. Just wanted to get to cruising speed."

"Uh-huh," I said. It was a weak attempt at snark, but I was still catching my breath. A look down revealed all of New Montreal, done in somber colors and with the flashing headlights of slower-moving cars below.

Huge holographic ads splashed through the sky, and we zipped by a few ad-blimps with even more ads on their sides. "I know the view's great, but you asked me for help?"

I stopped staring. "Right. So, did you read the stuff I sent?"

"You mean what your AI sent? I listened to the abridged version."

There was an abridged version? "We're going after these mercs, called the, uh . . . fuck, it doesn't matter. They're the ones that grabbed Katallina, the samurai girl."

"No samurai name for her?" Gomorrah asked.

"Never met her in person," I said. "So, they took her. Don't know if she's still with them or not, but if she's not with them, then they're the next link in the chain, you know?"

Gomorrah nodded.

"The plan, as far as there is one, is to kick in the front door and ask some very pointed questions," I said.

"Aren't you a stealth specialist?" Gomorrah asked. "Can't you sneak in?"

I frowned as I thought about it. "Probably? Might not be a bad idea. They might get spooked if we burn down their front door."

"I can always wait as backup," Gomorrah said. "Also, hang on, we're going down."

Then the car flipped upside down; Gomorrah pulled the joysticks back and aimed us nose down.

I screamed a little.

CHAPTER TWENTY-TWO

REACTION TIME

If you ever have to fight a samurai, and that's already a losing proposition, then the very best thing you can do is make sure they don't have time to react.

They have an infinite arsenal at their disposal but only a finite amount of time to pick which tool to use.

Strike fast. Strike hard, and never strike the same way twice.

—Anonymous writer, from a dark web guide for assassins, 2052

"Fuck fuck fuck fuck fuck."

Gomorrah twitched her hands to the side, and we juked out of the path of a cargo craft so fast that even my cybernetic eye only caught a passing glimpse of the life insurance ad on its side.

"Shit shit shit!" I added as Gomorrah started to pull up, then encountered the rising, warning-light-covered smokestacks of New Montreal's industrial district.

My everything clenched as she flung us to one side to avoid a pole, then tossed us in the other direction to keep from ramming a chimney.

"Tight," Gomorrah said before rolling the car to the side to slip in between two metallic blurs. I didn't even see them until we were shooting past them.

"Fuck shit," I agreed.

Gomorrah snorted and leveled us off. She smoothly guided the Fury down between the megastructures nearest the industrial sector and wove down into the main traffic lanes. She was still ducking and weaving around slower cars, but it wasn't at a speed that had my lunch considering a violent exit.

"Where did you learn to drive, and can someone sue them for incompetence," I said.

"Come on, no one's died from my driving," Gomorrah said.

"I feel there should be a 'yet' at the end there," I said. "Maybe in italics."

The nun laughed. "I got my license early, so I used to drive the church van around a lot."

"Bringing people closer to God by means of heart attacks?" I asked. "You know, at this rate I expect you to just crash into the mercs' hidey-hole."

"That's one way of doing it," Gomorrah said. "But nah. I'm going to park us a few blocks over, and we can make our way down on foot."

"Is it a nice enough neighborhood to leave this thing parked on its own?" I asked.

"No one's going to steal my car, Cat."

"It's a nice car," I said.

"It can handle itself," Gomorrah said. "Right, Fury?"

The car chimed a positive-sounding two-tone note.

I shrugged. She was probably right. It would take someone with serious balls to try to jack a samurai's ride. We veered out of traffic a moment later and glided down a few levels, past billboards and ads and a few sky bridges between the buildings towering above us until Gomorrah came level with a hangar door in the side of a building.

"It's one of those pay-per-minute parking spots," Gomorrah said. "The cheap ones, you know?"

"Yeah," I said. "What's the rate like?"

"Forty-five credits per minute. Countdown starts when you move in, ends when you're finally out," Gomorrah said. I noticed her head twitching, the telltale sign that someone was navigating some menu. "It's got some vacancy."

"You know, this might take a few hours."

"That's fine," she said.

"'Cause you're not planning on paying?" I asked. I sure as hell wouldn't.

Gomorrah looked my way for a moment. "What? Of course I'll pay. It'll be what, a few thousand credits at most?"

I shrugged. It was her credit.

The hangar opened and we slid into the poorly lit interior. Gomorrah hovered past an automated car racking system and headed toward a more traditional parking lot by the back. Gomorrah tucked in between a sedan and a soccer mom van.

I stepped out with a sigh. Gomorrah's driving was a bit much for me, and it was nice to have both feet on solid ground again. "Okay," I said as I pushed Fury's door closed. It hissed and shut itself on its own. "So, I'm a bit disoriented. Where's that merc hideout?"

"Three buildings down," Gomorrah said. She moved to the back of her car, the trunk opening as she approached it. "It's near ground level." A set of mechanical arms came out of the back of her car, carrying a very familiar flamethrower that Gomorrah grabbed and, with a tug on its strap, hung off her shoulder.

"Cool. Myalis, can you give me waypoints?"

Certainly.

I nodded, taking in the faintly glowing green balls set a couple of meters apart in my vision, all of them leading over to an elevator bank at the back of the parking garage. A three-dimensional wireframe of the building pointed me more or less in the right direction too.

"Are we really just going to knock on their front door?" Gomorrah asked.

"No. But we'll get within a building of them before we start planning properly, I think. Myalis, can you make it so we don't ping anything on the way over? I don't want them to see us coming until we want them to know."

I can do that. Though I can't account for organic observers, or for that matter closed-circuit systems or a few other methods of observation.

"Just do your best with what you've got," I said. "Let's go!"

Gomorrah caught up with me and we walked over to the elevators side by side. I slapped the right floor number and leaned against the wall as the elevator rumbled its way down. "Do you know how you'll get in?" the nun asked.

"Not yet," I said. "I don't suppose the place has suspiciously large air vents able to hold my weight?"

Not unless you're considering losing quite a few kilos.

I snorted. "Okay. Back doors? Windows maybe?

One moment, I'm going to send you and Gomorrah the schematics to the building. Keep in mind, these are the official schematics, not something taken from a scan. It's entirely possible that the building has been changed.

A three-dimensional model appeared before me of an entire megastructure. Hundreds of rooms, corridors, small homes and shops, all stacked up one atop the other, with supports marked in orange and walls in translucent greens. Faint blue lines marked out what I suspected were the building's wiring.

"Can you highlight the mercs' place?" I asked.

Here you go.

A stretch of the building some three stories tall lit up in purple. I toyed with the controls built into my augs until it was zoomed in a little and I could see it better. The section the mercs were using wasn't perfectly square. Some of the rooms from other parts of the building poked into their space, but it was a near thing.

"Looks like a sort of garage on the first floor. Living spaces on the second, and . . . maybe those are offices on the third?"

Indeed. The bottommost floor occupied by the Hour Men is the fifth floor of the building.

"Where are the entrances?" I asked.

Five doors were highlighted in red. Three emergency exits leading into a stairwell that crossed a decent portion of the entire building. A door by the offices, no doubt leading into a sort of lounge, and the main door of the garage.

"Those fire escape entrances look to be in pretty quiet spots," Gomorrah said.

"I really doubt they're viable entrances," I said. "They have to be locked up, or else bricked over. Unless these guys are complete idiots, and I doubt that."

"You think that highly of them?"

"No. I just don't like the idea of underestimating someone so much," I said. "I think the garage is too obvious, and the main entrance is a bust."

"Unless you go in with a disguise or something."

That . . . was an idea. "Maybe. Let's look at other things first. Myalis, they have an entire wall that's on the exterior, right?"

They do.

The garage-side wall lit up. "Any windows?"

Four windows flashed the same color as the entrances.

"Well, there's another option," I said.

"How important is it that you get in physically?" Gomorrah asked.

The elevator dinged and its doors opened out into a little lobby with cracked tiled floors and heaps of trash shoved up against the corners. "I guess we should figure out what we want to do with them before breaking in, huh?"

"That might save us some time," Gomorrah said.

"Right. Priority one is the girl. And I guess her dog. We need to find out if she's there. If she is, then we extract her."

"Just the two of us?" Gomorrah asked.

I chewed on my cheek, then shook my head. "No. That's too risky. If she is there, then we get some other samurai to help. Someone like Deus Ex could probably fry everyone in the building from a dozen kilometers away without hurting her. It'd be safer."

"And if she's not there?" Gomorrah asked.

"Then we find out where she is. If that means finding someone to ask questions to, then so be it."

CHAPTER TWENTY-THREE

PHONES

Phones! For well over a hundred and fifty years, humanity has been brought closer together thanks to the wired, and eventually wireless, communication networks that followed wherever we congregated.

Perhaps the most iconic of these is the smartphone. So called because the device was meant to be smart. Not in the sense that it had any kind of learning or adaptive AI, but in the sense that it allowed someone to be more productive and achieve more.

That turned out to be a lie.

Phones significantly reduced a person's attention span and ability to focus, introduced constant para-relationships and entertainment on the go.

That's why today we use the successors of the handy smartphone instead.

Augs!

Linked between your optic nerve, the inside of your eye, and an implanted processor, the modern aug (or, as it is properly called, ocular augmentation) allows you to do anything you could with a cell phone, but with only a thought!

There can be issues, though. That is why one should always ensure that their augs are the top of the line, run the latest updates, and keep with their rental fees.

Having your eyes shut off for missed payments is no joke!

—Part of Freezerburn Electronics'
"stealth" advertising campaign of 2031

"Windows it is," I said. I patted myself down, making sure everything was in place, and stepped out into the little lobby we'd dropped down to. Myalis's waypoints led out ahead and to the left, and I wasn't about to argue with that.

Finding your way around in a mega building was a strange sort of skill you needed to hone pretty well if you were going to live in the bowels. There were some efforts to make things fit a certain mold, but those usually fell flat when every other building had a different company building it.

It reached the point where you could kinda tell who built what based on the way the building's innards were arranged.

I couldn't name any of those construction companies, of course, but I could recognize a pattern. Some had lots of tight corridors in the center and bigger rooms on the outside, others the opposite. One group had a sort of open space in the middle that often reached out all the way to the sky above and was used as a sort of extra space for walkways.

It never ended up as fancy as it sounded.

I kinda recognized where we were going a few corridors down. I'd never been here, but I'd been in enough places like it that it wasn't hard to figure it out. We crossed through one passage with peeling wallpaper set over cement walls and shoved through a doorway into a street.

Not a street in the old sense, like a passage at ground level where cars went, but a proper modern street. That was a place with shops and houses along both sides, and enough foot traffic to keep things lively.

Myalis's waypoints hovered a little higher, pointing to the end of a long passage that, under the banners, stickers, holographic ads, and shop fronts, was little more than a wider corridor under all the dressings.

A few auto-shops were selling stuff from ramen to microwaved meals to anyone with the credits to spare. There were bigger lines at the stalls with actual people behind the counters, though. Something about being served by a machine always felt wrong to me, and it was the same for a lot of folk.

Vending machines spamming incessant jingles tailor-made to act as earworms and a few unmarked doors leading off to who-knows-where lined the sides. In the middle were a few squared-off plant boxes with benches on their sides. Not that I'd be caught dead sitting there. Judging by the yellowness of the plants, the place wasn't exactly maintained all that often.

Gomorrah reached up and pushed her mask in. "I can never get used to places like this," she said.

I turned, walking backward a few steps. "Why's that?" I asked. "These places are filled with life."

"They're . . . I don't want to say filthy, but, well." She turned to the side, and I could tell she was looking over to a pair of girls, teens if I had to guess, both in neon shorts and bikini tops and little else. Joygirls, probably. Looking for a gullible Joe to fuck and/or rob.

"It's a bit low-class for you?" I asked.

"I'm hardly from a rich background," she said.

I shrugged. A place like this had a community around it. The folks here knew each other, even if just in passing. They wouldn't stop to help if one of them was bleeding out, but they might spare a friendly nod or something.

It was the kind of place I'd wished I'd grown up in. The lower-middles, where there was still work around if you knew where to look, and where the occasional idiot who'd pulled in a big win would spread the joy around a little.

You wouldn't live long, but your life wouldn't be complete shit.

"Are you hungry?" I asked as we crossed a shop where some pimple-faced teen was dropping slices of vat-protein into some sort of bread cone. There was an entirely fresh slab of pseudo-meat rotating on a spit behind him, perfectly square and sweating under the heat from a couple of red-hot elements.

"Not anymore," Gomorrah said.

I shrugged. I still had that steak from earlier working around in my gut, but I figured it was a bit too healthy for me, and I had to balance it out with something more my class. "You do you," I said.

The waypoints led us to a four-way intersection, then off to the right down a street without half as many lights and twice as many ads hanging off the walls.

I slowed my pace down a bit. "Keep sharp," I said.

"What?" Gomorrah asked.

"The ads. Cigarettes, vapes, pills, and guns," I said, gesturing to the holograms. Half of them were of very sexy, very digital women smoking while trying to catch our eyes or of action-hero sorts endorsing guns that were made for people really into compensation.

"What of them?" Gomorrah asked.

There were fewer people around. Not as many beggars, more girls, and the occasional boy next to intimately dark entrances. No manned food stalls either. "You can tell a lot from ads," I said. "The folks that put them up have a vested interest and make sure they target their audience, you know?"

"I suppose."

"Around your part of the city, I bet there are lots of ads for Bibles or . . . I don't know, Jesus wine? TV evangelists? Whatever it is you religious types like. Back there, there was food and insurance and job sites. The kind of stuff that the people living there need."

"And here it's drugs and guns," Gomorrah said. She wasn't dumb. "So the people here need those things."

"The people here have proven statistically likely enough to buy those things that it's cost-effective to put up ads for them," I said. "At least, that's how it was explained to me."

Gomorrah nodded, and I saw her hunching a bit. She brought her arms up, sliding her hands into her opposite sleeves. I didn't think it wise to make oneself small, but we were just passing by, and it wasn't time for street living lessons.

There were two ways to move through a dangerous part. Three, really. You moved fast. You moved like you fit in. Or you made yourself small and tried to look unappetizing.

The way we were dressed, even if we weren't covered in chrome and spit-shined like some fancy corporate stooge, still hinted that we had a few credits to spare. It was better to make it look like that was because we weren't to fuck with than looking like someone that had followed their GPS to the wrong corner.

Catherine, could you look to your left? Behind the hologram of a woman with a cheap rifle.

I let out a sigh when I noticed a kid staring at us from behind a dancing holographic woman using a rifle as some sort of marital aid. He had one eye glowing with the telltale sign of someone with some cheap aftermarket aug.

"Myalis, why did you pick this road?"

It is the route to your destination that requires the least time spent lingering in gang-infested areas.

"Hmm, fair enough, I guess." I looked at the kid again and made sure to focus on his eyes. "Any way you can tell me what he's up to?"

Sending a live feed of you and Gomorrah to three young men with surprisingly varied criminal records who happen to be waiting in an alley some hundred meters away.

"That's nice. Any chance you could tell them not to pull off whatever they're thinking of doing?"

Only if I get creative. None of them have augmentations. They're using a tablet of all things to see the feed from the child. Give me a moment, it might take some convincing them, at least if they've consumed as many narcotics as I suspect.

I reached into my jacket and pulled out my Trench Maker. "We might need to do some negotiating," I said.

CHAPTER TWENTY-FOUR

CHOOSING TO DIE

Modern policing is very successful. As long as you're in a sector that is deemed safe (often marked with the color code "white"), then the rate of violence is actually some of the lowest ever recorded in human history.

Occasionally, policing forces will descend into areas with higher levels of violence (also called "brown" zones) in order to secure the citizens there against potential violent criminals.

There are many tactics that the modern cop uses to tell if a person is a threat. That includes surveillance AI routines, automatic record scrapers, and the good old M.I.N.O.R.I.T.Y. technique for determining if the cop will be suspended for firing upon a potential suspect!

There's no longer any need to worry about corruption! Our own internal auditing and reporting system has cleared every one of our officers of any suspicions.

—Ad for Dirty, an international policing agency, 2052

"Look at these fine ladies," one of them said.

Our greeters were seven young men. Most were barely out of their teens, but two of them looked like they were pushing thirty or so. Pretty old for street rats. That meant they were important, tough, lucky, or had fallen in late. All but the last were usually a bad sign.

I'd spoken to some middle-class sorts before. Mostly through the obligatory socializing parts of my shitty schooling where we had to talk to other kids on similar programs across the country. Of course, the school programs listened to everything we said to make profiles of us later, but that was a given.

When I talked about street rats, the middle-class sort always had the same mental image. Guys with crazy hair, lots of leather, and too many spikes on their clothes. The image wasn't entirely wrong; some gangs really went for that straight-to-streaming look.

But the average street rat? They weren't going out and buying ten-thousand-credit pseudo-leather jackets and dyeing their hair. They were lucky if a single thing they wore wasn't picked out of a secondhand pile or off someone else's fresh corpse.

These seven were that sort. The only sun they saw was in the glow of neon ads, and their teeth had more colors than their hair.

I looked at Gomorrah, but she was quiet, mask fixed on the nearest of them. I like to imagine she was unimpressed under there.

I wasn't so blasé. These sorts might have spent nothing on clothes and less on hygiene, but when they did have cash, it went into one of three things. Drugs, ass, and guns. And these guys only looked a little high, and very horny.

Shifting my shoulders, I looked for whichever one stood out as the leader of the bunch. "You sure you wanna do this?" I asked.

One of them grinned. He shouldn't have. "Yeah, girl. You're a fine-enough-looking piece, and that arm of yours." He whistled. "Wouldn't mind that wrapped around my member."

I sighed. "Gomorrah, I know you're fine with killing Antithesis, but how are you on killing normies?"

"You mean human beings?" Gomorrah asked. "I was about to bring it up. While murder's never been something the average Christian is against, I find it a bit distasteful when it's of human beings."

"Right, right," I said. "But won't all of these idiots have a much happier life in . . . heaven or whatever?" I asked. "We're just speeding things along."

"Cute," she said. "It doesn't work that way. And I doubt heaven would want anything to do with this bunch, half of them have records."

"So, we talk our way out, then shoot if things go sideways," I said. Nodding, I turned back to the group. "Y'all know we're samurai, right?"

"Yeah, so what?" one of them said. He looked particularly intelligent and wise with his pants needing to be tugged up after every sentence, like an entirely new and horrifying sort of punctuation. "We don't believe the shit the corpos spout. 'Specially not 'bout you guys."

"That's . . . well, that's up to you, I guess," I said. I looked to the others, trying to spot one I could talk to that wasn't brain-dead. One nearer the back looked like he'd never come back from an overdose before. "What about you? You willing to risk it?" I asked.

He was a bit younger. Maybe my age. Not old enough that the cops wouldn't beat him bloody but young enough that maybe he could get his shit together. "Um, yeah, yeah, I'm with my boys. Just two of you."

They laughed, shifting submachine guns around and fiddling with their little handguns.

It was weird. A week ago I'd have been scared shitless about this and try-ing to hide it. Now I was just annoyed.

One of them reached out and grabbed my flesh-and-blood arm with his greasy hand. "Come on, put up a bit of a fight at least."

A twitch and my augs pinged the guns on my back, both of them deploy-ing and aiming at the nearest idiots. My new arm wrapped around the ass-hole grabbing my forearm and squeezed.

I was pretty sure the bones in his arm weren't meant to make splintery noises. "First one of you who puts his finger on a trigger gets to test out my new railgun," I said. "It's a virgin gun, you know. Never took an asshole's head off. You'll get to be its first."

The guy that had been grabbing me scoffed and pulled on my arm. Not screaming from his arm being crushed? Either he was hyped up on some-thing good, or he had augs to suppress pain. He was a heavy guy; when he tugged me toward him, there was little my skinny ass could do but follow. That was, until my railgun hummed for just a second, then made a sound like someone exhaling hard.

The man stood still for a while, the loonie-sized hole smoking where the bridge of his nose was slowly filling with melted brain gunk and sizzling from the heat along the edge of the new piercing.

I tugged my arm free and pulled my Trench Maker out just as his body collapsed. "Guess who just learned their last lesson about respecting peo-ple's personal space?"

The other six tugged their guns up. It looked like it had just clicked with them that shit was real. "You bitch!"

"We told you guys that we don't want trouble," I said. My railgun started to hum again and my tail whipped around to my side, spikes deploying from it and the end sparking to life with blue flames. "That's one of your friends dead. We're not here to clear the place of rats, so how about you move on?"

"You're just a human, like us," one of them said. The same idiot that didn't believe in samurai, or whatever.

"You're not wrong," I said. "But you're underestimating how much of a bitch I am. See Gomorrah here? She likes lighting things on fire. But she's nice. She'll preach your ears off before killing you. I won't. I've never cared for anyone that wasn't one of mine, and none of you are one of mine."

"We'll be telling the bosses about this!"

"You'll tell your boss that you ambushed a pair of samurai minding their own damned business and threatened them?" I asked. "Are you a fucking moron? Your bosses will hang you for being brain-dead."

"You know, I'm starting to think maybe I could light them up," Gomor-rah said. She raised a hand, and a foot-long beam of searing-hot flame snuck out from her sleeve and wavered before her.

"Yo! You can't, like, burn people. That's against the Geneva Convention thing!" one of them said.

I . . . wasn't expecting that kind of reference. "It's more of a Geneva suggestion for us," I said. "Now, we have business elsewhere, and you're wasting our time. So, if you could kindly fuck off, that would be really appreciated."

The rats looked to each other, then came to the unanimous decision to run away. They did it with a swagger, as if trying to convince anyone looking that it wasn't a full-on retreat, but they still left us be.

"Did you really have to kill him?" Gomorrah asked.

"Probably not," I said. I didn't dwell on the body next to me much. "I haven't exactly invested in nonlethals, though, and I don't know if I could take someone of that size one-on-one. Also, my head isn't as bulletproof as the rest of me."

"You really need to see to that," Gomorrah said. "It's the only part you can't replace. It should be the part you're the most keen on protecting."

I sighed. "Yeah, I guess. Don't really like hats, though."

"Get a shield, or a helmet. One of these days one of those sorts of punks will pull one of those anti-Antithesis guns from somewhere and your head will be mulched."

"You can do funeral rites, yeah?"

"No, no I can't. And I wouldn't for you. You'd think someone like you would have better survival instincts."

I frowned. "What does 'someone like you' mean? And are you really shitting on my survival instincts, Miss The-Lanes-Are-a-Suggestion?"

Gomorrah humphed and continued on. I had to jog to catch up. "You know, I kind of expected you to just kill them all."

"Should I have?"

"It wouldn't be appropriate of me to say yes. But at the same time, they didn't seem like very virtuous people."

I rubbed at my lip a bit while thinking of an answer. I understood her wanting to off the idiots. I wouldn't shed a tear for any of them. At the same time . . . "You know, this is gonna sound really cheesy."

"What is?"

"When I was a kid they had these, uh, re-reruns, I guess, of these old comics. When I got to the orphanage for the first time. That was before I found Lucy. This older kid gave me this collection. All pirated, of course. I lost it when I switched augs at some point. But . . . yeah. I used to read these stories about old samurai. Street warriors. Heroes. And they'd always try to do the right thing. I kinda wanted to be like that."

"That's . . . kind of cute."

I glared at the nun.

"No, really. It's naïve, and that's coming from a Christian, but it's kind of endearing. I guess that's why you were chosen to become a samurai."

I shrugged. "I don't know. Maybe. Anyway, it doesn't feel right to kill idiots when you don't need to, and where we are now? We're doing what we want to do, because we want to. The choice is all ours."

CHAPTER TWENTY-FIVE

RAMEN BREAK

Certain traditions are fated to fade away. Sometimes they are kept alive by historians and dedicated practitioners, but as technology moves on and culture shifts, the need for some traditions just ceases.

Some, on the other hand, especially those that were able to adapt, to become commercialized and commodified, not only survive but thrive. New cultures adopt them, they become a symbol of something greater, and in so doing, they are immortalized, at least for the moment.

When I was a young man in Japan, I, like many others, enjoyed the quick-and-dirty foods of the convenience store and street vendors. None of these more than the ramen that kept me fed through years of schooling and bachelorhood.

That is why, when I saw the rise of automation, I saw my chance to take on an old tradition, a symbol, and help it evolve into something new.

It was a grand risk, but I believe the rewards have been worth it.

—Minato Watanabe, CEO, founder, and sole employee of Automata-Ramencorp International

Because of the way the building was laid out, the mercs' place was set at the end of this long corridor. To one side was a long wall with nothing on it but a few little vents and a couple of cameras. Along the opposite side was a Korean nail salon, of all things.

Gomorrah and I never got to that corridor, of course. When we reached the building the mercs were staying at, we went up a few floors and picked some seats at this shitty little android-operated ramen stand.

The bot behind the counter wasn't one of those fancy models trying to look human. It was just a cheap assembly of hard plastic over poorly oiled actuators and servos. Most of the cooking was done through a conveyor system, so all it had to do was handle the transactions and put bowls in front of customers.

Gomorrah paid.

I slurped up a few freshly overboiled noodles and blinked as my eyes watered from the heat on my tongue. "Ah, okay," I said. "So, the front entrance is obviously a no-go."

"Obviously," Gomorrah said. She opened her third pack of spicy sauce and dumped it into her bowl. "There's brazen and then there's brazen."

I nodded and spun my chopsticks around, ignoring the ads scrolling along their sides. "Yeah. So that leaves my first less-dumb idea. We, or at least I, go in by the windows on the outside."

"You're not afraid that they have those monitored?"

"All of them?" I asked. I shrugged. "Yeah, you know what, they might. They had some pretty good gear, and it took a lot to track them to here. Wouldn't surprise me if they went overboard with the safety stuff too."

"Could your Myalis disable the security?" Gomorrah asked. "My AI isn't strong with that, but I have a few points to spend."

I can. While we're playing telephone, do you mind if I connect with Gomorrah's AI directly?

"Go ahead," I said.

Gomorrah looked at me quizzically for a moment before her mouth twisted. "Ah," she said. "Pleased to meet you, Myalis," she said.

The ramen bot juttered, then spoke with a familiar voice. "A pleasure to meet you as well," Myalis said.

The bot shifted to the side; its head, which was a boxy thing with a pair of sensors and a couple of gang tags sprayed across it, turned toward me and spoke with a new voice, masculine and smooth. "Greetings, Stray Cat, I am Atyacus, Gomorrah's AI assistant."

"Oh, uh, hey," I said. I waved to the bot. "Are you two just . . . going to share a body?"

"It does simplify things to a degree. We're sharing data as we speak, and most Vanguards do seem to enjoy having something to address physically while they speak," Atyacus said. He—and it definitely sounded like a he— had a cultured sort of voice. Like one of those fedora-wearing guys in those black-and-white movies.

"Cool," I said. "While you're in there, can you get me another bowl of ramen? I wanna try the pork one."

It was Myalis that replied. "What is Lucy going to say when she tries to pinch you and finds more than she bargained for?"

I glared. "I won't get fat. I've got an orphan's metabolism."

"Is that even a thing?" Gomorrah asked.

I shrugged. "Sure. So, the plan? We use Myalis to shut off security, and then I slip in through a window?"

"Do we even need to enter the building at all?" Gomorrah asked.

"Unfortunately," the ramen bot who was currently Myalis said, "we do. Other than their connection to the water and power grids of the main building, I can detect only one communication line into the building. Specifically, to a router on the topmost floor."

A square opened in my vision, footage, live I guessed, of the back of a cubicle. There were a few posters pinned to the wall, and a calendar, but not much else.

"That's the most I can get from it. The rest of their network seems to be wired, and it's a closed loop. I can access one of their printers, but they haven't used it for anything very sensitive."

"Okay, so we need to get in, and then we can connect to their network?" I asked.

"You might not necessarily need to enter the building," Gomorrah's AI said. The whole sharing-a-body thing was weird. "If my colleague only requires access to their network, then it's possible, likely even, that some of their wiring is in their walls. In which case you could connect to their security with nothing more than an incision."

I rubbed at my chin, then poked at some sort of pseudo-meat floating in my ramen broth. "Yeah, okay," I said. "Gomorrah, can you manage that? Like, do you have something to see wires?" I noticed that the lower part of her mask was raised for the first time. It made it look like her mouth was right over her nose.

"I can manage," she said after she finished chewing delicately. "Will you be coming in from the outside at the same time?"

"That depends. I do like the image of rappelling down the side of their building and busting in through a window, but, well, I've got bombs too. Those would work on their front door, I think."

"Are you really choosing based on which one makes you feel cooler?" Gomorrah asked. The disappointment really came through when she wasn't wearing a mask.

"No?" I tried.

The nun sighed and got to her feet. "Where would be the best place to try to cut through the wall?" she asked the ramen bot.

The robot shifted, and then Myalis came through with a reply. "I suspect . . . here."

The wireframe of the building returned, now with a blinking red circle on the floor with a garage.

"That's two down from the front door," I said. "It'll mean if they try to run, you'll be there."

"We could pinch them in, keep them from making a run for it," Gomorrah said.

I nodded. "I really wanted to try the windows. Oh well. Get into their system with Myalis's help, and then if we can spot the girl, we leave and call for the big guns. No girl means we break in and ask them all some questions the old-fashioned way."

"The old-fashioned way?" Gomorrah asked.

"With high explosives," I replied.

She shook her head and started to walk off. "I'll keep in touch," she said. "Atyacus, you staying in that bot?"

"Of course not," the ramen bot said.

I turned to it a moment later. "So, any idea of what we should be doing?"

"Have you tried our two-for-one special? Two meat flavor packs for the price of one!" the bot said.

I rolled my eyes, tipped the rest of the broth in my bowl down my gullet, then did the same to Gomorrah's leftovers because wasting was a sin, and then I got up and moved off. "We need somewhere to hide in the mean-time," I said. "Somewhere close to the baddies' front door."

The nearest business is a nail salon. There are a few other stores on the same floor.

I brought my hands up and looked at my nails. "You know, I've never really cared much for nails. More of a Lucy thing. Can I even paint my cyberarm's nails?"

The nails retract to allow plasma cutters to deploy.

"I bet they don't have that color at the salon," I said. "Right, let's go waste some time, then."

Some ten minutes later, when I walked in—with Myalis fudging the results of any camera looking my way, of course—the little old lady behind the counter took one look at my organic hand, then started babbling.

"I don't speak, uh"—I looked to the nearest poster, which was covered in some Asian writing—"Whichever squiggly language that is."

I think that might be racist.

"Is it racism when you're mocking someone's language?" I asked.

Yes.

Oh. "You learn something new every day," I muttered. "So, lady, can you make my fingers pretty? I need to look extra girly before I go blowing things up later."

You don't strike me as the girly type.

I grinned. "Well, if I'm real lucky, and Lucy's in the right mood, these fingers might end up somewhere girly later."

Disgusting.

The lady didn't know why I was chuckling, and somehow, that only made it funnier.

CHAPTER TWENTY-SIX

RED CARPET TREATMENT

After the end of the Second World War and the advent of more advanced weaponry, there was a noticeable shift in the way armed forces reacted. It still took some decades for what is essentially an entirely new SOP to take effect, but by the late 1990s most modern militaries understood that a small number of well-equipped soldiers could be used to greater effect than large units of poorly trained conscripts.

In many situations, a small team of well-trained soldiers could make a large, impactful difference.

Whether that is taking down a VIP or sabotaging enemy infrastructure, going in silently is not only more effective, it also allows for a degree of denial on the assaulter's part.

The samurai generally don't fit that bill.

Almost universally, they dislike being quiet.

Something about their mentality just does not agree with the idea that a problem can be solved without explosions, lasers, or explosive lasers.

—Excerpt from *An Analysis of the Capability of the Modern Unit vs. the Samurai,* 2029

I raised my hand and turned it this way and that. My nails shone pretty and rainbow. There was a bit of a holographic effect with them, little hearts in the middle that only showed up at certain angles. "Neat," I said.

"Yes yes, very very pretty," the old woman said.

I grinned back at her and looked at the time. It had been a nice way to spend ten minutes. I bet that Lucy would love that kind of pampering too. Maybe we could order one of those massage people in our hotel room. That was a thing that was done . . . probably. I wasn't up to date on how the rich wasted their credits.

"Myalis, can you transfer over some credits to the nice lady?" I asked.

This will basically empty your account.

"Yeah, but Lucy will like it."

The woman looked at me quizzically for a bit, and then something in her eyes glowed and her smile only grew. "Thank you, honorable customer. You go pinch many bottoms now."

"Damn right," I said as I shoved off her chair, then stretched. "Any news from Gomorrah yet?"

Atyacus has kept in contact with me this entire time. They've reached the appropriate location, though it took convincing a guard to look the other way.

"A merc guard?" I asked.

No, the location where Atyacus proposed breaking through the wall is a warehouse for medical supplies. It has twenty-four-hour guards and surveillance. I suspect that the Hour Men encouraged the placement of a high-security facility next to their offices to act as a sort of additional deterrent. Atyacus disagrees. We've been going back and forth for what for you would be subjective years.

"You do that a lot?" I asked. "Argue with other AI?"

We need to do something to pass the time. Arguing online is one of the few hobbies we share with humanity.

"That and trolling people."

I would only ever troll you, you know that.

I rolled my eyes and came to a stop next to the exit of the nail salon. I leaned against the counter and tapped my feet, and then, because there was nothing else to do, I logged on to my media feeds.

It had been . . . maybe forty-eight hours since I'd last checked. That was practically a lifetime.

Normally I was pretty reserved, only looking to see if anything neat had happened maybe once an hour. I couldn't remember the last time I'd gone so long without looking, but then the last couple of days had been a little hectic.

And, as the site checked my biometrics and auto-logged me in, my vision was filled with gifs, ads, stills taken from a friend of a friend, more ads, news posts, news posts that were actually ads, government warnings about the incursion, and then ads made to look like government warnings about the incursion.

You have over six thousand private messages. All from the last day.

"I'm popular," I said.

Ninety-two percent are targeted ads. Two percent are offers from various corporations aware of your status as Vanguard. Three percent are from people begging for assistance; the remainder are poorly designed malware.

"Annnd I'm already bored," I said.

That might be for the best. Gomorrah has spliced into the office's internal network. Their security software isn't terribly impressive.

"I guess they were placing their bets on it being hard to access instead of difficult to hack into. Probably the smarter option," I said. The media feeds disappeared, and Myalis replaced them with camera feeds from all over the inside of the Hour Men base. For the most part it matched the layout of the blueprints, with a few extra doors and what looked like a couple of windows installed in others.

There were also lots of half walls, and what looked like choke points built into the office space. The top floor was all desks and cubicles and a few meeting rooms. The next floor down had bunks, a small interior range, an armory and some showers and a break room. The bottommost floor, the garage, was the largest of the lot, mostly open space with a couple of nondescript cars tucked away next to an honest-to-God hovertank.

"How many people?" I asked.

Thirty-two have appeared on screen. Every room has a camera, though there are a few blind spots.

"I can't see Katallina," I said.

She doesn't seem to be present.

"Can you connect me to Gomorrah?" I asked.

A moment later I heard my favorite nun breathing as if she were leaning over me. Probably a microphone in that mask of hers. "Any ideas?" she asked.

"Girl's not here. Myalis, you see any sign of her in their software?"

Some traces, yes. Or perhaps calling them possibilities would be more accurate.

Atyacus's voice came over the line. "It seems as if the Hour Men accepted four contracts in the last forty-eight hours. They don't keep any detailed notes on these. In fact, a lack of paperwork seems to be part of their operating procedures."

"So we need someone to ask some questions to," I said. "I guess I'll knock at their front door."

"Seriously?" Gomorrah asked.

"I mean, we need to find out, and I don't feel like chasing leads all day. So we ask. Can you take out that tank?"

"I can," Gomorrah said. "Most things made of metal will melt eventually, but that's besides the point. How are we going to do this?"

I leaned to the side and looked down the corridor where the front door of the Hour Man offices was tucked away. It was a heavy-looking door. All steel and bolts. Not terribly decorative either, and I guessed that the walls were filled with fold-out surprises.

"I fling a bomb at their front wall, then when the dust settles ask to speak to their boss?"

"That sounds like a bit much," Gomorrah said.

I rubbed a finger under my nose. "They kidnapped a kid. I don't think we need to go in soft and polite."

"But soft and polite might get us farther," Gomorrah said.

"Hmph." I tapped my fresh nails on the counter for a moment, then nodded. "You know what, sure. But you send them a message or whatever. I'm not expecting them to exactly roll out the red carpet."

These guys had to know what they were doing, and what the reaction of the average samurai would be. In their place, I'd start running the moment I found out a samurai was on my tail, and if that meant fighting my way out, then so be it. The dead couldn't be punished.

"Sending now," Gomorrah said. "I'm close enough to their lower exit to stop anyone trying to escape that way."

"Yeah, I'm within spitting distance of their front door," I said. I looked around and spotted my crossbow leaning against the backside of the counter. Nearly forgot about it. Would probably have made the old lady rich if I did.

I grabbed the crossbow and pulled the bolt on its side back before flicking its safety off with a twitch of my augs. There were a few explosive bolts left in it.

"Did you send the—" I began.

The feeds of the cameras inside the building started to flash. Some sort of silent alarm had gone off and the lights flickered in response was my guess. The fine folks inside the building started running around, picking up weapons and armor even as guns deployed from the walls and ceilings.

"Well, it doesn't look like they're agreeing to anything just yet," I said.

I stepped out into the corridor. Maybe they would see me standing outside and reconsider things.

I kind of expected the guns that deployed from next to the door.

I didn't expect the twin punches to my gut that sent me tumbling back with a heavy cough.

Lying on the ground, I panted for breath, then touched my chest to confirm that I wasn't bleeding or anything. I found two coin-sized bits of metal flattened over my armor. "Okay," I said. "Bombs it is."

CHAPTER TWENTY-SEVEN

SOMETIMES A GIRL JUST WANTS TO BLOW SHIT UP

There are ten billion people on Earth right now. And, by our best estimates, approximately one in ten thousand is a samurai. That's .001 percent of the world's population.

We see samurai all over. Getting one to act as a mascot for a corporation is considered a huge victory, and even those that try to avoid the spotlight will still be plastered in gossip rags and talked about on Mesh and internet forums. Samurai are natural-born celebrities.

For all that, the likelihood of any one person actually meeting a samurai in their lifetime is minuscule.

I think that this nearly mystical level of rarity just adds to the occultism around the samurai.

—Excerpt from *The Cult of the Samurai*, 2044

I had a bit of a problem.

For one, I was on the floor, chest heaving and feeling like I was a bit past the point where I was meant to die.

I wasn't dead, though, which was nice.

That would change very soon if the turrets placed next to the doors decided to open fire again. I had no idea if they could break through my armor, and I didn't feel like finding out. Also, one of them had shot me in the tit and I was betting that would leave a bruise.

I raised my cybernetic arm toward the door, and with a flick of my augs, I had the top of it open to reveal the rocket launcher within.

The rocket came out with a sound like a hollow fart and whistled across the corridor.

Then, with an impact that made the floor skip under me, it turned the front wall of the mercs' hideout into a nice big crater.

The old lady at the nail salon came rushing out. "What is this?"

I coughed, turned over, then pushed myself up to my feet. "Me being a bit dumb," I said. "Myalis. A helmet, please."

Certainly.

New Purchase: Mark IV TIGER-C Helmet

Points Reduced from . . . 8,426 to . . . 8,366

A box appeared by my feet and I scooped down to pick it up.

"You're samurai!" the lady said.

"Yup," I said. "Nearly a dead one too." The helmet, of course, had a pair of cat-ear slots on the top, and a sort of masklike front with a visor over the top of the face. It was sleek: gunmetal highlights, a sapphire visor, and that familiar blue steel covering the majority of it. It also had whiskers. "Really?"

Those are very sophisticated devices. They analyze the composition of the air around you and reproduce it within the helmet without any harmful effects. They also detect minute vibrations in the air, making up any losses of audibility caused by covering your ears.

I rolled my eyes as I tucked the helmet under one arm, then tied my hair back in a loose bun. On the helmet went. It was a bit snug, but not too much so. The moment it was on, the insides inflated and it felt as though someone had buried my face in a layer of pillows.

It would do.

I stretched a little and pulled my Whisper off my shoulder to tuck it up against my chest. "Go hide away," I said to the old lady. "Or maybe close up for the afternoon? I figure we're going to have a lot of curious people around soon."

The lady nodded and jogged off to her shop. Soon the shutters were rattling down over the front.

I took off toward the mercenary base. My rocket had really screwed up the front door. The turrets that had tagged me were scattered everywhere in bits, and the heavy door was crumpled as if it were a cardboard box and someone with a bat had gone to town on it.

"Gomorrah?" I asked.

"I'm here," I heard her reply. There was a faint crackle in the background. Gunfire? "Are you meeting any resistance?"

"Uh. Yeah. I got shot in the tit."

"You didn't need to be so specific," Gomorrah said. "Are you all right?"

"Fine," I said. "I'm about to kick in the front door. We're trying to keep anyone important-looking alive, right? 'Cause I'm somewhat in a 'blow stuff up' mood right now."

"I'm well. Still at ninety-plus percent with my flamer fuel. The tank's inoperable, by the way. And yes, we want to keep some of them alive. I hope you have better luck than I've had. These men don't seem keen on surrendering."

I brought Whisper up. "We'll have to see. Stay in touch."

I kicked the door. Then when that didn't do much, I kicked it again.

I sighed. "Myalis, I need one of those black-hole bombs."

I think I have something for that.

New Purchase: Mark II Dimensional Shunt Bomb

Points Reduced from . . . 8,366 to . . . 8,361

I caught the grenade Myalis spawned for me out of the air and figured it out at a glance. Timer, trigger, little safety pin. Easy.

Moving way back, I flicked the grenade over to the base of the door. It rolled off to the side a bit, but that wasn't a big deal. I aimed down the length of Whisper and waited.

The world around the door warped, shifting in on itself like looking through poorly made glass. When the twisting finally stopped, everything in a rough circle, maybe two meters wide, was just gone.

I stared at the openmouthed face of a man with a bulletproof vest on the other side. He raised a rifle and aimed it at me.

My finger twitched and a bolt appeared in his shoulder. And then he exploded.

"Oh, shit," I said. I twisted Whisper to the side and opened the bolt. "What kind of ammo do I have?"

Explosive-tipped. Standard explosive.

"Shit, I need something a bit less lethal."

How nonlethal?

I blinked. "What does that even mean?"

Nonlethal only means that the person hit isn't dead in the end. That leaves a lot of room for variation.

I started forward. "Got something like a gas, maybe?"

To compensate for your awful aim. That's a good idea.

New Purchase: Gas-Bulb, Knock-Out-Bolt

Points Reduced from . . . 8,361 to . . . 8,358

I picked up the magazine of bolts, dropped the one that was in Whisper, and slotted the new one in place. "Okay, then," I said.

I had to hop over a hole in the floor near where the grenade had gone off. I could see the floor below, but mostly just the top of some vents and such. It probably wasn't the best thing to do to a building's structural integrity to blow holes in it.

The entrance opened out into a lobby, a large desk, all square and brutalist, a pair of doors leading off to the back, a bathroom off to the side. No benches or anything, but then the type of people coming here wouldn't be sitting down and waiting.

I stepped over the bottom half of the guy I'd shot, Whisper swaying from left to right as I scanned the room.

No one. I was kind of expecting someone to show up, maybe a guard or two? Or maybe they were running down to meet Gomorrah. "Can I have that security feed?" I asked.

A trio of video feeds superimposed themselves over the top of my vision. The next room over front and center, the next rooms after in the next two boxes. That at least explained where the people were. There were guys dressed in the standard uniform of a lifeless corporate goon. Slacks, a button-up shirt with some cutesy pattern, a too-tight tie.

The vests and assault rifles they were grabbing were a bit unusual, though.

The two men and one woman carrying a crew-gun to the center of the room, where they shoved aside a potted plant and hooked the gun onto a plate on the floor, were somewhat more concerning than the rest.

I noticed one or two guys dressed more impressively being ushered down some stairs to the floor below.

"Right," I said. "I guess those guys are the VIPs. So let's go get them."

You might want to note that the room you're in is currently filling with a nerve agent.

"What?" I asked.

You're wearing a mask. It's a non-issue.

I begged to differ. It at least explained why no one was waiting up front. They didn't want to get caught in their own gas. It also explained the masks with rebreather-looking-things the office workers were putting on.

"Gomorrah," I said. "Watch out for gases and such. They're using them up here."

"Noted" came her reply. "I'm going to pull back and buy something for that. Can you keep the pressure up?"

"Sure thing, love," I said.

The doors leading into the office proper weren't slabs of reinforced steel, just plain old smart-glass doors, currently set to opaque.

I made sure my shoulder-mounted guns were ready, then paused. "Wait, they've got masks. I need a different sort of ammo. Again."

I was going to point it out. The gas your bolts use is likely to bypass their rudimentary masks, but it will still take longer to affect them.

I sighed. "Man, I just want to blow things up. Why does everything need to be so complicated?"

CHAPTER TWENTY-EIGHT

THE OPPOSITE OF REASSURING

In the early 2000s there was a fear that the interconnectivity of the world could lead to trouble. Hacking was portrayed in the media as a new and terrifying crime.

The reality was a little more pedestrian at first. A good programmer with malicious intent could maybe steal some files, mess with some machines, or perhaps spy on someone, but other than the occasional virus there wasn't too much to it.

Then augmentations became a new standard. Everyone had one, and the world became far, far more digital. By the 2030s one in ten people in the world had an aug. By 2040 that was up to four in ten. When 2050 rolled around, nine in ten people had an augmentation of some sort, most of them used to keep connected to local or international networks, social media, and other feeds.

Hackers, those who knew what they were doing, could now turn a person's entire life into a living nightmare.

—Excerpt from The Rise of the Aug, 2052

My plan, insofar as I had one, was simple. Burst in, fire a few bolts into the room, then unload my railgun into the turret they were still setting up.

It was a nice plan because I got to shoot things.

I raised a booted foot, prepared to kick at the door, and then I hesitated. It didn't look like a door with an actual lock on it.

After making sure that my shoulder-mounted guns were set properly, I held Whisper close with one hand, then turned the door handle. A shove had the door moving in and got some of the office workers inside to look up. "Hey, guys!" I said.

My railgun thumped and the gun emplacement in the middle of the room burst apart as a tiny bit of metal moving absurdly fast poked a hole through the middle of it.

Whisper came up and I aimed more or less in the direction of the first idiots to bring their guns to bear. The first bolt I fired thumped into and through a cubicle wall; the next rammed into a projector box and fritzed it out. "Myalis, masks," I said.

Fortunately, Myalis seemed to get what I meant. The gun on my opposite shoulder burped, twitched, then burped again. All across the room, masks were shredded apart as Myalis fired through them.

I was expecting the room to fill with gas or something, but there wasn't anything like that. The nearest office worker opened fire with an SMG and I ducked back out of the room and moved away from the doorway before I got sprayed.

"Myalis, why isn't that room filled with gas?" I asked.

It should be. If you're wondering why you can't see it . . . you are aware that not all gases are visible to the naked human eye, right?

"Oh," I said. "I was expecting . . . I don't know, orange-yellow gas or something."

So that anyone you face can see the gas and react to it?

"It's always colorful in the movies," I said.

I'm sure.

I snorted and moved over to the door opposite the one I'd barged in from. Bringing the camera feed back revealed that two of the office workers on the other side had already slumped over, and the rest looked drunk. A clever one by the back had switched his mask out for a less holey one, but he was still stumbling about.

Opening the door slowly and quietly, I flicked on the invisibility on my jacket and held Whisper close. There was a neat puncture that was visually warped where I'd been shot earlier. Annoying, that. I'd need to replace the jacket at some point.

A stop by the nearest office worker revealed that while he was slumped over and noodly, he was still breathing. "Nice," I muttered.

"Stray Cat?" Gomorrah asked.

I shuffled past the gun emplacement, heading toward the back rooms. "Yeah?" I asked while looking into the offices I passed. Most of them were empty. Just desks with a few knickknacks and workstations. No decorations beyond the occasional bland calendar. No pictures of family, no toys or models or anything.

Most corporations wished that they could have offices this bland, but something about being human made you more productive when you had a bit of color around, and at least some things that helped you pretend you weren't some fleshy automaton.

"I've cleared the garage and all the rooms around it. Also, three of them surrendered. I have them sitting next to a firebomb."

"That's . . . okay," I said. "I'm only at the entrance of the main office space. Still need to check some of the rooms around here."

"I see. I'd keep clearing things, but the access to the middle floors is heavily reinforced. I don't know if I can break through with what I have. And from what I can see, they have some nasty armaments on the other side."

"Can't you just buy some bigger toys?" I asked. The next bit of the top floor was separated by an intersection. To the left were the washrooms and a small lunchroom and kitchen. The cameras there were pretty extensive, especially in the washrooms. "Creepy," I muttered as I turned left instead.

"I could," Gomorrah said. "But I don't like the idea of running into people prepared to face me. We're not immortal, you know?"

"Hmm, yeah," I said. "Any access to their ventilation system? Power? We could siege them.'

Gomorrah hummed. "I think I had a similar idea, yes. Once you find the access from above, we could try to negotiate with them."

"Stuck between two hard places, huh?"

"I don't think that's how the expression goes, but something like that."

The hall was lined with bigger offices. With actual desks and better workstations. One long conference room had a nice table floating on a pair of lifts in the middle. The front offices had looked like they were bought with a budget, and I was guessing this was where the actual budget went.

"All right," I said as I finally found the stairs leading down. At least, the door leading to the stairwell. A door currently barricaded with thick metal shutters. "Found the stairs. No resistance or anything so far. Not even a second set of turrets."

"Check the feeds from the second floor," Gomorrah said. "They have corridors at the end of both staircases. With crew-operated guns at each. I'm counting about a dozen men in some very nice gear too."

I rubbed at my chin. "Any way we can ping their augs? Send them a nice friendly message?"

"I'll try," Gomorrah said. "Give me a moment."

I nodded and backed away from the door. "Think we could have broken into their augs from the start?" I asked Myalis.

Perhaps. Though most people who can afford it don't place augmentations in their bodies without at least some security measures.

"Fair enough," I said.

> **NOTICE**
> All individuals within the Hour Men mercenary building are now officially notified that the following samurai wish to question you:
> *Gomorrah*
> *Stray Cat*
> Please surrender. Lower all weapons, remove all offensive equipment from your person, and prepare for arrest and questioning.
> Refusal to comply will be met with the wrath of God.

"Damn, G-girl," I said. "Way to be polite and nonthreatening there. Very diplomatic of you."

Vanguards are not chosen for their diplomatic abilities.

I let out a rather inappropriate giggle at that.

A message was just sent out. Unsecured transmission. It's addressed to you and Gomorrah.

"Huh," I said. "Can I hear it?" I asked.

It's text. Displaying it now.

> Dear Stray Cat and Gomorrah,
> Go fuck yourselves.

Gomorrah sighed. "How polite. So do we just burn them all or are we going to try something else?"

I considered it for a moment before replying. "I'm going to set a bomb up here by the door. Myalis, are they watching us?"

Negative.

"Right. So, bomb by the door here. Then . . . I think I might come in through a window after all. If we can knock them out peacefully . . . ish, then we can ask them some questions later. While they're tied to a chair or something. Got that, Gomorrah?"

I could feel her hesitating for a moment. "It might work. I don't like the idea of you hanging off the side of this building while they know we're assaulting them."

"Ah, don't worry," I said. "I've never done anything like this."

"That's the opposite of reassuring."

Snorting, I knelt down next to the door and flicked off the coms between Gomorrah and me. "I'll need a grenade. Motion sensor activated. Maybe . . . more knockout gas? Something that'll keep people rooted here. Oh, those sticky bombs would do."

Certainly.

Two purchases later, and down to 8,350 points, I was setting up a surprise for anyone that came upstairs.

"All right," I said as I got back up. Bringing up the building plans helped pinpoint where the windows on the floor below were located. The nearest one that matched above was in the conference room. "Time to swing on down and say hello to everyone downstairs."

CHAPTER TWENTY-NINE

SPIDER CAT ~ SPIDER CAT

The rich get richer. That's kind of just a thing.

The super-rich get higher. Not just metaphorically, but literally too.

Life on Earth is generally acknowledged to be rather awful. So why not leave?

With over twenty low-orbit installations, and an entire resort on the moon and Mars,* Tesla-Travel Corp has you covered!

*As of 2039 all Mars expeditions are canceled.

    —Ad for Moon Colony Alpha and former Mars Colony Beta, 2039

New Purchase: Tree Cat Grapple System

Points Reduced from . . . 8,350 to . . . 8,003

The system was built like a backpack with some straps that went around the chest. It was fitted for me, which was handy because I couldn't imagine fitting something so tight on without it bruising my already sensitive chest.

I stared at the two hooks that stuck out from the backpack with some degree of confusion. They were bulbous things, with little glass bits and a bunch of slots on them. "Okay," I said. "I have no idea how these work."

They're multifunction hooks. Pressing them against a stud will launch a drill that will grab on. Leaving them loose will deploy some hooks from within, and the end is a sort of sponge that can fill with a powerful adhesive to cling on to a surface. They're meant to be usable in any situation.

"Well, that's neat, but where do I hook them if I don't want to die?"

Please look at the wire-map of the building, I'll highlight the location of load-bearing supports. Press the hooks against those walls and they will grab on.

Seeing as how I didn't feel like falling to my death, I followed Myalis's instructions, setting up the two hooks to burrow into the walls, and then I trailed out the lines, still connected to the pack, all the way over to the window.

It wasn't the sort of window meant to be opened. No one sane wanted to get a fresh breeze of smog into their air-conditioned office. So I got Whisper out, loaded one of the explosive bolts into it over the sleeping gas bolts, and blew one of the windows off.

"What's taking you so long?" Gomorrah asked.

"I'm trying to make it so that I don't turn into mulch on hitting the ground," I said.

"Well, hurry up," Gomorrah said.

I stepped onto the windowsill, the cords from the grapple system trailing out behind me, and then, with a step over the edge, I placed my foot down on the wall below and dropped out of the building.

The system gave me just enough slack that I was able to stand "straight" on the side of the building, my front facing the long drop below and my feet, with my awesome boots, planted on the wall.

I had to take a step as a blast of wind shoved me to the side.

The rear of the building was overlooking a street with cars shooting past some dozen meters above. The other buildings nearby turned the area into a sort of tunnel where a constant wind rumbled through.

This wasn't one of those nice building fronts with fancy decorations. It was pure utility. Vents stuck out of the sides of gray-on-gray buildings, and the headlights of the passing cars flashed across mirrored glass. At the bottom were rows of semi-trailers moving along sluggishly.

I was thankful for the mask; it kept the stink of the city away as I got used to basically standing horizontally.

I took a step, and the grapple system gave me just enough rope to make it feel as though I were walking normally. It still felt all sorts of wrong, though. "All right, I'm outside," I said.

"Good," was Gomorrah's reply.

"Testy much," I muttered as I continued to walk down. There were three windows on this level. One about a foot tall and three wide led to the armory; another was rather normal-sized and led into the break room; and the third looked like it was boarded over on the other side, metal rails the only thing I could kinda see behind the glass.

Planting my feet over the armory window, I flicked over to the display of the camera inside the room. Two guys, both checking out some rifles.

I held Whisper close, then reached into my jacket and pulled out my Trench Maker. Even when using my off hand to aim, I could still hit a window that was at my feet.

Three booms echoed out and a trio of fist-sized holes appeared more or less grouped together in the glass. The guys in the room jumped out of their skin and looked up at the window.

I tried to bite down on my Trench Maker, bumped my mask, was thankful that no one saw that, then slid it away into its holster to bring Whisper to bear.

One shot later and a bolt was buried into the armory's floor.

I crab-walked away from the window while keeping an eye on the two mercs in the room. They jumped away from the bolt, one of them grabbing a helmet from a rack and tossing it onto the shaft in the time it would take someone else to blink stupidly.

It only took a few seconds for them to start stumbling around. There wasn't any audio on the camera, but I could hear them with my new ears.

"Gas? Some sort . . . of, ah, crap."

"The door!" One of them staggered over to the door and pressed a button next to it. "Okay, okay," he said as he wavered. His thumb landed on an intercom button. "This is . . . uh . . . gas! Windows. They're using gas!"

He slid down the wall, flopping to the ground alongside his buddy.

It had taken about ten seconds for both of them to go down. Decently fast.

From the camera feeds I could see those without masks scrambling to put them on, and someone jumped to a screen against one wall and started inputting a bunch of commands.

They're increasing the speed at which air circulates and are pulling more air from what looks like an internal storage system.

"To negate the gas," I said. "These guys are pretty impressive."

They're decent, for poorly equipped humans.

I moved over to the lounge window. They were clearing out of that room in a hurry. That was fine by me. I took my time loading an explosive bolt into Whisper. Then I aimed for the middle of the window.

The glass burst apart, sending shards flying all over. I leapt "up," the grapple system loosening enough that I dropped down to above where the window had been, then fell into the room.

I was really not good at three-dimensional movement, I realized when I crashed onto the floor on my knees.

Rolling over, I slid up behind a couch, then undid the clasps at the front of my backpack.

"They're here! In the lounge!"

"Barricade those doors!"

"Did they come from above or below?"

"Cameras are still down."

I snorted as I left the grapple pack on the ground next to me and stood up. "They're really panicking, huh?"

It seems so.

"Get the rocket launchers!"

I frowned. "Hmm." That didn't sound like something I could tank. "Myalis, I need a gas grenade."

Certainly. Do you want the gas to be colored?

"I mean . . . that would be pretty cool," I admitted.

New Purchase: Knock-Out Gas Grenade: Pink

Points Reduced from . . .8003 to . . . 7998

I picked up the grenade off the floor before me and primed it. "Thanks." A jog over to the door later, and I leaned Whisper to the side, pulled out my Trench Maker, and punched a couple of holes into the door before flinging the grenade into the room.

You know, I don't think you deserve any title related to stealth after all.

"It's proactive stealth," I said as a plume of pinkish smoke wafted out of the hole in the door. The one problem with colorful gas was that it made seeing enemy movement on their cameras a real pain.

Seeing them panic and rush away from the gas was kinda funny, though, in a cathartic way.

The guys at the gun emplacements rushed back into the main corridor, then stumbled back and away from the spreading pink cloud.

The ventilation system was doing a good job of sucking it away, but a few unlucky idiots had still been caught in the smoke and were dropping here and there. I kicked the door in, then rushed into the corridor. My cybernetic eye did something that turned the world to monochrome but made it easier to see through the smoke.

The mercs had moved to two rooms: an office and a washroom of all things. The washroom had one of those doors with a vent at the bottom. A kick and it bent in, so I fired a bolt into the hole and moved on just as they opened fire on the door.

Moving fast, I rushed over to the office, rammed the door with Whisper's butt, then fired a bolt into the room while the guys within panicked.

I kept moving, not wanting to stick around when they tried to shoot back.

"Gomorrah," I said as I moved to the end of the corridor. There were some automated turrets here and there, but they were all conspicuously quiet. "I think the floor's cleared."

CHAPTER THIRTY

BLUEPRINT FOR SUCCESS

With samurai providing the blueprints, all sorts of technological advancements once thought impossible suddenly became possible. Though just because humanity, or at least some parts of it, knew how to build these things didn't mean that they could.

Exotic materials, incredibly tight and precise machining requirements, and the need to build entire facilities just to build the parts to build the devices we wanted took some time to develop.

A lot of the technology we have blueprints for we simply can't construct yet.

—Excerpt from *Building the Future*, 2041

My idea of a "cleared floor" did not, apparently, satisfy Gomorrah in the least.

I wondered if she learned how to nag at nun school while listening to her complain about how I hadn't even checked every room and corner before declaring the area safe. She poked her head into every room, looked at every nook and cranny, and casually melted the turrets that Myalis had deactivated.

I left her to it and started dragging the mercs over to the lounge I'd burst in from. I figured the me-sized hole in the window would help with ventilation. Their guns were tossed into the armory, which had a door Myalis could lock on command.

In the end, we had a dozen mercenaries, all stacked up in one room and with no gear that looked dangerous.

Gomorrah paced for a bit, then pointed to one guy in particular. He had a bit of a five-o'clock shadow and was wearing a rather sleek suit that was getting crumpled on account of him lying on the floor. "That guy seems important. He was moved down here by the others, and I saw him giving orders."

"So he's the boss," I said.

"Maybe? Atyacus hasn't found much about him. His social media feed is pretty much empty. There's not much to find about him other than birth records and some medical things. Nothing interesting unless you want to know that he had a hernia a year back."

I snorted and bent down to pull the guy up. The bastard was heavy; even dragging him by his lapels onto the room's couch was a strain. Once he was sitting down I tapped his cheeks, but that didn't seem to work. "Myalis, what do I need to wake this guy up?"

The knockout gas you used will wear off within another four to six hours.

"Oh, sure, I guess we'll just make ourselves comfortable, then," I said.

The snark is unnecessary.

"I find it fun," I said, defending myself. "So, anything I need to wake this guy up within the next couple of minutes? We've been fooling around a bit, but we are on something of a schedule."

Of course you do. There's a rather cheap product from your Class I Medical Utilities that can solve this. It's only one point. Overuse of it has some rather terrible consequences on one's health, but I don't think that's an actual concern here.

"All right, gimme one."

New Purchase: Wake Up

Points Reduced from . . . 7,998 to . . . 7,997

A box appeared on the sofa next to the comatose guy. On opening it I found a plastic device the size of an inhaler, with a soft pad on one end and a large button on the other.

Stick over exposed skin, then depress the button.

I tugged the guy's jacket sleeve up to expose his wrist and placed the device over it before pressing down. There was a bit of resistance to the press, like emptying a syringe. The man shook a bit, started to shiver, then woke up with a gasp.

"Hey there, buddy," I said.

"Ah, shit," he said as soon as he locked eyes on me and Gomorrah. His gaze wandered to all the mercenaries on the floor around him, then to the hole in the wall. "Do you have any idea what it means to make enemies of us?" he asked.

"Uh," I replied. "Not really. Didn't cross my mind. Do *you* have any idea what it means to kidnap a samurai kid? Because I have the impression that it's a whole order of magnitude worse."

He just kept glaring. "We have often assisted samurai with missions both clandestine and not. If you think us unable to call in favors, then—" He finally stopped when I grabbed his jaw in my cybernetic arm.

"Okay, let's start from the top. I'm Stray Cat, that's Gomorrah. Do you have a name?"

I let go. "My name is no business of yours, you—" Then I grabbed him again.

"All right, your name is now Potty Mouth," I said.

The look of indignity that crossed his face was great. It was a little strange to think that a trick that worked on the kittens was working on a grown man, but I wasn't about to complain. The snort from Gomorrah was only further encouragement.

I leaned in close. "Look, Potty Mouth, we didn't just burst in and knock your friends out for fun. I've been tracking our missing girl for nearly a day now, and my patience is starting to wear thin. We got this far. We know you're the ones who kidnapped her. So, you tell me where she is, and we leave. You've got insurance for fixing the place up, right?"

I let go of his face again. Potty Mouth worked his jaw, still glaring up at me. "We can't tell you about our work with any client."

"We can empty all of your bank accounts," I replied.

That got a twitch out of him.

"And I do mean *all*. Hell, I'm pretty sure we could just bulk-sell all of your assets to the quickest bidder. And what we can't sell we can lock up. Is this your only base? I kinda doubt it. The others must have other things worth selling, right? And just how loyal are all the employees here? Will they stick around after they learn that payroll is now a pipe dream? How long until one of them squeals for a few million?"

Potty Mouth shifted on the sofa and his eyes wandered around as if he was looking for a way out. "If we betray a customer's trust, we're done for as a business," he said.

"If you piss me off and keep stalling, you're done for as a person," I said.

Gomorrah raised an arm and a gout of bluish flames burst out from her sleeve. "They say that burning to death is one of the worst ways to go. But usually someone dies from asphyxiation long before they cook. My fire produces no fumes."

I stared at her. "Damn, that's cold."

"It's literally the opposite," she said.

"Fine," Potty Mouth said. "Look, I don't know everything that goes down, all right? I'm just upper management, not the CEO. But, but I know who contracted us for the capture-and-confinement job."

"Capture and confinement?" I repeated.

"Sounds like a euphemism for kidnapping," Gomorrah said.

I shook my head. "Corporate slang. Nasty. So, who was it? And where's the girl now?"

Potty Mouth squirmed. "I don't know where she is. I can tell you where she was delivered, but that's it. But, but," he said when Gomorrah lowered her arm to point it at him. "But, they were a lot sloppier than we were. And you found us, so . . ."

"Right," I agreed. "And the who?"

"Sunrise Weapons," Potty Mouth said. "They make light-based weapons. Chemical lasers and electrical arc emplacements. Experimental stuff from blueprints bought off some samurai."

"And they wanted the girl, why?" I asked.

He shook his head. "We didn't ask. They wanted her intact. Any new samurai intact. Along with anyone near them. We took the dog because it was close and she seemed attached to it."

"No shit," I said. Standing taller, I reached to rub my eyes, remembered that I had a helmet on, then let my arm drop. "Damn. Okay. You got the drop-off location?"

"More importantly, do you know which division of the company you worked for?" Gomorrah asked. "They have a few installations that are on public record. I doubt they have cells in their accounting offices, but I'd like to narrow it down some more."

Potty Mouth hummed. "It was their R&D, I think. But not the main one. I think they got a second group just for this. Most people wouldn't agree to work on a samurai."

"I wonder why?" I said, voice as flat as it could go. "Myalis, you remember that big gun I bought the other day? The one that I never got to fire?"

Are you talking about the decoy railgun?

"That's the one. I need a bomb from the same set. Something with decent motion sensors on it."

I think I understand.

"Wh-what are you doing?" Potty Mouth asked.

I patted him on the head. "You'll see," I said.

New Purchase: Decoy Bomb

Points Reduced from . . . 7,997 to . . . 7,995

The "bomb" was an elaborate affair, with a steel case and a few canisters connected to a screen in the middle. A silvery ball sat atop it, spinning around and scanning the room with a red beam like one of those barcode scanners at a grocer's.

I placed it on the coffee table in the middle of the room. "Right. You stay here, Potty Mouth," I said. "We'll be activating this as soon as we're out of the room. Maybe don't move?"

I gestured to the door with a thumb, and Gomorrah walked out ahead of me.

"I've got your number," I said before shutting the door. It didn't do much to stop his protests.

A loud beep from the bomb shut him up, though.

"Let's go see Sunrise about a girl," I said.

CHAPTER THIRTY-ONE

OBSOLETE WORRIES

Never question a samurai about what they might think are personal things.

This means that you should avoid the following topics:

- Religion
- Abortion
- Politics
- Economics
- Sexuality

These are subjects that tend to spark debates with our clients, and that can worsen their mood and generally make them uncomfortable.

In the very worst cases, they might decide that they ought to do something about a perceived issue. We at Welcome Inn International do not want to be held responsible for the destruction of any religious organizations or the toppling of local governments.

Remember your three Cs:

Courtesy,

Care,

Common Sense.

—Part of a training manual for Welcome Inn International staff, 2046

It felt a bit strange to just walk out of the Hour Men headquarters. We just went up one floor and left out the main entrance. I even waved to the old lady at the nail salon on the way out. There was a squad of Police-Tech enforcers rushing over to the scene, but when they saw us they averted their eyes and rushed to cordon off the area without so much as trying to stop us.

Gomorrah stretched her arms up until her back popped audibly. "That was interesting," she said.

"It was, I guess," I said. I shifted a bit to get the grapple pack I was carrying to sit better over my shoulder. "I wasn't sure we'd get anything out of it, but . . . yeah. A name and all that."

"You were told to find the girl by someone, right?" Gomorrah asked.

I nodded. "Deus Ex. It was her job, but she dropped it on my head because she's a little shit."

"In that case you should probably inform her of our progress so far. Make sure we're all on the same page."

"Shouldn't I call her after we save the girl?" I asked.

Gomorrah shook her head. "No, this way if something goes wrong, you get to share the blame around a bit more. Haven't you ever had a job before?"

I chuckled. "No. At least, nothing more than doing odds and ends. That's a weird way of looking at things. They teach you that at the convent?"

"It's a lesson you learn from experience rather than from a book."

We left the building, took an elevator up a few floors, then continued on our way back to Gomorrah's car. The area had cleared up of people. Maybe they'd gotten the warning about samurai mucking about. I certainly would have taken off if I knew there was a samurai fight going down. At least, I would have before becoming one.

"You ever find it weird that you're a samurai?" I asked.

Gomorrah glanced my way for a bit. "I don't know? I suppose it is a little strange, but I can't say I've given it that much thought. I just am now."

"Yeah, I'm kinda rolling with it too. But then sometimes I'll forget and all those worries I had come back, you know?"

"Worries?"

I reached up to scratch the side of my nose, then remembered my helmet. "Yeah, you know. I have all these kids to take care of. I mean, they're not mine, but they're kinda my responsibility? And . . . I guess I was planning to kind of run away from all that, try to make a life for myself. Didn't have much going for me, though."

"Uneducated orphans aren't in high demand?"

I snorted. "Yeah, pretty much. I mean, there are some jobs available for anyone, but they don't pay all that well. I'd be in debt over my head just trying to get an apartment or something. Could become a joytoy, but that's not something I'd want to do."

Gomorrah shook her head. "No, I think I understand. You had all those worries, and now they're moot."

"Moot? Uh, yeah, I guess. I have . . . less than a hundred credits to my name. I couldn't buy a soda right now. But it's not a problem anymore. It's just—I don't know—weird. Same with the kittens. That's the brats Lucy and I watch over. They were on a fast track to getting fucked over, but now we just don't need to worry anymore? Lucy was talking about getting them to school. That's just so weird."

The nun patted me on the shoulder. "It's fine. I think this is probably what people who win the lottery feel like."

To be entirely too pedantic, the likelihood of becoming a samurai isn't as random-based as the likelihood of winning a lottery. There are characteristics and experiences that make some candidates more likely to become samurai.

I hummed. "So you're saying I was chosen for my good looks?"

No. Nor did your awful sense of humor factor into it much.

"You wound me," I said.

Of all the billions of items I have that you could purchase, none are able to fix your inability to be funny.

Gomorrah giggled next to me; she even turned away when I shot her a glare. Was Myalis transmitting to her too? Not that I was actually angry; Myalis could be a bit of a pain, but she was kinda funny. "You should try using some self-deprecating humor, Myalis," I said.

I would. But even doing so would still leave me leagues above your petty human-ness.

"Your AI has quite the attitude," Gomorrah said.

"Atyacus isn't like that?" I asked.

"Not even remotely. He's quite polite."

I grinned. "Wanna trade?" My shoulder-mounted railgun deployed, then spun around and smacked me behind the head. "Okay, okay, I get it! Sheesh!" I said between laughs.

We arrived in the parking garage only to find that there were a lot more people here than before. That was fine. The problem was they were gathered around Gomorrah's car. One of them was on his back, with a buddy smacking his face and one of those plus-shaped wrenches in hand. It looked like they were trying to undo something on Fury.

"Someone's trying to jack your wheels," I said.

Gomorrah's fists tightened.

I recognized some of the punks as we got closer. They were the same ones that we'd run into on the way down, plus maybe half a dozen members. "Yo!" I called out. "Did you never watch one of those kids' shows that teach you about not touching other people's shit?" I asked.

We got quite a few glares. One of them, one that hadn't been there earlier, stepped up. He was a mountain of a man, covered in glowing tattoos and equipped with a pair of cybernetic arms that looked like they'd been torn off a cargo-lift bot. "You killed one of ours," he grumbled. "We can't let that kind of shit fly."

I reached over my shoulder and unslung Whisper. Without actually raising the weapon I turned off the safety with my augs and pulled the trigger.

A bolt smacked into the ground, then bounced off the cement floor with a clatter.

A few of the punks giggled.

"If you knock them out, I won't feel good burning them," Gomorrah said.

"You mean you wouldn't feel bad burning them otherwise?"

She shrugged. "If they put up a fight. They tried to steal Righteous Fury."

The big guy at the front grunted as he crashed to the floor. Some of his buddies went down quietly, but a few of them tried to run. They didn't make it far before whatever amount of knockout gas was in them took them out.

"That's a bit much. It's just a car. A very nice car, but still."

"I don't think you understand the relationship a woman can have with a vehicle this gorgeous," Gomorrah said.

I shook my head and stepped over a few bodies on my way to the passenger side. "You make it sound like you want to marry this thing . . . Please tell me you don't actually get off to a car. I mean, there's kinky, and then there's just weird. And you already have that pyromania fetish."

"I don't have a pyromania fetish. And I don't get off to my car. That's just weird."

"Do the seats have a massage feature?" I asked as I ducked in. I tossed my gear to the back, then looked at Gomorrah, who was grabbing the wheel.

"I mean, technically."

"Damn, Gomorrah," I said with a laugh. "Are you that repressed?"

"I'm not repressed," she said a little too fast.

"Sure, sure. You get your lover moving, I'll call up Deus Ex."

"Fury isn't my lover."

"Fine, your mobile sex toy, then."

"It's unchristian to hate someone, but I might make an exception for you."

CHAPTER THIRTY-TWO

BASSE COUTURE

Car culture is strange.

Samurai car culture takes that to a whole new level.

They tend to be at least mildly competitive, which means that we occasionally get to observe two samurai trying to one-up each other with increasingly wild rides. These cars don't tend to stay cars for very long, not when walking mecha, flying tanks, literal airships, and space-capable craft are some of the easier ways to escalate.

—J. P. Kafka on the evolution of car culture, January 2038

I leaned back into the molded seat and tapped my fingers on the armrests as I thought. Fun and games aside, we were on a mission. We had to run over and save Katallina. It felt as if we were getting close. Deus Ex had dumped the mission on my lap that morning, and now we were nearing the early evening.

What was Katallina thinking? Stuck, captured, and no doubt far from comfortable for well over a day now. I'd be losing my mind in her place.

The problem was, samurai needed points to solve all their ills, and she couldn't have more than a few dozen from what I'd seen.

"You're quiet," Gomorrah said as she let go of the controls. "We're cruising. I set us on a circular path until we figure out our next step."

"Mmm," I agreed. "That's fine. I was just thinking. Myalis, can you gather up everything we've learned so far in like, a packet or something? Send it to Deus Ex and Longbow. The nerds too."

"Nerds?" Gomorrah asked.

"Lag and Dial-Up," I said. "They're a pair of samurai that basically live in the Mesh."

"You know a lot of samurai," Gomorrah said.

"Just the five," I said.

"That's more than I know," she said.

"I guess I get around," I replied with a grin.

Gomorrah crossed her arms. "Disgusting," she muttered.

Incoming call. One moment.

The car's dashboard, already covered in displays and analog switches and all sorts of buttons and screens, lit up as a hologram appeared standing above it. A foot-tall Deus Ex wearing a frankly adorable pout as she sat on one of her huge floating guns. "Stray Cat, I saw your package."

I stared. "You going to rephrase that?"

"What?" the girl asked. "No? I got the information packet your AI compiled. Just finished looking through it, in fact. Sunrise Weapons looks like the likely culprit for the kidnapping. I set my AI to digging into them as soon as I got to that part and we've found some interesting stuff about them."

"I sent that like, a minute ago," I said.

She rolled her eyes. "You're still thinking at meat-speed. You'll catch up eventually." A few screens flicked to life around her, most of them maps. "Pinpointed a few likely spots of their corp to place the girl, so I sent a few drones out to scan the buildings."

"Um . . . why didn't you do that from the very start?" I asked.

"I only have so many drones, and their scanning process gives people cancer. Anyway, point is I found her here." One of the maps grew bigger but I wasn't paying attention to that.

"Wait, back the fuck up. Did you just give cancer to a few hundred people? What the fuck?"

"A higher chance to *develop* cancer. Probably lower than just breathing the air outside," Deus Ex said. "I don't actually have anything that can directly give people cancer. That would be a useless weapon."

"That's really fucked up, Little D, and I don't think it would be anything approaching a useless weapon."

"I have quantum-tunneling plasma guns that could fry people a light-year away. I don't need a cancer gun. And besides, those scans worked despite the shielding they have up."

"Still fucky," I said. "I know some of them are dicks, but others don't deserve that kind of crap."

"Fine, I'll pay into their life insurance or whatever," Deus Ex said. "They're not important; the girl is."

"You need therapy," I said. "But that can wait until after we've saved the kid. And her dog. Do you have a plan or do we just barge in and take her back?"

"I'll send you the scans to look at them yourself," Deus Ex said. "But looking at the place . . . I don't think we'll need much preparation. They're scientists. The only security in place isn't on the floor where the girl is kept, and those are rent-a-cops. The cheap kind. The moment they learn a samurai is on the scene, they'll clock out and leave."

"Good security, that," I said.

The hologram shrugged. "I'm up north right now. About an hour's flight away if I take my time. I have a couple of things to finish up here. Try to get her out before then, and I can take care of things once she's safe."

"You don't want to help?" I asked. "It's your mission, after all."

"Stray Cat, there are literally only a dozen people in place, and they're all normies. My drones could probably take care of them all with their cancer scanners and a few hours. But you're closer. Just make sure she's safe in the end. Collateral doesn't matter. See you in a few hours. Deus Ex out."

The hologram winked away.

"Friendly one," Gomorrah said. "Not too sure how pleased I am with her taking on God's name that way."

"She's a right little brat," I said. I didn't comment on her disregard for human life, but I was certainly thinking about it. "I'm not as . . . is the word bloodthirsty?"

"You mean the way she didn't seem to care about casualties? No. Blood-thirst would mean she wants more people dead. I think she's just callous."

"Right. She really does need therapy. Anyway, I say we fly on over there and I'll see about sneaking in. Can you keep close, just in case?"

"I'll park God's Righteous Fury near them. I can always just launch a few rockets at the building and drive in if I want."

"Now who's bloodthirsty."

Gomorrah sniffed. "I paid for the rocket launchers, I intend to use them."

I raised both hands in surrender. "Fine, whatever. Just don't blow me up, all right."

The twin joysticks slid out from the dash before her, and Gomorrah grabbed on. Soon we were dropping out of traffic and shooting across the city. I was almost used to her insane driving. Almost. I winced as Gomorrah cut a corner so close that the side of the car clipped through a holographic ad hovering next to a building.

"Right, I need a distraction. Myalis, can you bring up the blueprints that Deus Ex got?"

Certainly. I've color-coded it for ease of understanding. And I've replaced all the big words with little ones.

I chose to take the high ground and not comment on any of that as I took in the map hovering before me. It wasn't an actual projection, just a display on my augs that moved as if I were looking at a fixed object.

The base . . . lab . . . thing was a smallish complex set on a single level that took up the majority of a building's floor plan. It had a few officelike spaces near the entrance, then was divided into sections. One looked like a set of labs; the next had break rooms and washrooms as well as a few con-ference areas and smaller offices, and then a second lab area, this one less of an open-concept area and more a series of small rooms connected by a T-shaped corridor.

Katallina was in one of those rooms, in one that was divided in half with a cell at one end and the entrance at the other.

There were cameras here and there, but they had blind spots, and the only place with any sort of security was the main entrance.

"Yeah, that looks easy to break into," I said. "Not very secure. Could it be a trap?"

It seems as though someone embezzled some of the funds originally intended to keep the complex secure. It has recently been used mostly to test a few nonlethal light-deterrent weapons. Nothing that would excite the competition too much. I think the main thing keeping the complex safe so far is the lack of interesting things to steal from it.

"That's one way to keep safe," I muttered. "But now they have a kid samurai. What the hell are they planning?"

According to the project lead's files, they want to indoctrinate her, then use her to purchase low-tier weapons and blueprints only slightly above the company's current manufacturing capabilities. He wishes to make these inventions seem as if they're innovations from Sunrise Weapons R&D.

"That's . . . it?" I asked. "It's not a company-wide thing?"

It seems as if few members of the upper echelons in the company are in on the plan.

"They're moronic," I said. "Wait, how do you know?"

The complex's networks are connected to the internet. The lead researcher's password is his cat's birthday.

"You mean this entire thing was started by a bunch of fuckwits?"

Was there any doubt?

CHAPTER THIRTY-THREE

STEALTH, BUT FOR REAL THIS TIME

While it's true that every samurai is very much unique, you can still observe some patterns in their collective behavior.

Notably, their spending habits tend to fall into two broad categories:

Those who purchase new equipment frequently.

And those who find a tried-and-true style, and keep to it until they need to adapt.

—Excerpt from *On the Habits of Gods*, 2046

Gomorrah parked near ground level, right up against the side of a building and halfway into a traffic lane. Something in her car had all the trucks behind us funnel around to give us some room.

"So, you'll go up, and I'll see about clearing an escape route?" Gomorrah asked.

"That's the whole of it, yeah," I said. I stepped out of God's Righteous Fury, then took off my coat. It had a few holes in it, annoying ones that I found way too obvious even when the rest of it was invisible. "Can you stay here for a bit?" I asked.

"I can," Gomorrah said. "What's up?"

I flung my coat onto the passenger seat, then stretched a bit. "Need new gear."

"Do you have the points for it? Also, that jacket had better not be dirty," she warned.

"It's probably not," I said. "And yeah, got . . . just shy of eight thousand to spend."

"Christ!"

I leaned down to look into the car. Gomorrah had a hand over the mouth of her mask. "You stub your toe or something?"

"That's a lot of points. Why haven't you spent them yet?"

"Catherine," Myalis said from the car's speakers, "is exceptionally frugal for a Vanguard. Foolishly so."

"That AI would have me burning all of my points as soon as I get them," I said. "Money and points are for saving. You never know when you'll need them. Like right now."

Gomorrah leaned back. "Well, hurry up. And please don't take off any more clothes than you already have."

"No cameras on the outside of your ride?" I asked.

"There are plenty. I don't want to soil them with images of you undressed." Gomorrah flicked a switch and the door next to me snapped shut with a hiss.

I showed the side of her car my finger, knowing that she could see it in full 8K from where she sat. "Rude," I said. "So, Myalis, I need gear."

I'm always ready to accommodate. You're looking for stealth-specialized equipment?

"And a new jacket," I said. "I think I'll give that other one to Lucy? The bullet holes give it a certain look when it's not invisible."

Shall I inform Lucy that you want to see less of her?

It took me a second to get it, but when I did I snorted. "Good one. But nah." I waved Gomorrah off and started for the entrance. "I need a cool coat. That's, like, Samurai 101. But before that, got anything like a disguise . . . thing?"

How very precise. But yes, I do have many things like a disguise thing.

"Not my fault my language is so great."

Your language is a festering mess. It's a miracle I can even understand it. And I'm smarter than most of your species combined. The pitiful nature of humanity aside, I have one suggestion in particular that I think would suit you well. It's a small module that is worn on a belt. It deploys micro-drones with projection units. They can overlay a full-color, high-resolution image over a surface, including your body.

"So you can make me look like a potted plant?" I asked.

You certainly have the intelligence of one already. You would fit right in.

"Walked into that," I muttered as I moved over to the nearest entrance. The building's first floor was a dilapidated mess. Myalis unlocked the door without having to be asked and I stepped into an abandoned lobby. A glance at the graffiti-covered elevator doors and I made my way over to the stairs. I'd ride up once I was a few floors away from the ground and there were less-suspicious elevators around.

The projectors can render a fully realized image atop your body. A projection of details that aren't real. Essentially, you can look like someone else, as long as that person is reasonably bigger than you are.

My eyebrows rose. "That's impressive," I said.

It won't work on many Antithesis models, so it is somewhat uncommon. Many cameras and scanning devices will see right through the hologram as well.

"Still," I said. "How much?"

Fifty points.

I nodded. "I'll take it."

New Purchase: Hex-Projector Light Drone Camouflage System
Points Reduced from . . . 7,995 to . . . 7,945

I snapped up the box that appeared out of the air and popped it open, revealing what was essentially a large metal device with holes behind it to clasp onto a belt. It had three slits on each side.

"I'll need a belt," I muttered.

I figured as much, yes. You are also likely going to purchase a more stealthy weapon. Perhaps a holster for it?

"Aren't we going in the wrong order?" I asked. I paused at the next landing to catch my breath. I wasn't exactly out of shape, but maybe my diet could use a bit of improving. Also, my body could handle being shot less often. Which reminded me . . . "And I need a cool jacket. All right, I need a list."

A list of the things you need? How long ahead are you thinking?

"Just for this mission. I think I can sit down after and find a few things to buy," I said.

In that case, might I propose the following:

I blinked as a bullet-point list appeared before me.

- *Handgun (currently have 1x holsters empty)*
- *Coat. Possibly Stealth-Tech.*
- *Ammunition (Trench Maker + arm launcher)*
- *Additional protection*
- *Additional firepower*

"That looks like a serial killer's shopping list," I said.

These are the few things I suspect I could convince you to purchase before you arrive at your destination. The next landing's the exit, by the way.

I huffed up another flight of stairs, then pushed through the door there and into a little corridor that opened up to an interior plaza. This building was one of those fancy hollow ones, with patios on the inside.

"Let's start from the top, then," I said as I started toward an elevator. It was one of those big cage-y ones that you could lose an arm with by sticking it out through the bars. "Why do you think I need a second handgun?"

You have two arms and two slots in your holster.

"That's a great reason to have more guns," I said. Wasn't exactly hard to convince me. "I want something really cool."

How incredibly vague.

"And not cat-themed."

That significantly reduces my options.

I chuckled. "Come on, there has to be something else?"

Very well. Perhaps as an alternative to your Trench Maker, which can use nearly any sort of ammunition, a more specialized handgun? The Victorious Model Seven. It's a handgun that fires subsonic osmium rounds through a barrel that is essentially one large suppressor.

"So it fires a big heavy bullet but doesn't make much noise?" I asked.

Any noise. Also, the gun only fires smart rounds. They have small ailerons that can turn and adjust the trajectory of the round midflight in order to curve toward your intended target. Perfect for someone whose aim is as creative as yours. Adjustable rate of fire. Cyclical, single-use twenty-round magazines. The only issue is the gun's weight when fully loaded. Though that does help with its recoil.

"Sounds cool enough," I said. "How much?"

Eighty points.

That was getting a little expensive. Not crazy-expensive, but on the higher end of things. Then again, it wasn't even a hundredth of what I had. "Sure, and enough magazines to fill my holster."

New Purchase: Victorious Model Seven

Points Reduced from . . . 7,945 to . . . 7,865

I paused and raised both hands just in time for a neat little box to fall into them. Popping the surprisingly hefty box open revealed a sleek handgun. All angular and sharp, with a rectangular barrel and angled grip. The top had a sort of tiny scope, glassy at one end and flat at the other. I held it out before me and a holographic sight appeared above it.

"Nice," I said.

There wasn't much to shoot at, though, so I stuffed it away into my shoulder holster after making sure the safety was on.

I picked up the next two things to drop before me. Two rather heavy magazines that I handed to the little grabby arms of my holsters even as I walked out into a space with wall-to-wall vending machines and a few dozen street rats mingling around.

They eyed me; I grinned back. They couldn't see it through the helmet, but I liked to imagine that some of the expression came through.

"I need a jacket," I said. "A badass one."

Another wonderfully precise description.

"You're usually pretty good," I said. "And no cat themes."

You're ruining my fun.

"Deal with it."

CHAPTER THIRTY-FOUR

THUMP

For a period of time, it was common practice to think of the human element as the weakest link in any security system.

That changed when technology grew complex enough that no one could predict the exact loyalties of their own devices.

As it turns out, humans might be a weak link, but they're one that is understandable and predictable.

—Anonymous commenter, during a virtual hacker conference, 2054

"You know what I want?" I asked as I wove through a line that cut across a corridor. It ended at one of those corporate soup kitchens. People filled out forms on some tablets at the end of the line, then got their vouchers for a free meal.

I can only guess.

"Well, I need a new jacket for one," I said. "Something . . . like my last one, maybe? A bit cooler? Maybe semi-armored? But yeah, I need that. But what I really want is a grenade launcher."

You want a grenade launcher. Somehow, that wasn't what I expected to hear, but I suppose it makes sense. You are aware that you are essentially on a stealth mission?

"Do you expect this mission to not involve high explosives at some point?" I asked.

That is a very fair point. I have a few questions to narrow down exactly what sort of launcher you need. How accurate do you want the weapon to be? What are your tolerances for size? Are there any particular things you want this weapon to do?

I thought for a second. "I want something that makes that cool thump sound. Maybe some rapid-ish fire? And something that's easy to reload?"

I see. I think you may need to purchase a new catalog for that. Might I suggest the rather generic Explosive Launchers class? The first tier costs seventy-five points.

"All right, fine."

Class I Explosive Launchers Unlocked!

Points Reduced from . . . 7,865 to . . . 7,790

Now, as for an actual weapon. I suggest the Icarus Mark II. It's a one-hundred-point grenade-launching rifle. Rather slim, with a titanium chassis. The magazine holds eighteen rounds, which can be fired in single shot, or in three-round bursts.

"That's a lot of grenades," I said.

They pack just as much punch as larger ones. I think you'll find the weapon enjoyable. It has a rather high skill ceiling, but you'll learn. And there are special ammunitions that you can purchase that have multiple uses. More standard explosive rounds are significantly more expensive, of course, and you can use any kind of explosive from your Class One Esoteric Single-Use Explosive Devices catalog.

I paused for a moment and glanced at the wire-map of the area to make sure I was heading the right way. "Does it look cool? No cat stuff on it?"

. . . Certain changes can be made to remove any such decorations.

Snorting, I moved over to an elevator bank, then waited for one to come down. "Sure, then."

New Purchase: Icarus Grenade Launcher Platform

Points Reduced from . . .7,790 to . . . 7,690

A box appeared by my feet, startling a beggar lounging against a nearby wall. I opened it to find the Icarus within. It was about two feet long, with a bullpup sort of configuration and a very boxy frame. The top had a rather tall but narrow scope, and there was a grip under the squarish front. It looked a little stubby for a rifle.

Picking it up, I found it rather rear-heavy. It made sense when I pulled at the magazine tucked into the top of the stock, then shoved it back in.

The gun connects to your augs, but it also listens to your voice. Saying one of the following will change the way the ammunition acts: High Explosive. Knockout Gas. Flashbang. EMP or Fragmentation.

I pulled the gun up, then found the strap on its side and looped it over my shoulder. "Nice," I said just as the elevator dinged. "Now, I need a cool coat, and some sort of additional protection stuff."

I see. Perhaps something that meets both goals. The Mark III Neo is a long coat that has a system of projectors built into it. It can mimic light sources, like your previous coat, and this one can also displace carbon wafers into the path of any oncoming projectile.

"Carbon wafers?" I asked.

The physics required to explain how to use quantum tunneling to displace an object from one location to another, then lock that object in space would require an order of magnitude more education than what you have.

"As long as it looks cool," I said. "And will stop me from getting dead."

New Purchase: Mark III Neo

Points Reduced from . . . 7,690 to . . . 7,540

Another box by my feet. I idly wondered if anyone would use the darned things I kept leaving around all over. When I popped it open it revealed a long trench coat, folded neatly into the box.

I pulled it out, admiring the cool shoulder pads and the split back. The material was super dark, some sort of light-absorbing cloth I guessed, and the armored plates here and there really looked great.

What didn't was the cat-head-shaped pauldrons, and the big image of a grinning Cheshire cat on the back under the stenciled words "Stray Cat."

"Seriously?" I asked.

You didn't say not to.

I sighed. "Myalis, you bitch."

I still slipped the jacket on. It might have been a bit catlike, but the damned thing was cool. I tugged the lapels forward and felt it settling over my shoulders just right. A glance into the chromed elevator doors had me looking my reflection up and down.

"Cat pauldrons are still a bit much," I said. "But the rest looks nice enough, I guess. Extra preem drip. Very much on fleek."

. . . That was painful to process. They're thematic. Think of it as being on-brand. And judging by the parts of your brain that just lit up, you have no reason to call it unflattering.

"Uh-huh," I said. "Just don't go too far."

I would never.

She totally would. The door opened and I stepped out into a rather plain corridor. Clean floors, plaques on the walls pointing toward different businesses, and all the hallmarks of being a safe house for midranking corporate stuff.

I never liked places like these. They were way too . . . I supposed the word was "orderly." I didn't feel like I belonged here, not with the near-rags I usually wore, and not now in my samurai gear. It had the same feeling as walking into a church while all those around you were in their Sunday best. I didn't belong in the corporate cult culture.

"At the end of the next corridor, right?" I asked as I took off to my left. The new coat swished quite satisfyingly as I walked.

Indeed. Now would be a good time to test your new cloaking device.

I agreed. With a twitch of my eye, I brought up the menu for all of my gear with my augs and looked at the new icon for my cloak. It was just a floating image of the belt-buckle-like device. The menu that brought up was a long list of options. It was like looking at an extended list of Halloween costumes.

"Ah," I said. "That's a lot of choices."

I have access to their network. Do you want me to create a cover for you that should get you past their security?

"Sounds perfect," I said as I flicked out of the menu. Too much choice was too much.

The entrance to Sunrise Weapons' R&D lab was a plain lobby. A pair of sliding doors that led to a security checkpoint, then a corridor deeper into the labs. Just as I rounded the corner, I noticed my everything shifting and when I looked down, it was to see that I was wearing something different. Clothes on top of my clothes.

It looked like I was in a plain overall, with a logo-covered jacket atop it, and the gun bouncing by my side now looked like a case.

I stepped into the first room, then had to wait a moment until one of the guards by the front desk waved me in.

You already have an appointment here, and I've cracked their security. Just act natural and you should be fine.

Moving up to the security desk, I faced the sleepy-looking guy behind it and waved. "Hey there," I said, trying to sound friendly but professional. Just an eager young technician or whatever.

"You're from . . ." He paused and looked at his screen. "SuperCat, Animal Care and Grooming Co.?"

I flinched. "Y-yup," I said.

"What's with the helmet?"

I glanced to the side. On the cameras behind the guy's desk was an image of me wearing a plain white helmet, still with the cat ears. "It's for, uh, protection. While handling animals."

"Really?" he asked.

"Yeah, really. Corporate protocol, you know?" I was going to drown Myalis, the fact she was in my head be damned.

"Hmm, yeah. Wanna pass through the scanner? Put your bag on the side there." He pointed to an x-ray machine, with a walk-through scanner next to it.

I put my gun on the black threads, then stepped through the scanner. The x-ray that I saw on his screen looked nothing like a high-tech grenade launcher, and a lot more like a bag full of stuff.

"Right, you can go."

I made it halfway down the corridor before I huffed. "I hate you."

I sent the recording to Lucy already.

"I really hate you."

CHAPTER THIRTY-FIVE

DOG GONE WRONG

At some point, the last of the Boomers finally passed away, and the traditions of the workspace largely faded with their passing. This ushered in a new era of business philosophy, where the styles of the late 1900s were largely discarded.

In some ways, this was an improvement. Management was generally more aware of issues with the environment, the mental health of their employees, and the kind of issues that could be caused by social movements.

Their answers were to hide any environmental impacts, to preemptively fire any stressed employees, and to quash any social movements before they took off.

—Business Outsider, 2047

My entire life, I'd walked into places where I really shouldn't have been. Usually in parts of the city that weren't welcoming to a one-armed girl whose only weapon was a sharp tongue. More recently, as a samurai, I'd been a bit more liberal with my traveling. Running around as if it didn't matter that I wasn't allowed to be where I was.

It was a bit weird, but, in those moments, I was still myself.

Now I felt off. I was essentially in a costume, marching down the corridors of a complex and getting a bit lost while crossing by scientists and technicians who never gave me more than a second glance.

If they noticed that I felt uncomfortable, they didn't comment on it at all.

My eyes twitched as I brought up a map of the facility. It wasn't big enough to really get lost in, but there were more doors sealing off the different sections than I'd expected. Not that they impeded me much. The doors had electronic locks so laughably cheap that I probably could have broken through with a crowbar. Having Myalis break into them was just overkill.

I reached the back of the facility in a little while. There were fewer peo-ple here, and those that I saw were often sitting in little labs, or typing away in front of computers. For all the lab coats I saw, there didn't seem to be that much science-y stuff going on.

I was expecting a whole lot more bubbling solutions and Bunsen burn-ers, but maybe I shouldn't have been setting my standards based on pirated cartoons. There were a lot more workshop-looking places, so for all I knew the place was doing more engineering-ish science than . . . other sorts of science.

"God damn it," I muttered.

Is something wrong?

"Lucy was right."

She is rather clever, so that isn't too surprising. What was she right about this time?

"My education's not great," I said.

That is correct, yes. Are you considering going to school?

"Urgh," I said. I stepped to the side and moved over toward a janitor's closet as a trio of guys moved by. Two of them were in suits, the last in a lab coat. They barely looked at me as I opened the door to the closet and looked inside, trying to look busy. They were heading in the same direction I'd been moving in, which was a bit annoying. "Yeah, she might be right, but I don't know about that," I said.

If they heard me, they'd probably assume I was on the line with some-one, which wasn't technically wrong.

Perhaps a nontraditional education then? The human propensity to teach people in groups is efficient on a large scale, but given the opportunity, being taught directly is far more effective for a given individual.

"So, like, online classes?" I asked. Those were pretty popular. We'd taken some at the orphanage whenever a new pandemic sprang up.

With the right additional augmentations, and perhaps some liberal use of certain drugs, you could cram a few years' worth of education into a few days. There are catalogs that allow you to essentially download vast amounts of information into your memory.

"That sounds fucking awful," I said.

Or you could enroll in a local school? I'm certain some of the better private schools would love to have a Vanguard in attendance. You might not even have to wear their uniform.

"And that sounds an order of magnitude worse. Right, I'll think about it," I said. The three guys had moved on and around the bend, so I moved out of the janitor's closet and set off toward the end of the corridor.

My goal was just to the left, which unfortunately was where I found the scientist and his two business buddies. I skipped back around the corner and twitched my ears to listen to them. All three were right before the door holding Katallina.

"The subject has been somewhat cooperative," the scientist was saying. "But it could be better."

"We don't care about cooperation, we care about results."

"Hey now," Business Dude #2 said. "Results are the end goal, but if we can get them without risking the girl, or better yet, while getting her to want to work with us, then that would be for the best, right?"

"What, you're planning on giving her sick days, maybe a 401(k)?" Jerkwad asked.

The scientist cleared his throat. "Whatever the case, the subject hasn't actually produced anything yet. So far we've been trying the nice approach under the assumption that other enhanced forms of encouragement can't be undone."

"Enhanced forms of encouragement?" I repeated in a whisper.

I suspect that it's a euphemism for torture.

"Oh," I said. "Well, that makes this a whole lot more justified."

I spun around the corner and brought my brand-new grenade launcher, the Icarus, up to my shoulder. The stock was actually quite comfortable. A menu appeared in the corner of my vision with the different options for explosives laid out in an easy-to-use wheel menu.

I selected "Fragmentation" because I figured HE might accidentally blow up the girl in the next room over.

"Hey, do you have permission to be here?" Business Dude #2 asked.

I raised my off hand in a "wait one moment" gesture.

Would the fragmentation go through the wall? I wasn't entirely sure.

"Hey!" he repeated.

"Shut up, I'm deciding how to shoot you," I said as I flicked through the menu a bit more.

Jerkwad turned to the scientist sort, then pointed a finger right at me. "Who's this? Is she one of yours?"

"No sir, she, uh, might be a contractor?" the scientist asked. He really didn't sound certain.

I flicked the menu over to the knockout gas option. Worst case with that, I'd put the girl and her dog to sleep. No biggie.

"Are you an idiot?" Jerkwad asked. "You can't just let anyone in here."

I rolled my eyes, then brought the gun up. It made a handy little red line appear in my vision, arcing where the grenade would go. So I made it overlap with Jerkwad's head. A squeeze, and the Icarus shook three times as a trio of grenades thumped out of it.

The first smacked Jerkwad in the side of the head and sent him tumbling down with a scream.

I snorted as the hall filled with the hissing of pressurized gas. "Sleep tight, assholes," I said as I lowered the launcher and started forward.

They looked like they wanted to protest, but they were too busy stumbling around drunkenly to do anything of the sort.

By the time I reached the door they'd been standing before they were on the ground, drooling and insensate. "Can you break into their augs?" I asked Myalis. "Kinda curious to know who these idiots are."

Easily done. Anything you want to know in particular?

I thought about it. "No, not really. Just empty their bank accounts."

Into your own?

"That makes me sound greedy. Split it into thirds? A chunk for me, one for Gomorrah, and the rest to the girl." I poked the door. It was a heavy metal thing, more fit for a prison than a room. The electronic lock next to it flashed green the moment I glanced at it. Myalis's work, I guessed as I pulled it open.

Just like Deus Ex's scans showed, it wasn't a very large space. Half the room had a few cupboards and some chairs. The other half had a cot and a little toilet behind a thick plastic wall.

A girl was on the cot, her head rising as she looked over at me.

She glared.

I stepped in and closed the door. "How's the gas in here?" I asked.

I suspect the air on her side is filtered, otherwise she would be knocked out already.

"That's annoying," I said. "How long will we have to wait?"

The gas is meant to stay around an area for some time. It's more effective that way. I should note that while I've shut off the facility's security, there's a chance someone will notice the bodies.

I nodded along. "Hey, kid, can you hear me?" I asked.

She glared harder, which was a yes in my book. A dog's head rose up from the blankets next to her. They hadn't killed the mutt. That was nice.

"Right," I said. A flick through my augs and my disguise flicked off. "My name's Stray Cat. I'm a friend. You ready to blow this joint?"

She's not a Vanguard.

I froze for just a second. "You sure? Wait, yeah, of course you are. Then . . ." I moved closer to the glass door. No matter what, I'd still save the girl. "Hey, kid, you were near another samurai during that incursion, right?"

She swallowed, then got up. Her outfit had been replaced by some scrubs at some point, all off-green and tacky-looking as hell. "I don't care who you are, fuck you!"

"Oh, great, another kid with an attitude," I muttered. "This day's just perfect."

CHAPTER THIRTY-SIX

CATKILLER

Our weakness? You want me to just tell you what samurai are weak against?

Well, I suppose . . . awkwardness?

—Guillotine, interview with *Star-Spangled Monthly*, 2029

There were all sorts of things I could have handled. Katallina being angry at me. Her throwing a tantrum. Having her curse me out. All reactions I'd seen from my kittens plenty of times. They were outlets to anger and sadness that I got. I could deal with snark, it was how I did emotions.

Katallina looked at me, and then her eyes got wet and she started to cry.

I didn't do crying. Lucy did crying.

If a kitten cried, it was Lucy that did the hugging and the shushing and all that junk.

"Ah, fuck," I said. "Uh, shit, it's okay, kid?" I tried.

Somehow that didn't work.

I looked around, but other than her dog, there wasn't much to see. "Shit, uh, look, you're safe, all right?" I asked. "I'm gonna slip you, and your dog I guess, a mask, and we can both leave this place, okay?"

She bawled harder.

Interesting.

"What?" I asked.

I started looking for catalogs that could improve maternal instincts or help people in emotional distress, but other than some drug cocktails I can't find anything very relevant. It's an oversight I don't think we were expecting. A complaint has been filed.

"That's nice," I deadpanned. I reached up to run my hands through my hair, bumped my helmet, then groaned. "Okay, okay. Hey, kid, you hear me?"

The girl nodded. She was ugly crying, and she was just old enough that it wasn't even passably cute.

"Okay, look, I've got some questions, all right?" I asked.

Katallina snorted some and I sighed as I backed up.

"Myalis, can you connect me to Gomorrah?"

Certainly.

"Thanks," I said. Something pinged and I sighed again because I was in that sort of mood. "Yo, G-girl," I said.

"I recall telling you not to call me that. Or some variation thereof," Gomorrah said.

"Yup. I recall not recalling that. So, uh, found the girl, and the dog. Neither are Vanguards. I . . . wait, Myalis, is the dog?"

No. The dog is not a Vanguard.

Gomorrah hummed. "Interesting. So, where is our wayward samurai?"

"That's a question, isn't it?" I muttered. I tapped on the glass of the chamber. "Hey, kid, uh . . . shit, I don't know where to start. Look, we're looking for someone, a samurai. The one that gave you that gun you had. Do you know where they are?"

"He's dead," Katallina said. "The monsters ate him."

"Uh," I said. "Do you know who he was? His name?"

She nodded. "Randall, he was from 2B."

I blanked, but Gomorrah was on the ball apparently. "Randall from 2B. That's an older teenaged boy from the same floor where Katallina lived. Male, sixteen. Good, clean record. Babysits others on occasion from his social feeds . . . and the cleanup crews for that building have tagged his body already."

I rubbed at the nape of my neck, then stood up and stretched. "Welp, that's fucked," I said. "Can you tell Deus Ex?"

"You don't want to tell her yourself?"

"Not particularly. Make some space in your car for a girl and a dog, would you?"

Gomorrah was quiet for a little while. "You want to put a dog in my car?"

"I'm not leaving the kid here," I said. "She's in a fucking cage."

"That's fine. But the dog?"

I started pacing. "Gomorrah, you can't just abandon a dog. Even I know that."

Gomorrah groaned, a very un-nunlike sound. "God give me patience. Fine. I'm going to contact Deus Ex. Ping me when you're done, and I'll blow off a wall to pick you up."

"We could leave from the front," I said.

"Look, this whole thing has been a little disappointing to me, and I have missiles primed to fire already. Don't take my fun away from me."

I surrendered to the crazy pyromaniac nun with the missile launchers on account of her being crazy and a pyromaniac and having missile launchers. "See you in a bit, then," I said.

Once the line cut off, I moved closer to the glass wall of Katallina's cell.

I didn't want to speak my next question out loud, so I opened a text box with a twitch of my eye and typed it out. "Myalis, her parents?"

All dead. I found their insurance and have filed a claim on it in her name, to be transferred to an account she can access. The insurance company didn't want to pay out, but I persuaded them otherwise.

"That's nice of you . . . how did you persuade them?"

Footage of you at the Hour Men base. For the record, no, she doesn't have any extended family capable of taking care of her.

If it worked it worked, I supposed. "Hey, Katallina," I said. "I'm going to get you out of here, okay?"

The girl snorted. "Who even are you?"

"Uh, I'm a samurai," I said.

"Samurai are supposed to be cool."

Never mind being shot twice, my worst injury of the day had just landed with critical damage. "First, good insult there, but wrong target. Second, you're like, in your teens, stop acting so young."

She straightened a little. "I lost everything," she said.

"That happens sometimes. Now, you can stay in the cage with the creepy scientist dudes until they figure out that you're not a samurai, or you can come with me. I . . . basically run an orphanage at this point."

"I don't want to go to an orphanage," she said. She sniffed a last time and wiped her nose on the sleeve of her beige shirt. "I can take care of myself."

"Very cute, but no, you really can't. City's got to be full of refugees right now. You'd be swallowed up on the streets in no time. At least come with me for the day; we can figure things out tomorrow."

"What about the assholes that kidnapped me?" she asked.

"I'll give you a share of their money once I'm done bankrupting them," I said.

That perked her up. I had the terrible impression that she might just fit in with all of the kittens. I shuffled over to the glass and tapped it, expecting a screen to show up somewhere.

"The door's wireless," Katallina said.

"Right," I agreed. "Myalis, two masks, one for the kid, one for the dog. Can you make them appear on the other side of the glass?"

I can.

"Are you talking to yourself?" Katallina asked. She looked concerned.

New Purchase: Hazard Mask

Points Reduced from . . . 7,540 to . . . 7,520

New Purchase: Hazard Mask—Canid Modified

Points Reduced from . . . 7,520 to . . . 7,510

Two boxes plopped onto the ground of the cell, and Katallina jumped. "You actually are a samurai," she said.

"What did you think?"

"Shitty cosplayer."

"God save me from little shits with attitude," I muttered. "Put on the fucking masks."

Do you have any idea how ironic it is that you want saving from children with attitudes?

"You calling me a child?" I asked.

That would be insulting to children everywhere.

I scoffed but couldn't hold back a chuckle. "You ready?" I asked. Katallina was strapping a mask over her dog's muzzle. It seemed very okay with the bulbous mask. Its tail was wagging, anyway, which I figured meant it was all right.

My experience with actual dogs was pretty limited. I'd petted one or two when I ran across them, but for the most part I spent more time seeing dogs in my media feed than interacting with them. They were something of a luxury, needing space, and food, and grooming. The sort of person who had time for that wasn't the sort of person living in the same space as the orphanage.

"What's its name?" I asked.

"The dog?" Katallina asked. "He belonged to Miss Rupert next door. She was nice, let us play with him and take him out for walks. She died. His name is Catkiller."

I groaned. My life was a joke. Myalis got the door opened, and judging by how neither the girl nor the dog fainted, the masks worked well enough to protect from the knockout gas. "Let's go," I said as I brought my gun up.

A glance at my map of the building showed me where Gomorrah would be coming from. It also revealed that the red dots of security personnel were moving a lot more than before.

"What's up with the security?" I asked.

I can't see what alerted them. One moment . . . ah. It seems that one of them spoke to another and neither recalled your appointment. I'm afraid that I don't have the tools to rewrite memories.

"You have a gift for being terrifying," I said.

"Who are you talking to?" Katallina asked.

"The alien voices in my head," I said. "Let's get the fuck out of here."

"There're guards."

I blinked, then raised my grenade launcher while my shoulder-mounted guns deployed over my back.

"Oh," she said.

"Come on, if you behave you'll maybe get to see an asshole blow up."

On leaving the room, Katallina took a moment to punt the scientist sprawled in the floor right in the face.

She'd fit right in with the kittens.

CHAPTER THIRTY-SEVEN

CASH MONEY

Been doing some morally ambiguous shit?

Afraid people will catch on to how skeevy you are?

Using child labor? Selling people? Using indentured servitude on your employees? Selling weapons to the wrong sort of people?

If you think that your business might get fucked over by the first uptight samurai that passes by, then consider getting AoG Insurance!

We'll cover your dumb ass, no matter what.

But skip a payment and we'll fuck you up.

—Acts of God Insurance Corp. ad, 2050

I had time to think as Katallina, the dog whose-name-I-would-change, and I moved through the R&D lab's corridors. Sure, there was security coming for us, but I had a lot of knockout gas grenades and access to the cameras so I knew where they were coming from before they turned around the corner.

That meant walking over a lot of sleeping idiots on our way out.

It felt a little cheat-y, but I was fine with that. Cheating was all right in my books, as long as it wasn't done against me.

Besides, I was busy thinking, and Myalis jokes aside, I did like a bit of quiet to think in.

Our mission was essentially over. Not in the ideal way either. It left me with a girl, and a dog, to take care of. I didn't think that someone like Deus Ex would particularly care for Katallina now that it was revealed that the girl was just a normal girl.

She was an orphan too. Whom I'd saved. By some weird twisted logic, that kind of made her my problem.

Because I didn't have enough problems—or orphans—to look after.

Lucy was going to be so much fun to deal with. I sighed and absently fired another burst of grenades through a glass door. The idiot hiding behind it panicked, throwing a jacket over the canisters spewing gas into the room, but not quick enough to stop himself from face-planting a moment later.

There were other things. Money problems. Problems of reputation and such. How would this company react to us blowing up their lab?

"Fuck it," I muttered.

Is something wrong? The hormone balance in your brain suggests that you're in something of a foul mood.

I took a deep breath. "Nah, I'm fine," I said.

"Huh?" Katallina asked. She looked a bit lost in thought too.

"It's nothing," I said. "Just talking to someone else."

Is there anything we can buy to help you?

I barked a laugh. "I don't know. What do you think Sunrise's reaction will be to us, uh, doing this?"

Likely denounce everything, cut ties with whoever plotted this, then funnel resources into shell corporations before going bankrupt in order to not have to save face. For many smaller human corporations, it only takes a few days for them to essentially cease existing, then return as an entity with the same employees and a different logo.

"Damn," I said. "Shit's really not fair, is it?"

Not usually.

I stretched a bit. I was developing something of a stress headache. I was way too young for that kind of stuff, though. "Who'll profit from all of this? I mean, in the end, who's responsible?"

The chain of legal responsibility would stop at the person carrying out the kidnapping on the behalf of the company. The moral responsibility is a little more loose to define. I suppose that in the end, those who run the company are those responsible.

"So the CEO?"

That is merely a well-paid employee, not the end of the line.

I rubbed at my neck through the material of my suit. "Do you know who the big shareholders are?" I asked.

I do.

"Do you know if they knew about . . . this?"

They seemed aware. At least, those who own considerable shares. Those with only a fractional share didn't seem to have been informed. Most of Sunrise Weapons was owned by Switzer Corp.

I nodded. "Right, in that case. Those who knew, empty their accounts. Split half of it with the company's employees. We're keeping the other half. Liquidate the rest, I guess. How much is that?"

Seventy-three million credits. Before dividing it in half. I wasn't able to reach some accounts in such a short time, I'm afraid.

I tripped.

"Uh, you okay?" Katallina said.

"Fucking fuck," I replied sensibly.

That's thirty-six and a half million for you. I'm rounding it down to big numbers, of course. I don't want you to have an even worse headache.

I absently fired off more grenades down a corridor, then stopped around the corner from the wall Gomorrah was planning on blowing up.

If it helps, you're not even in the top half of the wealthiest Vanguards.

"That doesn't help," I said. That kind of money . . . A burger was five hundred credits. That meant that . . . "How much is thirty-six and a half million divided by five hundred?" I asked.

"Seventy . . . three thousand," Katallina said.

I blinked at her.

"What?" she asked. "I'm not an idiot."

That was a lot of burgers. No wonder Deus Ex was just casually able to rent a penthouse. The girl had been a samurai for a while. She was probably loaded. The amount I had was just too damned much for me to wrap my head around. "What am I going to do with that kind of money?" I muttered.

It's about the amount someone in the top five percent would earn in a year's time. While significant, it isn't a grand amount. Also, anything you could purchase with human currency could be purchased with your remaining points, but at a much lower price and greater quality.

"Yeah," I muttered. "I guess I can continue renting that hotel room for a bit."

Only a few years. But yes. That would be an appropriate use for that money.

A few years? How much was the damned room going for? I decided that I didn't want to know.

"Hey, uh, Stray Cat?"

"Just Cat," I said.

Katallina nodded, then pointed to the side. "Can I bring that with me? It was Randall's."

I followed her pointing finger and looked into a lab, one with a window all along its wall. Inside were some benches and a large steel tank at one end with a gun pointing into it. The same gun she had in the videos I'd seen.

Giving a gun to a kid was a terrible idea. But then, I wasn't keen on ideas that weren't terrible. "Yeah, sure," I said. I kicked the door to the lab open. It was just a small detour.

While I fiddled with the clamps holding the gun in place, a text popped up from Gomorrah, asking me if I was quite ready. I sent her a thumbs-up emoji.

Her response was an explosion that made the floor skip out from under me.

The dog barked, Katallina screamed, and I felt a bit guilty for not warning her. I pushed the rifle into her hands. "Come on, our ride's here," I said.

Gomorrah had parked in the middle of the corridor. Or at least, she was hovering there, the dust and loose debris of the hole torn into the side of the building wafting past us as the air pressure from the bottom of Fury pushed them by.

A couple of confused scientist sorts ran past. They didn't seem to know what the hell was going on but had the common sense to be somewhere that wasn't near the sleek black samurai car that had made itself at home in their lab.

"Whoa," Katallina said. "That's a nice car."

"It's kinda hot, yeah," I said as I moved to the passenger side. The door opened, and then the panel right behind it folded out and slid back, revealing two very small seats at the back where my Whisper was resting.

"If that dog ruins my seats I will be giving you a religious epiphany," Gomorrah said in greeting.

I helped Katallina up into the back, then let the dog jump up where he snuggled up next to the girl. The doors closed up as soon as I fell into the passenger seat and rearranged my coat for comfort. The soundproofing was good enough that as soon as everything sealed up I couldn't hear the rumble of the wind under us.

"So, where to now?" I asked.

Gomorrah turned my way. "I thought you knew?"

I reached up and pulled off my helmet, placed it on my lap, then ran mechanical fingers through my hair. "Yeah, no, I really don't. Did you contact Deus Ex?"

"I sent her what you learned."

I appreciated her circling around the topic. Didn't need to set Katallina off again. "Right. So . . . man, I need a break. The last day has been way too damned busy."

"Burnout happens," Gomorrah said. "Not often with samurai, but it's not impossible." She reversed us out of the hole in the side of the building, and then we shot off toward the flowing traffic above. She moved past a couple of cop cars, but Gomorrah didn't seem to care about them and they left us alone.

"Yeah. Think you could bring us to the hotel?"

"I suppose," Gomorrah said. "It's a bit of an anticlimactic end to everything."

"Meh. You could come up with me? Meet Lucy, the kittens."

"The kittens . . . those are the orphans you take care of?" Gomorrah asked.

"Yeah. They're pretty cool. Sometimes. Some of them." My eyes narrowed. "They mostly behave."

"I suppose I don't really have much to do," Gomorrah said.

I leaned back into my seat. "What do you do for fun?" I asked.

"I used to have chores at the church, but they've been . . . honestly, they've been babying me recently. I swear if one more person starts calling me a saint I'm going to bring them closer to God the fast way."

I laughed. "Well, you won't have to worry about that with the kittens."

CHAPTER THIRTY-EIGHT

KITTENS!

The NA Ministry of Child Protection prides itself in providing only the very best care to the children in its charge.
—Statement from the NA Ministry of Child Protection, 2031

Gomorrah did a fine job landing right next to the sidewalk leading into the hotel and shutting her car down as if she had no intention of moving from that spot.

I didn't mind. It meant less walking. I'd been doing some thinking on the last bit of the trip back. "Hey, Gomorrah," I asked.

"Yes?" she asked.

"Can you give me and the kid a minute?" I nodded to the back of the car where Katallina was sitting pressed up against her dog.

Gomorrah glanced back, then nodded and stood up, leaving Fury and shutting the door behind her.

"Um," Katallina said. She didn't continue with that thought.

I took a deep breath, then turned so that I could see behind as best as I could. "We need to talk, just a little."

"About what?" Katallina asked. She sounded wary. And weary. I could understand both.

"You don't have any close family, right?" I asked.

She shook her head. I didn't remember exactly how old she was. Thirteen? Fourteen maybe? Older than most of the kittens, but not all of them. Junior's age, more or less.

"I . . . look, I know what that's like. And no, I'm not being some asshole adult pretending to sympathize. I'm an orphan too, you know? So, uh, yeah, I've been there. And when I was there I was flung off to some shitty orphanage with no choices. Well, I could have left, but that was a non-choice. Look, I don't want that to happen to anyone, but I'm just me, all right?"

"Okay?"

"Fuck, I'm bad at this," I muttered. "If . . . if it were up to some of the people I know, I think they'd just hand you over to the government. Maybe some would make sure you ended up in a nice orphanage, but it'd be the same mess, you know? Only with nicer bars in your cage. I ain't keen on that. But I've kinda been assuming stuff."

"Assuming what?" She was petting her dog, the big lump drooling merrily on Gomorrah's leather seats.

"That you'll just do as I say, I guess. So I'll lay it out for you, all right?"

She took a moment before nodding, her thumb rubbing at the side of her gun. "All right."

"I've got these kids. The kittens. There's a bunch of them. Nose, and Junior, the Twins, and . . . yeah, a few more. All little shits. All orphans, like me. They're family, you know? Not by blood, but by circumstance."

"You want me to be one of them?" Katallina asked.

I shrugged. "I'm inviting you, I guess. I'm not the boss. I call them my kittens, but that's like saying, uh, my country, or something. But yeah, I won't make you do anything. You want to get emancipated and run off with some cash to figure things out, that's on you. You want to be sent to some governmental place, that's up to you too. I kinda robbed the people that kidnapped you a bit, and some of that cash is rightfully yours. It's not retirement money, but it's a good amount."

Katallina shoved herself off the seat and started scooting to the door. "I'll see," she said.

I shook my head and pushed the door on my side open. Was I a magnet for snarky little shits? Did I deserve it? My eyes narrowed. I totally deserved it. Dammit all.

I stepped out of the Fury and stretched my fleshy limbs while taking a deep breath of the kerosene-filled air inside the hotel's hangar. Gomorrah was waiting by the door, arms crossed, feet set, and looking like someone who was really done with the world around her. The people around her were purposefully moving toward the farthest door from where she stood.

Maybe I could ditch the cat theme and go full nun. I was sure people would leave me alone then. Also, Lucy had a thing for serious women in uniforms.

I picked my helmet out of the Fury, then grabbed Whisper from the back and slung it over my shoulder opposite my Icarus. I was starting to have a nice collection of things that could blow things up. I almost forgot to grab my newfangled grapple system too.

Katallina and her dog waited awkwardly next to Gomorrah until I ran over. "You're going to leave your car parked there?" I asked.

"Who's going to move it?" Gomorrah asked.

It was a fair point.

We moved into the lobby where I noticed a fair number of people looking our way. It was still a bit strange to be the center of attention like that, but as long as they didn't try anything, I didn't particularly care. Katallina started walking a bit closer to my side.

We moved past one of those little stand-up signs that say "NO PETS ALLOWED," then stepped into a free elevator.

"You mentioned that you have a big family?" Gomorrah asked.

"Yup," I said. "You'll like them. Well, one or two of them. There are so many that statistically there's bound to be one that doesn't annoy you."

"That's not reassuring," Gomorrah said.

"You'll like Lucy," I said. "Uh, are you into women?"

Gomorrah slowly turned to stare at me. "What?"

"It's an innocent question," I said.

"I'm literally a nun."

I shrugged. "That would just make it kinkier. Anyway, if Lucy pinches your bottom just tell her not to. She can get handsy, but she's nice. If any of the kittens ask you to give them a weapon, don't. If they're annoying, just threaten them. Uh, make it look serious, though, because I've been weaning them off fear for a long time now, and they're pretty . . . fearless."

"Christ," Gomorrah said. "Are they people or feral dogs?"

"They're poorly raised children," I said. "I was pretty much the only one around that wasn't insane."

Gomorrah stared so hard I could feel it through her mask. "God, watch over my soul."

"The kittens aren't really religious," I said.

"I can't imagine," she deadpanned.

I patted her back, and then when the elevator door opened, I started out into the corridor. We still had guards stationed by the doors, and the place still looked way too clean for the likes of the kittens to be staying there.

Katallina's head was on a swivel, and the dog . . . was doing dog stuff. I don't know.

I could just make out the kittens talking on the other side of the apartment door; they were talking over a television playing some sort of cartoon, if I had to guess. Someone was doing something in the kitchen, and I decided that I had had enough spying on the kittens for a day.

The door unlocked as I reached for the handle, and I stepped in with a yawn. It was only early evening, but I was ready for a rest already. "Yo! I'm home. And I brought guests."

"Shut up! TV's on," Nose shouted back. He didn't even turn away from the flashing colors on the floor-to-ceiling screen.

I glared, then stared at the TV, connected to it through my augs, and flicked it off.

"Hey!" came a chorus of whines.

"Myalis, can you ping all the kittens and tell them to come over here? Be as creatively threatening as you want."

With pleasure!

"I have the feeling that being here is a mistake," Gomorrah said. "Why is this place more fearsome than breaking into a mercenary base?"

"Because kids are scarier than neckbeards with guns," I said. The kittens, spurred on by Myalis's threats, gathered up in the . . . I didn't know what the huge room that encompassed the kitchen, the living room, and an area with a piano was called. I looked over the sea of little shits, then narrowed my eyes. "Where's Lucy?"

I didn't alert her. I suspect that sending threats to your girlfriend would cause some issues.

"She's sleeping, dipshit," Junior said.

"Oh," I said.

Daniel wobbled into the room and then came to a stop next to the island in the middle of the kitchen. "Hey," he said. "Nice seeing you alive. That the girl you were trying to save?"

"Yup. Gomorrah, Daniel, watch over the kittens, I'm going to go wake Lucy up," I said as I took off. I pretended that I couldn't hear Gomorrah's "What?" even though I'd picked it up plenty well.

"So, are you a nun, or is that just some cosplay, because if it is just cosplay, you got an Instagram or something?" Daniel asked.

I left it up to Gomorrah to decide whether to choke him.

I went over to our bedroom and carefully opened the door. It was well oiled and didn't so much as squeak.

Lucy was on the bed, partially covered by a blanket and hugging a pillow. She was in jeans and a T-shirt and looked like someone who had just flopped down for a quick nap. I couldn't help but smile as I shuffled over and took off my coat, then the holster beneath. I sat next to her and started to run my hands through her hair.

She had wavy hair that always got tangled up if she didn't take care of it. It was beautiful, but a bit messy, and high maintenance. I would never tell Lucy that it suited her very well.

"Hey," I said.

Lucy groaned and buried herself deeper into her pillow. "Just eat whatever," she said.

I snorted. Did she think I was a hungry kitten?

She blinked and looked up to me. It took a moment for recognition to flash in her eyes. And then she shoved her head back down. "It's good you're back; wake me up later."

"Really?" I asked.

She sighed, yawned, and rolled over. "Fine," she said. "How was . . . everything? What time is it?"

"Who cares?" I asked. "Uh, we have guests."

She blinked some more. "We have guests?"

"Yup. You might wanna get up."

"Dammit all," she said. But she did get up.

CHAPTER THIRTY-NINE

WHERE THINGS GO

He that is without sin amongst you, let him yeet the first stone.

(John 8:7)

—Excerpt from *The New Youth Bible*, 2044

"Do you want me to lay out the situation for you?" I asked as I helped Lucy to her feet. She paused, then stretched, and for a moment I was distracted by that little bit of belly that appeared when her shirt rode up.

"You make it sound serious," she said.

"It sorta is," I said. "We saved that girl, and uh, now she's here. And she's a bit of an orphan."

Lucy turned and looked at me. "You're so predictable."

"What?" I asked.

She pulled me over, gave me an unfortunately chaste kiss, then used my shoulder as a place to rest her head while hugging me. "Predictable," she muttered. "You saw the girl, felt bad about it, then decided she needed saving, right?"

"Well, I mean, at a certain angle you could certainly paint the situation to look like that," I said.

She pinched my butt, or tried to. The armored undersuit I was wearing made that a little hard. "Hmmph," she said as she was robbed of one of her favorite pastimes. "Well, whatever. We should have some funds, and as long as the girl doesn't mind sleeping in the same room as the Twins it should be okay."

"Right, speaking of funds, I made lots of money."

"Okay?"

"Like . . . multiple millions."

Lucy pulled back and looked at me. "I guess that'll help."

"I thought you'd be more excited," I said.

"Can we spend some of that on cute clothes?"

I rolled my eyes. "Yes, Lucy, we can."

"Good. The rest . . . I guess rent? We'll need proper food too. I don't know if we can stay in this much luxury forever."

"We could," I said. I'd find a way, if it was what Lucy wanted.

"It's just a bit much," she said. "But whatever, it doesn't matter. I'll find some school stuff for the kittens soon, including the new girl, and . . . I guess we'll see where things go from there?"

"Yeah, sure," I said. "Maybe we can buy some other goodies? Or, uh, help people, somehow? Speaking of, I left Gomorrah in charge of the kittens."

Lucy was confused for a moment, and then I saw understanding flash in her eyes. "The nun?"

"The pyro nun, yeah," I said.

"Cool! Let's go say hi, and make sure the kids didn't get themselves toasted."

I was actually expecting . . . one of two things:

Gomorrah buried under a pile of kittens, suffocating under their prying questions and being completely lost. Or, one to ten dead kittens, and a faint odor of charred kids.

Instead I found the kids all sitting in the living room, with Gomorrah resting on the edge of one sofa and telling them all a story. They were being attentive, most sitting cross-legged on the floor and looking up to the samurai with wide eyes.

"Wow," Lucy whispered.

". . . And so on the sixth day, God created the heavens, the sun, and the planets. He did this with His own will, and without assistance from any extraterrestrial or intergalactic force."

"When was that?" Bargain asked.

"That was many thousands of years ago," Gomorrah said. She seemed happy, relaxed, and quite content.

Bargain's eyes narrowed. "Give me a thousand credits and I won't discredit you in front of the others," he said.

"I've literally seen her burn things alive," I said. "I really wouldn't fuck with her God-given patience. Anyway, Gomorrah, this is Lucy, my girlfriend. Lucy, this is Gomorrah, she's a nun, a samurai, and, when she's not being testy, she's pretty fun. Also, she's hot under the mask. Figuratively and literally."

"How hot are we talking?" Lucy asked.

"I give her . . . point-eight Lucys."

"I'm a measure for hotness now?" Lucy asked.

I nodded seriously. "When you're in the room? Definitely." This time, instead of a pinch, it was a smack. The armor did its job, though, and Lucy shook her hand, looking mighty displeased.

"It's a pleasure to meet you," Gomorrah said as she stood. "Cat . . . hasn't spoken too much about you, but what she said was always very fond. I can tell that she really cares for you, despite your nonstandard relationship."

Lucy and I looked at each other and we both decided not to poke at that. It was 2057, for fuck's sake.

"Right," I said. "So . . ." I looked over the kittens until I spotted Katallina standing a bit to the side of all of them. "Right, everyone's met Katallina?" I asked.

There was a lot of nodding.

"Awesome. Katallina, wanna come with me and Gomorrah and Lucy, just to the kitchen?"

We all shuffled quite awkwardly over to the island in the kitchen. Fortunately, the kittens started to be noisy soon enough. The TV came back on, the phones and augs came out, and they started to play and argue, creating a familiar hum of background noise, occasionally punctuated by indignant screams and the malicious laughter of children.

We settled down except for Lucy, who moved over to the fridge. "What do you guys want? We have . . . literally everything."

"Just water," Gomorrah said. She reached up and undid her mask fully, then set it on the table next to her.

"Taking it off?" I asked.

"I assume that since this is your home, most of your points went into securing it," she said. "It should be fine, right?"

I chuckled nervously and earned myself a suspicious look from the nun.

Lucy returned, setting some bottles on the table. Water for Gomorrah, soda for the rest of us. When she took in Gomorrah's face, sweaty blond hair, delicate nose, and all, she paused. "*That's* a point eight?" she asked. "Cat, were you trying to moisten me up for later by using some sort of weird compliment?"

"She loses points for being a nun," I explained.

"How so?" Gomorrah asked as she took a pull from her bottle of water.

"Nuns have natural resistance to lesbianism," I said.

The water went everywhere.

I started opening cupboards until I found some paper towels (not even the thrice-recycled sort; this place was really fancy) and started wiping down my face and the counters. "That was a reaction," I said.

Gomorrah finished catching her breath, then glared at me.

"Ohh, she's even hotter when she's angry," Lucy said. "That's just so cruel."

"Can either of you take anything seriously?" Gomorrah asked.

"You're seriously cute," Lucy said. "I'm seriously contemplating inviting you to a threesome."

Gomorrah's mouth worked while blood rushed to her face. She couldn't seem to decide on whether to glare or just blush herself to death.

I laughed and bumped shoulders with Lucy. "All right, we can tease you later," I said. "We do need to, uh, talk about stuff? Mostly I wanted you here because the kittens can be annoying in large doses."

"What about me?" Katallina asked.

"Well, I wanted to see if you liked the kittens. You can still say no, you know?" I asked.

She looked to the table, then carefully took the soda Lucy had given her and sipped from it before answering. "I guess I could stay? I can leave if I don't like it, right?"

"Of course."

"And I can keep Catkiller?"

Lucy blinked. "What?"

The dog, probably hearing its name, strutted on over while leaving a fresh line of drool on the carpet. One of the kittens whined at it leaving, but the dog didn't seem to care much. It dropped its head onto Katallina's lap and drooled there for a bit.

"A puppy!" Lucy squealed. She teleported to the other side of the island and was soon rubbing herself against the dog, who seemed to thoroughly enjoy the sudden loud attention. "Who's a good boy? Who's a good boy? Your name is Catkiller? That's a good name, yes it is!"

"It's an awful name," I said.

"I think it's a nice name," Gomorrah said.

I huffed. "Can we change his name?" I asked Katallina.

The girl looked at me, wide-eyed. "You can't change a dog's name," she said.

"It's literally called Catkiller! That's like . . . going to inspire violence with the kittens, or something."

"You let me keep a laser rifle," Katallina said.

"That's different," I muttered. I'm not sure anyone heard me over the cooing noises Lucy was making while petting the dumb dog.

Are you jealous of a dog?

"I'm the one she . . . you know what, I'm not finishing that," I said. Taking a breath, I cleared my throat. "Katallina. Welcome to the kittens, I guess. Don't shoot any of them, no matter how annoying they get, all right?"

"I'll do my best," she said. "And, uh, thanks."

I gave her a thumbs-up, then went to fetch a snack from the fridge. On returning, I placed another bottle before Gomorrah and slumped onto a stool. "So, tell me more about these home defense things?" I asked.

She closed her eyes. "How many points do you have?"

"About . . . seven thousand and change?"

The nun rubbed at her face. "You . . . are stupid. You could have saved us a day of running around with that amount of points."

"My bad?"

"All right, let me teach you the principles of spending points as a samurai, because it's obvious that you're not learning on your own."

CHAPTER FORTY

BICKER BICKER

Samurai are basically mad scientists when it comes to wherever they live. Sure, you might find out where that is, but trying to break in is likely to have you turned into a rat by some needlessly cruel defense system. It's just not worth it.

—Longbow, final interview given to a team of reporters that attempted to break into his home, 2049

When Gomorrah said she'd teach me, I was expecting her to just kind of informally tell me a few things, maybe drop a few hints, give a couple of tips.

I was not expecting her to drag me over to the one unused room in the penthouse—the office—and sit me down on a chair in the middle of the room. Lucy, of course, followed. I think the dog would have followed too, but one of the kittens dropped something in the living room, and he proved his shortsightedness by abandoning all love for Lucy in favor of chasing down floor food.

"You, as we have firmly established already," Gomorrah began, "are an idiot."

I blinked. "Okay . . . that's a bit rude."

"Do you have anything that protects you from your own explosives?"

". . . No?"

"My point is made," she said.

"Myalis never suggested anything like that," I said.

You never asked.

Gomorrah pinched the bridge of her nose and then, upon letting go, went through some calming exercises. "Okay. Okay. This is really something you should have learned early on."

"What is?" I asked.

"The Protectors, God bless them, are wonderful, but they are not entirely human. Don't get me wrong, they probably understand human psychology better than any human does, but that doesn't mean they use that knowledge all the time."

"Uh, okay?"

"I don't get it!" Lucy cheerfully jumped into the same boat as me.

"You have an excuse," Gomorrah said.

"It's okay if I don't get things because I'm cute?" Lucy asked.

Gomorrah rolled her eyes. "No, you don't have an AI in your mind. Stray Cat . . . Cat here, does. She should have been told this by now."

"My role models so far have been Deus Ex, who's a little shit; Longbow, who is a LARPer; and you," I pointed out.

"God Almighty."

I snorted, and then Lucy giggled, which made me chuckle, and soon she plopped herself onto the same seat as me, both of us bouncing as we laughed.

Gomorrah sighed. "The point I'm trying to get at is that the Protectors only protect if you ask for it. The AI will not prompt you to better yourself, merely provide the tools to do so. Exceptional ones, but still just more tools."

"So I need to ask Myalis for stuff?"

"A wild oversimplification, but essentially correct." Gomorrah started to pace. It was a nice office for pacing in. One wall had a floor-to-ceiling window that overlooked part of the city. It was only with my cybernetic eye that I could tell it wasn't an actual window but a stupidly high-def screen. "There's a list of things you should be asking for."

"Is that list common knowledge?" I asked.

"Among samurai? More or less. It tends to change from area to area, and no one respects it entirely because . . . samurai and rules," Gomorrah said.

"Aren't you included in that?" Lucy asked.

"I am a terrible nun," Gomorrah admitted without batting an eye. "The list goes something like this, in order of priority . . ." She looked about, saw the window, then gestured at it and a list appeared.

Secure your home
Secure yourself
Obtain greater equipment
Obtain the means of producing your equipment
Secure the assets you care about
Obtain comforts

"There."

I tilted my head to the side to try to figure the list out. "Yeah, it needs examples. Maybe some cartoonish drawings on the side in corpo-art style to help me figure it out?"

Lucy poked me with her elbow. "Don't be difficult," she muttered. "Gomorrah is trying to help. So, Miss Nun, you said the first thing is protecting our home?"

"Generally, yes," Gomorrah said. "There are limits. Anyone with sufficient explosives can take out a building like this, and in that case nothing in your price range will protect this apartment. But there are ways of protecting you against anything up to that. I have turret emplacements around the church, with an electronic warfare system in place, as well as a few drones that protect the building."

"How much did you sink on that?" I asked.

"I've been a little cheap. The church is a somewhat public place, after all. And if it's destroyed, well, I could move elsewhere. I'm attached to a few of the sisters, but they're not exactly family," Gomorrah said. She managed to sound uncomfortable without her expression changing at all. "I've put two thousand or so points into defensive measures."

I whistled. "That's more than I've spent, total . . . I think."

She nodded. "I expected as much. You're very frugal."

"Hey, I don't know where my next points might come from."

"What you can't buy with points you can obtain with hard credits," Gomorrah said. She wiggled a finger at me, completing the image of an annoyed nun. "More points can be obtained later. Worst case, get some blueprints for something new and sell those to the highest bidder."

I raised my hands in surrender. Well, one of them, the other was being held on to by Lucy. "Okay, fine. So let's say I put two . . . maybe three thousand into home defense stuff. That leaves me with about four thousand points?"

"That's enough for some self-modification," Gomorrah said.

"Did you get any?" I asked.

She reddened a little. I was beginning to think the mask was more to hide her blush than anything else. "God's Righteous Fury cost four thousand points. And the tier-two catalog wasn't inexpensive either."

"Wow, and you're giving me shit," I said.

"My car can serve as a perfectly valid residence, in a pinch."

"How very fiscally responsible of you," I said. "So, I should spend the remainder of my points on a big cool toy?"

Lucy poked me again. "Don't be silly, Cat, you can't spend all of them on toys. A few is fine, though."

"Like that toy in our bedroom?" I asked.

She nodded quite seriously, but I recognized the mischievous glint in her eyes. "When we get married, I want Mr. Tentacles to be the best man."

I couldn't hold back a grin. "Marriage, huh? Wait, is that even a man?"

"Cat. It has like, sixteen penises."

"Good point."

Gomorrah looked a little nauseated. "I truly do not want to know."

"That's fair," I said. "Wouldn't want to corrupt your no doubt pure and chaste mind. So, since I'm not obsessed with cats, maybe I should spend those points on other things? I wonder what Deus Ex spends her points on?"

"You should spend them on things that keep you alive," Lucy said. "If you die I might be a little upset and you wouldn't want that."

"You're right, upsetting you a little would be awful," I said.

"Also, you need to let me pick out some gear for you that looks cool. Your sense of fashion is terrible."

I squeezed her a little. "It is not," I said.

"Your helmet had whiskers."

"That wasn't me!" I said, defending myself.

Gomorrah stopped her pacing and stretched a little. "It's getting late," she said. A glance outside revealed that the sun was well on its way to setting. "I should head back home soon. Do put up some defenses around your home here, please. I'd be mildly disappointed to learn that someone enterprising killed you in your sleep."

I lifted Lucy up and plopped her down next to me. She squirmed a little at the treatment but stopped as soon as I got up. "All right. I'll uh, walk you to the door?"

"I'd appreciate that," she said.

Lucy jumped up behind me, then pulled Gomorrah into a quick hug. "Thanks for taking care of my Cat," she said. "I know she's a lot of trouble, and a bit stupid, and sometimes she's a bitch, but I still like her."

"You're welcome," Gomorrah said over my indignant grumbling. "I think she's becoming something of a friend."

We escorted Gomorrah past the kittens, some of whom were polite enough to say goodbye; then, once we finished repeating our goodbyes again, and the door was shut behind her, I found a nice place to rest, leaning up against Lucy for support with my head leaning against hers. "I'm tired," I said.

She laughed. "I can tell. Do you want to do that security stuff first? I'm sure I can keep you energized until then."

"That sounds fun," I muttered.

Somehow, we made it over to the bedroom without tripping over each other; unfortunately, Lucy tended to be a work-before-pleasure kind of person, and she just sat down on one of the cushy seats in the corner of the room. "All right, let's buy shit!"

"All right, all right, where do we start?"

The door clicked open and a Dumbass skittered in. "Do forgive the intrusion," it said in Myalis's voice. "But I did wish to be able to talk to both of you without needing to resort to Lucy's frankly atrocious augmentations."

"Oh, come here," Lucy said. She made wiggly hands at the drone, who quickly settled onto her lap.

"Right, so home defense stuff," I said as I settled onto the edge of the bed. "Where do we start?"

"From the top," Myalis said. "If that's what you wish."

CHAPTER FORTY-ONE

BIG OL' MECHA-CATS

On every governmental document, there is a tiny checkbox, entirely hidden in the document's code.

This checkbox can only be checked off by solving a complex cryptographic code, the sort that adds a few megabytes to the size of the document's file.

It essentially reads as such:

If you are a samurai, check the following box:

Once checked, the document is considered "complete" regardless of how much or how little was filled on it. An analyst will check to determine if the provenance truly does belong to a samurai, and will then file the document accordingly.

—IRS *Blue Book* instructional manual

To be entirely honest, I really didn't feel like working, and yes, contrary to what Lucy believed, shopping for stuff totally counted as working.

Mr. Tentacles was over in the corner, doing nothing, and both Lucy and I had a lot of free time all of a sudden. There were at least a dozen very fun things we could have been doing instead.

But no, I had responsibilities and stuff to take care of first.

I sighed. "Okay, from the top, then," I said.

"Wonderful!" Myalis said. "If you wish to follow the list Gomorrah outlined for you, then the first purchase you should look into is a method by which to secure your place of residence."

Lucy leaned back, still hugging the Dumbass close. "That might be tricky," she said.

"What's that?" I asked.

"We don't exactly have a place of residence."

I blinked, then gestured around the lavish room. "What's this, then?"

"A hotel room? It's really nice, and I'm sure with your crazy samurai money you could keep us here for a while, but it's not permanent," she said.

"What'll happen if you get hurt? Will we get kicked out? What if we want more kittens? They're already two or three to a room, which is fine since we have big beds here, but that's a temporary solution."

I leaned back into the very comfortable bed. "Damn. All right, so we need a house. Like, a proper place to stay in. Myalis, can you give me an idea of what a place would cost?"

"The range of prices for a home is rather huge, you are aware. Perhaps a few additional factors to narrow it down? I'm assuming you want to stay within the same hemisphere?"

"Uh, right, that's true. Same city? Maybe . . . a place with enough room for all the kittens, and then a few more." I sat up, then pulled my legs in and started to pull my boots off. My feet were . . . completely fine. It felt as though they should have been achy, but my alien boots were too good for that, apparently. "Maybe we can buy a place and renovate it?"

"The good news in that case is that quite a few buildings were recently evacuated and are being dealt with by local insurance companies. Some small businesses have also surrendered their leases."

"Oh," Lucy said. "That's great! We could buy like, an entire penthouse floor."

"I can't imagine the top floor of a building being cheap," I said.

"There is only one for sale right now within your price range. It happens to be one you're familiar with."

It took a moment for that to click. "No way," I said. Then again, the damage had been fairly extensive, and I couldn't imagine the folks that had been there with us not suing the ever-loving shit out of the idiots who ran the place. And I recalled Longbow being a bit miffed too, what with some of his gear being messed with.

"Its current going rate is two hundred ninety-eight million credits."

I worked my jaw. "Uh. That's a bit more than what I have. Is that to buy the building?"

"It's to buy the topmost floor. Not including yearly utilities. As a samurai, you wouldn't need to pay taxes, of course."

"That's a bit much," Lucy said. "Like, a big bit much."

"Yeah," I replied. But I was still thinking about it. It was a nice enough building. And I bet we could add some decent security. Longbow would probably be fixing that roof-mounted gun of his, which was a nice bonus. And there was parking on the roof and out front. "I'm really tempted," I said.

"You can't be serious," Lucy said. "That place was huge."

"Exactly. Plenty of space to build rooms for the kittens. It might be really neat. And it needs renovations anyway, so we could armor it up or whatever." I nodded, liking the idea. "It'll make for a really cool place to live."

"You did catch on to the fact that the price tag has nine figures, right?" Lucy asked.

"Yup," I said. "You don't like the location?"

She giggled. It was a strange giggle, though. "Oh, wow, uh, yeah, it's a nice location, I guess."

"Myalis, can you get in touch with the company selling the place, then tell them that we're interested?" I asked. "And do you know how to negotiate to lower the price?"

"I can certainly manage," Myalis said. "Though I have to say that securing a place to live, while wonderful, doesn't help in securing the location where you're living."

It took a moment for me to untangle that one. Myalis was right, though; having a place to live didn't mean we were in any way safe. "Right, we need security stuff," I said. "We need security stuff that we can eventually move over to somewhere else."

Lucy clapped her hands, which was a good sign she'd come up with an awful idea I'd eventually agree to because she was Lucy. "Giant killer robot cats," she said.

I flopped back down to the bed and covered my head with an arm.

"Aww, come on!" Lucy said. "Hear me out!" She came over and bounced onto the bed, and then, because the huge expanse of mattress wasn't big enough, she ended up on top of me, straddling me with her face over mine. It wasn't a sexy straddle, though; it was the "Lucy wants something silly" straddle. "Giant cats, but they're mecha, with like . . . laser guns inside them. And they can walk around and murderize things."

"There are a few options that would fit those rather loose criteria," Myalis, the traitor, said.

"Seriously?" I asked. "It sounds ridiculous."

"It's entirely on-brand. You need to think of the branding! Also, the kittens wouldn't be afraid of them, and we could move them over to wherever we go to live later."

"Hmm," I said. "It wouldn't cover everything, though."

"Buy different kinds. Like, Gomorrah said we'd need some sort of electronic warfare sort of thing, right? Buy a cat like that. Oh, and one that's all shields and stuff, and one that's got, like, a cannon."

"This is sounding expensive," I said.

"Approximately four hundred points so far," Myalis said.

I reached up and pulled Lucy down onto me. "You're lucky I'm such a softy," I said.

"You really are," she said.

"Okay, let's take this a little more seriously," I said. Mostly because the sooner we finished, the sooner I could ravish the girl pressing herself up against me. "Let's say we spend five hundred points or so on home defense. Mobile stuff, like your giant cat drones. That's . . . a fair amount of points, but not too many. I think . . . yeah, we should diversify things a little. Maybe a couple of more mobile drones, and a few specialized ones?"

I heard the Dumbass that Myalis was controlling move closer to the bed. "One electronic countermeasures drone. One heavy-weapons platform, and three simpler weapons platforms?"

"Maybe replace one of the simpler ones with a drone that can use non-lethals?" I asked. "As a sort of first resort."

"Nonlethal for someone trying to mess with the house, or the kittens?" Lucy asked.

"Mostly because I don't want the kittens to get caught in the splash damage," I said. "Or for them to see someone's head blow up." Though I watched the same shows as them; it wasn't too shocking to see that kind of thing, even in real life.

"I see. I have picked out what I hope are the best options for what you're looking for," Myalis said. "Do you want me to project an image of what they would look like?"

"Oh!" Lucy said as she rolled off me.

Myalis was such a fucking clam-jammer. I sat up just as five fuzzy holograms materialized, then sharpened into more precise images.

The drones looked like cats. Giant mechanical cats, without any fur and made of metallic plates in a dull black that I suspected the holograms couldn't do justice.

"Those look like they're pretty big," Lucy said.

"Approximately the size of a Bengal tiger," Myalis said.

The five looked pretty similar, though one had a broader back, and another had a lot more fins along its sides and where its ribs would have been were it an organic creature. The heavy-weapons platform and the electronic-warfare one, if I had to guess.

"These are Se-Cat-Urity Drones, Mar—"

"Wait wait." I cut her off. "Se-Cat-Urity drones? Were you even trying with that name?" Lucy giggled, which didn't help any.

"Very well then, I'll send a ticket to have them renamed . . . Sent. Acknowledge. Accepted. The drones have officially been renamed. They are now classified as Personal Use Security Systems, Model Y."

Lucy's giggle turned into a full-blown laugh, and I started to look for something to throw at Myalis.

CHAPTER FORTY-TWO

INVASIVE

If you're going to kill a samurai, make sure to double-tap.

—Anonymous

I reluctantly got off the bed and walked around the five large cat mecha sitting in a row. The holograms flickered whenever I walked between them and the Dumbass that Myalis was using to project them, but I still had a good idea of what the machines looked like.

"These are pretty intimidating," I said.

They were. With scowling eyes and a build that made them look like one of those cloned tigers the super-rich had in their mansions. No stripes, but the way their armor was jointed hinted at something similar.

The holograms flickered, and suddenly the mecha were bristling with weapons.

"Every unit has a pair of basic firearms. Belt-fed, five-point-six-millimeter machine guns mounted in the ribs. The combat units have larger guns. These are rail-fired magnetically propelled grenade launchers. With customizable payloads."

The railguns twitched this way and that.

"The face of most units can open up, and the jaws are strong enough to break bone. The claws all have arc-jets in them. Effectively electrical welders to soften nearby targets. The heavier model has a hellfire, belt-fed missile launcher instead of the railgun, and the electronic countermeasure unit, I'm afraid, focuses mostly on E-war applications, and therefore lacks the room for deployable weapons."

"Is this what shopping is like for you all the time?" Lucy asked. "Because I'm a bit jealous."

"The nonlethal version," Myalis continued. One of the mecha started to spin slowly. "Is equipped with Tasers, gas deployment systems, and guns that can spray an irritating adhesive. Contact from the latter to a human's skin should cause them debilitating pain."

"That doesn't sound very nonlethal," Lucy said.

"While they may wish for death, they won't be dead," Myalis said.

I nodded. "How much for the five?" I asked.

Myalis was quick to answer. "Four hundred and ninety-five points. Just shy of your five-hundred-point budget."

I looked at Lucy, and she nodded.

It was a big purchase, but it was meant to keep the kittens, and Lucy, safe. When put in that light, it really wasn't much.

"Let's do it, then," I said.

New Purchase: P.U.S.S. Model Y—Security Mecha (Various)—Five Models

Points Reduced from . . .7,510 to . . . 7,015

Five boxes appeared across the floor, all in a neat row.

"Oh! Like Christmas!" Lucy said as she catapulted herself off the bed. She landed with a stumble, legs wobbling a bit, so I caught her in a quick hug to keep her steady. "Can I open them?" she asked as she assaulted me with big wet eyes.

"Yeah, sure," I said.

The boxes were the same cheap-looking plastic that all of my stuff came in. Lucy had to scramble with the sides of the first a bit before she found the edge and tore it off.

Inside, tucked in nice and neatly, was a folded-up mecha-cat. Its eyes sparked and glowed, and it stretched itself out of the box while Lucy cooed at it.

I was kinda impressed that it had fit in there, but then, cats were mostly liquid, and it looked like a cat.

Lucy patted it, then moved on to the next box until we had five mecha roaming around the room. They were deathly quiet, and scanned every-thing as if it would jump out and try to eat them without a moment's notice.

"I'm going to go tell the kittens not to be afraid," Lucy said. She patted her hip and whistled, as if the cats were dogs, and they immediately formed up and followed after her.

"Should I be disturbed that she knows how to control them so easily?" I muttered.

Does that same trick work on you? It might just be an ingrained habit.

I wanted to be angry, but Myalis was probably at least a little bit right.

"What're we looking into next?"

I have received a reply from the real estate agent currently in charge of the museum. They're a rather luxurious company, in charge of selling and buying high-end properties across the East Coast of the continent. They wish to set up a meeting with you, on-site, at your earliest convenience.

"Huh. Do you know when the incursion zone will be cleared for civilians?"

Myalis was quiet for a moment.

Reconstruction is slated to begin tomorrow morning, with heightened security until the end of the week.

"Fast," I said. "Ask them if they want to show up tomorrow morning . . . no, tomorrow afternoon."

Message sent.

Lucy returned wearing a rather smug smile. "The kittens love them. Catkiller not so much, but he'll get used to them."

"Awesome," I said. "How's Katallina?"

"The Twins are all over her," Lucy said. "She seems happy. Or at least distracted."

"Almost as good," I said. "Are the rest of the brats distracted?" I asked.

Something must have snuck into my voice because Lucy gave me a *look*. "We're not done shopping yet," she said. "Right, Myalis? What was the next thing on Cat's list?"

"The next item is personal protection," Myalis said, switching back to speaking from the drone. "I think Vanguard Gomorrah meant more than just the surface level of protection here. This should encompass everything from protective gear to further bodily modifications?"

"Oh, bod mods!" Lucy cheered.

I rolled my eyes. "I've got the arm and the ears already," I said.

"Don't forget the tail," Lucy said. "I like it. It gives me something to grab onto."

"No," I said. "I'd like less . . . uh, obvious stuff. Also, the tail's not stuck to my body or anything."

"You are deficient in a few places," Myalis said. "Even if we focus mainly on organs and modifications that are less apparent, there is a lot that can be done to help you. Notably, you might want to focus on items that improve your digestion, assist you in removing toxins and other unwanted elements from your body, and systems that can improve the rate at which you heal."

"Healing is good," Lucy said. "Got anything that'll give her abs? Big, sexy ones. Like a cheese grater."

"Hey," I complained.

Lucy pulled me into a quick hug. "You know I love you, handles and all." She pinched my stomach, where I very much didn't have handles. "But abs are really fucking hot."

I poked her in the stomach. "What about you? Huh? All that rich food."

"We just need to do some more cardio," Lucy agreed.

"We have many options to improve your physique, although it has been noted that self-improvement of one's own body does produce slightly better results in the field over faster methods."

I squirmed a little. "So, how invasive are we talking here?"

"Generally speaking, not invasive at all," Myalis said. "You've done more invasive things with Lucy here in the past day or so."

Lucy snorted.

I shook my head. "Idiots, the both of you. Now, that self-healing thing, what's that all about? And is it a separate thing from the, uh, anti-poison one?"

"Anti-toxin, and that is entirely up to you. If you want to avoid any complex surgeries and want to keep the number of purchases to a minimum, I would advise investing a few more points to purchase a single module that covers as wide a range of options as possible. It is unlikely to do them all as well as specialized prosthetics and replacements to your current organs, but it would likely be a solution that covers a lot of ground."

I nodded. "Okay, all right. And I'd need to be operated on?"

"For a few more points, the organ could be transported directly into your body."

"Wow, that sounds awful," Lucy said. "Where will the, uh, stuff that's already there go?"

"They would be mulched by the new organ as it sets itself into place, then passed with Cat's normal waste removal methods."

"You want me to shit out my liver?" I asked. I wasn't sure if I should be horrified or fascinated, so I settled for a bit of both.

Myalis took a worrying moment to respond. "Technically it would be a liver, as well as both kidneys, and a lower rib."

"How big is this thing?" I asked.

The Dumbass projected a hologram of a metal thing, with a sack on one side, and a lot of little pipes sticking out of it. It looked about as big around as a football, though one that had been deflated a little and then sat on.

"This is from your Sun Watcher Technologies catalog. It's a versatile replacement organ. It can pump, filter, and replenish your blood, create small repair nanites that it can fuse to your white blood cells, and it has a sophisticated hormonal control system that allows it to assist your body's functions. It is, as you can imagine, a little more durable than normal human organs as well."

"How much healing can it do?" Lucy asked.

"It assists in clot formation, can more efficiently produce the materials the body uses to heal itself, and it can generally pinpoint various ailments and act to rectify them. Mostly, it will prevent sickness, though it will not stop everything, nor will it do things like regrow limbs."

"So, cuts heal faster and I wouldn't get a cold?" I asked.

"Yes to the former. The latter is technically accurate. If a small cut takes a week to heal until it is no longer visible with your unaugmented body, this would reduce that time to a mere few days."

"So no instant-regrowth stuff?" I asked.

"That would require far more invasive, and numerous, systems," Myalis said.

I groaned. "Fine, fine. Walk me through how to install that thing."

CHAPTER FORTY-THREE

COMFY MORNING RITUALS

Indentured servitude isn't as bad as people make it out to be. After all, the person in charge of an indentured person—the use of the word "slave" should be avoided at all times—is legally obligated to care for that person.

That means that the minimum standards for living, such as (limited) entertainment, food (up to a caloric amount calculated based on the indentured person's BMI) and living space, must all be provided alongside fulfilling work that can, at a reasonable pace, cover the cost of those living expenses, as well as a certain percentage of the indentured person's debt.

Servitude just means that someone is willing and able to serve in order to pay off their debts! That's it!

—American IS Bureau pamphlet, 2047

I woke up when the bed shifted and lazily made my ears twitch. My new ears let me sense things with a sort of echolocation, and that meant that I didn't need to turn my head and open my eyes to see what was going on.

Someone very pretty was climbing into bed, bare feet slipping in and brushing past my calves. They were a little cold, but I didn't mind much. She laid herself down behind me and wrapped an arm around my middle.

Lucy usually liked being the little spoon, so I enjoyed the reversal while I could.

"Are you awake?" she whispered. It tickled the base of my neck in a very pleasant way.

"Mmm," I replied as I shifted back a bit.

I was sore, so the movement wasn't all that comfortable. Some of that soreness was the fun kind—Mr. Tentacles had gotten a workout—but some of it, especially around my gut, was a bit strange.

Installing that artificial organ thing had been almost traumatizing. If it weren't for Lucy's careful ministrations afterward I might have found the whole thing awful.

Lucy placed an arm over me and pulled me in closer. She was only wearing an oversized shirt, which made the snuggling a whole lot more fun. "Where were you?" I muttered.

"Checking on the kittens," she replied. She sounded as if she was already nearing sleep.

"Mmm," I agreed.

At some point my breathing became even, and I dipped back down into sleep.

I woke up a second time when Lucy started snoring into my ears. It was a reverberating noise, only broken up by the occasional snort.

Sighing, I turned over and faced her. She was sleeping with her mouth open and looked incredibly dumb with her hair poking out this way and that. I made sure to take a picture with my cybernetic eye.

I wanted to stay under the blankets and just sleep the entire day away. The counter in the corner of my eye telling me it was eleven in the morning could get bent for all I cared.

But I really had to piss.

I wiggled out of the covers, trying hard not to wake Lucy up, until my feet touched the floor. It was warm, because of course the hotel had heated floors. I padded to the bathroom and did what I had to do. By the time I was done, sleeping was no longer an option.

My boots were tossed across the room, and I was too damned lazy to fetch them. I just found a shirt in one of the drawers, then some underthings, and I moved out of the room.

I wasn't alone in getting up so early.

Katallina was filling a bowl with some milk. I watched her for a moment, then found my own bowl and set it next to hers. I grabbed the cereal, shook the box to make sure it wasn't empty, then took the milk when she was done with it.

We crunched away for a bit before she interrupted the quiet by pointing to the box. It had Longbow's face on it, of course. "When's that going to be you?" she asked.

"When I'm desperate for cash," I said.

"There's a meme of you online," she said.

I blinked. "What?"

"Yeah. There's this van, and you do a thing to throw it off the side of this building, but you almost fell off with it. They're memeing it."

I groaned and chewed harder. I was going to have words with Longbow. "How did you sleep?"

"All right," she said.

Wonderful conversationalists, the both of us. "Cool, cool. If any of the kittens give you trouble, you tell me, all right?"

Katallina nodded, which I figured was good enough.

I had just about finished when Lucy trudged into the kitchen while wiping the back of her hand across her mouth. "Hey," she said. "You're up?"

"Yeah," I said. "Sleep well?"

"No. It got cold after you left." She looked at my bowl, then scowled and opened the fridge. Soon enough she was burning eggs on the stove and there was bread being roasted in the toaster. "What're you doing today?" she asked.

You have an appointment in a few hours.

I blinked. "Right, I have an appointment this afternoon, in like, a bit. Want to come?"

"Come? What's the appointment?" she asked. I followed her with my gaze as she returned to the fridge, especially when she bent over to pull something from a bottom rack.

"Mmm? Oh, it's to check on a house. For, uh, us," I said. I was way too young to be saying such adult-y things.

Lucy stared at me. "Really?"

"Yeah. The museum Myalis mentioned?" I said. "Just checking in with some real estate agent, I think. Maybe they wanna give me a tour? I don't know, exactly. Want to come?"

Lucy nodded. "Sure, let me eat and then I'll get dressed . . . I only have one change of clothes. Uh, the kittens too."

"Oh," I said. Going on three days with the same clothes on, that was going to stink soon, not just metaphorically. "Right, we'll see about ordering some stuff for everyone. I have enough for that." A glance to the side, and I caught Katallina looking my way. "We'll secure your things too, if we can," I said.

She nodded, then got up and left. Her dog padded out from under the counter where I hadn't noticed him and followed after her.

"So, just the two of us?" Lucy asked.

"Yup. You trust the cat bots to babysit the kittens?"

"Better than Bitchbot," Lucy said.

That was a fair point. The kittens were pretty self-sufficient, and I was pretty sure the cat bots could keep them safe. "Hey, Myalis, if something happens around the bots, can you inform me?"

Of course. By the way, you still have things on Gomorrah's list to purchase.

"I know, I wanna see the museum first. Might need to sink points into remodeling or whatever," I said.

That is reasonable. Shall I obtain transportation to the museum for you?

I nodded. "Yeah."

Lucy shook her head and headed out, presumably to get changed.

"Something comfortable this time," I said.

Of course. I actually like Lucy.

I snorted but couldn't argue. I liked her too. I finished up by tossing everything in the dishwasher, and by resisting the urge to steal from Lucy's plate. Instead I looked around, spotted one of the cat bots, and pointed to the plate, then my eyes. It nodded, which was pretty cool.

I returned to our room and started looking for my clothes. They'd been tossed here and there the night before, so I had to crawl around to find some things, but at least I got to help Lucy find her own things at the same time.

Twenty minutes later, with only some of that time lost to fondling and other such distractions, we were both heading out. "Oh!" I said. "I forgot to give you my old jacket."

"You're giving me your hand-me-downs?" Lucy asked as she followed me to the kitchen.

"It can turn you partially invisible," I said. "And it's got big bullet holes in it. Looks pretty rad."

Lucy took the coat and looked pretty pleased with herself until she poked at the holes. "Hey, wait, you were shot?"

"It happens," I said as I led the two of us out of the penthouse and locked it up behind me.

"Cat!" Lucy barked.

I regretted giving her the coat. "It's nothing," I said.

"Is that why you had a bruise on your breast?" she asked as she lined the coat up. It was a bit loose around her shoulders, and tight around the chest, but it still fit her just fine. We were used to second- and thirdhand clothes.

I declined to answer as I moved over to the elevator.

"Hey!" she said.

"It was nothing," I said.

"No, getting shot isn't nothing!"

"It's part of the job. A little bit. It's one of those high-risk, high-reward things," I said. "Look at how much things have gotten better, and it's only been two days."

"And none of that would be worth anything if you died," Lucy said.

She crossed her arms, set her shoulders, and glared.

It was a long ride down to the lobby.

CHAPTER FORTY-FOUR

KINDA CUTE

Samurai, on account of being perfectly human, despite what some people would think, and how some media portray them, have as much need for companionship as anyone else. They can fall in love just as easily, and their sexual desires are just as keen as you would expect from a healthy human.

That means that relationships between samurai and normal people occur.

Statistically, these don't tend to last. The vast gulf of difference, not just in experience, but in responsibility, tends to erode away any bonds in a relationship.

It is far more likely that samurai will have short-term flings, or that they will connect with another like-minded samurai, and form a strange, quasi-dependent relationship with them.

That doesn't mean that there's no hope for those aiming to find love with a samurai. There have been some long-term relationships, marriages even, that have lasted for years between normal folk and samurai.

—*Gold-Digger Weekly*, issue 147, 2038

I actually managed to placate Lucy a bit by the time we reached the hotel lobby. She wasn't super happy yet, but she was no longer glaring at me for having risked my life.

It was my life to risk, of course, but saying something like that to Lucy would just have pissed her off even more. As far as she was concerned, my ass was hers. I was a little annoyed too, but that was probably just . . . annoyance making more of itself, or whatever.

Relationships were complicated.

"I'm sorry," I muttered.

Lucy glanced my way. "What was that?" she asked.

I sighed. "Lucy."

"Fine," she said before her shoulders slumped. "Yeah, fine. Just . . . don't die, all right?"

I couldn't help but grin a little. "I'll do what I can not to."

"Do more," she said. "I wouldn't want to take care of the kittens on my own."

"Meh, you'd manage."

She jabbed her elbow in my gut and I coughed. "Hey!"

I ignored anyone in the lobby looking our way. We probably both looked a bit like samurai, what with Lucy wearing my coat. I made a note to give her any other gear I ended up replacing too. Sure, it was secondhand, but it was the sort of secondhand that most people only wished they could get, and for all that Lucy was worried about me dying, I had a few things keeping me alive, Lucy was operating on her 1.0 hardware.

I'd have to see about changing that up later. If I could get redundant mechanical organs shoved into me, so could Lucy.

Blinking, I determined to word things more carefully in the future.

We stepped out into the lot out front, where valets were helping clients out of their cars and taxis were stopping and going near constantly.

One moment, I'm moving your vehicle closer.

I brought an arm around Lucy's shoulder and pulled her into my side as we waited. It didn't take very long until a sleek black car pulled up before us. It wasn't a sports car or anything, but it was really nice. I could imagine an executive being chauffeured around the city while doing . . . taxes, or whatever rich people did.

"Looks like that's our ride," I said as I moved up to the back door and opened it up for Lucy. I even gestured her in with my new arm.

She laughed and climbed into the back before I followed her in. The moment the door was closed the car started to move, and a chime sounded from somewhere.

"Welcome, honored customer, to Charon Limo-Taxi. This is vehicle One-One-Seven serving the New Montreal region, and of course, serving you," a smooth, feminine voice said.

Lucy ooohd. "Fancy. Do you know where we're going?"

The chime sounded again. "Your destination has been entered as the Rose Briar Museum. Warning: this location is within a yellow incursion zone. The Charon Limo-Taxi cannot guarantee the safety of our honored clients within that area."

"That's fine," I said.

I figured, from Lucy's profile, that she would enjoy this treatment a little more.

A glance over at Lucy, who had found a screen to poke and prod at, proved that Myalis was essentially spot on.

I leaned to the side, my shoulder pressing into Lucy's. I took off my helmet, figuring I wouldn't need it in the car of all places, and I allowed my new ears to twitch a little. They made combing my hair a real pain in the ass, not that I did much to care for my hair at the best of times.

The taxi wove into traffic and seemed to insist on following every law in the book. Gomorrah would have gotten us there already.

I was almost dozing off when I felt the car tip down and blinked awake. We were dropping toward the skyline, buildings rising up around us, many of them torn and shredded, others sporting car-sized holes in their sides, or with the corpses of Antithesis creatures jammed into them.

It was a surprisingly busy area, with hover platforms slowly working their way up the buildings with orange-wearing indentured workers aboard. Clearing crews, I guess, searching out and disposing of any dead aliens.

If they were around, that meant that most of the aliens were dead.

The taxi turned and spun around the top of a rather familiar building.

The knot in my stomach at seeing the museum was unexpected, but maybe it shouldn't have been. Lucy's fingers slipped through mine, and her grip tightened.

We came down for a slow and gentle landing on one of the cleared landing zones on the roof. There was only one other car there, though judging from the streaks and boot prints covering the ground, there had been plenty of people around recently.

It was, of course, raining, because it was always raining. Fortunately, it was the slow, weak sort of rain that was more annoying than anything. Just scattered drops, smacking the ground and the windshield with intermittent taps.

The car shook a little on contact with the ground.

"Charon Limo-Taxi wishes you good luck in your business dealings. We shall be here, awaiting your return," the taxi said.

I opened the door and slipped out, then helped Lucy out.

Reaching into my coat, I pulled out my gun, the new one that was meant to be stealthy. "Here," I said. "It's called the Victorious. It fires smart rounds, so you don't need to aim too much."

"Uh?" Lucy asked.

"Just in case. There's a safety thing, uh, I think it'll connect to your augs. Myalis, can you do some tech wizardry?"

Of course.

"Yeah, but why?" Lucy asked as she held on to the gun as if I'd just handed her a sick puppy.

"In case you need to shoot something," I said. I'd have given her my Trench Maker, but it needed more aiming, and was a bit cumbersome besides. "Just shove it in your pocket and keep it around, okay? Hell . . . Myalis, I need a holster that'll fit on Lucy. And one of those, uh, what did you call it, that defense thing my jacket has?"

A quantum projection system? I could provide something like that, yes.

I nodded. "And one of those stealth thingies. The ones that make you look like a plant or something."

That would make going after Lucy a bit harder.

"Cat?"

I believe I can find all three prerequisites in one item. Would Lucy prefer a belt holster or a waist holster?

I eyed Lucy up and down. "Belt," I decided. Taking off her jacket in the rain would just give her a cold.

"Catherine, what are you doing?" Lucy asked.

"Keeping you alive," I said. "Probably should have thought about it before leaving the house."

New Purchase: Multi-Projection Security Belt (+Holster)

Points Reduced from . . . 6,515 to . . . 6,415

The box that I caught out of the air had a simple black belt within. I pretended not to see the cat-head-shaped buckle as I gave it to Lucy. There was a holster to one side and a blocky device on the other. "Here, put this on."

"Cat!" Lucy protested.

"Don't make me put it on you," I said. "That would involve taking your current belt off, and who knows what kind of fun that might lead to?"

She jabbed a knuckle in my gut, then snapped the belt out of my hands. "Fine," she muttered. "I'm no hypocrite."

Once everything was buckled, and her old belt was tightened around one leg in a way that somehow managed to look good—because when you looked as good as Lucy, weird fashion shit just looked quirky, not weird—Lucy slapped her new gun into her holster and crossed her arms.

I grinned at her and slid my helmet on. "You know, you're kinda cute when you're all pouty."

"*Kinda* cute?" she asked.

I pulled her to my side, and we started toward the steps leading to the front of the museum.

CHAPTER FORTY-FIVE

REAL ESTATE-ING

The housing market was turning into an increasingly dangerous bubble in North America in the end of the 2010s.
As it turns out, all that was needed to pop that was an alien invasion.
—Anonymous commenter, on the price of homes, 2022

I stayed by Lucy as we made our way down the side of the building and toward the museum's entrance. I idly noticed bullet holes here and there, and stains on the ground where Antithesis had bled out.

Signs left over from my fight here a few days ago?

I supposed that the carrion Antithesis had grabbed most of the bodies at some point, or a cleaning crew had come around already.

I was a little worried that a stray gust would pick Lucy up and fling her off the side. Which was silly, of course, but it didn't stop me from placing myself between her and the drop. If I was blown off the edge, I had options, she didn't, and she was still new to the whole walking-without-crutches thing.

We did make it to the bottom safely, though Lucy paused to catch her breath.

"You okay?" I asked.

"I need to do more cardio. And maybe eat a little bit less," Lucy said.

"I can certainly think of a few ways to get your heart beating," I said.

She snorted. "Not out here."

"Hah! No, it's a bit chilly for that."

We found someone waiting for us at the front of the museum, a woman, maybe in her midthirties, wearing a nice corporate-style long coat and shades. She had a suitcase by her side and was staring off into the sky in the way someone looking at their media feeds did while bored.

"Hey!" I called out.

The woman snapped out of it, looked to us, then put on a smile that I immediately pinged as fake. "Hello," she said. "You're right on time."

"Cool," I said. "I'm Cat, this is Lucy."

"I'm Jessica Washington, from Washington, Smith and Associates. It's a pleasure to meet you."

She extended her hand, and I hesitated just a moment before shaking with my cybernetic arm. "Yeah," I said. "So, we were kinda interested in the place. You intend to give us a tour or something?"

"Of course," Jessica was all smiles. "At Washington, Smith and Associates, we prize our clients above all else, but we're also very discerning about who we take on as a client, and to whom we will sell their property. We only want the best for the city, of course."

My eyes were practically glazing over at all the corporate talk. "Uh-huh," I said. "Point being?"

"Well, Miss . . . Cat, your credit score isn't quite able to meet the demands of purchasing a floor in a building such as this one. You can imagine our concern for our client's well-being."

"You, uh, do know that I'm a samurai, right?" I asked. "I thought that bit was, like, really obvious."

"I'm aware, yes," Jessica said. "But your status as one of humanity's protectors doesn't ensure that you will be capable of meeting payment requirements, and the potential losses of time and money for our client need to be accounted for when viewing any potential contracts and agreements."

My eyes narrowed.

Then Lucy jumped in. "What she's trying to say, I think, is that even if you're a totally cool samurai, you're still a newbie one, and they're not sure you can make all the big payments for a place like this. It is a lot of money. So she's trying to ease you into paying even more so that they don't need to worry."

"A guarantee, or a larger sum paid for the lot, would do a lot to reassure my clients," Jessica said.

"That sounds like bullshit," I said.

Lucy shook her head. "No, no, it's 'cause you're thinking about it wrong. This lady here isn't working for us, she's working for her clients. The polite act's just an act."

Jessica's smile broke off, and she sighed. "That's essentially correct. My clients heard that the person interested in purchasing the building was a samurai, and they insisted that we bring up the price as a consequence of that."

I pinched the bridge of my nose. "That makes sense, I guess," I said. Of course people would get greedy. It just made sense. "What's the price now?"

"Three hundred and fifty million credits."

"That's . . . it was at two hundred ninety-eight million credits last night. That's one hell of a jump," I said.

"They wanted to double it outright, but we convinced them not to. Doubling the cost would make it disproportionately more expensive than the value of the buildings around this area. It wouldn't make sense to buy this one at that price, then."

"And three-fifty is reasonable?" I asked.

Jessica tilted her head from side to side. "It's not far from it. Were the building in perfect shape, without any recent incursions, then yes, it could go for that kind of price given enough time on the market and some interest."

"But the place looks like shit now," I said.

"That's why its initial offer price was so low at just under three hundred million."

I scoffed. "That's just silly. Did you guys talk to Longbow yet?"

The woman blinked. "The man on the cereal boxes?"

"The samurai, yeah," I said. "He had a gun emplacement on the roof."

She nodded. "That was a factor leading to the price being so high."

"Yeah, but someone in the building sabotaged it," I said.

Jessica twitched. It was really minute, and I almost missed it, but there was definitely a flinch there. "Really?"

"Yup. And the vaults in the back of the building are fake. Like, literally made of cardboard. Myalis, you got anything on that?" I asked.

"Myalis?" she asked.

"My AI," I explained.

I do indeed. If your goal is to intimidate the woman, then I'd advise allowing me to enter the conversation. A low-cost drone would be more than enough.

I nodded. "That sounds great."

New Purchase: Light Communications Drone
Points Reduced from . . . 6,415 to . . . 6,410

A box appeared before me, and I snapped it out of the air, popped it open, and let the tiny drone within whizz out. It was no bigger than a closed fist and looked about as durable as some of the thirdhand toys we'd played with at the orphanage.

"Greetings," Myalis said. "I'm Vanguard Stray Cat's assistant, Myalis. She has asked for my assistance regarding some things."

"A pleasure," Jessica said. "Should we step inside? If we're going to be negotiating, I'd rather do it within the building. Privacy and all. Also, it's not as cold."

I looked to the side and noticed Lucy hugging herself for warmth, then nodded. "Yeah, that's a good idea."

The android that had been in the front entrance the first time we came was long gone, and the security doors had been torn right off their hinges. Still, the lobby was a bit warmer, and there were chairs along the sides next to posters of various samurai in action and some poorly disguised ads.

"So, did you intend to tell folks that the vault in this place is fake?" I asked.

"Technically, it meets all specifications to be considered a vault," Jessica said.

"Are you shitting me?"

Myalis's little drone slid closer. "She is, technically, correct. The guidelines on what can and can't be considered a vault are lax, and the interpretation of 'a large room with minimal survival equipment' could be accepted as enough to consider the room in this building as a vault."

I shook my head. "No way. I don't care what any law says, that vault isn't real. It's fake."

"We could lower the price in consequence of—"

"And I haven't spoken to Longbow yet, but I'm pretty sure he was still pissed about his AA system being fucked with. Pretty sure he's going to turn around and hit whoever owned the place for that particular fuckup."

"I . . . will inform my clients of that," Jessica said.

Lucy smiled. It was one of her terrifying smiles, the sort that was also a little hot. "Go ahead. Of course, I'm sure Cat could help cool Longbow down. In the end, they need to weigh how much they'll lose versus how much they have to gain in trying to sell this place."

Jessica rolled her eyes. "You two might think you're being clever, but I see what you're trying to do. Truth is, I'm only getting a commission on this place, and it's not that great to begin with. Still, I need to make ends meet, so even if this place had been a baby-skinning factory, we'd still try to sell it at a price that was at least fair compared to the current market values. You can threaten and posture all you like, and you might even have the right of it, but unless you plan on just stealing the place, then we'll have to insist that you pay a fair price."

I stared at Jessica. The woman had brass balls. Though, to be fair, she was kinda right. Just 'cause the place had nearly been the death of me didn't mean I could just take it.

My temptation to be a bitch warred with my sense of what was fair for a bit, and then I crossed my arms. "Fine. Let's talk prices, then. *Fair* prices."

CHAPTER FORTY-SIX

IMPECCABLE MATHEMATICS

You want to distract an entire forum of people for a few hours? Mention a samurai's weapons, then point out some random detail.

Just be sure to be somewhat wrong about it.

Hours of pleasure, guaranteed.

—Anonymous commenter, 2021

"Okay," I said. "So, two ninety . . . whatever," I said.

Jessica nodded.

"Now, we need to factor in a couple of things," I said. "Whoever buys this place needs to renovate it. A whole lot. Not to mention cleaning the place up."

"That's factored into the price," she said.

"I doubt it," I said. "You know, I almost bled out over here? Hell, I used flesh-eating nanite grenades in there."

The real estate agent blanched. "Pardon?"

"They're designed to melt flesh so that the Antithesis can't use it anymore," I said. "The nanomachines don't last that long, don't worry, but you'll still need specialists to clean up."

"I will make note of it," Jessica said.

"Now, there are two other things you should tell your clients. One, they're on the hook for fucking up Longbow's gun. Two, Deus Ex had to come over here for stuff, and she's a vindictive little bitch. Like seriously, just yesterday, she gave a couple dozen people cancer because it was faster than poking at them herself."

Jessica nodded slowly.

I leaned back, then hummed. "How much can you bring the price down by?" I asked. I'd done my share of negotiating for stuff before. I wasn't great at it, but I could manage in a pinch. Buying stuff from a street vendor wasn't quite the same as buying anything worth hundreds of millions, but I figured some of it would cross over.

Jessica looked straight past me for a moment. "We could, if we lower our expectations, and convince some of our clients to make a smaller profit, lower the price of the building all the way down to two hundred and seventy-five million."

I snorted. "That's barely a discount."

"It's a significant drop in price. My clients will barely make any profit at that rate."

I shuffled a little. "I'll give you one hundred million," I said.

"That's a solid no," Jessica said. "I can't drop the price by that much."

I gestured for her to wait. "Calm down, I can spice it up a little," I said before turning to Myalis. "Hey, which one of my catalogs has the most valuable stuff? That is, if I were to sell it on an open market?"

Myalis's little drone bobbed up and down. "That depends, the market is somewhat fickle. Though I can generally make some predictions."

Notably, your Cyberwarfare tier-one, Medical Utilities tier one, Stealth tier-one, and finally your Sun Watcher Technologies tier-two catalogs all have items that could sell for a good amount of credits.

I nodded along. "Yeah, I can imagine. Hey, Jessica, do any of your clients own any biotech firms? Or weapons . . . manufacturing . . . things? Hell, do any of them want to live longer?"

Jessica perked up a little. "Do you intend to trade blueprints for the building?"

"That . . . could be an option," I said. I had seven thousand or so points, but I didn't want to spend them all here. If I valued the building at about two hundred million, and only wanted to spend . . . say, five thousand of those points, then I'd need to make sure each point was worth . . .

I opened up a calculator app and plugged in the numbers with a few twitches of my eye. Forty thousand credits per point. That was . . . a lot.

"Myalis, can you put together a list of blueprints to sell? Assume that each point is worth . . . about fifty thousand credits, all right?"

"Of course," Myalis said.

That would actually be significantly above the credit-per-point value usually used by Vanguards.

I nodded. "Send that over to Jessica here. Let's see if her clients will bite, yeah?"

I opened a text app and started writing to Myalis. "Maybe, but how many samurai have things available this way?"

There are a few hundred Vanguards who offer items on a per-point valuation system online. Usually at rates hovering around the twenty-five-thousand-credits-per-point rate. Some Vanguards will trade points between each other, usually for thirty to thirty-five thousand credits each. Your advantage here is that you're offering blueprints, which are somewhat rarer, and you have two catalogs that aren't offered by any of the other Vanguards selling things.

Lucy stepped up. "I don't know if it's a good idea," she said.

"Pardon?" Jessica asked.

Lucy nodded, and I would have thought her serious if I didn't know her. "Yeah. Selling to the real estate agent directly, or to your clients, I suppose, isn't as smart as just selling directly on the open market. Cat, you've got some pretty exclusive stuff, right?"

"I think I'm the only samurai with the Sun Watcher tech tree," I said.

Myalis decided to pipe in. "I can confirm that."

I nodded along. "Yeah, we could make more that way. I don't quite have the two hundred and seventy-five mil on me right now, you know? That's a lot of change to carry around."

Jessica looked to the side, then back to us. "Could you give me just one moment? I think I need to contact some of my clients. In the meantime, perhaps you can tour the building. It's in a state of disrepair, I'm aware, but it shouldn't be so dangerous that you can't explore it. Um, unless those nanites . . . perhaps not?"

"Oh, if they start eating Lucy, I'll do something about it," I said. "And I'm pretty sure I'm resistant to that kind of thing."

"Of course." Jessica bowed to us, then moved over to the door. She didn't talk aloud, but from the way she was twitching and moving her head, she was using her augs to their fullest.

I nodded over past the entrance, and Lucy followed me over.

The museum's main floor looked like crap. Some of the displays had been moved, but most of them were just plain abandoned. The huge hole in the ceiling above, still with a big lump of Antithesis meat stuff jammed against it, didn't look stellar.

"Bit creepy," Lucy said as she looked over the floor.

I had to agree. It had a very . . . carnival-after-dark look to it. "You need to look past all the junk and stuff," I said. "There's a lot of room here."

Lucy nodded, then looked over her shoulder. "Think she'll take your bait?" she asked.

Myalis hovered over. "Some of her clients were actually listening in and communicating with each other. There was something of a bidding war behind the scenes. Some wished to get rid of their shares of the building the moment you came in, others wished to purchase those."

"Really?" I asked. "Bit weird, no?"

"I suspect that it's more a matter of potential risk. As it is, the share price has skyrocketed. I could influence it downward, but such an obvious manipulation would be noticed."

"So the value of the building just went up?" I asked. "That's the opposite of what I want."

"The value of anything is entirely based on a person's willingness to pay for it. In this case, the owners of this building seem entirely willing to write off the monetary value of the building if it means obtaining something that is, to them, more valuable still."

"She's saying that the bigwigs want a go at your shiny shiny alien tech," Lucy said. "And it's worth more than this drafty old place."

That made sense, I supposed. Buildings were plentiful; exclusive blueprints to alien tech weren't. "So, think we can get a better deal out of it?" I asked.

"Oh yeah," Lucy said. "Just pretend that you'll borrow the money from someone else, and then when Jessica back there panics, say that you'll be willing to trade the place for, like, peanuts."

Myalis wavered from side to side a little. "As much as I would find that amusing, some of the clients on the line aren't entirely clueless about the value of what's being offered. They're the ones trying to hold the price steady where it is. Others are driving it up, likely in hopes of selling their shares soon, and still others are selling now while they can. It's an interesting little scenario."

"Awesome," I said. It was starting to dawn on me that maybe I'd be the proud owner of . . . a place that needed some really extensive renovations. "What am I getting myself into?" I asked.

"The usual amount of trouble," Myalis said.

Lucy giggled. "'Usual' means that there's also an unusual amount somewhere."

"I have a tier list," Myalis replied.

Lucy pulled me in for a hug, and I easily reciprocated. "You all right?" she asked.

I nodded. "I'm fine," I said. "It's just a lot, you know? But . . . hey, we might have a place all to our own soon. A really expensive one."

"It's kinda cool," she said. "The kittens will love it."

"It's kinda stressful," I replied. "And yeah, they will, which isn't an endorsement of anything, I've seen the kinds of things they love."

A cough from behind me had me turning. Jessica stood there, somewhat awkward. "Miss Stray Cat, I think we're ready to continue our negotiations."

CHAPTER FORTY-SEVEN

CLOSING A DEAL

Interior of homelike space. Ruins in the back. Sections on fire. Sheets and furniture from Le Très Beaus' autumn collection are scattered on the ground.

EAST BLADE bursts into the room and looks around. His suit is dirty, his gun is smoking.

EAST BLADE: Rose? Where are you, my sweet Rose?

Camera pans to side, revealing ROSE's legs. Bare. She is partially buried in some rubble.

EAST BLADE: Rose! Oh no, Rose!

ROSE coughs. She is hurt.

ROSE: East? Is that you, my blade? What happened? I was enjoying a cool, refreshing Neocola when everything exploded!

EAST BLADE rushes to assist Rose. Highlight can on ground.

EAST BLADE: Don't worry my love, I'm here for you!

—Excerpt from screenplay of *Katanation Street*,
season 30, episode 4357, January 2052

I really shouldn't have been enjoying myself at someone else's expense so much. It felt . . . wrong. Mean, at the very least. Like stealing candy from a kid.

Now that I thought about it, I was pretty sure I'd stolen candy from kids before.

Jessica was sweating. I wasn't that keen on reading people, but even I could tell that she was stressing out to the max. Her hair was plastered to her forehead and she kept chewing at her bottom lip. "That price isn't entirely reasonable," she said.

I shrugged a shoulder. "We could buy some other building. I'm fond of this one for . . . reasons, but there are others. Right, Myalis?"

Myalis's drone wobbled. "Within the next twenty blocks, there are seventeen more areas for sale with a similar footprint, two of which are on the top floors of their respective buildings."

"See," I said. "Not too sure how much those are going for, but it's a buyer's market, right?"

I had no idea what a "buyer's market" actually was, but it sounded right.

Jessica nodded. "That's true. Would you consider keeping the price at four thousand points?"

"That's a lot," I said. "Half a day's worth of fighting aliens, easy. Three thousand is a lot more reasonable."

Jessica fidgeted. "I think my clients would appreciate a higher price than that."

I nodded. "That's nice."

As we spoke, Myalis was helping me keep track of the building's value, the graphs, which I could only just barely understand, filling the edges of my vision. The building's top floor was now hovering just under one billion credits in value, with three big companies holding the majority of the shares for it, and a few dozen stragglers hovering by the edges.

Of course, that wasn't the actual value of the floor. That was the very much inflated value that some idiots had placed on it. As far as I could figure out, Jessica's company was basically splitting however many points I bought the floor for evenly among those who owned shares of the floor.

The things fluctuating so much were parts of the ownership of the floor. Which was a bit weird. You either owned it or not, I figured, but maybe there was some accounting bullshittery going on that I wasn't aware of.

Point was, if they closed the deal with me, then a bunch of corps would get some exclusive blueprints and such. If they didn't, then . . . actually, I wasn't sure what would happen if they didn't; that wasn't my area, and I didn't care all that much.

"Let's meet in the middle," I said. Jessica perked up at that. "But, but, I'll be looking over the crap you guys want with those points; if I see anything too skeevy I'm vetoing it, all right?"

Jessica nodded along. "That sounds very fair. Let me just confirm with my clients, and I'll be back."

I waved her off, then backed up a bit before slumping. Fortunately, I had a Lucy to slump onto. She was the perfect height for that.

"Tired?" she asked.

"It's not even two yet, and I already want to go back to bed," I muttered.

"You're such a baby," she whispered. "You know, all those fancy sorts are probably watching you right now. What'll they think?"

"I don't care," I said.

Lucy giggled and pulled me into a hug. "Here, this'll help."

Part of me wanted to protest, but I'd be damned if it didn't help a little. "Thanks," I said before planting a kiss on her head. "So, what do you think we should do with this place?"

"Clear some space to have lunch, maybe?" she asked.

"I don't know if anyone would deliver all the way over here. I mean, with the incursion cleanup. Maybe we can pick up something on the way back? The kittens would like that."

"We have really good food in the apartment."

"Yeah, but it's not fast food," I said. "Filet mignon is good and all, but burgers."

"That's your entire argument? Just 'burgers'?" she asked.

"It's a winning argument," I said. "Jessica looks like she's ready."

Lucy let go of me, and I walked over to Jessica with an easy smile on my face. She was smiling too. It made her look a whole lot less severe. "My clients are ready to accept your proposal. In exchange for three thousand five hundred points' worth of equipment and blueprints, rounded in your favor, we at Washington, Smith and Associates are happy to close the sale of the top floor of this building."

"So . . . this is mine?" I asked with a wave to the room around us.

"As soon as everything is signed. We have a notary expediting everything as we speak. The full contract will be sent to you for verification."

"Ah, right, Myalis can do legalese, right?"

"I can manage," Myalis said.

"Cool, once that's all done, I guess you can arrange for pickup of all the stuff your clients want to buy?"

Jessica nodded. "Perhaps when we sign the final contract? At the rate things are moving, that might be tomorrow. Although I don't want to put any pressure on you."

"Tomorrow's fine," I said. So I didn't own the place yet. Just . . . mostly did. I extended a hand to Jessica, my meatier one, and she jumped before shaking it. "Thanks, Jess, this was almost fun."

"Ah, well, thank you, Miss Stray Cat. I don't get to do business with samurai often. If you're ever in the market for a new home, or a new building, do remember to call us!"

Jessica looked quite pleased with herself as she sauntered off. I waved at her back, then turned back around. "Weird one," I said. "Wonder what's got her so happy?"

"The deal she just struck might not have been worth as much as the building was in sheer monetary value, and in so doing, her company might have lost some potential revenue, but I suspect that the clout of having bargained and, ostensibly, won, with a Vanguard will improve her company's reputation."

Usually, when people dealt with me they had pretty crappy reputations, and they didn't get better just from associating with me. "All right," I said. "Got that list of things drawn up?"

"I do. To be clear, there are some items that would best be kept in the hands of a Vanguard and not spread to the public at large. Those were removed from consideration. I also drastically reduced the number of weapons available."

"That's fair," I said. "What kind of stuff isn't for normal folk?"

"A lot of software and many of the components of your Cyberwarfare catalog. Nonregulated AIs are something of a nuisance. Some items from your Stealth catalog as well."

That sounded reasonable. I moved over to Lucy, then pointed to the main room. "Wanna explore our new place?" I asked.

Lucy grinned. "I'd love to!" she said. "Oh, are you going to princess-carry me through the threshold?"

"I don't think that's the right tradition for this occasion," I said.

"So what, we smash a bottle of champagne against the side?"

I barked a laugh. "Only if you plan on turning the place into a ship."

"Hmm, nah. One of the kittens would fall off the side. Oh, we'll need guardrails."

Lucy and I took maybe an hour to explore the whole floor. There was that big museum room, shaped like a stubby L that took up all of one side of the building. The rest of the floor had a few dozen rooms. One was a storage area, another a place for staff that linked up to the lobby.

There were a pair of doubled washrooms, and that one little nook where we'd stopped a few days ago to debug my aug-gear. The corridor that had the shelter at the end was lined with offices on both sides, some of them still filled with officey junk.

"The main floor can be turned into some sort of open space," I said. "Maybe a mega-playroom?"

"That sounds like a bit much," Lucy said.

"Eh, we can chop part of it off, turn that into a kitchen or something."

She nodded. "All right. And the offices can be turned into bedrooms. They're about the right size for one-person rooms."

"Not enough of them for all the kittens," I said.

"Some of the bigger rooms could be filled with a few bunks. Like we had back at the orphanage, but less . . . you know, moldy."

It was dawning on me just how much work we'd just bought for ourselves. Still, it sounded like fun.

CHAPTER FORTY-EIGHT

A DATE

Pick your battles.
—Bloodsuck, 2027

I wanted to do something nice for Lucy. Not for any reason in particular, it was always . . .

I'd had a dream once, while scrolling through my media feeds and looking at videos of some celebrities living the high life. People with a lot of money and a lot of fame, just doing things and probably not realizing that there were people like me, so, so far below them wishing they were in their shoes.

It was a stupid sort of daydream at the time. A "what if I could go to that kind of place?" or "what if I pulled up somewhere in that kind of supercar?" Idle fantasies to forget that life sucked, if just for a moment.

Life didn't suck so much anymore, though.

"Ready to go home?" I asked Lucy.

She turned, coat swirling around her, and for a moment clinging to her sides and hips in a way that made my heart skip. "Aren't we home here?" she asked with the kind of dimply smile she always had when she was being cheesy.

I looked past her and to the museum, our home. "Yeah, but not yet," I said. I wouldn't say something like "wherever you are is home." She'd poke me and call me sappy.

"All right. Do you know if the kittens are all right?"

I blinked a few times, navigating through the menus in my augs until I found the status screens for my new cat mecha. They were all green, and the preview windows that showed me what the robots were seeing revealed glimpses of the kittens in the penthouse, playing games and being lazy little shits. "They're fine," I said. "C'mon, food!"

"Food!" Lucy agreed with a cheer. She brought her arms up and made a familiar grabby gesture. With a roll of my eyes I turned around and didn't protest when she jumped onto my back.

"You're not twelve anymore, you know," I said as I grabbed her under the knees and pulled her up.

"I refuse to believe that," Lucy said. "I am eternally youthful and adorable."

I laughed as I carried her out the front of the museum.

Our ride, the Charon Limo-Taxi, was still waiting for us on the roof. It was a bit of a pain getting up there with Lucy weighing me down, especially since she kept complaining about my back-mounted guns digging into her stomach. Not that that was enough to get her to let go, of course.

"All right, now get off," I said as I stopped next to the taxi.

"Not gonna tuck me in?" she asked as she leaned her chin onto my head.

"Nope, but I might drop your skinny ass."

She mock-gasped. "My ass isn't skinny, it's perfect and plump and all that is right in the world."

We got in the back seat, and I gestured for Lucy to give me a minute. "Just need to check something real fast," I said. "Here, play with Myalis." I placed Myalis's little drone on Lucy's lap.

"Are you using super-advanced alien technology to distract me?" Lucy asked.

"Yes," I said.

I flicked through my augs and found a text box to write in. "M. I want to bring Lucy somewhere nice."

I see. What sort of place are you thinking?

Glancing at Lucy from the corner of my eye, I held back a smile. "Someplace with good food," I wrote. "Something fancy."

Understood. There are a few reservation-only places in the region, all within half an hour's driving distance from your current location. Cross-referencing reviews, and dismissing those that were paid for or solicited, then eliminating places with menus that wouldn't agree with either of you leaves you with four options. Might I suggest La Maison des Rois?

I nodded. "Sounds good," I said aloud. "Okay, we're heading out now. What do you want to grab for the kittens?"

"Oh, we should go to one of those nice places, the ones that give you a little toy with your meal. You know, Choking Hazard or something?"

I nodded. That was a favorite of some of the kittens, though mostly for the ads. We couldn't exactly afford that kind of food ourselves. "Sounds good," I said.

Leaning back, I listened to Lucy prattle on about this and that while the taxi took off and led us out of the incursion zone and back into the flows of traffic around New Montreal. We climbed higher and higher, into the nicer, faster lanes usually reserved for people a dozen tax brackets above normal folk.

We started arguing over how to decorate the house. I was almost more keen on low-tech, old-school decor. Nice and square and simple, but Lucy liked things curvier. If I let her have it her way, the place would be colorful and bubbly. It would still look great, because Lucy had an eye for that kind of thing, but it was really not my style. "What if we invite some samurai over?" I asked. "It'll look like a kid's place."

"It'll look awesome," Lucy corrected. "And so what if they think it looks a bit immature? It'll basically be an orphanage."

"Well, yeah, but those aren't cool."

Lucy snorted. "Your idea of cool is graffiti on the walls and, like, a decorative dumpster in the corner."

"That would be kinda cool, in a sort of ironically tasteless way."

"You just know some of the kittens would put actual trash in it," she said.

I crossed my arms. "Grunge is a perfectly acceptable style."

"It's not a style, it's what happens when you can't afford anything nice, but still look good under all the clothes," she said.

"You saying I look good under all the clothes?" I asked.

She nodded. "I'm only with you because of your looks," she said without an ounce of sarcasm.

The taxi slowed to a stop behind a really fancy car, some fire-red Italian thing that looked fast while standing still. Lucy started to look around, but by the time she knew to start searching for clues we were pulling down and onto the pavement on a covered driveway built into the side of a skyscraper. It was near the topmost floor too, one of the bigger ones. The restaurant looked like it took up most of the floor, which was something I'd come to appreciate the cost of a little more in the past few hours.

"Um?" Lucy asked.

I grinned. "I thought we could grab a bite, you know, before grabbing burgers for the kittens."

Lucy looked out the windows. Some men in nice suits and women that had to be models were waiting in a line to enter, a serious-looking man at the door checking them off on a floating tablet. "This place looks a bit extra."

My grin wavered a little. "You'd rather go somewhere else?" I asked.

Lucy hesitated, eyed me, then smiled back. "Nah, this is fine. Wish I'd come dressed for the occasion."

"You look fine," I said.

"You're biased."

I jumped out of the car and ran around the back to open the door for Lucy and to give her a hand out. She giggled at the gesture and stretched. Our little taxi was fancy, but it was outfancied by all the rides parked around the multilevel parking machines on the other side of the driveway.

It was one of those with glass sides so that people could gawk at everyone's hundred-million-credit supercars.

I entwined my fingers with Lucy's, and we skipped up the steps to the front. "Do we have a reservation, Myalis?" I asked.

Of course.

"Cool!" I said as I walked past all the fancy sorts and up to the waiter-guy at the front. "Yo!" I said. "Reservation for Stray Cat and Lucy," I said.

The man paused in the act of talking to someone important-looking. "Um, the line is right there, ma'am," he said.

The dude in front of him, some chubby guy in a suit with a New Montreal pin on his lapel, glared at me. "Rather rude," he said.

"I've been called worse," I said. "So, we got seats?"

"Ma'am, you're supposed to wait in line," the waiter said.

"I don't do great with lines," I explained.

The man nodded. "I understand. La Maison des Rois can be a very exciting place. Nonetheless, regardless of status, we ask that all of our guests have the common courtesy to wait their turn. Please."

I pouted and Lucy giggled, but the guy was right. So I went to the back of the line and pretended not to notice some folk smiling at the bit of drama.

"You're an idiot," Lucy said.

"I thought we could cut in," I said.

"This isn't some cinema," she said. "It's a proper fancy place."

"Yeah yeah, laugh it up. We'll see if you think it's all that when you can't read the menu on account of its fanciness."

CHAPTER FORTY-NINE

BEING HELLA FANCY

Friendship is what we do here at Broccoli's.

You want naughty dragons? You want cures for your hysteria? Marital aids? We don't know why our new friends want that kind of stuff so bad, but we have it for them!

Our inexpert staff will try their very best to help you have the most fun you can possibly have! All while staying nice and safe. Don't forget to use your friend's rebate!

—Ad for Broccoli's, an exotic toy store, 2025

I'd eaten at restaurants before. Who hadn't?

The problem was, most of the time . . . all of the time, those restaurants were cheap little places, with shitty plastic benches angled so that no one would sit on them too long, and hundred-credit menus filled with near-foods that somehow managed to taste as real as they were but were also really addicting.

Those places weren't this one. Hell, I couldn't even pronounce this place's name without sounding like I was pretending to be fancy.

"This way," the waiter said as he led us through the main floor. There were tables here and there, each with a bit of space around them, and walls on three sides with opaque glass and what was probably real wood as trim.

There were plenty of people, which might have explained the line out front. This place had enough room for twice as many tables if they were willing to squish people in a little, but no, everyone had a nice chair and like, a candle.

I felt entirely out of place.

Lucy bumped her shoulder against mine, and I looked over to see her smiling coyly at me. She knew, of course.

"Right over here, misses, watch the step," the waiter said as he brought us up a little platform and to a round table with two seats, one on either end. It was small, not too small, but enough that we would almost be bumping knees.

I swallowed and jumped ahead to pull out a chair for Lucy.

She went to the other side and pulled out her own chair.

I saw the waiter's lips twitch as I tried to save face and plop myself down across from Lucy.

"Your menus are here," he said as he placed two booklets down. Physical menus? Weird, but all right. "If you are curious about anything at all, do ask. Ring the bell and I shall be with you within moments."

"Right, thanks," I said as I kinda gestured aimlessly in his direction. He bowed again and stepped away, disappearing around the corner a moment later.

There's a privacy field around your booth. Low-level electromagnetic interference. Not enough to stop any really advanced listening devices, but a nice touch.

I almost jumped at Myalis's intrusion. I sent her a quick text, just in case she couldn't read the mood, which, as smart as she claimed to be, I didn't doubt that Myalis was able to miss some signs. "This is a date, M. Don't do M things."

Well, I suppose I can remain quiet and merely observe your fumbling. Do enjoy.

I tried not to let my frustration show as I grabbed one of the menus and opened it up. It was bound in leather, with the restaurant's name stamped onto the front. Each page was some sort of thick, soft material and it looked as if the items were written by hand. But by someone who knew how to write really well.

"This is hella fancy," Lucy said.

"I know, right?" I asked. "Is this how rich people eat all the time?" I glanced at the first item. The page was for . . . avent-gouts, whatever those were. The first thing on the list, which was in alphabetical order, was Anemone of the Sea, for the low, low price of twelve thousand credits. "You could rent an apartment for a week at that price," I muttered.

"Are you looking at the, uh, first-page things?"

"Yeah," I said.

"That'd be a really crap apartment."

She was right, but still. "Yeah, but it'll last longer than however long it takes to eat this," I said.

Lucy laughed. "You're the one that wanted to come here," she said.

I looked away. "Well, yeah, I guess."

Her leg poked mine. "You okay?"

"Huh?" I asked. "Yeah, it's just, I don't really know what to say?"

Lucy stared for a long moment, and then she started to laugh. Big guffaws interspersed with little snorts, and I was pretty sure her legs were thumping the floor below. "Oh, Cat! You're cute."

"What?"

Lucy just shook her head and reached across the table. Her fingers wiggled until I gave in and entwined my hand in hers. It was a good thing I had a second hand now, I could still hold on to the menu. "So, once we're settled in, what do you want to do?"

"Uh, I don't know," I said. "Samurai stuff, I guess."

"That makes sense, yeah. I think . . . I want to go to school," she said. "Like, not an online one, but an actual school."

"Really? That's . . ." I cut myself off before saying "weird." "Not something I expected."

"It's a bit weird, right?" she asked. "Oh, they have this plate that's nothing but teeny-tiny burgers."

"Yeah," I said. "Why do you wanna go to school? I mean, what kind of classes do you want to take?"

"I think it's partly me just wanting to see what that's like, but I wouldn't mind taking classes to become a teacher. Or a caretaker. Do you need a degree for that?"

I shrugged. "Probably," I said. "We could figure something out. The museum is in the middle of the city, kinda, I bet there are a bunch of schools nearby."

Lucy smiled and pulled up her menu. "So, what are you having?" she asked.

"Uh." I looked down, and my eyes glazed over at all the weird words. They had too many accents and marks on them to be real words. "I have no idea," I admitted.

Lucy laughed and squeezed my hand a bit. "Maybe ask for whatever's most popular? It can't be that bad if they're serving it here, I figure."

"I wonder if the spoons are made of actual silver?"

"Should we steal them?" Lucy asked.

I nodded. Definitely. A glance around, at all the woodwork and the marble statues and . . . if my four ears weren't mistaken, what was an actual pond near the side of the room, had me feeling as if I'd just snuck into some forbidden place. But Lucy was there, so it wasn't all bad.

"Do you think people would be scandalized if we started making out?" Lucy asked.

"Uh," I said.

Then the waiter returned with a well-timed clam-jam. "Hello, ladies, have you chosen?"

Lucy nodded and pulled her hand back so that she could hold up the menu and point at things on it. "I'll have one of these. And I don't know what this is, but it sounds good. Also, do you have caviar? Does it actually taste good?"

"I can assure you that ours is only the highest quality that can be obtained, and it is prepared by only the finest chefs," the waiter said.

"Awesome. Can we wait until after to order more?" she asked. "I want to be rolled out of here."

"Certainly," he said with a bow. "And for you, miss?" he asked me.

A glance at the menu didn't help any. I hadn't exactly been focused on reading. "Do you have some sort of . . . meal thing? Like, it's set up already?"

"We do. Might I suggest the international meats platter? It has seven varieties of meat from all of the best farms around the world, prepared in seven distinct, local fashions. It's a little heavy but quite popular."

"That sounds perfect," I said.

Lucy and I handed him our menus, then ordered some drinks. Really, it was just water. It didn't feel right to order energy drinks to go with the caviar.

"So," Lucy said once the waiter was gone. "Why this?"

"What do you mean?" I asked.

She gestured around at the fanciness around us. "I don't mind it, it's kinda cute, but why?"

I shifted a little. "It's going to sound stupid," I said.

"Mm-hmm," she agreed. "But I wanna hear it."

I tried to be angry, failed, then rolled my eyes. "I wanted to treat you to something nice. You know, like . . . we never actually went on a date."

"We've been on plenty."

"Going to the corner store together or stealing from an automated burger joint doesn't count as dates," I said.

"Sure they do!" Lucy said. "They were the best dates."

"Maybe, but I wanted to bring you to a place like this," I said. "It's uh . . ." I looked for something to do with my hands while fighting the creeping warmth of a blush.

Lucy giggled and placed her hand on the table again for me to grab. "You're such a softy."

"I'm not," I said.

"You are."

"Bitch, I kill things," I said in mock indignation.

Lucy laughed at me.

I was saved, quite fortunately, by the arrival of the first course and our drinks. I had the impression that Lucy wasn't done teasing me, but at least for the moment there was good food to keep her busy.

CHAPTER FIFTY

SALAD

It's not just fine dining that changed with the arrival of the Antithesis. The first incursions popularized the purchase of long-lasting nonperishables, for good reason, but that had little impact on the worldwide market for food.

The biggest change appeared in 2023, during the central-Brazilian incursion: an incursion with few civilians dead but one that landed quite close to some of the country's largest agricultural areas.

Nearly one hundred million head of cattle perished during, or shortly after, the incursion, and with fears about possible biological weapons around incursion zones, the worldwide market for beef took a large downturn.

Shortly thereafter, large food conglomerates switched to using synthetic meats in full, something that had only been experimented with before that.

—Excerpt from *You Aren't What You Eat*, 2032

Lucy ate her salad while making these little noises that were—quite frankly—making me a bit jealous. I'd never heard her sounding so . . . pleased before. Ever.

Was I being outdone by a salad?

"This is so fucking good," she said, mouth still full. "How's your thing?"

I looked down at my plate and at the seven circles spread out across it. Each one had a little piece of meat, with some sauce expertly drizzled on it, and a little side of vegetables or greens or . . . stuff. I'd eaten one of them so far, a sort of slab of pork that was so soft that it came apart as soon as my fork (which was in fact silver) touched it. The other six were all different, but for the most part each was pretty small. "It's good so far," I said as I turned the large plate a little bit.

"This isn't even the main course and I'm loving it," Lucy said. "It was a good idea to come here. Cat, you need to find out if this place would sponsor you so that we can eat this every day."

I snorted. "I don't know, it sounds like a bit of work. Won't the fun wear off?"

"Sex is a lot of work, but it's never worn off, I can't see how this is any different," Lucy said.

"Should I be worried?" I asked. "You and that salad . . ."

Lucy nodded. "You should be. If this salad had an ass as nice as yours . . . well, sometimes a girl has to make difficult choices in life."

I *was* being outdone by a salad. That was effeminating.

I jabbed at some sort of brown meat. There was no way to know what it was, but it was juicy and soft and tasted stupidly good. "Mmm," I started to say before I swiped the back of my hand across my mouth. "So, you think I should do the sponsor thing?"

Lucy tilted her head as she considered it. "I guess? Isn't that what samurai do?"

"I mean, some of them have to be sponsorless," I said.

She shrugged. "I guess. Just figured that's the way you'd go. It's basically free money, right?"

"Yeah. Don't know who I'd accept as a sponsor, though. I wouldn't just slap on anyone's logo."

"Can you imagine doing a commercial for like, Pear headphones, and then the week after you learn that they're using child labor again," Lucy said. "Oh, which company was it that had concentration camps with like, minorities working in factories?"

"There's like, six," I said.

"Urgh," Lucy said. "Right, so you don't want to work for one of those. Probably get Myalis to look into whatever corp you end up working with."

I grimaced. "I don't know. I don't want my face on a cereal box. Or like, someone's underwear or something. It's too cringey."

Lucy giggled. "I love you, Cat, but I wouldn't wear you-themed panties, no matter how much you paid me."

"I know," I said. "Maybe like . . . uh, I hate myself for thinking this."

"Ohh," Lucy cooed. She leaned forward. "Tell me, tell me!"

I rubbed at my brow. "I could be sponsored by one of those companies that do animal products."

It took a moment for Lucy to catch on. "Oh, like a cat food company?"

"Not cat food! Shit, that's worse than having your face on cereal."

Lucy grinned. "Give your kitty some Cat, the best-tasting pussy food around."

I flung a napkin at her and she laughed. "You're awful," I said. "That wasn't even a double entendre. It was like . . . a single entendre."

"It's the salad." Lucy took another bite. "It's making me feel things I've never felt before."

I laughed and picked up a knife to cut into some sort of fish-looking thing. "Do fish count as a meat?"

"If plants can count as meat, why not?" Lucy asked. She finished a bit before me, then stole a few veggies from my plate until I finished. The moment I was done, the waiter returned and took our plates away and brought us fresh water.

Then he returned with dessert.

"Oh," Lucy said as she looked down upon a thick wedge of cake that wouldn't be surviving the next few minutes.

I laughed and picked away at my own dessert, some pie that sounded fancy and that tasted pretty good. "So, uh." I hesitated a bit. What could we talk about? I didn't want to go into anything heavy, not if it meant ruining the moment. "Did you ever want to try, like, new hobbies or something?" I asked.

"New hobbies? Like what, knitting?"

"No, no, like . . . I don't know. What do rich people do for fun?" I asked.

"Golf?" Lucy asked. "Eat *really* good salads? Hire whores? Mock the poor and downtrodden?"

I laughed. "Okay, so not that. I don't know, but right now we don't need to focus so much on . . . you know, surviving. We can do other things for fun."

"I do want to buy a tennis outfit," Lucy said.

"You want to try tennis?" I asked. That didn't sound very Lucy-like.

"Hey, I've got bouncy legs now. Also, you get to wear those really short skirts." Her eyebrows wiggled at me. "And then you get all sweaty."

I swallowed a bite of my pie. "Yeah, uh, I'm sure we can find something. I think I might get into shooting."

"Shooting? Like trying to hit things with bullets?" Lucy asked. "Don't you already do that? You know, samurai and all?"

"Yeah, my aim is . . . bad. Awful bad. Myalis keeps mocking me about it. But so far I've been pretty much pulling the trigger and hoping for the best most of the time. I'd like to actually learn how to aim."

"Wow," Lucy said. "That's terrifying." She smiled. "You're so incompetent."

"Hey!" I said.

We finished our desserts, then slumped back. The meals hadn't been too big, but they were enough that I was feeling full. Lucy kicked her feet up under the table and managed to only just place them on my lap.

I felt like I could almost fall asleep. There was a faint bit of music playing in the background, nothing too exciting, but a nice lilting song on some string instrument that was accompanied by the clink of glass and utensils. I twitched my new ears and fiddled with their controls. Soon, that music was accompanied by the steady drumbeat of Lucy's heart.

"Do the ladies require anything?" the waiter asked.

I jumped a bit, having entirely failed to notice him. "Oh? Uh, no, I'm good," I said.

Lucy pulled her feet back and sat up straighter. "Me too," she said. "We should probably head out soon."

I reluctantly agreed.

The waiter nodded. "In that case, here is the check." He placed a piece of paper on the table, then bowed and left.

I pulled it over and winced at the number. There was a barcode next to it, to scan and send the money over via electronic transfer.

"Bad?" Lucy asked.

"Huh? Nah, just forgot that I can afford these kinds of things now." I got up while my augs worked out how to pay.

I'll take care of it.

I nodded and reminded myself to thank Myalis later as I moved around the table and helped Lucy up. She leaned against me, arms hugging mine close.

"Let's go home."

"Home?" I asked.

"To the kittens," she said. "We need to pick something up for them."

"Yeah," I agreed.

I made a note for Myalis to see, telling her to tip the waiter appropriately, and then I walked side-by-side with Lucy, all the way out front where our taxi was just pulling up to the curb.

Opening the back door, I waited for Lucy to get in, but instead she paused, turned around, and climbed to the tips of her toes to plant her lips against mine.

She tasted like cake and sweetness and Lucy . . . and maybe that salad. Damn, it was a good salad.

"Think we can fuck in the car?" she murmured.

I felt myself flushing a bit, even as I tried to hold back a grin that was no doubt a bit goofy. "Let's find out," I said.

INTERLEWD TWO

I barely took in the interior of the cab, too busy wrestling Lucy's tongue with my own as we slid into the long back seat.

"Greetings, honored customers," the taxi said. "Was your meal satisfactory?"

"Mmh," I said. Lucy was scooting toward the middle of the seat, but she still had one hand around my neck and was making sure that my ability to breathe and think was a little on the short end.

We broke apart, for just a moment. "Yeah," I said. "Hotel, bring us to the hotel. Myalis, turn off any observation stuff."

I wish I could turn off my own. There are some things I don't want to see.

I snorted, then was cut off when Lucy grabbed the front of my jacket in a fist and pulled me closer. She was on one knee on the seat, her other leg extended to the floor to keep her at an angle.

I shifted, sitting up properly. "Lucy," I said.

She paused, and panted, her warm breath whispering past wet lips. "What?" she asked.

"Sit?" I asked, patting my lap.

She rolled her eyes. "Softy," she said. "Fine."

I grinned as Lucy shoved over and plopped herself down on my lap. I wrapped my arms around her, pressing her close to my chest. Lucy could call me a softy all she wanted; this, having her in my arms all soft and warm, was the best.

My head dropped to the nook of her neck, and I started peppering her with soft little kisses. I knew that it annoyed her a little. Lucy was always a bit . . . rougher with her affections, and she liked it like that in return.

The taxi started to move, both of us swaying just a little with the shifting momentum. I felt Lucy's rear wiggling a little, pushing down onto my lap as I continued to press kisses into her neck and hair.

"Cat," Lucy whined.

I loosened my hug a little, one hand slipping under the stealth jacket I'd given her. It was warm under the coat. I pressed my hand over her stomach, then up until it was atop a breast. I squeezed, just a little. Lucy squirmed some more.

"For fuck's sake, Cat," she muttered. "I wanted to fuck, not just some cuddles."

"Cuddles are important," I said.

Still, I could accommodate a little. Lucy was always very straightforward about what she wanted. It was one of the things I loved about her. She could play coy too, but it was always easy to read through.

This kind of kissing and cuddling and hugging, it just got her worked up, which might have annoyed her, but it always made things a lot more fun later.

Lucy pushed back into me. "Cat," she muttered.

I reached my free hand lower, passing over her belly and down toward her crotch. Lucy was quick to undo her belt for me, and I chuckled as she shifted and raised herself up a little. I reached my hand down, into the warm interior of her pants, then paused.

"Cat, come on," Lucy said.

I nuzzled the collar of her coat aside and nibbled down on her neck. She gasped, chest heaving out a little. I squeezed a bit harder as I started peppering her with kisses again. My other hand dipped lower. I could feel the soft, synthetic cloth of Lucy's panties, the band on the edge elastic and springy. I hesitated a little before moving my hand over the panties rather than in.

Lucy leaned to the side and turned her head so that I could better kiss her.

My searching fingers dipped down between her thighs and over soft warmth. I caressed something velvety and damp. "Wet already?" I asked.

She giggled. "It's the salad, I swear."

I laughed and pressed another big kiss onto her cheek. "That damned salad," I said as I started to move my hand up and down in a long, oval motion.

Lucy took a deep breath and shifted a bit, legs open wider and back arching just a little. She was like a cat pressing into a petting hand. I continued the motion absently while fondling her breast with my other hand.

She had great breasts. I could say that with no bias at all.

"Having fun?" Lucy asked. Her voice had dropped a little, becoming more sultry.

"Mm-hmm," I said. "I'm just contemplating how lucky I am to be able to play with these." I squeezed again.

"You're just playing with the one," Lucy said. "The other's going to get all lonely."

"I'll kiss it better later," I said. My fingers continued to trace little circles, sometimes pushing in a little deeper. Lucy might have been acting a little casual about things, but I could tell she was really starting to get worked up.

Not that I could blame her. I'd gotten nothing more than a few good kisses in, but I could already feel my underwear sticking to me. There was an aching, tingling sensation in my core, a want that had my heart thumping just a little faster. Feeling Lucy sitting on me, all soft and warm, only made it worse.

There was always this sort of . . . zap, when things started getting steamy. It was this sensation that started in my toes and raced up my back. I knew that my face was a little on the warm side, my ears burning up.

It was nice, it was hot, and it left me feeling . . . empty? Like something was missing. I wanted Lucy to grab my ass the way she always did, I wanted her to squeeze my breasts and press her tongue into my mouth, I wanted to feel her fingers slipping into me.

At the same time, the moment before all of that fun happened, the moment we were in right now, with me slowly teasing Lucy, that was the best. I could hear her heart beating wildly, felt every shift of her hips on my lap as she got worked up. She was getting more and more wet and that felt great too.

Maybe I was weird, but I imagined that need that she had, the same emptiness for something that I felt, and I imagined that she wanted *me* to be the one to fill that emptiness. She needed me, she wanted me, and of course, I was there for her.

It was probably a bit creepy to think that way. It was why I never really told her. Lucy was a lot more straightforward about that kind of thing than I was.

"Oh fuck, the food," Lucy said.

I snorted, then laughed, a cold wash moving down my spine and pushing back some of the fog. "Right, I forgot," I said. "Uh."

Lucy turned a little and looked up to me. She was a little flushed, though it was hard to tell on her darker skin. "Do we have to stop to grab something?"

"My hands are already full," I said.

She jabbed me with an elbow. "Idiot. I mean . . . fuck, can we just order something?"

"Yeah," I said. "Myalis?"

Yes?

"Food, for the kittens? Like, don't blow our budget. I . . . just, like, burgers and stuff."

How succinct. You know, it's not my job to help you order fast food for your charges, right?

"Please, Myalis," I asked.

For some reason, I could imagine the AI rolling her eyes.

The sacrifices I make.

The taxi banked, and the world outside went dark for a moment even as we slowed down. "We're here already?" Lucy asked.

"Oh," I said. I could see the hotel's front door just outside, a valet already moving to open the door for us. "Oh shit."

Lucy jumped off my lap, then arched her back and tugged her pants up to redo the button on the front. There was a certain smell in the cabin now, one that I hoped no one noticed.

The valet opened the door, and I stepped out. I was hyperaware of the wetness in my pants, and I could only imagine that it was worse for Lucy, who followed me out. I shoved my hand in a pocket; my fingers were damp.

We didn't say anything as we crossed the lobby, though Lucy did hang off my arm as we walked, just like she used to when she forgot her crutches before. "Holy shit," she said.

"What's wrong?" I asked.

"It's leaking down the side of my leg; I swear if you don't do something about this I'm locking myself in the bathroom with Mr. Tentacles."

I chuckled, the squirming warmth in my stomach twisting at the thought.

We got to an elevator. It was empty.

The moment the doors closed Lucy shoved me against one wall and got onto the tips of her toes, her mouth jammed against mine even as her hands reached out behind me and started gripping onto my ass so hard it hurt a little. "Fuck, Cat," she said as she broke the kiss for just a moment. "Can this thing move faster?"

The doors opened and we stayed where we were for a moment, at least until we had to break apart to breathe.

I noticed that one of the hotel guards next to the door was red-faced under his little helmet. I'd have been a little embarrassed, but my mind was too foggy for that.

We raced over to the penthouse and shoved the door open. I saw kittens in the living room, a couple of them draped over the large mecha-tigers as if they were huge toys rather than war machines.

"We ordered food from . . . somewhere," Lucy said as she ran ahead of me. She dipped into the kitchen, opened the fridge, and pulled out a pair of water bottles. "We're busy," she said.

I grinned at the kittens, made sure none were dead, noted that Katallina was sitting with Junior on one couch with Catkiller's head on her lap, then waved before moving to the bedroom.

We made it one step in, and slammed the door behind us before we were back to ravishing each other. Lucy flung the water bottles to the middle of the bed while we walked over, mouths barely coming apart for more than a second.

My core was burning, my entire body tingled, only finding a bit of relief whenever Lucy's arms and hands brushed by.

I flung my coat off and Lucy did the same with hers. I was wearing my skintight armor underneath, and it took some squirming to get out of it. We separated for just a moment as we tore our clothes off. I kept an eye on Lucy the entire time, though.

Her old T-shirt flew off to the side, leaving her in nothing but a ratty bra that wasn't quite sized right. She tossed that aside with just a moment spent with her arms bent back.

My boots came off, and then I shoved the bottom half of my suit down my legs. I glanced up and saw Lucy using the edge of the bed to keep balanced as she tugged her pants down. She was trailing juices down the inside of her thigh.

My mind was a little foggy as I stepped up behind her and hugged her close. Skin on skin, so warm it burned. I gasped in the scent of her and she pressed into me for just a moment before she started to turn around.

I pushed her back, catching her forearms as she squeaked and I lowered her back-first onto the bed, her knees right on the edge.

Sliding a foot forward, I pushed her legs aside and fell down atop her, my head landing right between her breasts. "Which one did I miss earlier?" I asked.

"Cat," she protested.

I kissed her breast, then worked a trail of pecks over to the nipple of the neglected breast. I nibbled on it.

"Cat!" Lucy squeaked. She was trying to push herself up farther onto the bed, but I grabbed onto her hips, stalling her motion so that I could leave a trail of kisses down her stomach and across her abs.

She was still wearing panties, the dark gray, store-bought things marred by a proud wet spot on the front. I tugged them down across the soft skin of her thighs.

I dipped in, and slowly, carefully, licked her from the bottom up. There was that familiar taste, the one I'd come to associate with a really good day. Lucy's thighs shifted, squeezing her legs shut before me. It was just something she did whenever she got too excited.

I knelt lower, lifted her knees up, and placed one on either shoulder before diving in again.

A glance up and I saw that Lucy had her eyes closed, her bottom lip bit, and both hands kneading at her breasts. I grinned as I pressed in. Slow and gentle, teasing. Lucy had once described it as starting like a butterfly landing on a flower, and ending like a dog drinking out of a bowl.

I had free hands, so I brought both of them up and spread Lucy open just a little more, and then I started to press circles into her opening with the end of my thumb.

I'd look up every so often, Lucy's face, the way her cheeks puffed, the way her eyes squeezed shut whenever I pushed a finger just a little deeper in, it all made me feel warmer and warmer inside. Hell, I'd once gotten off on just teasing her for long enough.

Her thighs tightened around my head, and I felt her tensing, stomach going taut for a moment even as the flesh around my finger tightened for a bit, almost pulling my finger in deeper.

"Oh, fuck," Lucy whispered.

Not a full-on orgasm, but close.

My free hand dipped down to my crotch. I still had my panties on, but they were easy enough to push to the side.

It was a little like rubbing the top of my head and my stomach at the same time, but I managed.

"Is it my turn yet?" Lucy asked.

"Hmm? No," I said as I came up. "Not until I have you panting for real."

Lucy huffed and spread her legs wider while sitting up. She sat on the edge of the bed, reached under my armpits, and pulled me up. Or, well, she tried.

I gave in with a laugh and climbed down atop her until I was resting over her, my face over hers. "You didn't like it?" I asked.

"No, I just want my turn," she said. She pushed me to the side, and I didn't resist as I rolled onto my back and Lucy climbed atop me. "Mr. Tentacles," she said. "Come over here."

CHAPTER FIFTY-ONE

FASHIONING A HOME

There has been a noticeable shift in style and fashion. Not to say that fashion wasn't changing rapidly already. By the mid-2000s, international communication, the internet, and the easing of travel restrictions allowed fashion from different cultures to come together and be mixed, occasionally homogenized, and often brought to extremes.

Now, this shifting has become so rapid that to stay on top of the latest trends means keeping a constant eye on the fashion feeds and paparazzi rags. A trend can start, flourish, and die in the space of an afternoon.

—Fa-Fa-Fashionista, *On the Evolution of Trends*, 2057

I walked over to the other side of the display and leaned forward to look at the wire-mesh interior. It showed most of the museum—and we'd have to find a better name for our new home soon—in red, with a few sections in green.

Myalis had determined that all of the red sections would need to be replaced and reconfigured sometime soon, preferably before anyone moved in.

"So, this is the final floor plan?" Lucy asked.

I nodded along. "Yeah, I think so," I said.

The floor plan gave us ten double bedrooms, good enough for a pair of kittens each, two bigger dorm-style rooms with a few beds in them for any newcomers, and a main bedroom one corridor over. Not too far that we couldn't run over, but not right next to the kittens either.

The main museum area would be split into a kitchen and dining space, a playroom that was frankly absurdly large, and another little area that could serve as an office or library of sorts for the quieter kittens.

We had one bathroom for every two rooms, with showers in each, and a smaller washroom next to the kitchen. The old vault was right where our bedroom would be, with the rear half of it marked to be replaced by a small armory where I could store stuff.

The outside wasn't going to be touched much. We'd hire someone to remove all the ads and signs, and maybe we'd add a carport over the parking space for . . . well, we'd have to buy a van or something. I'd pick whichever old beater would give Gomorrah the biggest headache.

Lucy nodded. "I like it. We'll have to see about getting nice furniture too."

"I think we can afford that," I said before glancing to the side. We had brought over the Dumbasses, both to guard the museum and to allow us to better communicate with Myalis. It was one of the drones that was projecting the image of the building's wireframe, and another was sitting nearby, waiting patiently. "Have you found any reliable contractors yet?"

"I have," Myalis said. "From looking into their records, I have found three suitably accredited teams with overlapping specialties. I would suggest hiring all three."

"All three?" I repeated.

"Indeed. One has done satisfactory plumbing work on past installations, another has an entire team of electricians, and the final construction company has experience working with both Vanguards and glass-fronted skyscrapers. The other two lack experience in both."

"Ah," I said. So hiring specialists to do the specialist-requiring . . . stuff. I was so far out of my depth. "That sounds reasonable. Do you have an idea of their price range?"

"Seven, nine, and twelve million credits, respectively. That's not including the entirety of the material cost, but I'm assuming some of that will be defrayed by the use of Vanguard-grade materials."

I held back a wince. That was . . . twenty-eight million? An insane amount of money. "So, for the materials, we can't build this whole place with samurai-grade stuff, it'll take way too many points."

"That is accurate," Myalis said. "To purchase enough material directly to rebuild this entire area would cost—assuming you want to purchase quality materials—something close to nine thousand points."

That was a lot lower than I'd guesstimated. "That's just normal materials, or fancier stuff?"

"Materials that are of a higher quality than commercially available, of course. Glass that can resist temperatures high enough not to melt on contact with your local sun and able to resist considerable impacts, hardened plates for the walls and floors and ceilings, doors that read a person's biosignature, temperature-regulating systems, and a few more commodities of that sort."

"Fancy," I said.

"Standard for a Vanguard's abode" was Myalis's reply.

"Sounds nice, but kind of expensive," Lucy said.

The Dumbass that Myalis was speaking out of shifted, and the wire-frame of the museum changed to a hovering image of some sort of confusing machine. It looked like it was the size of a minivan, with a large hopper on one side and a large screen on the other. "This is a Mark II Creation Engine. It takes in raw materials, sorts them by their atomic structure, then fabricates any needed material, components, or items."

"Oh!" Lucy said. "I've seen something like that! It's a big fancy printer. You toss stuff in, and it makes stuff out of it. They have them in some of the really fancy arcologies."

"Where'd you see that?" I asked.

"Media feed" was her quick reply. "How much will that cost, Myalis?"

"Aren't I the one supposed to ask that?"

Myalis bobbed Dumbass up and down. "The first-tier catalog—Matter Reconfiguration Machines—will cost a mere seventy-five points. The second tier costs one of your tokens, as well as an additional four hundred points. The device itself will cost two thousand one hundred points."

"Yikes," I said. "But I can make anything with it, right?"

"Not quite. The device defaults to allowing you to only make anything from a blueprint you have purchased, as well as a host of items that would be considered tier zero. That is, items that require no catalog to make, such as simple tools and basic materials. That extends to things such as cement mixtures, metal structures, glass panels, and other similar devices. Essentially, it would allow the contractors to make all the materials they need."

I crossed my arms and thought about it. It was a damned big purchase. At the same time, if I got blueprints in the future, which were usually a bit cheaper than outright buying something, I could have . . . basically infinite stuff from those blueprints. Bullets and ammo and things that I'd be reusing a lot were a no-brainer. I'd recover those three thousand points in . . . well, last time I'd spent maybe a hundred points on ammo, so it would probably take thirty more incursions before I had a return on my investment.

That didn't quite seem worth it. But I could also get guns and maybe it could be used to make stuff the kittens would need. If I died out in the field, Lucy could use the machine to mass-produce things. Maybe. "Anyone can use it, then?" I asked.

"Anyone you authorize. I can monitor the machine and only allow the contractors to pull materials they need."

"And can you authorize Lucy and the kittens?"

Myalis bobbed the Dumbass up and down. "That can easily be done. Perhaps a ban on the purchase of weapons for the children."

"That's reasonable," I said. I opened a text file and sent a message to Myalis. "Can it run even after I die?"

Are you worried about your charges being able to care for themselves? In either case, yes, it can. I will ensure that Lucy and your kittens are always authorized by your security protocols, even if you die.

"That sounds cool. Maybe we can place it where the armory would be?"

"We'll need another way to get to it, then," Lucy said. "We don't need people walking through the bedroom just to get a hammer or whatever."

"We can add a door to the armory linking back to the main room."

"Shall we continue with the purchase, then?" Myalis asked.

"Uh, yeah, I guess," I said. "Let's . . ." I looked around; we were still in the main museum room. "Let's move over to where the armory will be, that way we won't have to move anything. Also, we'll have a bunch of cash left over, right?"

"A significant amount, though less than half your initial amount."

"Right, let's set some of that aside for decorations and furniture and stuff. We'll need tables and chairs and . . . wait, we can just fabricate those, right?"

"With the correct blueprints, yes."

I rubbed at my nose. That was annoying. "It'll probably be cheaper to just buy normal things, then. Don't need to get a blueprint for a dozen beds."

"Not even our bed?" Lucy asked.

I considered that. A samurai bed . . . "Okay, so we get one bed, but the kittens can sleep on whatever we can afford for a few million."

"Speaking of monetary concerns, the list of requests from companies who sold you this location has come in."

"Oh? Can I see it?"

Myalis connected with my augs and I soon had a list hovering before one eye.

Quantity or Type	Name	Details	Purchase Cost
Blueprint	Anti-Adware Suite	Basic Cyberwarfare Catalog—Protects simple devices from nonauthorized ad intrusion	45
Blueprint	Anti-Spyware Suite	Basic Cyberwarfare Catalog—Protects simple devices from nonauthorized spyware intrusion	75
Blueprint	Micro Acoustic Listening Device	Stealth Catalog—Miniature listening and recording device	25

Blueprint	Clothing Creation Fabricator	Decoy Catalog—System to create clothes from modeled template	1,275
Blueprint	Hard Light Projector	Decoy Catalog—Miniaturized hard light projector for small cosmetic items	720
Blueprint	Decoy Super Aug	Decoy Catalog—A false version of the Vanguard customizable eye gear	260
Item x 35	Nano- Regenerative Suite	Medical Utilities Catalog—A suite of nano machines that circulate through a person's body and fix it rapidly	525
Blueprint	Feline Cat Reflex Augmentation	Sun Watcher Technologies—Reflex-enhancing brain implant	290
Blueprint	Prosthetic Ears	Sun Watcher Technologies—Ear augmentation	285
		Total:	3,500

"Nearly all blueprints, which, all right, and . . . lots of decoy stuff."

"From the bickering I was listening in on, it seems that some companies came together and desperately wanted to buy a clothing fabricator system. I suspect you might cause a bit of a fluctuation in some global markets. Congratulations."

"Wonderful."

CHAPTER FIFTY-TWO

FAB

Fandoms are an interesting social phenomenon. People who enjoy a piece of media or a celebrity congregate together to discuss the things they like. At the onset, this is completely normal human behavior.

What makes the phenomenon more interesting is how modern society's trend toward mass communication allows this communication to spawn new artwork, new memes, and new subgroups. It turns into an echo chamber, where ideas are reinforced and repeated and reiterated upon.

It isn't terribly uncommon for early fandoms to focus on something entirely new, for example a freshly emerged samurai. They will find, research, and dissect any bit of information they can about the new object for their obsession.

This can come as a shock to some samurai. For example, Hairumas, a samurai interviewed in 2034, said, "I didn't expect it. All of a sudden these guys and girls with Afros just kept asking me to sign stuff. It was wild!"

—Excerpt from a *Scientific Yesterday* paper, 2036

"Okay," I said as we reached the vault. It was in about the same condition as I remembered, minus the dead bodies. The floor had little pockmarks as if something had eaten away at it, mostly around where I remembered the corpses being. That felt like it had been months ago. "We'll start by paying the corps their due, I guess."

"Huh?" Lucy asked.

"Yeah, Myalis gave me the list of shit the building sellers want. It's all blueprints except for a bunch of nano-regen things," I said. "Think there's a box around here we could dump them in?"

The Dumbass following up piped up at that. "The containers most items come in are stackable. Shall I inform the broker that the thirty-five Nano-Regenerative Suites are ready for pickup?"

"Yeah, sure," I said. "We can leave them at the door I guess, with one of the dumbasses."

"What else did they buy? And what do those nano-whatsits do?"

"They inject these little bots in you that unmess you up. I think that's what I gave you for your MS, right? Crap, I can't remember. Anyway, I guess some rich dudes just want to live longer or whatever."

"Nano-Regenerative Suites can alleviate a lot of the ills caused by aging. Issues with joints, with eyesight, minor stress issues in musculature and in the cardiovascular system. Even an outwardly healthy human has hundreds of very minor issues that can be repaired," Myalis said.

"As for the other stuff they bought . . ." I looked over the list again. "Just blueprints. A lot of clothing stuff from my decoy catalog, some cyberwarfare stuff. Uh, mostly looks like protection stuff."

"I limited the offensive options," Myalis said. "Giving offensive electronic warfare packages to just anyone seemed like a bad idea."

"No shit," I muttered.

Lucy shrugged. "All right, then. So we're buying that big machine that makes stuff?"

"Yup," I said. "Blueprints and nano stuff first, though. Can you not swarm my augs with messages, though? That little chiming noise is a bit annoying."

"Very well."

New Purchases: Blueprints x 8—Various. Nano-Regenerative Suite x 35
Points Reduced from . . . 6,410 to . . . 2,910

I winced at seeing my points total dropping so low.

"The blueprints have been sent. You retain the original, of course. The purchasers have received copies."

"Ohh, so we can make stuff!" Lucy said. "Can I see the list?"

"Yeah, sure," I said.

Lucy grinned. "Okay, so . . . Boring, boring, creepy, oh, is a Clothing Creation Fabricator a thing that makes clothes?"

"Based on a template, yes. I suspect that the corporations purchasing it will be stymied, at least temporarily, by the complexity of the models required to get the machine to function."

"But we have you," Lucy said. "Could I show you pics of cute things, then have you make them with this thing?"

"Certainly," Myalis said.

I rubbed at my temples. "So, let's change up the design of our room a little," I said. "We're going to need, like, a walk-in closet."

"Does it make shoes?" Lucy asked.

"The Clothing Creation Fabricator can, yes."

"A big walk-in closet," I muttered.

We moved over toward the back of the room and where I imagined the armory would be. I never fancied myself much of a gun nut or anything like that. But the idea of having a room in my house entirely dedicated to weapons was kinda hot.

"Right, Myalis, can you place the creation engine right here?" I gestured, raising and lowering both arms as if dropping a big box on the ground.

"Certainly. Let me just verify that the structure can support its weight."

"How big is this thing?" I asked.

"It's approximately two meters long, two high, and three wide."

"Damn, that's big," I said. "We need like, a couple of feet of clearance all around, right? Where's the bit where you dump stuff in?"

"The front, as is the area where materials and items can be picked up."

"Ah, all right," I said. "We can squeeze it in a bit more."

"I have modified the blueprints to your armory and room in accordance with the room required to fit everything in. Is this suitable?" Myalis asked as a wireframe hologram appeared over the Dumbass she was using. Our bedroom was a bit smaller, with a long, narrow room added to the side that was no doubt the walk-in closet. It wouldn't be as big as the penthouse bedroom, but still, it was bigger than any room back at the orphanage.

"That looks great!" Lucy cheered.

I nodded. "That'll do. Okay. Big machine time!"

New Purchase: Mark II Creation Engine

Points Reduced from . . . 2,910 to . . . 335!

The machine took a moment to appear, longer than when I'd summoned . . . anything else. When it did appear, the pause made sense. It was a big, lumbering thing. It reminded me a bit of the front end of one of those moving vans, the ones with a flat front. A large screen took up a decent portion of the front, currently running through some idle animations. To the side was a heavy-looking door and below that a sort of hopper thing with little coasters. It looked a bit like the place where toys would fall out from one of those old coin-operated gacha machines.

"Shiny," Lucy said.

It was pretty shiny, all chrome and rivets and brass-colored knobs.

"To utilize the machine, tap the screen. It will verify your identity, then bring you to the main controls. From there, you can pick the thing you wish to build. The Creation Engine's matter content is currently at optimal levels. In the future, you will need to either add items to be reclaimed or purchase more raw matter through point expenditure."

Lucy stepped up and poked the screen. A digital kitten ran after a rolling ball of digital yarn.

"Did you customize the loading screen?" I asked.

"I may have," Myalis admitted. "I also added a loading screen. It's quite unnecessary."

I rolled my eyes and refocused on the screen. There was a list of options for Lucy to pick from. All of the blueprints I'd just bought to buy the museum, and one labeled "generic materials."

Lucy picked the "Prosthetic Ears" option and scrolled through that for a bit. There were some two dozen options, and the ability to customize those further, from adding color to tweaking how the prosthetic worked. "Do you think I'd look cool with cat ears?" she asked. "Yours are really cute."

"They're embarrassing," I said. I couldn't help but flick them back.

"They wiggle a bunch when you're about to get off," Lucy said without even glancing back.

My more human ears felt warm. "They *what*?"

"It's cute!"

"Dammit, Lucy," I groaned. "You should have told me."

She shook her head, then pointed to the screen. "Pink?" The ears on display were an ear-searingly bright pink, like someone had gone nuts with a radioactive highlighter.

"That's a bit much," I said.

"Yeah, I should go for something that matches my hair," she said before tapping a color-wheel option.

I shook my head. "Are you really getting cat ears?"

"Do you not want me to?" Lucy asked.

I huffed. Me telling Lucy not to do something had never prevented Lucy from doing something she already wanted to do. I couldn't see how that would change now. "It's up to you, I guess. Don't see why you'd want that, your ears work fine."

"So do yours," Lucy said. "I just wanna be on theme."

"On theme?"

"Well, yeah, there's you, Stray Cat, with the tail and the ears and the cat-themed jacket. And then there are the kittens, and then there's me. I'm the only part of the equation that's not cat-themed."

I stepped up and hugged Lucy from behind. "You're such a moron," I said.

"I am not," she protested. Not that she tried to move out of the hug.

I was enjoying the moment when Myalis twitched. "Catherine, you have a visitor."

"One of the contractors?" I asked. Already?

"No. It's Deus Ex."

"Oh, fuck," I said.

"The little laser girl?" Lucy asked as she pulled out of the hug. "Did you have business with her?"

"No, but she's the sort to dump some trouble on me. Come on, let's go see what the pipsqueak wants."

CHAPTER FIFTY-THREE

PALACE

Samurai are incredible. But they are not infallible.
—Two-Slices, June 2023

Deus Ex somehow chose not to act like the little laser gremlin that she was and waited outside for Lucy and me to come and greet her. Maybe it was a courtesy thing. Or maybe samurai didn't step into each other's bases without permission because of . . . common sense or something.

That might make sense, actually.

I opened the front door and held it open behind me for Lucy and the Dumbass that Myalis was currently controlling. Across from me, on the wide surface of the landing area that took up a chunk of our floor, was Deus Ex, the girl sitting on one of her twin laser . . . hover . . . things.

"Yo!" I said.

Deus blinked. "Oh, hey," she said. "New place?"

"Yup, bought it yesterday," I said.

She nodded. "Nice. I have work for you."

I crossed my arms. "You know, most people work up to their requests. Maybe a bit of small talk? Some questions about the family? Polite shit."

"Do either of us care about that?" she asked.

"Well, no, but it'd be nice to pretend."

Lucy waved. "Hi, Deus Ex!"

"Hello," Deus Ex said. "Fine, I guess we can do the small-talk stuff. I need a bit of a breather. And I guess the work's not until tonight anyway."

"What work?" I asked.

Lucy poked me. "You literally just agreed to do small talk first. Come on, Deus! We have vending machines left over. We can grab you something to drink. What do you like?"

"Ah, um, anything, I guess?" Deus Ex said.

I eyed the girl for a moment. She wasn't being as rambunctious as usual.

Then again, last time I saw her she didn't have bags under her eyes either. "Have you been sleeping?" I asked.

"Not since the New Montreal incursion started, no," she admitted. "I'm running on stims. Or I was; they're wearing off. I took a cleansing solution to wash them out. I should be fine by tomorrow."

"You need sleep," I said.

"I do," she agreed. "But until the work is all done, I really can't afford it."

Shaking my head, I moved over to the door and held it open again for everyone to file back into the museum. Deus Ex paused past the lobby and looked around with obvious confusion. "Is that a scale model of an Antithesis?" she asked.

"Yup," I said. "We, uh, don't know if anyone will be picking that up, actually. I think all the valuable displays are long gone, though."

"So you bought an entire museum. That's actually a rather unique home for a Vanguard," Deus Ex said. "I'm sure you could make a lot just charging for tours."

"Ah, actually, we're converting it to a normal home. Well, normal-ish. An orphanage," I said. "You've seen some weird homes?"

The girl nodded. "A couple of samurai live in bunkers dug into mountains. One that I met on the West Coast lives in the Pacific. Really deep underwater. The Antithesis incursions have landed in the ocean before. Those tend to be nastier than urban fights. Lots of biological stuff for the aliens to eat, and you need to fight in three dimensions a lot more."

"Nasty," I said. "I'd rather avoid that, thanks." I didn't exactly have a fear of drowning, but I did hold my breath any time a character was underwater in a movie or game. I couldn't imagine fighting underwater, even if Myalis had . . . okay, she definitely had something to allow me to breathe water.

"It's not bad." She looked around again. "You own the whole building?"

"Just this floor," I said. "And that bit outside, and some passages that are kinda on this floor, and kinda on the floor below. It's a little strange, on account of that museum part being lower than the rest."

"That's not bad. I'd suggest buying out the lower floors sooner or later. Probably not a priority yet. A whole building must be fairly expensive."

"You don't own the place where you live?" I asked.

She blinked. "Oh, no, I do."

"Which city is it in?" Lucy asked.

"It's in space," Deus Ex said with the casual ease of someone saying "It's in the next town over." "Technically it's in low orbit. It brushes Earth's atmosphere, so reentry isn't that bad."

"Wait, you live in fucking space?" I said. No one told me that space was an option.

She nodded. "It's fairly safe. Some Antithesis can get to it, but most humans can't. No one can really spy on my house, and I'd see anyone trying to mess with me coming long before they could do anything. Well, I suppose there are faster-than-light weapons that could hurt my house, but those are usually my specialty."

I was feeling a bit . . . I don't know what the term was exactly. What guys feel when they discover that some Chad has a bigger car, a cuter girlfriend, and a nicer house than they do. I wanted a space palace . . . Well, maybe later.

We moved over to the little cafeteria area, Deus Ex sitting down while Lucy grabbed the Dumbass and brought it before the vending machines to threaten some drinks out of it. I sat across from the littlest samurai. "So, you mentioned a job?"

"Not a job. Work. Being a Vanguard is a job. What we do is work," she said.

"O-kay," I said. "So what's the work?"

Lucy returned with the front of her shirt turned up to form a pouch, which she'd filled with ice-cold drinks. She set them on the table, then flopped down next to me. "Ah, that was annoying. Now my belly's all cold too."

I grinned and tugged her closer so that I could better rub her stomach. To treasure its warmth, of course.

Deus Ex rolled her eyes as she picked out the drink with the most caffeine and sugar from the bunch and popped the tab. "During the last incursion, the one that hit New Montreal, we had some difficulty tracking the landing area for most of the Antithesis pods," she began.

"Don't samurai have great equipment for that?" Lucy asked.

"We do, but it's a bit scattered. It really depends on the city. New Montreal was last hit, uh, I don't know, a decade ago? The system currently in place was built right after that. It's not as good as it could be."

"All right," I said. "So you don't know where every bit of alien goop landed."

"Not all of them, no. Those that fell from high orbit are easy to track. We have overlapping scans of them coming down and can extrapolate from there. Then those in lower orbits were mostly visible from hovercar dashcams and street sonar. So we know where they went too. But it took a while for someone to decide to look into all the footage to make sure we weren't missing anything."

"And you missed something?" I asked.

She nodded. "There are samurai that don't like high-risk work. They tend to come in after an incursion to help with the cleanup stuff. It means killing a few aliens and clearing the sewers and the area around a hive, usually with drones and stuff. They're useful Vanguards, but they grow really slowly."

"But it's safe," I guessed.

"Yeah," Deus Ex said. "I don't like that kind of work. It's not rewarding enough. Maybe half the Vanguards out there become that sort. Anyway, one of them tracked a bit of Antithesis debris to—actually, can I use your drone?"

"Go ahead," I said.

Myalis hopped onto the table with catlike grace. "What do you wish to display?" she asked.

"Oh, it's your AI. Nice. Ah, these maps, and this file, as well as this," Deus Ex said. "Thank you."

"She's more polite to Myalis than to you," Lucy mock-whispered.

"The AI deserves it," Deus Ex said. It stung all the more since she delivered it as a plain fact.

Myalis projected a holographic image of the Earth, then moved in on North America and finally the area we were in. Little black dots hovered in the air, and I recognized Antithesis pods. They were falling slowly toward the city below.

"That's a reconstruction made from hundreds of recordings," Deus Ex said. "Look at this piece."

One pod burst apart when a line of AA fire moved past it. Not through it, though. From the wreckage came something that looked fleshy and that sprouted wings, and that then turned blurry.

"Bad angle?" I asked.

"No. Organic electronic countermeasures. A stealth Antithesis. Maybe a new model. Lower active-combat threat rating, but in this scenario more of a long-term threat. It glided all the way over to . . . here."

The map shifted, showing a red dotted trajectory that went north, shifting here and there so that it was never quite a straight line until, finally, it hit near a small town.

"That's Black Bear. It's a mining town with a population of about three thousand in what used to be the Mastigouche nature reserve. And about three hours ago, all contact with the town was lost. We think there's a small stealth hive growing near there, and we need someone to go blow it up."

CHAPTER FIFTY-FOUR

PHOENIX

It's a polite and accepted fiction that an incursion is defeated when the samurai swoop in and kill the last alien trying to ruin humanity.

The truth is a lot more complex, mostly owing to the mechanism by which our alien invaders function. They adapt. They are not a singular living organism, but a collection of different types of creatures that can evolve and change to best accommodate any given circumstance. These changes are generally fairly slow, but they are fast enough to be troublesome.

The truth was discovered in 2022, when the Ohio incursion returned from the ashes and humanity discovered that the Antithesis could burrow and hide and scheme while we expected them to remain dead.

—William Hart, excerpt from "Essay on the Recursion Factor of Antithesis Incursions," 2028

I leaned back in my seat and stared at the map. The ex–nature reserve, according to the Wikipedia article Myalis brought up for me, was sold to an organization that was all about protecting nature and such. That organization was a shell owned by a mining consortium that immediately set up shop to mine . . . "What the fuck is vanadium?"

Lucy shrugged and Deus Ex blinked a few times. "It's a metal used to make alloys of other metals. Why are you asking that?"

"Says here that Black Bear is set up near two mines. One's a vanadium mine, the other titanium. I know what titanium is."

"Does it matter?" Deus Ex asked.

"Well, maybe it was like, a uranium mine or something? Radioactive Antithesis doesn't sound like something I'm keen on dealing with."

She nodded. "Right. Those are annoying. I really shouldn't argue against doing more research. Anyway, Black Bear is the priority. There's one Vanguard already on the scene, but he's not the greatest when it comes to defensive actions. That's why I wanted to send you."

"Um, I love Cat, but I don't know if she can take on all the aliens on her own," Lucy said.

"It's a stealth incursion," Deus Ex said. "They'll follow different rules. Most big incursions are swarming ones. The Antithesis produce as many creatures as they can and spread out quickly while fighting off whatever resistance they're up against. A stealth incursion is significantly slower. There's going to be a hive, but it will look very similar to the nature around it."

"So why don't we just use some fancy tech to find the hive and carpet-bomb it?" I asked.

"That's . . . exactly what we want to do." Deus Ex stared at the Dumbass still standing on the table, and soon it displayed an image of the globe. Just the hemisphere that we were on. "The incursion is here." A red dot appeared. "So we're going to strike . . . like this."

Blue dots appeared around the red one, forming a circle that went most of the way around it. Then another set of dots appeared closer. Then another. Each set overlapped with the previous one a little, and each new circle was closer to the middle until finally a single dot hit the red dot dead-center.

"Are those bombs?"

"Orbital strikes," Deus Ex explained. "We don't use those in cities. The earthquakes they cause tend to be bad for infrastructure."

"I imagine," Lucy said. "So why do you need Cat if you're going to bomb the place from orbit?"

"It's a strike, not a bombing, technically. And we need Vanguards to protect Black Bear. If the city went off the grid, that means it's being attacked already. They might not even know it yet. The one Vanguard we have on-scene is . . . not very useful for that kind of thing. Basically, make sure the civilians are safe while we bomb the hive, then help with the cleanup after."

"That sounds doable."

"It's the kind of thing that's good for newbies to do. It's not too danger-ous, will get you some points, and it doesn't require that you be too strong."

"Wow, thanks," I deadpanned.

Deus Ex nodded. "You're welcome. You can take Gomorrah with you, if you want. It would be nice to have even more boots on the ground. The military should be rolling in this afternoon to do a full visual inspection of the area."

"Is this common?" Lucy asked. "The whole stealth incursion thing?"

"It can take years to completely clear an area," Deus Ex said. "Even with a lot of Vanguards looking for them, the Antithesis tend to be able to sneak by and form new hives. They're usually spotted as soon as they start, which means we can destroy them quickly, but there's almost always another ready to form somewhere else."

"That's disturbing."

"They're an infestation," she said. "Like cockroaches, but worse. Sometimes they'll hide as parasites in animals for years, sometimes they'll burrow into the ground and wait, other times they'll spit pollen mist in the air that'll be carried a long way with the wind. If you don't dispose of the bodies correctly, then they'll regrow, and if you don't pay attention, they can burst out of an area with a bigger, stronger force than even an initial incursion."

"Damn," I muttered.

"About a quarter of the incursions you hear about are just remnants of an old one that resettled in an area with lots of biomass and that formed a new hive." Deus Ex shook her head. "We're getting better at tracking them. More satellites, more arrays dedicated to spotting them, and more Vanguards overall to do cleanup work."

I hugged Lucy a bit closer and tucked my face in the crook of her neck. She smelled like those fancy shampoos in the penthouse bathroom.

Refocusing a bit, I considered the job. The overall details weren't my problem. Deus Ex just wanted me to pop over to that little town and keep the folk there safe, maybe kill off any aliens that were annoying them. It was . . . not a terrible idea?

It would mean more points, at the very least, and I was running kinda low on those. "Do I get paid for this?" I asked.

Deus Ex blinked a few times, then shrugged and took a swig from her drink before answering. "I guess. You probably won't make many points, so it's fair. Uh, I don't know how much your time is worth."

"A million an hour," I said.

"Okay."

I stared. That had been a joke. Well, part joke, part wild stab in the dark. "Uh, okay, then," I said.

Deus Ex flicked her hand to the side and her empty can sailed through the air and landed dead-center in a garbage can across the room. "I need to get home and sleep," she said. "I might just autopilot my way there at this rate." She yawned, and for a moment it was easy to forget that she was a hardened alien killer.

Then she scrunched her nose cutely, sneezed, and a helmet unfolded out of her collar and covered her head. "You all right?" Lucy asked.

". . . I'm fine. I'll see you tomorrow or something. Get to Black Bear within the next couple of hours, they really need the help."

Lucy and I got up and escorted Deus outside where her big laser hover things were waiting. She stepped onto a little platform between the two, waved at us, then took off. Soon, her little platform was pointing straight up and with a burst of light she jetted off into the sky until I couldn't make her out as anything more than a distant twinkle.

"She's kinda nice, deep inside," Lucy said.

I snorted. "She's a bit nuts."

Lucy leaned in closer. "Are you going to go?"

"It's good credits, and I could use the points," I said.

Her grip around my arm tightened. "It's dangerous."

"Yeah, but everything is," I said.

"Don't be like that, you know what I meant."

I sighed and turned to plant a kiss on her forehead. "I'll be fine," I said. "Promise. Plus, Gomorrah will be there. I think the most dangerous part of the whole thing will be holding back from corrupting her."

Lucy snorted as she pulled me into a hug. "Fine, then," she said before her hands started to wander. "Just come back, okay?"

"Sure thing," I said.

We went back into the museum, and I split from Lucy for a moment to make a call. She had plenty to keep her busy, especially since Myalis was there to help her contact all the contractors we'd be needing to get the place fixed up. At least we had more cash secure for that, or would soon enough.

I searched through my contacts until I found Gomorrah's number. It rang once before she answered. "Cat?"

"Heya, Gomorrah," I said. "What's up?"

"Not very much, is something wrong?"

"Yup," I said. "There's an incursion up north. An hour's flight from New Montreal near some little town. Place called Black Bear. There's a samurai there already, and they're about to go all orbital strike on the hive, but the folk there need some people to keep them safe."

"Are you serious?" she asked.

"Yeah. Dead serious. Wanna come over to my new place? We can chat in person, then head out if you want to. There's more points to be made, and you know, civilians to protect and all that."

Gomorrah took a moment to reply, and when she did, it was with a big sigh. "I'm on my way."

"You're the second best," I said as I hung up. It made Lucy smile. I made sure to send her the museum's address too.

Now I just had to wait . . . and maybe get all of my gear together. I had the impression that things would be a bit more hectic than what Deus Ex implied.

CHAPTER FIFTY-FIVE

MAKING AN ENTRANCE

Post-2020 saw a massive surge of people moving into the cities and new megacities appearing all over the world—a surge that hadn't been seen since the height of the industrial revolution.

Despite that, the small town didn't just disappear. Entire businesses formed that catered specifically to people living in rural towns across the world. They became popular places for the rich to spend their retirement years away from the pressure of the city, and for the lucky few that retired to live out the rest of their lives in relative quiet.

That does not mean that small towns are perfect hamlets of civility. All the issues of poverty, hunger, and the gulf between rich and poor are just as prevalent in these towns, especially in the many, many "corpo-burgs"—corporate-owned towns—that started to appear near larger cities.

—*Commentary on the Shift in Small Town Thoughts*, Tim Butcher, 2038

I gave Lucy a kiss before going. Then, because Gomorrah hadn't arrived yet, I gave her another, then another.

Unfortunately, we were both still dressed when Myalis pinged me to inform me that Gomorrah had landed out front.

"Be careful," Lucy ordered.

I gave her a last hug for the road, pressing her close to me. She fit the way only Lucy did. "I will be," I promised before letting go.

I ducked my ears down flat on my head as I stepped out into the rain, then belatedly tucked my helmet on. Gomorrah had parked God's Righteous Fury right in the middle of our landing zone, the car all wet and sleek as if it were posing for one of those hyper-real commercials. I could almost hear the snobbish narrator telling the audience that they would never be able to afford a car this awesome.

I ran to the passenger side just as the door opened with a pneumatic hiss, then flung my Whisper in the back and placed my new grenade launcher on my lap as I fell onto the seat. "Yo."

"Are your feet in?" she asked as she pressed the gas. We were off the edge before the door had even sealed.

I leaned into the cushions as Gomorrah aimed us into the grayed sky. "So, uh, what's up?"

"You're really not good at pleasantries, you know?"

"Oh yeah, I know, but it's polite to pretend to be nice to your friends," I said.

"Hmph," she said. "Do you have any idea what the sisters at the monastery would say if they saw you calling me a friend?"

"They'd ask who the smoking hot girl you're with is?" I tried.

She shook her head. "If they didn't think I was some sort of saint they'd pull out the ruler and go on about bad influences for an hour."

"The ruler, huh?" I asked. "You should tell Lucy about that, she was always really keen on spanking disobedient girls . . . do you think Lucy could cut it as a nun?"

"No," Gomorrah said. "How is it that we've been together for less than a minute and you're already being a pervert?"

I shrugged. "I've got a very simple mind. Half of it is filled with snark, the other half is loaded up with images of Lucy being lewd. Speaking of which, do you think I could borrow a nun costume?"

Gomorrah made a disgusted little noise. I figured she was actually amused by it all, though. "I'd need to burn it, like how they disposed of unclean things in the past. And it's called a habit, not a costume."

"I'll try not to make a habit of calling it a costume, then," I said.

She glanced my way, and while I knew she couldn't see my smug grin through my helmet, I liked to think that she could sense it.

"Where are we heading to again?"

"Black Bear, I think. Some little mining town about an hour north from here."

A map appeared, superimposed over the rainy city on the other side of the windshield. Our location was a glowing dot, and our destination another. Gomorrah manipulated the yoke and we shifted just a little bit. "An hour north, huh," she muttered.

I only just had time to grab on to my launcher before we accelerated forward and everything became a whole lot heavier for a moment. A glance at the speedometer before Gomorrah showed it shooting past the two hundreds, then the threes, before slowing down in the four hundreds.

"I guess it won't take an hour, then," I said.

"I'd hope not," she shot back. "So, details?"

"Right. Deus Ex was about as enlightening as usual, which is to say, not very. Basically, some stealth aliens settled down near the town. We need to keep it safe until the big guns hit the hive. Probably going to send the aliens running."

"So we'll be playing a defensive game, then," Gomorrah said. "I can work with that."

"Plenty of forests and stuff around too, I think. Means a lot of biomass, but also a lot of stuff that burns."

Gomorrah nodded and then angled us down. I felt my insides trying to become my outsides, and that fancy supper from the night before was considering leaving when she leveled us off about twenty meters over the tops of the tallest trees.

I relaxed. Gomorrah was a good driver. Or was it pilot? It didn't matter, she seemed to enjoy this kind of thing, and she was damned good at it from what I could tell. Her AI probably wouldn't let her crash into a mountain either.

We started to slow down, and I felt the seat molding around me to hold me in place against the pull of deceleration until Gomorrah and I were flying slow enough that the scenery outside was more than just a blur.

Homes zipped past. Little bungalows in neat rows with bigger apartments next to them. A few stores too. Mostly gas stations and convenience stores, but at least one grocery right on the edge of the town.

I tried to recall how many people lived here. It was a tiny enough place that had we still been moving at Gomorrah's preferred speed, we would have likely missed it with a blink.

Flashes of gunfire drew my eye, and I pointed toward the center of town. "You see that?"

"No, what? Ah, I see it."

There seemed to only be two schools in Black Bear, two older-looking buildings built across the street from each other, with decently large fields out back and parking lots filled to the brim with cars haphazardly tucked away.

Weaving through those cars were familiar forms.

Model Threes, running on all fours like a pack of hounds, some leaping onto cars, others slipping around them.

And facing them from behind a row of squad cars were some five or six police officers. They were right before the school's main entrance.

"Damn," I said. "Myalis, can you figure out what's going on?"

I believe so. The protocol in case of an incursion near Black Bear is to resume work until company representatives can verify the veracity of any claims, calculate potential losses, then allocate their employees to shelters. I will note that there are no shelters in the town that meet any major criteria.

"Shit," I said.

In defiance of this, it seems as if the locals have unanimously declared that none of their machinery was functional today, and have sought shelter in the local high school. Company police have acted against this. From their recordings, it seems they were at the school to clear it out when the first Antithesis arrived.

"Damnation," Gomorrah said. She flicked something on her yoke and a dozen crosshairs appeared on the windshield, then zipped around to aim more or less right at the nearest aliens. "Firing."

"Firing *what*?" I asked.

Then the Fury spat out a volley of screaming missiles that spun in the air, realigned with the ground, and blasted the town below, sending fire and concrete and bits of hovercars all over.

"Now they know we're here," she said.

"Shit," I said. "Okay, we need to defend this town . . . the entire town. How many people have made it to the school?"

Unknown. Certainly less than the entire population.

"Right . . . shit, Gomorrah, can you drop me off by the front? There's supposed to be some other samurai here. We need to get into contact. I'll talk to the locals in the meantime. Can you waste a few more of those rockets on any big pack?"

"And then?" she asked.

"I think we need to draw all the civvies to one place and barricade it in. It'll be easier to protect them that way. We can install turrets and mines and shit. Worry about clearing the town later."

"So I'll play air support?" she asked.

"Land Fury somewhere safe if you want," I said. "I'm not your boss. Just not keen on seeing folk die."

The nun nodded and spun us around while lowering the car. The passenger door opened when we were still a meter off the ground.

"Call me if you need me, I'll be farming points the easy way."

"See ya," I said as I stood, grabbed my crossbow from the back, then dropped to the ground to land with a crouch.

The Fury pulled up with a wash of warm air, leaving me alone in front of some half-dozen guys in blue uniforms. "Sup?" I asked. "Hear you guys had an alien problem?"

CHAPTER FIFTY-SIX

SMALL AND IN CHARGE

There are all sorts of reactions to someone seeing a samurai show up, and generally, these reactions will depend on circumstance.

Fear and terror are common among those doing things that are morally dubious. Seeing a samurai show up at an underground human auction is never going to please the organizers.

Awe and worship for those who encounter a samurai on the streets. It's a privileged encounter with a celebrity for most.

And finally, relief, most often felt by those fearing for their lives when a samurai appears and decides that whatever is currently a threat needs to be removed.

—Excerpt from a sociological study on the predictable responses to a samurai's appearance, 2028

I took a deep breath and tried to look confident. Then I recalled that the folk I was dealing with were little better than corporate goons. Worse, they were corporate cops. That was like dealing with a toddler that had taken one or two concussions too many and whose only skill was to figure out exactly how much of a minority someone was or how poor they were before shooting them. I didn't need confidence to deal with these dipshits, I needed a bigger gun.

Walking over to the barricade they'd made with their cars, I stepped onto a bumper, then the hood before jumping over to the other side. There were eight of them, a couple more than I'd counted at first. Mostly men, with navy blue uniforms and bulletproof vests and tacticool handguns and a shotgun or three.

"Which one of you's the asshole in charge?" I asked.

"I am," One of them said. He had a little logo on his shoulder that the others didn't. The police station's symbol, then the logo of the local mining company, then some badge.

"Wrong, I am the asshole in charge now," I said. "How many cops do we have, minion?"

All right, so it was rude and stupid, but the look on the guy's face was worth it, and I needed to cut past the bullshittery as soon as I could.

"Um," the captain—I assumed that was his rank—said. "We have twenty-four officers in this town, ma'am. Seventeen of them are here. We have a squad car down the road with two more on their way in, and four others are at the clinic."

I nodded. "Myalis, I need a map of this place, please." A map appeared. "I like the location label," I deadpanned. The huge yellow "You Are Here" was a bit much. Still, that gave me an idea of what the town looked like. It had a decent footprint, but most of the buildings were on the smaller side.

"Ma'am?" the captain asked.

"Right. The high school's the new rally point. Is there enough room here for every civilian in town?"

"The building capacity is just under two thousand," he said.

"Fuck capacity, I mean how many folks can we cram in here so that they're not in our way while we're trying to save them all?"

One of the officers, a younger woman, cleared her throat. "I think we could maybe move three quarters of the town in here, but it'll be really tight. Some of the classrooms have locked themselves, that would give us more room."

"All right. You." I pointed to one of the cops. "Find the principal, or whoever's in charge of the school. Tell them to unlock everything. I'll be moving all the cars outside around and forming a wall with them." I had the idea from their little barrier. "I'll be giving you guys some turrets too. Find roof access and place them up there; they should auto-target the nearest Antithesis. Do not try to steal my shit, or we'll be having words."

The man nodded and shot off, and the others seemed to untense a little. Good for them, I supposed. Having someone show up and start cracking the metaphorical whip must have been some sort of comfort.

The captain's mic crackled and he pressed a hand to his ear for a moment. I'd need to tap into that later, but I had other things to do first.

"Myalis, I need good turrets. Won't be able to reload them." I eyed the map, then looked up at the school. Two floors, made of reddish brick and with some smaller windows on the second floor. The roof looked to be flat above. "Maybe three of them? We can cover this side of the building ourselves."

That sounds reasonable. I suppose you need turrets that are somewhat mobile and easy to set up?

"Yeah, can't have anything too hard to move."

"Ma'am?" the captain said. "Uh, corporate just gave us orders."

"Orders?" I asked. "And they are?"

"We're to move some VIPs from here to headquarters, then deploy along the walls to protect the building."

I blinked, then eyed the map again. "Is headquarters the one with the walls?" I asked.

"They're anti-rioting walls," the female cop said. "With sonic and water-based weapons. There's a safe house in it."

"A shelter?" I asked. "Myalis, you said there weren't any shelters in this town?"

The safe house she's alluding to is an underground location meant to house approximately twenty people in relative comfort. I do not consider that an appropriate shelter.

"How many people could fit in the headquarters?" I asked.

I glanced across the parking lot and the little sports field on the other side of that. There were some homes in the way, but I could still make out the corporate headquarters. The building was maybe five stories tall, with a wall all around it.

"What do you think, Myalis, is that place safer than this school?"

It is, though not by a huge margin. The defenses around the headquarters are mostly to prevent and subdue riots. While that would theoretically work on a smaller Antithesis model, it wouldn't be effective. The walls might slow an adversary down, though, and funnel them to the main entrance. There is a bit more room across all the floors for more people as well. Fewer supplies, though.

I nodded. "Okay! That's the new plan. Minion captain, tell your company bigwigs that a samurai or three are heading over to the headquarters to protect them."

"Really?" he asked.

"Yeah. You, and you, and you. Run inside, get us some volunteers. We're taking all the food we can get from this place. There's a cafeteria, right? A nurse's station? Yeah, we're taking everything with us. We'll walk over."

"Just us?" the female cop asked.

"Huh? Nah, everyone. Those who can't walk we'll carry. It's like . . . What, about a kilometer?"

It's less than half of that.

"Half that," I corrected. "Pretty sure even a fatass could run that if you scare them enough. I need . . . six cops to help me . . ." I counted those that were left. There were three. Had one of them that I didn't point to run off? Well, whatever. "Okay, we'll need volunteers."

"Only certified personnel can ride in our vehicles," the Minion Captain said.

"What? Says who?" I asked.

"Company policy."

I stared at him. "Minion, did you miss the part where I'm the asshole in charge now?" I pointed to the female cop. "You seem less stupid, I'm promoting you. You're now the Minion Captain."

"Uh, yes ma'am?!" the officer said before snapping a quick salute.

My decision had nothing to do with me liking the look of a girl in uniform.

I nodded and stepped aside, then flicked through my augs until I found Gomorrah's contact info. It didn't even ring once before she answered. "Got everything under control?" she asked.

"Probably," I said. "I'm moving all these people from the school to the corporate headquarters. They have walls and defenses in place already. I'm sticking some turrets onto these cop cars too to keep people safe while we move. How're things on your end?"

"Fine. Haven't made that many more points. One moment."

I heard a distant explosion.

"Still making enough to justify the cost of these rockets. You said there was another samurai in town?"

"Yeah, any sight of them?"

"Not yet. I'll fly over your group once you get them moving. Try not to get people killed."

"Hey now, only people I want to kill tend to die when I try to . . . I'm not actually sure where I was going with that one. Anyway, see you in a bit, just keep the skies clear for us."

I hung up and finally walked into the school, my new minion captain on my heels. The inside looked . . . like a school in one of those shows. A big open hall with a trophy cabinet on one side, and what was obviously student-made art on the walls. There were pictures of graduates and a few banners hanging from the ceiling.

I could almost imagine all the cookie-cutter characters gossiping and doing rural high school shit. Instead, there were dozens of people, some of them looking terrified, others trying to smile and laugh despite it all, and more of them fiddling with their phones or augs to keep distracted. A group of small kids were playing together to one side, making plenty of noise.

"Crap," I said as I took in the number of people I'd actually be responsible for.

Nothing was ever simple.

CHAPTER FIFTY-SEVEN

GREEDY BITS

Sometimes, the greediest thing you can do is to give unto others.
    —*Riches to Rags: A Guide to Corporate Living*

"Minion captain," I began, "why is this taking so long?"

Initially, things had moved pretty quickly. People had started to rush about, the cops barking orders that were repeated by others. There seemed to be a local fire brigade out and about, some twenty volunteers who were helping to organize things, and some others were assisting them too.

I supposed that moments like these were make-or-break for a lot of people.

I had stepped out and, with Myalis's help, bought three cat mecha.

They were useful, mobile, and able to attack and defend fairly well as far as I could tell. That, and we could use them to corral people. They could even "speak" in that they had speakers built in that I could shout at people with.

I had considered turrets, but turrets could have been made by just about any corp out there. They didn't serve to remind people that there was a samurai on the scene, they just said, "Hey, the cops have even more guns than usual," and that was the opposite of reassuring. They also weren't mobile, and while they had more firepower per point, I figured being able to move was more important.

New Purchase: P.U.S.S. Model Y—Security Mecha—Combat Models—Three

Points Reduced from . . . 335 to . . . 35

We'd just need to stay mum about the name.

So, things had started off well. The cat bots were suitably impressive, there weren't any aliens coming around to chow on the civvies, and things were moving.

"Well?" I asked my newly appointed minion.

The policewoman hesitated. "We're nearly done. We were going to just move everyone as one big group, but, ah, we ran into issues?"

"Issues?" I repeated.

She shrugged. "People want to arrive at the headquarters in order of seniority. Others want to make sure the children are safest. There's some fighting upstairs."

I wanted to pinch my brow. "Everyone knows that if we don't get moving soon, everyone here will become alien chow, right?"

She took a moment before nodding.

"Right," I muttered. I stepped past her and into the lobby. "Myalis, can you connect me to the intercom?"

Certainly.

I cleared my throat, and the sound of it carried across the entire lobby. I could even hear it on the floors above. "Okay, everyone. Form a line right here in the lobby, three people thick. Keep your children close, and try to help those you can, we're leaving. Not in ten minutes, not in five. Right now. If I have to come back to pick your sorry ass up later, I *will* be making you regret it."

It took a second or two for people to snap to it, but soon enough we had a line forming up with minimal shoving and pushing.

"All right! Let's move," I said.

I took the lead, and noticed the cops running ahead a bit and forming something of a cordon. One of them had already moved some of the cars that would be in our way.

The cat bots paced along the sides, glowing mechanical eyes glaring out at the town and back-mounted guns shifting around.

"Minion captain, take the lead," I called out to the policewoman before stepping to the side when we reached the field behind the school.

The line stretched back a ways. It wasn't exactly inconspicuous to have that many people walking along, and there was plenty of coughing and a murmur of nervous conversation, but no one was screaming or shouting.

I wasn't going to jinx myself by saying that it was going well, but so far, I could see the plan working.

A hum from above had me looking up to see Gomorrah's Fury hover near the school's roof. I waved her way, but doubted she'd noticed.

If anything came up, she could tell me about it. Or just bomb it from the air. Either one would be helpful.

I felt something like a fist in my chest, twisting just under my ribs. Stress, maybe? I'd heard all about that before. The corps hated it when some rando employee got too stressed and showed up at work with a 3D-printed assault rifle, so there were tons of shitty ads about dealing with that kind of thing.

I eyed the people moving in, then started following after the head of the group. So far, no aliens. I could live with that.

"Minion captain," I said as I caught up with the policewoman. "When everyone is in the headquarters, we'll need to keep them all calm; think your force will be able to handle that?"

"NeoPinkerton subjugation officers all have to take preemptive de-escalation classes," she said. "We should be able to handle a few rowdy people."

"Uh-huh," I replied. "Just settle people down, reassure them that there are samurai around who are eager to kill some xenos, then share whatever food and water you have. Maybe Myalis can set up a livestream from Gomorrah's Fury. Seeing the aliens get turned to giblets might calm people down."

"I . . . don't know if everyone would be calmed down by that kind of thing," she said.

I shrugged. "It would work on me."

Being at the front of the crowd meant that we were the first to arrive at the headquarters.

The building was one of those places designed to look good on a pamphlet. The front had this big cement pillar, curved in at an angle and with a skeletal framework wrapped around it. All of that covered in mirrored glass. I could only-just make out the fountain in the middle of the space beneath, some modern-art statue that looked like nothing and that probably had a descriptive plaque welded to it with text written by some wordy English major.

It was an entirely meaningless shape, surrounded by architecture that was just as useless.

The rest of the building was good old brutalist. Square and plain. I much preferred that kind of look. You could always trust a square.

The fence around the building was decorated to look a bit less like a fence, with curvy bits of metal on the outside and spiked bars above instead of barbed wire. The gate, though, was just a massive slab of steel, one that was slowly opening as we approached.

There were weapon emplacements all along the fenceline. Mostly sonic weapons. There were more conventional kinetic weapons within.

A glance inside revealed quaint little statuettes at even intervals along the inside. They had benches next to them, and little water fountains for drinking. I'd bet a couple of credits that those were to hide the guns they'd use on anyone dumb enough to riot.

A man ran out of the compound in full gear. Armored chestpiece and hard plastic plates over his arms and thighs. He even had a half-visored helmet on. "Hello," he said as he came closer. "Are you the samurai?"

"I'm one of them," I said. "There should be three of us here. Gomorrah's in the muscle car. No clue where the third one is."

"And you want to bring all of these employees into the headquarters?" he asked. His jaw set.

I sighed. There was the trouble I was expecting. "Yeah. Looks a whole hell of a lot safer in here."

The corpo cop paused. "Very well. We have authority from the higher-ups to allow any citizen of Black Bear into the headquarters. As long as they stay out of certain areas and remain calm, there shouldn't be an issue."

"Stay out of what areas?" I asked.

"Research and Development on floor three, the server rooms in the basement, and the NeoPinkerton armory on the first floor. We're collapsing cubicles on most of the office floors to make more room already."

"Oh," I said. That sounded . . . reasonable. "Well, okay then. I'll be leaving three of my mecha-cats with you guys. They should help if any aliens break past the walls, which they might."

The man nodded. "Thank you. We could use more AA support. The best we have are a few anti-drone countermeasures on the roof, but that's the best we've got against flying targets."

"Uh, I'll talk to Gomorrah, then."

You seem confused.

I nodded to the cops, then tapped the side of my head in the universal "I'm on a call" sign before backing away. The civvies were already filing in, escorted by a few more guards in armor who ran out to funnel them into the headquarters.

"I was expecting . . . corpo fuckery," I said.

Humans can be vindictive, needlessly cruel, and can lack empathy at the worst times. But they are generally quite good when it comes to doing what they think is in their best interest. Sometimes that math works out to meaning that the best thing to do in any given moment is to help those they can as best they can. In this case, some of the administrators of this company judged that assisting their workers would mean that those same workers would be able to return to work sooner, and with less ill will against the corporation as a whole.

"Thanks," I said. "It really helps when you point out where the greedy bits are in all of this."

You're welcome!

CHAPTER FIFTY-EIGHT

GIMMICK

Not all samurai have a gimmick, but nearly all of them do. These sometimes form from necessity or preference. A samurai adopting a certain kind of weaponry might specialize in that. Others prefer taking a certain role, and will purchase equipment according to that.

Still others will find a theme and, over time, will push and develop that to its sometimes illogical extreme.

—Fa-Fa-Fashionista, *On the Evolution of Trends*, 2057

"Cat?"

I jumped a little at the sound of my name. It didn't take much more than a second to place the voice, though. Gomorrah, talking to me through my augs. "Yeah?" I asked.

I was stationed just outside the headquarters in the middle of town, watching the last of the civilians running over. A few other families, and the rare single person, had been joining the file of people filtering into the big building behind me.

That meant that there were probably still hundreds of people in the town. I'd need to figure out a way to gather them all up and bring them over to the headquarters. Easier said than done, I figured.

"Cat, I found the third samurai. He's livestreaming things from the east end of town."

"Seriously?" I asked.

"Yeah. That's where the Antithesis are mostly coming from. It's probably for the best, actually; the headquarters isn't too far from the eastern edge of the town, so anyone who wants to find cover will have him between them and most of the aliens."

I nodded along. "We still need to let people know."

"I've been working on it," she said.

"Really?"

"Do you think I've been sitting up here enjoying the Fury's AC and twiddling my thumbs? Atyacus and I broke into all the televisions and phones and augs we could reach in Black Bear and have been directing people over to the company headquarters. I might have to swing around to escort some of the groups closer to the edges, they're too far to be able to run over here."

"Right," I said. It was easy to forget that I wasn't the only samurai around. "So now what? We sit pretty and snipe at any aliens coming our way?"

"I was thinking you could head over to our new samurai friend. We both know how great you are at making nice with people," Gomorrah said without a hint of sarcasm. She was pretty good at the whole deadpan thing, though.

I nodded along. "Fair enough. It'll mean being closer to the action too. I'll leave my cats here to guard the headquarters. Worst-case scenario, none of us should be too far away. Do you think Atyacus and Myalis can work together to keep an eye on the civvies?"

"They should be able to manage. Especially if your drones are around to see any Antithesis before they cause any trouble."

"Right, then." I shifted my shoulders and looked about. Most of the civilians on the street were running over. The last of the line had filed in and only the stragglers remained. The cops had mostly gathered out by the front of the headquarters, some of them were passing out riot armor and shotguns and such. They were gearing up for a protracted siege. I'd bet there were a few folks in the headquarters who would be willing to volunteer to man the walls, as it were, but so far there hadn't been all that many aliens to deal with.

"I had some time to look things up. In situations like these, with a stealth hive, there tend to be some patrols of lower-level Antithesis on the fringes. Then a lot more stronger ones closer to the middle of the hive. We might have trouble later."

"Would they even come this way?" I asked. "Sure, there's people for them to eat, but that's it. Aren't trees and grass and shit like that on the menu too?"

Myalis was the one that replied.

The Antithesis tend to prioritize things. First taking out any threats, then subsuming any local biomass that isn't dangerous. It's why they tend to attack people in an area first before focusing on retrieving bodies and other sources of biomass. A stealth incursion tends to function under similar rules, though with a much greater degree of restraint and subtlety.

"Can't say I'd call the Antithesis subtle about anything," I said.

They might surprise you, then. And that surprise may well be deadly. I would encourage you to be more careful than usual, but your usual level of care is nearly nonexistent.

I snorted. "Fine. Gomorrah, I guess I should head out and meet our new friend first. Maybe we can create a barricade or something to stop the aliens from coming this way."

"Our goal is to kill them, not just keep them out of the town," Gomorrah said.

"We can go around murdering them after the town's properly secured," I said.

"That's fair, I suppose. I'll be moving around and watching over the last civilians. Keep in touch if you see anything strange, or, God willing, a miracle happens and you have a good idea."

"Thanks," I muttered in reply. "If you're done being snippy, I'll let you go."

"Are you admonishing *me* for being snarky? It's half your personality."

I huffed. "Yeah, it's my gimmick. Yours is being a sexually repressed pyro-nun. You don't see me rubbing myself on people and then lighting them on fire while reciting verse, do you?"

"That . . . is a lot to unpack," Gomorrah said. "But I think a blanket 'fuck you' would work as a reply."

I laughed as I cut the connection. I'd have to think of some more insults as I walked. I stretched my back one way, then the other before finally setting off and around the headquarters' fence.

"Myalis, can you connect me to . . . uh, do the corpo cops have a number I can text?"

They do. Here, most of them are connected to this chat system.

My augs shifted and a chat box appeared, hovering before me. Plenty of chatter between different people, all of them with names like A-Green and M-Armstrong. I was tempted to snoop, see what they were saying, but all I could see were status reports and a few questions and answers being fired back and forth. Real professional stuff, without even a meme to liven it up.

S-Cat: *Will be heading east to meet other samurai and aliens. Keep me informed. Cats staying near headquarters.*

I waited until I got a few affirmatives, then minimized the chat box so that it was out of the way.

It was time, at long last, to be stealthy.

I shifted my Icarus grenade launcher so that it was tucked under my long coat, and then I brought my Whisper around so that the crossbow was cradled against my chest. And then I activated all of my stealth things.

My coat warped, then went invisible. I was now little more than feet and hands and a big crossbow. Presumably a head and helmet as well.

I tugged my coat on tighter and kept on walking. From the glimpses I caught in the windows of the homes and little businesses I passed, I wasn't impossible to notice, but I certainly wasn't as visible as I would have been otherwise.

"Not as stealthy as I'd want," I said.

You could be better, yes. You're mostly hidden, visually, but the parts of you that aren't will give away your position. You can also be identified using other senses. Many Antithesis can sense changes in air pressure, others can sense heat, and of course acute hearing is quite common across many models. And that only covers some of the more basic senses.

"Hmm," I muttered. "Yeah, I guess that'll be the next step. I'm sure there's shit for that?"

Of course. The solutions that cover every possibility do tend to be a little more expensive. Unless this incursion is far more profitable than I predict, I don't think that kind of expense would be in your best interest.

"Bit by bit, then," I said. "We'll patch whatever holes we find as they come up."

I shifted Whisper so that it was tucked against my shoulder and approached the next corner a little more cautiously. The streets here were vacant, some ads behind glass storefronts still playing, and the single red light strung over the intersection blinked, but otherwise there wasn't much of note.

Black Bear felt weird. Maybe that was just me being a city girl, though. The place was more open than I was used to, with no hovercar traffic and buildings that I could look up to without craning my neck back.

I kind of expected to see cows or whatever there was in the countryside, but I figured this wasn't quite that kind of place. "Myalis, can you slip into the town's cameras?"

There isn't much as far as security infrastructure goes.

"That's all right. I just want to have more eyes around us. Do you know where that other samurai is?"

The Vanguard is just ahead.

My ears twitched as I started to hear something. It was . . . music.

Heavy metal music, interspersed by the grumble of a chain saw.

I started to feel somewhat concerned.

CAUSE PLAYER

I snuck up to the next corner, back bent and body low until I was right up to the intersection. The buildings here were mostly homes. The sort of pre-built bungalow with a little picket-fenced yard that a lot of people probably dreamed of retiring in.

It was just too bad that they were right on the edge of town. Well, maybe the owners had insurance. I didn't know much about home ownership.

My ears did an all-right job of painting a picture of what was going on around the corner, but that picture was . . . confusing.

Someone was fighting with a trio of aliens. Model Threes, the little dog-like ones with the spiny backs and mouths that were too big for comfort. The Model Threes were rushing at a man who sounded large and who moved with sharp, sudden bursts of speed to bring a heavy bar around.

The roar of a chain saw didn't leave much to the imagination as to what, exactly, he was using as a weapon.

I figured anyone murdering aliens in hand-to-hand was an ally.

I came around the corner and raised Whisper to take a shot, but before I could really get to aiming my new chain saw buddy spun around, threw the corpse of one alien at another, then stabbed his saw into the third's head.

Bits of Antithesis splattered onto the ground, turned into so much chunky purée by the roaring blade.

The samurai was a tall dude, covered in plates of army green armor that looked scuffed and that left his biceps exposed.

He worked out.

Or maybe he cheated with the tech, but either way, the results were the same. His arms were as thick around as my head and looked like they were straining against his armor. The way his armor segmented over his chest gave the impression that he had abs too.

If I weren't gay, I'd think he looked pretty hot.

"Yo!" I called out.

The dude glanced my way, then completely ignored me as he walked over to the two alien bodies squirming a few meters away. One of them was still alive.

He dropped his chain saw, and the weapon faded into motes before hitting the ground. A projection? Or maybe some sort of nano bullshittery? It was definitely some alien gear.

Reaching over his back, he closed his hand over empty air, then pulled a shotgun from nowhere.

I wasn't well-versed in guns, but even I recognized a double-barrel. His was cartoonishly large. He pumped it—why hadn't he materialized it already loaded?—lowered the barrel to point it at the head of the last living Model Three, then fired.

I flinched back at the noise. I was used to gunshots. His shotgun was an order of magnitude louder than anything I'd ever fired.

It did the job, though. I stepped to the side as a bit of Model Three rolled by.

The big guy shifted his shoulders, then turned to face me. "Sorry about that," he rumbled.

I shrugged—realized he couldn't see my shoulders—then spoke up. "It's all good," I said. "Came over to see how things were going."

"So, you're the backup?"

"I guess so? More like I'm the cavalry."

He huffed, a sort of macho one-note laugh. "Right. Give me a moment."

Turning, the big guy looked up just as a small drone zipped closer. It was a tiny golden thing, no bigger than a marble with a pair of little wings fluttering on the sides.

"We will be taking a small break, everyone. Take the time to visit my merch store, or listen to these ads by today's sponsors . . . Lord VPN . . . Once we return, the carnage shall resume. Rip and tear, friends."

The dude paused, and then his shoulders slumped and he turned to me. "Okay, that's done," he said.

"You're livestreaming?" I asked before I glanced around. We were standing pretty much in the center of an intersection. The road past the samurai led off and out of town and into the woods surrounding Black Bear.

"Yeah, got to make a living, you know? I'm Cause Player."

I stared at him. "Your name's what?"

He shifted, shotgun dropping and evaporating before it even hit the ground. "I'm Cause Player. It's . . . a name. I do cosplay."

"Okay," I replied, because what the hell else was I supposed to say? Lucy had mentioned cosplay a few times. She followed some girls that dressed up . . . well, really, they weren't usually wearing much, but what they did have on belonged to some game or another. "Are you cosplaying something right now?"

"You don't recognize me?"

I placed a hand on my hip. "Oh yeah, totally. I know all the macho armor-wearing shooty dude characters."

I had the impression he wasn't too amused. "This is Doom Guy."

"Wow, that name's worse than yours."

"What are you here for? My ads are about to finish and I need to get back to work."

I raised my hands in surrender. "All right, sorry. Uh, mostly here to figure out what's going on. I haven't been running into any aliens at all. You seem luckier than me."

"I have a tool that attracts them," he said. "It doesn't work on most models, but these little ones will charge right over. I've been killing any of those that come into town. It's been pretty quiet so far. Little groups every few minutes."

"Huh," I said. "Well, we evacuated most of the civvies to the company headquarters and armed it up. Cat mecha and all."

"Stray Cat, right?" he asked.

"Oh right, yeah, that's me. Just call me Cat. You looked me up?"

"I saw the memes."

I paused, working over the implications of that. Memes? Plural? No, I didn't want to know. "Okay, then. So you're going to stay here?"

"Around here? I'm patrolling to keep the area safe. Give people time to leave. I marked a few places where there were more people, and I sighted a Model Nine but it left before I could catch up to it. They're fast little things."

"Don't think I've ever seen a Model Nine," I said.

"That's probably normal, they're stealth models," Cause Player said. "They look like long insects."

"They going to be a problem?" I asked.

"Probably," he said. "But I'm more worried about the other models. Not too many of them coming around, but there are enough that I'd rather stay on top of them."

"Right," I said. I eyed the street, then the woods beyond. They looked rather ominous, what with their trees and . . . plants and stuff. I was definitely not a country girl. "Crap, I'm not sure what to do from here."

Cause Player shrugged. "There are some civilians around. You could help them. I'm more of a solo player. And having someone else on my livestream might wreck the viewer's immersion. So . . . yeah. If you want to help, maybe find the Model Nines' mini-hives?"

"Mini-hives?" I asked. "That sounds like a nightmare."

"They are," he said. "Ask your AI. I need to get back to the show."

I rubbed at the back of my neck. "Right, fine." If he wanted to play actor for his crowd, that was on him. As long as he was still killing aliens I figured it wasn't any problem of mine. Dude needed to make a living too. "Myalis, Model Nines, they going to be a problem?"

All Antithesis models are problems on some level. Model Nines are, interestingly, the model that tends to irritate more veteran Vanguards the most. They are particularly adept at avoiding detection and often require a "boots on the ground" approach to be discovered and eliminated.

"Hmm," I said before turning back toward Cause Player. "I'm going to head back to the headquarters then, maybe try to herd some civilians back that way too. If you need anything, you call me or Gomorrah, all right? She's got a cool ride and can probably be here in a matter of seconds."

"Thank you," he said. He actually sounded sincere there. "I should be able to hold my own for a while. This isn't the best point farm, but it's not all bad."

"Yeah, cool," I said. I saluted him, then stepped back. I really needed a better invisibility system so that I could just disappear entirely. It would make for a cool exit. "Think you could point me toward the biggest group of locals that aren't safe?"

I can do that. I'll try to verify if I can see any Model Nines moving into town. They tend to be difficult to find via artificial means.

"How come?" I asked.

Their skin and fur can change colors and textures, similar to the Earthnative chameleon, though they are significantly better at it. They can also change shapes thanks to the way their prehensile fur is made. They are coldblooded, so infrared has difficulty seeing them, and they can release small spores from their down-fur that float in the air and will frequently give sensors false positives.

Sounded like fun. "Let's see if we can't catch us a couple of them, then!"

CHAPTER SIXTY

M9

The traditional family unit may have been displaced as time progressed, but it never truly disappeared.

A system by which a child had multiple guardians and siblings is still, in nearly every scenario, optimal.

A child needs constant attention and constant love to grow into a strong and capable adult.

Sometimes, that requires more time than their parents can give them.

This isn't because of a lack of love. That missing time is spent working hard to put a roof over your child's head and keeping them safe and fed.

Perhaps all you need is something to help with the more mundane tasks of raising a child?

—Nannyco Robotics ad, 2047

I glanced at my map of Black Bear really quick as I jogged along. Myalis had marked a few spots to check around town, mostly places where she'd seen civilians gathering. I wanted to get them moving to safety, but I was also on the lookout for nearly invisible ambush aliens.

Which I figured wasn't going to end with me finding any of them.

"Where to next?" I asked as I shot past an intersection. There wasn't any traffic, so I only gave a quick glance each way before crossing the road. It was a good thing too; it let me see some movement down the street a little ways. "Scratch that."

There was a small family milling around a van. An ugly old thing from the late 2030s. All curved and filled with unnecessary plastic body parts, and very much unable to hover. In a small town like this, though, that was probably fine.

There was a ramp extending out of the side of the vehicle, and what looked like an entire family was gathered around it. It looked like some picture-perfect bunch. The mom, dad, and a boy and girl who were in their younger teens.

It would have been picture perfect if the dad-looking guy hadn't been in a wheelchair, his kids fussing with him, while the mother ran around in a panic.

"Yo," I said as I approached.

No one noticed me.

That didn't bode well. What if I were an alien?

Then again, I was supposed to be stealthy, so I chalked it up to me just being that good before I screamed, "Yo!"

The kids and the dad jumped and spun around, looking for me. Then they started yammering as I walked closer. I flicked off my coat's invisibility just as the dad finagled a rifle from inside the van.

He paused in the act of fiddling with the safety and looked my way. "You're not an alien."

"I'm one hundred percent mostly human," I said. "What's going on here?"

"Oh, shit, she's a samurai," the girl said. She couldn't be older than thirteen or so, about the age of my kittens.

"Sweetie, don't swear," the mother said.

I don't know what she was talking about; the woman looked like she desperately needed a chill pill and maybe a margarita. "It's all right?" I asked. "You folks okay?"

"Who are you?" the dad asked.

I didn't actually know if they were a family, but if they weren't the resemblance was uncanny, and absent any actual names, that was what I was going to label them as. "I'm Stray Cat. Your kid's right, I'm a samurai. Just looking for stragglers. You folks should head over to the company headquarters, we have a samurai guarding the place already."

"Oh, wow," the son said. His sister looked like I'd just announced that Christmas was coming early. She whipped an old-school phone out, then frowned at its blank screen before stuffing it away.

"Yeah yeah, hero worship later. Your van's fucked?"

"Langu—" the mom started. She paused, then swallowed thickly. "The van won't start. It turns on, but I can't get it to move. And our phones stopped. Reginald can't walk anymore, not since he got hurt last year."

I nodded along. "All right," I said. "Myalis, is this something we can fix in a hurry, or are we going to escort this bunch around?"

It seems like the ground vehicles in this town all require a registry code to function. A DRM sent from somewhere in town. Something is likely interfering, or the company has shut it down, thereby preventing the vehicle from working at all.

"Can you fix it?" I asked.

Certainly.

The van rumbled to life and the family jumped. "Mom, it's working!" the girl said.

"There you go," I said. "It was just some software fuc—fudgery. Uh, you should be good to go? Head right toward the headquarters. It's not too far."

"Will we be safe there?" the mom asked.

"You should be. I doubt Gomorrah will be pleased if they don't let someone in." I moved over and helped the kids push their dad into the back of the van. "You good to drive?"

"I am, thank you," the mom said.

The lot of them tossed their stuff back into their car in a hurry, and then they were off. She actually stopped at the intersection and used her flashers to signal her turn. I shook my head. "That was nice; next group?"

Two blocks over. I'll mark it on your map.

I stared, then groaned as I realized the van had gone that way already. I could have hitched a ride.

I flicked my coat back on and took off once more. It got boring within ten steps. I could only get so much joy from seeing the shadow of my head bobbing on the pavement before that grew old. "Where are all the damned aliens?" I asked. "I don't think I've killed a single one yet."

There should be no lack of them in the region, but the Antithesis have little need to fight and kill the locals for biomass when there is so much still available naturally. Until the main hive is destroyed, it's likely that the local swarm will keep a low profile.

"Which means we might be here a while. We're going to need to evacuate the entire town to someplace else."

And scour the entire region.

"No chance that someone will decide to just nuke us?" I asked.

That would be exceptionally irresponsible. And while temporarily effective, it would likely spread some Antithesis elements far and wide. Radioactive ones.

"That sounds awful," I said.

Also, as a matter of common sense, we strongly discourage the use of weapons of mass destruction on a planet upon which your entire race resides.

"Common sense never stopped humanity before," I said.

Your race isn't unique in its idiocy, I'm afraid. Most others that have gone as far as humanity usually die out along the way.

"So you're saying we're tough?" I asked.

I was saying you're idiots, but if you wish to read it that way, I will not stop you.

I laughed as I picked up the pace.

My laugh froze in my throat as I came around a corner and saw the same van that had just moved away from me stopped at the end of the street. It was parked in the middle of a lawn, a fire hydrant spraying water up in a fountain.

Had the mom been distracted?

I hadn't even heard the crash. Or maybe I had and had simply ignored it. I was used to a city's worth of noise. A distant bang barely registered. I had to pay more attention. I might not have fought any aliens yet, but that didn't mean they weren't around.

Jogging over to the van, I expected to see the family moving about, maybe a bit disoriented. I had plenty of points to get some medical stuff if it came to that.

Instead, halfway down the street, I noticed the blood splashed across the inside of the windows.

Wait.

I stopped, then started to look around. If Myalis told me to wait, there was a damned good reason for it; she wasn't the sort to stop me from racing over to help someone.

My gaze traveled across the street, looking for something, the black of an Antithesis, maybe some monster lurking in the shadows.

I found plain homes, some with manicured lawns with little bushes, others looking a bit rougher around the edges. There wasn't much space between the homes, but they each had a little lot. Cars sat useless in driveways and some of the homes had lights on.

Stealth units.

My back-mounted guns unfolded, both of them coming to rest just over my shoulders. They scanned across the street.

"I want to check in on them," I said.

Go ahead. I am trying to see the Model Nine.

Myalis not being able to see the monster wasn't filling me with confidence.

I walked over to the van, eyes shifting around, searching for anything.

The wind shifted, blowing across the leaves of one of the few trees around, and the grass, and the bushes that twisted around.

My heart skipped a beat.

Spinning around, I raised Whisper.

It was far too slow.

The bush launched itself at me, entirely silent.

My plasma caster spat a torrent of burning pellets at the creature, but it couldn't track fast enough.

A claw crashed into my crossbow, and then two more smacked into a pair of hexagonal disks that flashed into existence before me. Those would have eviscerated me.

I stumbled back, dropping my crossbow and finally taking in the Model Nine as it regained its footing.

It looked . . . like a bush. Leaves and branches. But not really. The leaves were fur, too puffy and made of thin woven strands. The branches were more like additional limbs sticking out of a thin, muscular body.

I couldn't see its eyes, but I could make out the black claws at the ends of its many limbs. None more than a couple of centimeters long, some of them bloody.

I whipped out my Trench Maker just as the Model Nine jumped again.

Three barks sounded out as I fired into the Model Nine from point-blank range.

The alien crashed to the ground.

"What . . . what the hell," I swore.

CHAPTER SIXTY-ONE

MIMICS

You shouldn't believe just anyone's claims that they're a samurai. It is surprisingly easy to fake it.

One notable story is that of Fluff Dragon, the alias of a young man who obtained some basic body armor and some cosplaying supplies, then created a samurai persona for himself. This isn't entirely uncommon, and there are events and groups that "play" at being samurai. Fluff Dragon took it one step further by patrolling the streets and even participating in the periphery of some incursions.

He was discovered to be faking it when a group of Antithesis overran the position he was guarding and he was unable to procure more weapons or ammunition as samurai so often do.

Seventy-eight civilians died.

Be wary of false claimants, and don't be afraid to ask for proof. Most samurai will provide some evidence of authenticity if asked.

—Extract from "A Concerned Citizen,"
a series of pamphlets distributed in 2035

Targets Eliminated!
Reward: 25 points
New Total: 60 points
I panted for a bit, heart beating away in my chest as if I'd just spent twenty quality minutes with Lucy instead of just lightly jogging around. A ten-second fight with an alien did that, I supposed.

"Shit," I said for a lack of any better response.

I walked to the side a bit, then moved back toward the dead alien. The Model Nine looked like someone had dropped a potted plant on the street.

"Shit," I repeated.

You're distressed. More so than I'd expect from you after an ambush.

I shook my head. "I'm fine," I said. "Just . . . it spooked me is all."

I glanced at the real reason I wasn't feeling all that great. The minivan was just a few dozen meters away. The water pouring from the busted hydrant was slowing down, and over that I could just make out the car's engine still rumbling away.

"Shit." Third time now.

I bent over and scooped Whisper up as I started toward the van. A quick look over the crossbow didn't reveal anything obviously wrong with it. Maybe a nick in the paint? Nothing terrible.

I set the crossbow against my shoulder and started moving closer to the minivan, looking around for more trouble. Any bushes that gave me a weird look were going to get shot.

The van's doors were all closed, but the passenger-side window was broken.

I held my breath, then looked in.

Four bodies.

I didn't stare for all that long, but it was enough to know that none of them were alive. The Model Nine had hit me like a demented blender, all claws and striking limbs. I couldn't imagine fighting it stuck inside an enclosed space without any fancy gear. I didn't need to imagine the results of fighting in close quarters.

Felt a little sick, honestly. "Myalis, let's move on," I said. "Where's the next group of civilians?"

One block north, to the left at the next intersection. A group is moving on foot.

I nodded and started jogging over. There was no way people on foot could do anything against another Model Nine, not if one of them could wreck a car. Well, not wreck a car but . . . whatever.

I've found three Model Nines in your vicinity.

My boots scraped the ground as I stopped and started looking around, Whisper already tucked into my shoulder. "Where?'

Pardon me, English is an imprecise language. By "vicinity" I mean within two to three hundred meters of your current location. I have been observing the area and noting any visual artifacts caught on camera. Comparing the before-and-after images occasionally reveals new objects that are likely Model Nines.

"Anything I can shoot?" I asked. I was getting into a shooty mood.

Nothing in your line of sight. The civilians are approaching one of them. It is currently disguised as a standing mailbox.

I didn't even take time to swear, I just took off running.

Grabbing Whisper's strap, I flung it over my shoulder, then tugged my Icarus from under my coat. The crossbow was a weapon designed to take out targets from afar, sure, but it was a precision weapon. The grenade launcher had a whole other sort of precision to it.

"High explosive," I said as I tucked the launcher against my shoulder.

I could see the civilians, maybe a dozen of them in all. Some had rifles with them, but I doubted those would help.

A few turned around. Maybe they saw my head? My footfalls weren't making much noise.

"Hey!" one called out.

I ignored him to scan the road ahead. Trees, some bushes, a few cars waiting in driveways. There, near the middle of the road. A bright red box, nearly perfectly square and standing on four legs, but the logos on the side were only vague splotches and the legs were at a bit of an odd angle. The more I looked at it, the more it stood out as wrong. Not so wrong that I would have given it a second glance if I were driving by or anything, though.

I raised my Icarus until the line projected over my vision landed right at the base of it. I tugged the trigger back.

Firing while running meant missing. At least with my aim it did. Which was why explosives were the best.

The fake mailbox, the sidewalk next to it, and a chunk of the grass next to that burst apart. Clods of dirt and Antithesis bits rained down across the road.

The civilians screamed.

Targets Eliminated!

Reward: 25 points

New Total: 85 points

"Any others?" I asked as I looked around for anything weird. Strange bushes, weird mailboxes, talking animals, anything that stood out, but the place just looked like a mundane street, albeit one with a new crater in it.

"Who are you?" one of the civilians asked. He was pointing a gun at the ground between us.

Nothing in the immediate area.

I nodded and lowered Icarus. Didn't need to spook anyone into shooting me. "Hey. You guys heading to the headquarters?"

The civilians looked to each other. "Who are you?" the one in the lead asked again.

"Friendly . . . friendly-ish neighborhood samurai," I said. "Sorry about the explosion, that mailbox was an alien."

They didn't believe it.

I'd lied poorly before. It was one of those things you had to get good at as a poor crippled orphan kid, and to get better at lying, you had to know when someone didn't buy it. Which was kind of insulting. I was partially invisible and had a big gun. Did they need me to hack into their augs to announce myself too?

Obviously it was the mailbox thing that stretched their believability.

I flicked off the invisibility on my coat again and tucked my launcher away. Didn't need to give anyone a reason to twitch. "I'm Stray Cat. Based out of New Montreal. I'm here with a few others, we're securing the civilians around here."

Guns lowered some more. "Was there really a xeno behind the mailbox?" the guy I assumed was in charge asked.

"Yeah," I said. Close enough. "Where are you guys headed?"

"The old arena. A bunch of us are heading that way. It's our meeting place for when things go wrong." He rubbed the back of his hand across his nose. "Can you tell us how things are going?"

"In Black Bear? All right? Some casualties, but not that many." I held myself together fairly well, I figured. "The incursion near here's really small. We'll have some heavy hitters around soon, but we don't want normal folks out and about when that happens."

"We can't go to the headquarters. Most of us are subcontractors."

"I . . . don't see why that should matter?" I said.

"The company doesn't like us interfering with their things," he explained. "We live here, but half the town's basically off-limits to us."

Some of the folks behind him nodded, and I started to notice that they weren't all dressed to the nines. It was the middle of the day, sure, and I didn't expect people dressed to impress, but these people were all in jeans and . . . well, normal clothes that had been worn before. Not poor, but not far from it, maybe?

"Look, the company doesn't like you interfering, but they'd really hate it if I did. There's another samurai by the headquarters guarding it, Gomorrah. She's the nun with the flamethrower. She's very good at turning the unrighteous into charcoal, and she wouldn't leave a bunch of people waiting outside for the aliens to nab them. If the company gives you trouble later, you just reach out to me, all right?"

That seemed to work.

I figured I'd press my momentum while I had it, and I took off ahead of them, heading toward the headquarters. It was only a couple of blocks away. "Myalis, can you get one of my cats to come over? It can escort them the rest of the way once it gets here. Also, where's the old arena?"

Your P.U.S.S. Model Y is en route. As for the old arena, it's not on any of the official maps, but I suspect it's this building here.

A building flashed on my map.

Some older social media feeds call it the town arena. It predates the corporate acquisition of the town and doesn't seem to have been in use since.

"Well then, I guess we know more or less where we're heading to next," I said.

CHAPTER SIXTY-TWO

ARENA

The best thing you can do when there are aliens about is keep low and keep your head on straight. It's the best way to stay alive.

—Deus Ex, 2054

As soon as one of my cat mecha joined the civilians, I ditched.

Felt a little bad just leaving them behind, but they had a walking weapons platform watching over them now, and they were only a block away from the headquarters.

A glance at the map to make sure I was heading in the right direction, and I continued on toward the arena. From what Myalis was able to pull up in a hurry, the old arena looked fairly secure. It was a pre-incursion building, but like, way before the incursions started. It had a Cold War–era fallout shelter in the basement. Nothing up to modern code, I bet, but sometimes that wasn't a bad thing.

No cameras on or around the building, which was annoying, but Myalis said that she could triangulate a lot of phone signals in the area that hadn't been there a few hours before. People really were gathering there.

I'd be using that phone-tracking trick again. There were still a few pockets of people around Black Bear. If we did our job right, they'd be safe if they had somewhere to lay low for a while, I figured. Still didn't want to risk it too much. Having everyone in one place made it easier to defend them all. Plus, more guns manning the figurative walls.

It would suck if one of them had a cold and spread it around, but I'd take that over aliens eating everyone any day of the week.

I was just past the back of the headquarters when my augs told me I had an incoming call. Gomorrah.

"Yo," I said.

"Hey," she replied. "I reached out to Deus Ex, to get some news about that orbital strike. I think she was sleeping, but her AI wasn't. It directed me to speak with someone from the Family."

"All right," I said. Made sense so far. Pipsqueak needed her naptime.

"Long and short of it is that they'll be bombing the area in about five minutes."

"Five minutes!" I shouted. That was real fucking soon. I glanced at the sky but all I saw was a thick layer of gray, but that didn't mean they had to bomb the place now.

"The Vanguard I spoke to said the area of effect would only barely touch Black Bear. Though . . . Cat, I didn't have all that much confidence in the man from my one conversation with him. He sounded a bit stupid."

I paused. Was it wise to head out to the arena now? The headquarters looked a lot tougher and was closer to the center of the city to boot. More buildings around it to serve as cover. But that would mean abandoning however many people were at the arena. "Fuck. Look, I'm going to join up with some folks, then try to get them all into cover. What are you doing?"

I started to run ahead. Still looking around for Model Nines, but prioritizing getting my ass out of the blast radius more.

"I'm landing Fury now. I want it safe from the blast. I'll be in the headquarters. I'll see what needs doing after that."

"Right, did he tell you anything about what kind of bombardment we'll be dealing with here? Deus Ex said orbital, but that just means the bombs are coming from on high."

"He said Rods of God and some thermobaric explosives."

"Fuel-air?" I asked.

"You're familiar?" Gomorrah asked.

I could still vividly recall nearly cooking my eyebrows off a couple of days ago. "Yeah. Bombs are my thing. Shit, are they sure it won't hit the town?"

"He mentioned skirting the edge of the town. Starting here, then working over to the actual hive to make any Antithesis move away from Black Bear. Or something like that, I'm not sure I understood entirely."

"Skirting? Skirting is close," I said.

"Get to cover. We'll have to trust that our fellow samurai know what they're doing."

"I don't like trusting people I don't know," I said. "Myalis, you got anything on this?"

I'm afraid not.

I grumbled. "Fine, I'll get to cover with the civilians. Stay safe too, all right?"

"If you die I'll burn the one responsible, then scatter the ashes."

That . . . was morbid as hell, but also somehow really nice. "Thanks," I said, genuinely meaning it.

I found the arena off to one side of the town. A squat building, much longer than it was wide, with a tin roof painted some ugly green, and cement sides that rose up three meters off the ground. It looked a bit on the rustier side, and its age showed. Definitely something from the seventies.

Plenty of cars parked around the lot, a few of them pressed up against the front to serve as barriers around the entrance. An entrance that was slightly ajar with no one guarding it.

I looked around again, searching for a Model Nine, or maybe . . . anything that stood out as wrong. There wasn't anything. The cars were all older, maybe secondhand, lots of repairs; the air didn't smell like gunpowder or anything like that. There was nothing wrong, yet I felt a shiver running down my spine.

I flicked on my shoulder-mounted guns, tucked Icarus away, and pulled out my trusty Trench Maker. It was down a few rounds; had to keep that in mind.

Moving forward, I paused by the door and strained my ears. Voices? No, screams, but distant, more than one person crying, one sounded like a baby. Something mechanical being racked, air-conditioning units rumbling, people shouting confused orders back and forth.

"Shit," I muttered as I stepped in. I swept my gun around, looking through the lobby as quickly as I could.

Two bodies on the floor, looking like they'd been torn into. Bite marks, mostly. Not a Model Nine, then? I swallowed past the lump in my throat and moved on. Most of the noise was coming from deeper in.

I had to wonder why. The forest nearby had to have plenty of critters in it. Rabbits and birds and squirrels and . . . were there wolves here? Deer. Definitely deer, I was pretty sure those weren't extinct.

Point was, there had to be plenty of things to eat. And they were supposed to be able to eat plants and trees and the like.

Why go after the people here?

I got that they'd spread around and eventually butt up against humanity, and I was fine with murdering them to the last. I just didn't get why they acted the way they did. Coming after a town like this when there was plenty to be had around it with less risk.

Maybe I was overthinking it. Aliens had alien ways of thinking, big surprise.

I licked my lips as I pushed into the next room over. It was a small space, a corridor with windows lining one side, looking into a hockey rink. No ice. Too warm for that, and the stands looked a bit dusty. No aliens that I could see.

The corridor moved off a ways, and there were a few steps leading down at the end.

I followed the noises, moving slowly, keeping quiet.

Someone shot at something. First one shot, then two or three more.

"Shit," I muttered before sprinting ahead.

I bounced off the wall around the corner and found myself in another passageway. Locker rooms to one side, storage on the other, and a shitty barricade at the end.

Three Model Threes, running down the center of the corridor. Another jumped out of one of the rooms to the side.

I cursed and ran forward.

The plasma rifle on my shoulder opened fire, filling the air between us with flashing darts that pelted into the aliens' backs and sides, burning pinky-wide holes into the aliens. I didn't bother firing at them with my Trench Maker. I'd just miss.

The aliens went down, and I slid to a stop before the door they'd been coming out of.

I came face-to-face with a Model Three climbing in through a broken window.

It stared at me for just a moment before baring its teeth.

My railgun painted a line in the air, dust kicked aside in a tunnel that passed through the alien's skull.

"Sound bomb," I said.

Myalis provided a resonator dropping before me so that I could catch it out of the air. I turned it on with a flick of my thumb and stepped into the room. An office. Dust to one side, old drawers to the other, ancient cathode-ray screen rotting in the corner.

I underhanded the grenade outside and ran back into the corridor.

At least I was finally getting some action, I reasoned as I ran to the end.

Now I just had to try to keep folks alive too.

CHAPTER SIXTY-THREE

RODS OF GOD

There's no kill like overkill!
—Motto of the Family's unofficial Orbital Strike Squadron

I spun around the corridor and took in everything. It only took a split second to figure out what was going on.

There was a room at the far end of the corridor. Unadorned walls, thick, made of cement. The shelter. Before that were some doors, heavy metal things. Not vault doors, but the sort I'd expect to see in a well-secured warehouse or at the front of someone paranoid's place.

They'd built a barricade in the middle of the corridor, but the people guarding it weren't there.

For good reason too.

Three Model Threes, a single Model Four.

The latter looked injured, some of its tentacles shorn off, and it looked to be bleeding.

I raised my Trench Maker up, pointing it at the back of the nearest alien, the big Model Four. My railgun shifted, and my plasma caster turned to aim farther forward.

My finger twitched over the trigger just as my railgun bucked. A spray of superheated plasma shot out ahead with a snakelike hiss.

The four aliens went down in an instant. The one hit by the rail went thumping to the ground, a coin-sized hole smoking in its flank and the front of its chest busted apart; the Model Four slumped to the ground, the holes I'd poked into it with my Trench Maker the size of both my fists together, and the other two were partially aflame around the places where my plasma gun had peppered them with fire.

Targets Eliminated!
Reward: 45 points
New Total: 175 points

I stuffed my Trench Maker into its holster and let that get to work reloading it while I stepped around the bodies slumped across the corridor.

The guys running away kept running, but they were looking back, and soon their run turned from a desperate scramble to a confused jog. They stopped. "Are you a samurai?" one of them asked.

"Yup," I said. "You guys okay?"

There were some shared looks. "We thought," one began.

"We're okay," another said, louder. He moved toward me, a gun in hand, but not pointed anywhere near me, and by the looks of it, the magazine was missing from it. It was only a hunting rifle, though, all wood with a scope. These guys were armed, but not with anything fancy.

I glanced around, taking in six or so more dead Antithesis. They'd been holding them off, then.

"Did you see Bill?" the one walking over asked. "And Gaétan and John?"

"Who's Bill?" I asked.

"He—they were guarding the front door. Please, he's my son."

The guy looked old enough to be a dad. Maybe in his late fifties or so. "I . . . fuck, there were two people by the doors, dead, sorry."

He reeled back, confusion and anger, then hope. "Just two?"

"Fuck," I said. "Okay, everyone, get in the bunker, keep the doors closed until I come back. I'll knock. We need to get into cover soon, there's going to be a blast nearby. We can worry about other shit later, all right?"

I didn't give them much time to protest, spinning on my heel to run back down the corridor.

It was only a chance, but there might be some guy alive up there, and if he was, he'd be caught in the blast.

WARNING

Yeet-Stick Incoming!
You've got a minute to get under cover. The Rods of God are dropping.
—ZZ-Zeus

"What?" I asked at the prompt that appeared before me.

That was sent out to all communication devices within twenty kilometers of the hive's predicted location.

I started running faster, the corridors blurring past until I was back in the lobby. Two bodies still, no other aliens. I was relying on my shoulder-mounted guns, mostly. I looked around, didn't see anyone else, then ducked outside.

A blood trail gave it away. One I'd missed earlier, heading off to the side and into the back of one of the cars pushed up against the side of the building.

There was a dead Model Three there, slumped in the shadows next to the car.

I walked over to the vehicle and peeked inside. There was someone on the back seat. Breathing hard, a hand wrapped around their leg where an inexpert tourniquet had been tied.

He had a revolver in his other hand.

I knocked on the window, then ducked to the side when he brought the gun up.

"Hey! Hey, chill," I said. "I'm human. You need help." It wasn't a question, the guy was bleeding out all over the seat. It didn't look too bad. He might even survive all on his own with his makeshift bandage, but not if some alien showed up. I had the points to spare for some healing shit anyway.

He dropped his gun, and I reached over to open the door when I noticed the shadows around me receding. The world took on a reddish tint.

I spun.

A beam of light, no, multiple beams of light were piercing through the air, connecting the sky to the ground like massive pillars. They had to be dozens of meters wide to be seen from as far away as I was.

They cut through the clouds, leaving the overcast sky glowing red. It only took a moment for me to realize that they were moving, all the beams converging together to form bigger pillars, maybe some two dozen in all.

"Oh, shit," I said as they finally came together.

The beams flashed, then disappeared.

I tried to turn, but the ground was no longer underfoot.

My ears went mute a moment before a *sound* rocked past me. It felt like someone had dropped a fifty-five-gallon drum filled with cowbells onto the back of my head.

I was still stumbling, trying to catch my balance when the wind hit.

My jacket was whipped forward, and my vision, already confused by everything waving around, went black.

Not blindness, I realized: dust. A cloud of dust and dirt and ash so thick that it turned day to night.

I felt tiny particles pelt against my back, against my helmet and legs. None hard enough to hurt, or at least not hard enough to break through my armor.

What the hell had that been?

I rolled into a ball, the wind whipping past pushing me forward. I think I ended up under the car with the guy in it. That didn't provide much cover, but it was somewhere to hide.

Then the earth shook again.

Another strike? Had they launched them sequentially?

That minute was not nearly enough warning!

I was going to find that Zeus asshole and tear him a new one.

Are you well?

"Fuck!" I screamed.

I will take that as a no. Your undersuit's integrity is still at one hundred percent. Your vitals are fine considering the situation. You will survive, just hold tight and wait. It's just a little orbital strike.

Myalis was being comforting and sarcastic, which actually helped a little. I didn't believe in those breathing exercises they taught at the orphanage much, but it didn't hurt to try one now. The rumbling continued, and my ears unmuted themselves, allowing me to take in the torrential roar of wind around me. There were other sounds mixed in. Things crumbling, a dozen car alarms going off.

I was on the edge of Black Bear nearest the blast. That meant we were just about the hardest hit. Still, I could only imagine the town being a crater after this.

The wind settled. It shifted back, rushing in the opposite direction, though with only a fraction of the force.

It's over.

I rolled over, then started to crawl out from under the car. I wasn't even sure how I'd fit in so easily, it was a tough squeeze to get out.

Standing up, I looked around but couldn't see anything—that was, until I wiped at my helmet and cleared it of the dust and dirt caked on.

The wind was settling down, and with it the crap in the air.

The clouds, I noticed, were nearly all gone. They had to be, to make way for the multiple mushrooms dominating the sky right next to me.

They were bigger than any skyscraper I'd ever seen, massive bulbous things, dark gray and growing.

"Shit," I said.

I paused and looked around. I expected cars to be flipped and all, but it wasn't quite that bad.

A clod of dirt the size of my fist thumped to the ground a dozen meters away. Maybe it wasn't that bad, but it wasn't far from it.

I . . . didn't quite know what to do.

That man still needs assistance.

"Right," I said. That first. Then I could check on the civilians in the shelter. After that I'd figure out my next move. I had to contact Gomorrah and maybe Cause Player.

I had the impression that whatever that had been created more work for me, not less.

CHAPTER SIXTY-FOUR

AFTERMATH, BUT WE'RE REALLY BAD AT MATH

When the first incursions occurred, humanity as a whole didn't know how to respond to them. They were a threat unlike any other.

And so, naturally, no holds were barred when it came to unleashing humanity's collective arsenal on the aliens.

Often, that meant that the worst of the disaster wasn't created by the aliens, but by humanity itself.

—Excerpt from *A History of Disaster*, 2047

"Okay, press here," I said, gesturing at a point on the dude's leg.

He hissed as he put pressure on his wound, but it helped, keeping one of my hands free so that I could tug his leg up and wrap the bandage around it again.

I had plenty of first-aid stuff, but it was a bit pricey. Good bandages, though? With some sort of magic bullshit fast-healing stuff in them? Yeah, one point for a roll that had an adhesive strip on the ends and that would contract and breathe as needed.

"There," I said as I pressed the strip into the bandage. The edges flashed green and the entire bit of cloth tightened a little. "I'd kiss it better, but you're not my type."

"Thanks," he said.

I shifted back out of the car, ignoring all the glass crunching below me as I backed out, then gave him a hand to get out himself. He still hung on to his gun, which was great. It might come in handy.

"Let's get you inside," I said as I looked around. None of the cars around us had windows, and they were all turned an ugly grayish brown by the blast of dirt and ash.

Speaking of ash, there was a faint rain coming down from above. Too gray to be snow.

"What happened?" he asked.

"Some fuckwit didn't learn their lesson about blast radiuses, I think," I said. "Just hope this shit's not radioactive."

It is not. The HVW that struck nearby was an iridium rod. It is nonradioactive.

"Oh, so it's not fallout?" I asked.

It's fallout from the explosion, but it is not radioactive fallout. No more than any amount of soil kicked up would have, at least.

"That's good, right?" the guy asked.

"Sure," I said. "Let's get you inside, you can have a sit with your family."

The arena was fucked. The lobby was fine. A bit dusty, and some of the posters had been ripped off the walls, but nothing a janitor couldn't fix. The rest of it, though? The tin roof had been peeled back like a sardine can, exposing the hockey rink and letting in plenty of dust and crap.

Dust had made it all the way into the corridors leading to the shelter. The doors were shut when we arrived. Couldn't blame them, I'd have closed them on sensing the blast too.

I had to knock hard to get people to respond. Then I was practically shoved aside as the man who had asked me about his son grabbed the guy next to me and hugged him.

A nice, tearful reunion. Still, two others wouldn't be getting theirs.

I hesitated for a bit.

Should we move these people back to the headquarters, or leave them here? A quick look in the shelter revealed a low-ceilinged room, with hefty cement pillars here and there, and little rooms on all sides with cots. Maybe some thirty or forty people inside, most of them adults, but a few kids.

"Hey," I said to one of them standing by the door. He had an old hunting rifle by his side and looked ready to use it. "I'm stepping out. Just outside. Close up, all right? I want to see what's going on."

I waved them off and headed back upstairs. I wasn't as concerned about aliens as I had been. That blast should have done a number to anything outside, aliens included.

"Myalis, can you connect me to Gomorrah, please?"

Certainly.

I closed my eyes for a moment and just breathed. The line beeped and I heard Gomorrah talking to someone. ". . . Do what you can. Empty the infirmary. There should be more help coming soon. Give me a moment, I've got a call. Cat?"

"Hey," I said. "Did you feel that?"

"If by 'that' you mean the dozen orbital strikes less than ten kilometers away, then yes, we all felt it." She was a bit terse. Maybe I could cut back on the snark? A little bit?

"Everyone all right?" I asked. "Are you all right?"

"I'm fine," she said. "Everyone else . . . well, there aren't any dead. Biggest injury is a broken leg. One of the police officers climbed up the wall to see the light show. He was thrown off. We have a lot of smaller injuries. The entire side of this building facing the blast had windows. There's just . . . blood all over. We're trying to set things up. Get glass out of cuts and bandage them up."

"Oh, shit," I said. I hadn't considered that. "I heard you saying something about help. That's not me, right?"

"No. Army is coming in from New Montreal. They should be half an hour out. The army-army, not some PMC," Gomorrah said. She sighed. "I can't wait, this entire thing has turned into a mess."

"Yeah," I said. "I'm going to stay here for a bit. There's a shelter with a bunch of civilians in it. Once you get in touch with the army, can you have them send a few soldiers this way? We can escort them to the headquarters."

"You don't want to do that yourself?"

I shook my head. "Not in this mess."

The streets were covered in debris and a few trees had fallen. The power lines had snapped in a few spots too.

"Do you still have power?" I asked.

"Generator," Gomorrah said. "They have a smaller one here, enough for the lights. We're using the steps instead of the elevators too. Apparently there are bigger generators over by the mines."

"We'll see if we can't get the army to move them over," I said.

"That's an idea." Gomorrah paused. "I'm getting a request for a call with someone, I'm patching you in."

I didn't have time to protest before my augs shifted and suddenly I was looking at the face of a smiling man in a business suit. "Hello, Gomorrah . . . and Stray Cat? Pleased to meet you. How are things on the ground?"

"Gomorrah, who's this fucko?" I asked, politely.

Gomorrah snorted and the guy's face went through a few emotions. "This is the one in charge of the orbital weapons. No, he's not a Vanguard."

"I'm Lorenz," Lorenz said.

"That's nice. Why the fuck did you hit so close to the town?"

"Uh, that's where the hive is?" he said. "I actually stopped firing early. We were supposed to hit twelve times, then six more times in the center, right over the main body of the hive, but there's some tectonic instability in the region from the first hits. We'll need to wait for that to clear out first."

"Another wave of hits?" I asked. "The place is barely keeping together as it is."

Lorenz seemed to disagree. "We need to eradicate as much of the hive as we can now, before we send you in to weed out the rest."

"I'm sorry, what?" I asked.

"The Black Bear Mining Corporation has been using new technology to find mineral deposits," he said. "Instead of strip mining, they've been using tunnels to reach those deposits directly."

I squeezed my eyes shut. "Lorenz, what the fuck are you on about?"

"I'll admit, I'm curious too. This seems like an unnecessary tangent. We're trying to save lives here, we don't care about mining."

"Sorry, sorry. It's just that we think the local Antithesis hive has relocated into the mining shafts around Black Bear. Some of the scans of the mines we have don't match up to the official records the company keeps. For that matter, they've been extracting more ore than they should have."

"So the aliens are underground," I said. "That is, if you didn't collapse them in."

"The shafts should still be there. The next wave of HVWs should be stronger, with bunker-buster munitions. It will be a bit harder than the last blast."

"HVWs?"

Gomorrah was the one to reply. "High-velocity weapons. The kinetic strike rods they just used."

"Okay," I said. "So you want us to go skipping around in some mine-shaft, to kill some aliens, while folks around here are screwed over by your inability to aim?"

Lorenz looked a bit pale. "Yes? . . . Ma'am?"

"Lorenz, where are you right now?" I asked.

"I'm not supposed to disclose that."

His IP traces back to a Family-owned complex in Wyoming.

"Wyoming, huh? Lorenz, I've decided that I don't like you. So if you want me to do anything that isn't driving over to . . . wherever the fuck Wyoming is, then you'd better become real convincing real fast. I'm not in a good mood."

CHAPTER SIXTY-FIVE

POLITICS ACCORDING TO CAT

In 2022 a bill was brought up for consideration by members of the then-Republican and Democratic parties, in a bipartisan gesture. The bill would, in essence, restrict the ability of a samurai to participate in the open market. They would not be allowed to purchase or own stocks or shares in a company, they would not be allowed to own or operate their own business, and in theory, they would need to be affiliated with a company in good standing in order to file their taxes.

In 2023 a samurai named Blitzo accidentally detonated a chemical laser weapon above Washington, D.C. The beams projected by this device, all of them with temperatures of several thousands of degrees, and no wider than a hair, were fired across the city at entirely random angles.

Of the seventy-two casualties from this accident, seventy-two were politicians or lobbyists.

By sheer, scientifically proven coincidence, these were all lobbyists and politicians in favor of the bill.

The bill did not pass.

Blitzo was charged, tried, and acquitted of all charges. His defense, that the bomb was set off accidentally by a faulty fuse, and that the lasers could have gone in literally any direction, was impossible to disprove, regardless of how unlikely the results happened to be.

Judge Van Maners, who presided over Blitzo's trial, was quoted as saying, "Fuck all of that."

—Excerpt from *Samurai and Politics: A Simple Guide*, 2039

"Ah," Lorenz began with all the grace of a new manager meeting his first Karen. "We . . . you see . . . um."

"Um?" I repeated.

"Cat," Gomorrah said. There was a bit of a warning tone to it. "I think what Lorenz was trying to say there was that he's very, very sorry that he almost blew you up, and that he will make sure that the Family takes full responsibility for the damages caused here."

"I don't know if I can . . . I mean, yes. Yes, that's what I meant," Lorenz said in a hurry.

I snorted, but . . . yeah, I was basically bullying the idiot at this point. An idiot with an orbital gun, but an idiot still. "How many people are working with you, Lorenz?"

"We're a team of forty," he said. "For the North-America-near-orbit zone."

So he wasn't some guy in a basement pressing on big red buttons for fun. The background in his image kind of hinted at him being somewhere important. Lots of books and little photos on a shelf behind him, as well as awards and some knickknacks. Office shit, basically.

"And who's . . . Zeus?"

"That's the samurai that set up the orbital drop system," Lorenz said. "He's a member of the Family."

"Right," I said. So Zeus wasn't the one pulling the trigger? "Tell him that he needs to give his toys to more responsible people."

"I . . . will pass that along?"

I wanted to rub at my forehead. Instead, I settled for starting to walk in circles around the arena parking lot. "How long until the army comes in?"

"They're waiting for the debris to clear. They should be there in under half an hour. Though I'm not the one in charge of that side of things."

"Then who is?" Gomorrah asked.

Lorenz swallowed. "That would be the NA Coordination group?"

"How big is the Family?" I asked.

Lorenz blinked. "It's the biggest samurai-affiliated-and-run organization in North America?"

So a corp, but one run by samurai? "Dammit," I muttered.

"They're not that bad," Gomorrah said, likely reading my mind. "Lorenz, you've done an awful job of . . . a lot of things. Maybe you can redeem yourself by telling us about the mines?"

"Yes, yes, I can do that. I'm sending you the geological readings. The map might not be entirely accurate, but it should be close. It's based on the tremors caused by our orbital impacts. Each impact is offset by a few seconds, and based on the vibrations across the region, we can extrapolate . . . ah, never mind. We have maps."

"Yeah," I said. "And the Antithesis are in those caves?"

"Mineshafts," Lorenz corrected. "And it's very likely. The hive was difficult to see from orbit. Stealth hives tend to create a lot of 'chaff' that spreads quickly and makes scans difficult to run. It's also very easy to overlook the sort of static they create."

"Not here for a lesson," I said.

"Right, right. Um, yes. The hive was originally concentrated over a random part of the forest, but it then started spreading. That spread's speed slowed down considerably just as the hive reached a position above one shaft that happened to be relatively close to the surface."

I stopped pacing. "They slowed down because . . . well, they weren't slowing down, they were just growing down instead of out?"

"That's what we suspect, yes."

I chewed on my lips.

"It's a very small hive. The Family will be sending some of its best samurai to eradicate it tomorrow."

"Tomorrow?" I asked.

"In the early morning," Lorenz confirmed.

"The incursion here was only two days old and it was already threatening Black Bear. Give it a dozen hours and it might be able to start producing more models that will be a threat," Gomorrah said. "I don't doubt the Family can get on top of it, but why not act sooner?"

"That's what the second set of impacts are for. To weaken the Antithesis position."

"And wreck the town even more," I said.

So we had a choice. Let the Family basically nuke the place, then come in tomorrow to mop up. That option would mess the town up even more. Probably not too bad, actually. Anyone that was hurt was probably in cover already, and we'd have more time to warn people. The army would be here too.

That reminded me, I had to call Cause Player, see if he was still alive.

The second option was doing shit ourselves. Risky. And dumb.

But the points . . .

"What are you thinking?" Gomorrah asked.

"I wonder if I'm claustrophobic or not," I said.

"You don't know?"

"I've been in a few tight, warm places before," I said. "Lucy and I both found that very enjoyable. But this is different."

Gomorrah made a disgusted noise. "Do you really have to turn everything into a sex joke?"

"Yes?"

"Right, well I'm in favor of clearing it out ourselves," Gomorrah said.

"Really?" I asked.

"Tight quarters, small sightlines, flammable enemies. This is literally the perfect situation for my load-out," Gomorrah said. "Might not get another like this for a while. I could use the points."

I felt my good eyebrow rise. "Going to get a second car?"

"I'm a one-car kind of woman," Gomorrah said. "As God intended. No, I want some more defenses around the church. I had some people snooping around already. I'm not fond of that."

"You could buy one of the floors below my new place. Turn it into a . . . church thing, or whatever. Hell, you can slap a steeple on the roof. Lucy would hate it at first, but I think its phallic nature would win her over eventually. Plus she'd get to see nuns. And tease them."

"You have such a one-track mind," Gomorrah complained.

"Sorry, when I get fidgety," I explained. "Anyway, where you go I go, I guess."

Lorenz sighed. "That's great to hear."

I'd honestly forgotten he was even there.

"We're waiting until the army shows up," I said. "Not going to leave all these people out here without anyone to defend them."

"There's a whole battalion coming in," Gomorrah said. "Sounds like they're taking this seriously."

No PMCs, weird. My interactions with the government so far had been . . . sparse and traumatic. I hoped that the government's army wouldn't be similar. "Good, I guess. Once they get here, I'll head over to you. We can figure things out from there."

"Thank you, both of you. The Family will certainly appreciate your assistance in this matter," Lorenz said.

"Kissing my ass won't un-blow-me-up," I said.

Gomorrah actually giggled for a half second before cutting off with a cough. "Yes, well, see you soon."

"See you soon," I said. "And Lorenz, do call a girl before exploding her or things in her vicinity. It's just polite."

"R-right," Lorenz mumbled.

The line went dead and I let out a long breath before stretching my back.

An interesting conversation, and a great opportunity.

"To die in a hole, you mean."

I would encourage you to save some points to use in case of that sort of emergency. Or, alternatively, spend them on something that would save you in case of a cave-in.

"Like what, a teleportation machine?" I asked.

Yes. There are many ways of moving things from one point to another without crossing the space between the two points.

I blinked. "You can teleport stuff?"

The silence was very, very, long.

Catherine . . . how do you explain the items you purchase arriving before you?

"Oh, right. Obviously."

I spent the long minutes waiting for the army to arrive feeling particularly stupid.

CHAPTER SIXTY-SIX

TANKS AND SOLDIERS
AND GUNS, OH MY!

Most modern militaries in the early 2000s were designed to counter other modern militaries and minor uprisings.

The Antithesis changed that. Now most forces split their attention between crowd suppression, their traditional antimilitary role, and incursion suppression.

—Introduction to *The Three-Way Problem* by Professor Ivence, 2054

I don't know why, but when I imagined the army showing up, I was expecting a couple of troop transports. Maybe a few armored cars.

I wasn't expecting tanks.

My knowledge about tanks wasn't exactly great. I'd seen them in movies and games, and maybe in a history documentary or two. I knew they were big armored things. For some reason, it never registered that they'd be fucking enormous. I'd been inside that one mobile base, but that was a mobile base, not a proper tank-tank.

The tank that rolled onto the road with the arena was nearly wide enough to take up the entire street. It had smaller gun emplacements all around it, turrets with armored screens under them, and a main gun sitting on the back with a barrel I could have stuck my head in.

Wheels instead of tracks, though. Big ones, with hexagonal-patterned tires, four to a side.

The tank turned my way, casually rolled over the hood of some poor civilian's little sedan, then made a tight turn a couple of meters ahead of me and stopped with a hiss.

I stared up as a hatch hummed open. The inch-thick doorway was shoved up by a little hydraulic arm, just enough that a guy was able to poke his head out. "Are you Stray Cat, ma'am?" he asked.

"Yup," I said. "Nice ride."

The soldier grinned. "Thank you, ma'am! We're the only super-heavy here. Thought it would be best to have us break the tide, as it were."

"Super-heavy?" I asked.

He reached an arm out and gave the vehicle an affectionate thump. "One hundred and fifty tons of alien-killing beauty."

"Nice," I said. I think I saw the appeal. I wasn't a gun nut, but that cannon on the top. Well, bitches did love cannons. "You guys going to stick around here?"

"Yes, ma'am!"

I heard something off to the side and leaned back to see a few more vehicles coming over. Tanks, but these were no bigger than an SUV. Fewer wheels, and the asymmetrically set gun wasn't as panty-wettingly big.

"Cool. You're really freeing me up here," I said. "There are some civilians holed up in the arena. Saw some Model Threes and Fours around earlier. And watch out for Model Nines. They're nasty fuckers."

The tanker saluted. "Will do, ma'am. Do you need a ride anywhere? We have infantry being dropped off here."

I shrugged. "Sure," I said.

I wouldn't mind riding on a tank.

As it turned out, what he meant was that when a troop transport came around—just a sort of enclosed truck, lightly armored and unarmed—to drop off a couple of squads of infantry, it waited around for me to hop on.

I didn't complain. It saved me some walking, but I did kind of want to ride in one of the tanks. Lucy would trip.

I stayed standing in the cramped rear of the transport, eyes on the road passing by behind us. The town had taken a serious blow already, but a lot of it seemed somewhat superficial. Some cleanup, a bit of cash spent repainting homes, fixing yards and replacing all the glass, and Black Bear would be right as rain. More or less.

The transport rolled to a stop before the headquarters, and I leapt out of the back.

There were a lot more soldiers around than I'd expected. They seemed to be using the front of the headquarters as a staging ground, tents going up and blocky mobile homes with com-arrays on their roofs parking in neat rows.

I saw some of the local police around, mostly hanging out close to the main building itself. Either they didn't want the army going in or they were just focusing on keeping the civilians safe while the soldiers took the brunt of any potential attack.

The army certainly had the better equipment. More of those light tanks were parked here and there, sandbags already going up around them, and others were setting up AA guns on mounts on the lawns of the buildings across the street.

I found Gomorrah sitting on Fury's hood, one leg kicking back and forth while she stared off into the sky.

"You look chill," I said as I moved over.

The nun looked down, her impassive mask staring back at me. "I was. Just relaxing a little before we get back to work."

"We're taking the Fury?"

"We're not walking."

Fair enough. "Right. Before we go. Did you find a place to land us?"

"I figured I'd find the biggest hole and slip into that," she said. We were both quiet for a while, and then she sighed. "Don't say anything."

"I wasn't going to," I lied.

"Did you have a better idea?"

"If I say anything related to lube, you'll be pissed, right?"

She nodded.

"Right, right. So, I *was* actually thinking. The mine has to have an exit. Or at least, an entrance. The orbital strikes might have poked a few holes in the surface, but the company had to get in somehow."

"You're thinking of hitting the hive from that direction?" Gomorrah asked.

"It's an idea," I said. "If we drop into the middle of the hive, between . . . whatever dead end is in that, and the exit, half of them will be able to run away."

She shifted. "Unless we come in by the main entrance and then half of them leave from that new hole. Did you want to split up?"

"No. Let's stick together. And that hole is monitored. Any aliens coming out of there will be tracked. At least, I hope."

"And not those from the main entrance?" Gomorrah asked.

I shrugged, then made a crumbly gesture with both hands. "We could collapse it?"

"That . . . makes some sense. A few rockets by the entrance might do it."

"I've got a lot of options when it comes to bombs. Like, an unhealthy amount. I'm sure there's something I can buy for a few points that'll do the trick."

I stretched, then gestured to the Fury. "Let's go." I tossed my crap in the back. "Oh, and we need to call Cause Player."

"*You* need to call him. I've been talking to everyone today. And don't forget your cats."

I had forgotten about those. With what looked like a few hundred soldiers around, they were probably not as useful to have around. "Myalis, can you recall those? Would they fit in the trunk?"

"The trunk's not too big," Gomorrah said. "But you can try."

My mecha-cats trotted over, some of them surprising the soldiers as they sauntered by. As it turned out, you could fit them in the trunk, but it was a near thing. They had to fold themselves up all neat and tight, and I had to shove them in a bit.

I slumped onto the passenger-side seat and started looking through my contacts while Gomorrah gently took off and started to hover over Black Bear.

My augs rang, and soon enough, Cause Player picked up. "Hello?" he asked.

"Hey," I said. "You're alive?"

"Yeah. That blast nearly knocked me off my feet. Nearly destroyed my camera too, but I still got a good angle on everything. It'll make for a great VOD."

"Uh, yeah. That sounds cool. No injuries?"

"I have good armor," he said. "Are you okay?"

I allowed myself to grimace. No one could see it. "I'm fine. The hive's not entirely gone. It's currently settled into this mineshaft. Gomorrah and I are heading over there now."

"Can I come? Tight quarters like that make for a great show."

I considered it for a bit. "Sure. We'll take the side leading deeper into the hive, you take the other side."

"That's fewer aliens for me," he said.

"There are two of us," I said. "If the tunnels split again, we'll be able to handle it better. Plus we have mechas with us. I'm a stealth and bomb specialist; Gomorrah has all the flamethrowers."

"I guess. At least I'll be around if you two need help, or vice versa. Let me put my stream on pause."

"You don't want them seeing us?" I asked.

"Do you want to be seen?" he asked.

"One sec," I said. "Gomorrah, two things. Cause Player wants to come with. We'll be splitting up at each entrance. I think we could drop him off at the main entrance and take the other ourselves. And do you mind being on camera? This dude's got, like, a Twinge livestream going on."

"I don't mind people seeing me, or Fury, for that matter."

"Neat," I said. I opened a text box and started to send a text to Lucy. She'd want to follow Cause Player's stream, knowing her. "Cause Player? We're good. We'll swing around to pick you up in a couple of seconds, er—as soon as we know where you are."

"Cool. Do you have a map of the hive?"

"Ah . . . yeah, but it's shitty. Let me get one from the mining corp, they must have a map of their own damned mine."

We really weren't going into this as prepared as we should have been.

But I figured we'd be fine. Overwhelming firepower corrected a lot of wrongs.

CHAPTER SIXTY-SEVEN

EXPLORING NEW HOLES WITH YOUR FAVORITE NUN

"Okay, so you know how slave labor is all sorts of illegal, right?"

"Obviously."

"Right, so get this. Someone volunteering . . . isn't. An employee giving you time willingly, without asking for pay? Yeah, that's fine."

"Who's going to work for free?"

"No, no, see, that's the best part. You take note of who did volunteer work, make it public, and when promotions roll around, you tell those who volunteered a lot and who happen to get promoted that it's partially because they volunteered."

"So to get promoted you need to volunteer?"

"What? No, that'll just get idiots with too much time up the ladder. Nah, but when someone who did volunteer gets promoted, you make a big show of it. I'm telling you, about one-fifth of our employee work hours last year were entirely volunteer work. You can even use it as a tax write-off!"

—Overheard conversation at the AE New Montreal Head Office

Cause Player didn't complain about how cramped the rear seats of the Fury were. That was great.

He did complain about just about everything else, though. "Slow down!"

"I'm hardly going fast," Gomorrah said.

"It's relative!" he said as trees whipped by on either side.

"We're barely going one hundred," Gomorrah complained.

"That's really fast when you're only a few feet off the ground!"

I snorted. "Who uses feet? For measuring shit, I mean."

"I'd use liters for that," Gomorrah whispered.

It took me a second, but when I caught on I cackled.

"The road! The road!" Cause Player shouted.

Gomorrah looked ahead, twitched us out of the path of a tree, then turned to stare at Cause Player. "I didn't learn to drive yesterday, you know?"

"Wait, I vaguely recall you telling me you didn't know how to drive?"

"That was three days ago."

I looked out ahead, at all the trees whipping by. "Um, now I'm a little concerned too," I admitted.

Cause Player said something that was probably rude, but Gomorrah chose that moment to yank us up, spin Fury around, then come to a very quick hover on a flat patch of ground.

The forest was cleared for a ways, leaving plenty of room for the huge machines that were parked around the mine entrance, which was wider than most of the houses in Black Bear and twice as tall.

The Fury slid to a stop and hovered a meter off the ground, front facing the mine entrance. The entrance, and about a dozen Antithesis.

"Huh," Gomorrah said.

She flicked something, and a large gun unfolded from the car's hood.

The Fury's soundproofing proved its worth. I didn't even hear the machine gun going off. Soon, the few Model Threes and Fours lingering around were turned into so much pulp that they were hard to tell apart from a pile of roadside slush.

"This is your stop," Gomorrah said. "We even cleared the landing zone."

"Thank you," Cause Player said. "I think . . . I'll figure out how to get back on my own."

"Suit yourself."

I leaned to the side to see him open the back door. He looked strange, all tucked in with his heavy armor, knees almost at his chest. It was good that his guns were the teleport-y sort. "Stay warm," I said. "And if shit goes crooked, give us a call."

"I will," he said. "You do the same." With that, he squeezed out of the car and crashed into the ground, boots first. Heavy metal started to fill the air as he strode forward, and a large gun materialized into his arms.

"Really want one of those," I said.

"The music?" Gomorrah asked as the door closed.

"The magic gun thing," I said.

She nodded. "It's neat."

Gomorrah drove forward, then angled us up and over the rocky hillside into which the mines dove.

I have the survey information from the headquarters. It seems as if they sent information that doesn't entirely match the seismographic information obtained from the orbital strike. Either the company is lying, their information is out of date, or they are incompetent. I suspect it's a little bit of all three.

"Did you check around for any signs that they're lying on purpose?" I asked.

None that I could see, but there are some employees who have a history of bending the truth to better pad out the bottom line.

Well, that wasn't unexpected. "Whatever. We'll figure it out once we're down there. If the place is active, we'll want to deploy quickly."

"Rockets in the entrance?"

"Might make the place cave in on us," I said.

"That's fair. Do you have anything to prevent a cave-in from killing you?" Gomorrah asked.

"I don't," I said. "Well, bombs."

The nun sighed. "Bombs don't . . . well, I suppose technically."

I kinda wished she could see my grin. "Explosives fix most problems, when you're creative enough with their use," I said.

"Right, I've got a thing. I'll buy you one once we've landed."

"Really?"

"A hundred points to keep you alive is hardly much of a sacrifice."

I . . . felt a bit touched. "Thanks," I said, meaning it.

Gomorrah didn't comment; instead she wheeled us around a patch of what had been a forest. I hadn't been paying too much attention, but now that we were over the area closer to where the Rods of God had impacted, it became pretty obvious something big had hit.

Nearly every tree around was knocked flat on its side, like tens of thousands of narrow dominoes.

The hole we were looking for wasn't that hard to spot. A crack running across the edge of a hill, maybe fifty meters long and way, way deeper.

"Not finding much space to land on," Gomorrah said. "Maybe there?" She pointed to a spot some dozen meters from the crack, with a few rocks that looked kind of stable.

"Hover over?" I asked.

"Yeah, but we need to unload some stuff. I think that grapple system of yours is still in the back. I'm . . . very much not surprised that you leave stuff around in other people's cars."

"Oops," I deadpanned.

Gomorrah brought us down and set the Fury to hover. Stepping out was a bit tricky, with the ground being so uneven, but we managed.

I stared into the crevice, the whole thing feeling a lot larger, and a lot darker now that we stood right on the edge of it. "All right, let's unload the mecha-cats. Should we leave one with the Fury?"

"To guard it? No, I'll remote it up a few hundred meters. It'll target any flying Antithesis around, and it can serve as a beacon for us. There's not much normal reception around here."

I glanced to the skies. Dark. Dark and brownish. There were some fires here and there too, little white plumes reaching out to the clouds.

"Cat?"

I snapped out of it and rushed to the back of the Fury to help unload the mecha-cats stored within. "Going to be tricky to get these three to the bottom," I said.

"They're not so heavy," Gomorrah said. "Who's going down first? Oh, and let me get you that thing."

"Ah yes, the thing," I said.

As it turned out, the thing was a small pack with clamps. It was mildly complicated to put on and had a bunch of boxes around it. Gomorrah explained that they would deploy a sort of airbag around me if something went horribly wrong. It was more than just an airbag, but I got the gist of it.

"Myalis, can I spare enough points for, like, a stealth poncho? With a hood?" I asked.

A stealth poncho?

"Like, a thing that'll cover me more than just my jacket. I have my legs and head still visible."

I think I understand what you're looking for. Perhaps a cloak?

"A cloak of invisibility? That sounds kind of awesome. Always wanted one of those."

"For peeping in bathrooms?" Gomorrah asked as she helped me grab the last mecha-cat.

"Showers, actually," I said.

You only want something simple?

"It's all I can afford," I said.

"You know it's still weird to only hear one side of that conversation," Gomorrah said.

I shrugged.

New Purchase: Cloak of Inpurrceptability

Points reduced from . . . 170 to . . . 35

I picked up the box the cloak came in and opened it to find a long cape-like thing, with a deep hood that of course had cat ears sewn on. Kinda cute, though. I slid it on over everything else I had. Fortunately it was pretty light, because I was covered in a whole load of gear already.

"Do you think we should get like, exoskeleton suits, or power armor?" I asked.

"Isn't that the end goal?" Gomorrah asked. "Honestly, I think it depends on what you're going for."

Gomorrah and I set up my old grapple system, the drill heads digging into some of the larger stones as if they were so much butter. And then it was time to head down into the pit. "I'll go first," I said.

"Not even a debate?"

I grinned, then walked off the edge. "Nope!"

CHAPTER SIXTY-EIGHT

DARKNESS

Samurai Hunters Twelve!

Build your own samurai team and hunt Antithesis in the best MOBA of the decade!

Now with 178 new DLC characters!

—Nimbletainment ad, 2039

The darkness was . . . strange.

No, all right, it was normal darkness. Just a lack of light from above. The thing is, I could still "see" perfectly well. My cybernetic cat eye was pretty good about low light, and it was messing with my head that my meat eye wasn't.

Strangely enough, the ears helped me see more.

I hadn't noticed how accustomed I'd gotten to my new ears, I guess. They were supposed to have some sort of sonar to them, and I had noticed that I could see a sort of mental image of things that were around a corner, but it was all very subtle. A sort of impression that faded into the background when I wasn't paying attention. Something about the system had to be there to prevent it all from disorienting me.

Now, in the deepening darkness of the mines, that system came into play again. Or it would be more accurate to say that I noticed it more. I couldn't see into the deeper darkness, but I could sense what was there anyway.

Freaky.

Kinda cool, though.

My grapple system lowered me down meter by meter until finally my foot touched the ground. I'd left Whisper in the Fury, figuring that a long-ranged, low-rate-of-fire weapon like that wouldn't be of much use in a mine. Looking around, I had the impression it was the right choice.

The moment I touched down, I deposited the two mecha-cats I was holding. The suckers were pretty heavy, but at least they had little handles on them. The mecha deployed while I looked around.

There were big chunks of rock and stone all over, fallen pieces from whatever had caused the hole above, I figured, but the walls themselves were smooth, as if someone had polished them.

I unclipped myself from the grapple's harness, then used an aug-command to send the whole thing wheeling back up.

Reaching into my coat, I pulled out my Trench Maker, then tugged up the hood on my cloak. The cat ears on my helmet actually served to keep the cloak in place, which was handy.

Then with a flick of a switch, I turned on the cloak and faded away. My coat's invisibility came on too, and with the two combined, I figured I was nearly entirely covered. My head was invisible from any direction but straight ahead, my legs from the same. Only the bottom of my boots and maybe my hands and guns when I stuck them out would be visible. That was pretty decent, I figured.

"Myalis," I muttered. "Remind me to get a stealthy gun."

Gladly.

My Trench Maker was fun, but it was the loud kind of fun. "I'll need some silent grenades too."

I see three options there. Either chemical grenades that spread toxins or solutions to break apart Antithesis, or Flesh Melters; the nanites are silent. Both options are fairly slow-acting.

"And the third option?" I asked.

Black hole bombs, by dint of being what they are, do not let any sound escape.

"Huh," I said. "That's something." I didn't have the points for any gear like that just then, which was really starting to get annoying. I liked being able to buy my way out of trouble. "Let's wait for Gomorrah to arrive, and then we can look into farming for points."

Wonderful!

Gomorrah's timing was on point. I heard the faint whine of the grapple system from above, and my favorite nun came sliding down like a spider on the end of a thread. She touched down and swung her flamethrower around in an arc, the gun tucked under her armpit. Her other hand held on to the handle on the back of one of my mecha-cats. "Cat?"

"Hey," I said, bringing a hand out from under my cloak to wave.

"Didn't see you there," she said. "Honestly, I can't see much. Are we safe?"

"Safe-ish?" I tried. I couldn't see any Antithesis, but I hadn't been looking all that hard. The ground was a dusty mess, and thanks to that, it wasn't hard to see the trails left behind. Pawprints, or the nearest thing to paws that the aliens had, and other spots where things had dragged across the ground.

Gomorrah removed her mask, then pulled something out from within it. The insides? A box materialized by her feet, and she knelt down, opened it, and replaced the insides of her mask with a new insert.

"What's that?" I asked

"Night vision," she said. "Or dark vision? I'm not entirely sure of the mechanics. It lets me see in low light. And I won't be blinded by sudden changes in brightness."

"Neat," I said. "Why not just get a whole new mask?"

"I have modular gear," she said. "Most of it's covered by my habit."

Interesting. It only made sense that she'd have her own way of doing things. Probably less wasteful than my own, actually.

"That way, I think." She pointed off to one side.

"I'll go ahead. We need some way for you to know where I am."

"My friendly fire does tend to be a bit literal," she said.

With your permission, I can send microsecond updates on your relative location to Gomorrah, and with the assistance of Atyacus she will know where you are at all times.

"Sounds fair," I muttered. "Gomorrah, Myalis is sending Atyacus my location information. No need to try to get me hot and bothered."

"Adorable," she said. "I'll send you the same, I guess."

It took a bit of fiddling, but soon Gomorrah had an outline around her whenever I looked her way, one that moved whenever she did. It was kind of neat. "Ready?" I asked. The same aura appeared around my three cats too. They weren't stealth models, but they were pretty quiet already.

"Lead away."

I stepped out ahead, Trench Maker low to my side and attention out ahead. The mines got a bit cleaner as I moved past the spot with the opening above. Somehow, I didn't expect to feel the weight of all that rock above me pressing down. Not literally, just a sort of . . . awareness that there was a lot of shit above me, and it might not stay there.

Kneeling down a little ways into the tunnel, I brushed my meat fingers over the floor. "How is it so smooth?" I asked. It wasn't smooth-smooth, but it wasn't as rocky and pebbly as I would have thought a mine would be.

From the company records, it seems as though they adopted some Vanguard-level technology to mine. Mostly to discover mineral deposits, but they also use a plasma-jet system to burn into the earth.

"Hmm," I said. Some sort of melting effect would explain the smoothness. It reminded me a bit of melted plastic, like leaving a bottle on a heating vent for too long.

The company is supposed to backfill some mines once they are done extracting from them, but in most cases they mark the shafts as filled without doing so, or fill them with what seems to be industrial waste.

"How surprising," I said, my tone about as flat as the floor.

The mine bent a little, and it was as I moved forward around that bend that I noticed the first Antithesis to greet me.

A Model Four, one that seemed to be injured.

I raised my Trench Maker, then hesitated. Loud. It would attract all the rest, which was both good and not.

Then more aliens joined my new pal, some Model Threes that seemed a bit smaller than I was used to, and with a strange shuffling, a large worm appeared. A Model Eight. I hadn't seen one of those in a while.

The Model Threes surrounded the Model Four, and then on some unseen signal, they tore into it, chopping the Model Four apart and tearing limbs off before tossing them to the worm.

You missed out on some points there.

"What the hell?"

Antithesis have no sense of individuality. No more than a leaf on a tree can think for itself. This is the hive pruning itself for more resources. A good sign.

I tucked my Trench Maker away, then pulled up my Icarus. I had some options for the kind of explosive I wanted to thump ahead from the launcher, but really, there was an HE option and I was a high-explosives kind of person.

Lining up the shot took a second, and then I pulled the trigger and felt the launcher kick back with a satisfying "fwump."

The HE round landed right in the middle of the pack and I flinched back as an explosion rocked past me.

I hadn't considered what being in a tunnel would do with an explosion like that.

At least it was significantly worse for the aliens.

Targets Eliminated!

Reward: 60 points

New Total: 95 points

I grinned. The worm alien was missing its front half, and the Model Threes were scattered across a few dozen meters, the bits of them that were still recognizable.

I was going to pat myself on the back for a job well done when I heard some motion coming from deeper in the mine. A lot of motion.

"How many aliens are we dealing with?" I asked.

Likely several hundred to the low thousands, depending on how entrenched the hive is. As long as it has biomass, that number is likely to redouble every twenty-four hours.

"Ah . . . shit."

CHAPTER SIXTY-NINE

NICE

"You don't want to see us letting loose, uwu."
"We stop the buck!"
"You don't want that to happen to you, desu!"
"We'll fuck you up!"
—Hyper Cutie Zoom Ranger Sparkle Girl Bubble-chan!
and Neon Girl Happy-chan! in a 2040 joint interview

"This was a mistake!" I shouted as I ran.

Behind me, aliens were pouring out of a crack in the wall. Smaller ones, because that was all that could fit, but enough of them to give me pause. Little Model Ones, all sleek and batlike and hard to spot in the cavern, even with my ears, and Model Threes that looked slimmer than usual. Plenty of others too, but I wasn't going to sit down and observe them all when the entire hive looked like it was out for blood.

Charging down the bend in the corridor, I slid to a stop the moment I saw Gomorrah's outline ahead of me, and then I turned around and raised my Icarus.

The grenade launcher had an eighteen-round magazine. I'd fired one already.

The next five thumped out and arced over to the bend just as the horde started coming around.

With a quick flick of my eye, I switched over from HE to fragmentation, then launched the next two rounds before I continued to run toward Gomorrah. "Turn off notifications for a bit," I said. "And I'll need ammo soon!" My counter was down to ten rounds already.

"What?" Gomorrah asked.

"Pissed-off aliens," I said.

My mecha-cats, all three of them currently surrounding Gomorrah, tensed, guns unfolding from their back and eyes glowing red as they focused on the end of the tunnel.

"Does your helmet filter the air?" Gomorrah asked.

"What? Uh, I think?"

It does.

"Good."

Aliens started pouring out from the end of the mineshaft, and despite that, Gomorrah didn't slow down her slow, steady walk.

I jogged up and kept pace beside her, my shoulder-mounted guns deploying even as more aliens started running our way.

I fired up and over the front lines of the aliens, each blast going off behind them taking out three or four of them.

Then the mecha-cats opened fire. They seemed to mostly focus on the Model Ones above, their backs arching like a pissed-off cat's as the air filled with zipping tracers that skewered fliers across the breadth of the tunnel.

I clicked on empty with my Icarus and fell to one knee. "Reloading," I said. My railgun fired, punching a thin hole all the way through the horde, and then my plasma caster started to spit fire into the approaching aliens. They were getting closer than I'd like.

"I got this," Gomorrah replied.

I pressed the tab on my launcher's side to eject the magazine within, then caught a fresh one out of the air as it materialized next to me and slid it in under my gun. There was a bit of fumbling there, even with the correct buttons glowing a bit to help, but I figured I'd get used to it.

Then Gomorrah started speaking in Latin and she leveled her flamethrower ahead of her.

I hissed as a white beam shot out of the end of her oversized gun. The heat was palpable, like standing right up against the door to an oven. The white beam broke up a few meters away, splitting apart and spreading liquid fire onto anything it touched.

The aliens melted.

It was weird to see. Almost disturbing. So much flesh bubbling and going liquid a moment before sloughing off of bones. Eyes popped and lungs emptied with little squeaks. Not all of them died right away. Some fell to the side, still on fire, wriggling and fighting to move even as their fur and skin burned.

Gomorrah waved the flamethrower left and right, spreading the fire around in a curtain ahead of us.

For some reason, the worst part was the lack of screams. The aliens had to be in pain, but they were silent, dying without much of a fight.

Gomorrah paused in her chanting. "They're going around."

Around? I eyed the burning conflagration ahead of me for a moment before I saw what she meant. The aliens ahead were dead, but in dying they created a sort of barrier that Gomorrah's flamethrower had to burn through. The horde was splitting apart, rushing at us from both sides.

"Two cats, focus left, one focus the air," I ordered. The mecha-cats immediately shifted, the two on Gomorrah's left aiming down and ripping into any Antithesis that tried to sneak around, and the one behind us a little continuing to fire into the air, striking at the Model Ones zipping by.

I turned, flicked on HE and burst mode, then fired two three-round bursts into the pile of burning aliens ahead of us before I switched back to fragmentation and let loose on the right flank.

The HE rounds tore the wall of bodies apart, scattering flaming plant-meat around and opening up some room for Gomorrah to spray the aliens farther back.

I felt my cheeks straining as I launched round after round of fragmentation grenades into the aliens pouncing around our flaming barrier. Sometimes, the little shields built into my jacket would flicker on, stopping some of the frag from hitting me and Gomorrah behind me.

My rails twitched up and took out a pair of fliers with one burst, and my plasma caster kept switching targets, leaving burning lines in the dark that ended in the middle of the chest of dozens of fliers.

"Bigger ones!" Gomorrah shouted.

I emptied the last of my magazine, dropped it, and caught a fresh one from Myalis without having to ask. It gave me a little moment to look ahead.

Gomorrah was right, bigger aliens were coming. Model Fours and Fives. The latter would be a problem, they were tankier.

"Let's move right," I said. "We need a wall on one side."

"Got it," Gomorrah said.

She started sidestepping even as her habit shifted and a pair of back-mounted guns poked out over her head. The two new flamethrowers glowed a violent red for a moment before adding their own fire to the conflagration ahead of us.

I was sweating, armor sticking to me, and yet I couldn't help but want to laugh as I slapped a new magazine in and continued firing ahead.

I left it on HE. There was no going wrong with HE.

"Can't take out the big ones," Gomorrah said.

I squinted ahead. One of the Model Fives had fallen, burning and dead. So that wasn't entirely true.

The problem was likely the quantity of fire Gomorrah had to use to take it out; she'd focused on it, which thinned out our flaming barricade a little, even with her two back-mounted guns adding to the blaze.

"Down to thirty percent," Gomorrah said. "I'll need to reload."

"Got it," I said. I pulled my trigger faster, forgoing aim to put more dents in the number of aliens coming. "Myalis, next magazine, I want those monofilament bombs."

Understood.

It wouldn't do that much to hurt the really big guys, but it would create pockets that the smaller ones couldn't pass through. I glanced at my ammo counts. Only halfway with my plasma caster, and my railgun still had over ninety percent. The mecha-cats were nearing the halfway mark with their main guns and had switched from full-auto to picking off targets more carefully.

I clicked empty, dropped my magazine, and picked a new one that Myalis dropped right into my open hand. It was a bit heavier, but that wasn't an issue.

"Going to set up some traps," I shouted. "Then I'm switching to something with more boom, reload on 'Go.'"

"Got it," Gomorrah said.

I fiddled with the controls on my launcher, then aimed way, way up, a parabolic arc showing up in my augs that would be dropping the next explosives past the front rows of aliens.

Our little bit of cover was growing smaller as Antithesis jumped over their burning comrades and launched themselves at us.

I fired, starting from the left, and firing again every few centimeters as I turned. It left a racking arc of smoke lines in the air that crashed somewhere out of sight.

Then the blending started as the monofilament grenades went off and started whipping super-thin strands of some protector-tech wire around. I saw a few aliens being torn apart from the ankle up and grinned.

"Black holes," I said.

Are you certain?

"Set them to only go off with us outside their range."

Understood.

"Go!" I shouted.

Gomorrah stepped back, her flamethrower smoking, its barrel and entire front half red as a stovetop. I saw her drop to one knee behind me and tear open a panel on the side of her gun.

I stopped paying attention as I tore the used mag out of my Icarus and picked up a fresh one from Myalis.

Only six rounds.

"Got it," I said as I clicked the magazine in place.

Without Gomorrah's constant fire, the Antithesis were getting a lot closer.

I aimed for somewhere in the middle and fired, spacing out the shots in another arc.

The wall of corpses ahead of us exploded and a running Model Five charged across the no-alien's-land between.

Then the black hole grenades behind it went off.

I dropped Icarus, letting it dangle by my side from its strap as I whipped out my Trench Maker and sighted it at the Model Five.

It wasn't necessary.

The wind picked up, whipping past me and tugging me forward. The fire roared and shifted, flames dancing up toward the six black points hovering in the air just over the wall of fire.

Aliens started to be picked up and crushed into each other, and the Model Five before me slowed, then stopped, huge claws gripping at the ground even as it started to be pulled back.

I fell to one knee, lessening the pull of the wind.

The Model Five dug in, lowering its head even as the muscles in its legs flexed and it dragged itself forward.

So I shot it in the leg a few times.

It flopped backward soundlessly and crashed into the other aliens being sucked into the burning singularity.

The monofilament grenades behind them came loose and flew into the mess, still spinning and turning everything into a meaty blender.

Then it stopped and for a moment everything was quiet and dark as hundreds of kilos of compressed alien meat flopped to the ground.

Gomorrah slapped the side of her still-glowing gun closed. "Reloaded," she said.

"Neat," I said as I tucked my handgun away. "Let's keep at it, then."

CHAPTER SEVENTY

A PERFECT TIME FOR A PICNIC

Nutrition and dieting is hard!

Try Nutrimin-Os! Now with a percentage of your daily vitamin and mineral needs!

—Nutrimin-Os ad, before the 2048 lawsuit that resulted in the company's bankruptcy

I turned left and right, looking for any aliens.

Well, living aliens. There were literal piles of dead ones all around, some still crackling and burning merrily away and lighting up the mineshaft.

I imagined that the mining company would have to patch the mine up a little. We'd left a few holes on the floor. And the walls. And the ceiling.

Mostly that was me, but I'd share the blame around with Gomorrah too.

"Is that it?" I asked.

"Looks like it," Gomorrah replied. She looked around as well, then casually hosed one pile of dead Antithesis. One of them flopped around, not entirely dead yet. "There will be more, I'll bet, but I think we took out whatever the hive has acting as a mobile guard."

"So the next batch will be . . . what, the immobile guard?"

"No, probably the Antithesis that guard the hive itself. Bigger, meaner bastards. But I don't think they tend to move as much. Kind of like a last line of defense."

"To protect the queen or whatever?"

Gomorrah looked my way. "You need to pick up a damned textbook. Antithesis don't have queens. They're plants. They have root networks and flowers and seeds."

"Right, right," I said. Standing a bit taller, I stretched my back out until it popped. "Can I have five to reload things?"

Gomorrah nodded. "That's probably for the best. I think we could both use a small break. I skipped breakfast."

I'd eaten breakfast with Lucy and the kittens that morning, a messy affair with cereal and burnt pancakes and some actual eggs, but that had been . . . I glanced at my aug's time readout. It was nearing four in the afternoon. Not as long as it felt, but still a while ago. "Yeah, I could use a bite," I admitted.

Gomorrah stared at the ceiling for a bit, then tugged off a glove and held her hand up for a bit. "That way."

"Uh, why?" I asked as I looked down the way we'd come from.

"The air's flowing from that direction and pushing deeper into the mines. We'll be upwind of all the smoke."

"Upwind, right . . . which one's that?"

Gomorrah shrugged. "Up is where the smell's coming from, down is where it's going. More or less."

"Guess snacking with smoke in the air's going to make it taste bad."

"Oh, the smell isn't the problem," Gomorrah said. "I like the smell of burning Antithesis. It's earthy. It's the chemicals I use in Archangel's Kiss. They're all sorts of cancerous, and toxic, and generally liable to leave you dead from inhaling them."

"You named your flamethrower Archangel's Kiss?" I asked. "Is that . . . like, some of your repressed nature trying to come out?"

Gomorrah started walking off. "I was thinking of a more biblical angel."

"A hot dude with wings? Kinda disappointed, I thought you batted for the winning team."

She sniffed. "I bat for the winning team—God's team." She was quiet for a moment, and I didn't say anything. "That was far cornier than I thought it would be."

"Yeah, it was pretty bad."

"Also, biblical angels are more . . . wings and wheels and eyes. Here, I'll send you a document about it."

"I'm sure it's a fascinating read."

"It has pictures."

I snorted.

We reached a point some hundred meters away from the carnage, and I saw Gomorrah raise a hand just before she caught something out of the air. A blanket? She unfolded it and laid it on the ground, then sat down atop it.

I didn't even bother questioning it and just sat down next to her. It was nice to get some weight off my feet, even if my boots were stupidly comfortable. "Have you tried Protector food?"

"Uh, just the juice boxes," I said.

"You're going to love this, then. Anything you won't eat?"

"I'm a malnourished orphan, my list of foods I'm picky about is real small. Though I'm not fond of mushrooms, they're just rich-people mold."

"Right," she said as two boxes appeared between us. Both were roughly rectangular and made of a familiar plastic-ish material, though the hinges on the back were a bit different than the cases I was used to.

Gomorrah slid her mask off and took a deep breath. "That's better. The mask is comfortable, but it's a bit stuffy."

I reached up and undid the clasps holding my helmet in place, then pulled it off. My hair was a sweaty mess, and my head felt lighter without the weight of the helmet on it. It did feel nice. The air stank a bit of dust and smoke and gunpowder. Or maybe that was just my cloak.

Gomorrah handed me one of the boxes and I fiddled around with it for a bit before the case popped open and released a puff of steam.

I stared.

There was a small spork clipped to the top. The rest of the MRE had what looked like a square of shepherd's pie and a small sandwich, with some veggies here and there with some sauce drizzled on them. Probably a healthier, more balanced meal than I'd had . . . ever.

The problem was that the sandwich was cut to look like a cat's face, with little carrot-stick whiskers and a little cheese nose.

"Myalis, is this a joke?"

I didn't do anything.

I whipped around to stare at Gomorrah, a Gomorrah who was very pointedly not looking my way, and who had a suspicious quirk to her lips.

I picked up a whisker and bit into it angrily.

That was enough to break Gomorrah, and she started to titter.

"I didn't take you for a bully," I said.

"A bully?" she asked. "Really?"

"You're just kicking a girl while she's down."

The nun rolled her eyes, still holding back laughter. "Get over it."

"You know this means war."

"You are terrifying," she said. "Can I rub your belly until you feel better?"

I wanted to throw one of the little carrots at her, but they were absurdly good, and I wasn't going to waste food. "This is really good," I said as I took a bite from the sandwich. The bread was good, and the meat and sauce and cheese inside were also . . . good.

I lacked words to appropriately describe how it tasted, but it was definitely a whole order of magnitude better than some of the crap I'd tasted before. "Mmm, have you tried the little juice boxes?"

"Yeah, they're great. Which ones did you try?"

"There are more flavors?" I asked.

"The strawberry one tastes really nice. There's a milkshake one too."

"Oh, damn," I said. "Milkshakes give me the runs, though."

Gomorrah lowered her spork. "Could you not be quite that candid? Besides, I think there's a world of difference in quality from whatever you drank before."

"Pretty sure the ones I tried didn't have any milk in them. Though the 'shakes' part was entirely accurate."

"You're disgusting," she said.

I grinned over at her. "All right, I'll stop. But it's really fun to rile you up."

She shook her head. "Some friend."

I only smiled harder. "Yeah, actually."

The nun actually looked as though she was starting to blush before she wiped it all away with a scowl. "Do you have any plans for the rest of the hive?"

"We'll be fighting bigger, uglier bastards, right? I figure running in there guns blazing might be fun, but not all that safe. Maybe I can sneak ahead? Except this time I just plant a whole load of bombs all over and set them off all at once."

"And then we sweep in and pick off the rest," Gomorrah said. She took a bite from some veggie that crunched wetly, then nodded. "Simple, but it might work."

"Does your chuuni fire cannon need air to work?"

"My what?" she asked.

I pointed to the flamethrower.

"It's called Archangel's Kiss. And no, it doesn't require air to burn. But having an oxygen-rich environment wouldn't hurt. Why?"

"Because I have these neat thermobaric bombs, and I think they're pretty intense when they go off in tight spaces."

Gomorrah bit her lower lip in a way that I would have enjoyed had I been trying to be flirty or something. "That is a nice idea," she said.

"Uh, yeah," I said. I noticed that my MRE was done. I couldn't remember shoveling the last of it down, but I suppose I had. "Anyway, I need to reload on ammo for my handgun, and refill the cats. I guess I'll leave them with you while I range ahead?"

"That sounds fair." Gomorrah stood, then gave me a hand up too. "Now, let's burn this hive down, shall we?"

CHAPTER SEVENTY-ONE

CHLORINE TRIFLUORIDE

Don't use explosives in enclosed spaces.
Especially when you're in those spaces.

—Someone with common sense

I wiggled my head around to make sure my helmet was on snug. It slipped down a little more, then held on tight. Good enough. "All right, so, just give me like, half an hour? We can still chat in the meantime, I think we don't need to worry about signals."

"Very well," Gomorrah said. "Do avoid setting any bombs off until we're ready. You'll probably just kill yourself if you do."

"I'll try not to," I said. "I really want to use fuel-air bombs, but we might settle for some nanite bombs, or some that melt aliens."

"I don't see why we couldn't mix it up."

I nodded. "DDT on steroids or something," I said. I paused, looked at my mecha-cats, then down the darkened tunnel I would be traveling all on my own. I wasn't actually concerned for myself, but I did kind of feel bad about leaving Gomorrah behind. "The cats will keep you company, all right?"

"Of course."

"And if I bite the bullet, you take care of my kittens for me, okay?"

The nun placed her hands on her hips, her flamethrower left to dangle by her side. "You have no business being so fatalistic," she said.

I grinned as I stepped up and wrapped her in a quick hug.

I wasn't a hugger, no matter what Lucy accused me of, but . . . well, it felt nice. "See you in a bit, nun-girl."

Firing off a sloppy salute, I took off into the darkness. My coat's invisibility wrapped around me; then my cloak came on and I flipped my hood up onto my head.

I kept up a light jog, just fast enough to get my heart beating, but not so much that I'd exhaust myself. "Okay, let's talk bombs," I said.

I have two suggestions. First, seeing as how both yourself and Gomorrah are fond of large explosions and copious amounts of fire, an aerosolized agent could be a decent solution to clear out a majority of the mines.

"So like, a gas that burns and hovers in the air?" I asked.

Essentially, yes. There are many variations available, but I would suggest a rather stable one, one unlikely to be immediately detected by the Antithesis and one that will only ignite under very specific conditions.

"So I don't accidentally blow myself up, that's always great."

I would suggest aerosolized chlorine trifluoride. Bonded with a chemical agent that stabilizes it until introduced to either extreme heat or minute amounts of hydrogen fluoride, which is a by-product of the chlorine trifluoride reaction.

I frowned. "So it won't go off until introduced to some chemical that it produces when it's already going off?"

Hence creating a chain reaction, yes.

"Does it burn good?"

Yes. Chlorine trifluoride burns . . . good.

"Cool. So what was the other option?" I asked. I wasn't super smart, but I knew that setting off a big flaming explosion in the tight quarters of a tunnel I was in was a bad idea. There were ways to make it safe . . . safe-ish, and I intended to use those if I could.

The other options are slower-acting. Either an aerosolized acidic compound, pushed deeper into the mines to try to burn out the hive, or a more precise use of nanites designed to break apart Antithesis matter.

"That sounds handy. But slow."

It would be considerably slower than merely burning everything, yes.

I passed the piles of burned bodies that Gomorrah and I had created, then reached into my jacket and hesitated. Handgun or grenade launcher? I was trying to be stealthy . . . and I also had room in my underslung sheath.

"Need a handgun, something subtle."

I've been eagerly awaiting an opportunity to present this particular weapon, which is entirely silent, to you. It's from both your Stealth and Sun Watcher catalogs, as opposed to any of your weapon catalogs.

I slowed my jog down to a quick walk, then even some more when I reached the curve where I'd first met some aliens. I didn't want to come around and meet another group head-on; not if I could avoid it. Couldn't hear any of them, though.

The weapon system is called the Claw. It's not technically a gun but rather a range finder and teleportation system.

"How does it kill things?" I asked.

Within the weapon is a magazine filled with spring-loaded rods, each with ten blades held in place by a trigger. On deploying, these blades open up, and the entire rod rotates around its own axis until all of the kinetic energy within is spent.

"All right," I said. Myalis decided to send me a neat image of a silver cylinder that went from looking like a nice pen to turning into a spinning ball of knives for a couple of seconds. "Very stealthy," I said.

The Claw system teleports one of these rods into the target you are aiming at.

"Oh," I said. I watched as the video changed to what looked like an MRI of one of those rods going off inside a cow. It didn't seem to do more than chip away at bone. For anything else, it acted like an industrial blender set on smoothie mode. "Yeah," I said. "And it's noiseless?"

The vacuum created by teleporting the rod is funneled out of the Claw after each shot, it's the loudest noise created by the weapon, and it's no louder than your breathing.

"Does it look like a cat?" I asked.

It can be made to not look like a cat, if you insist.

"I think I do. How much is it?"

Two hundred and fifty points.

I winced at the price, but then . . . "What am I at?"

Current Point Total:

2,741

"Oh," I said. That changed things a little. "Sure, then."

New Purchase: Claw, Range-Finding and Teleportation System

Points Reduced from . . . 2,741 to . . . 2,491

The gun came in a little box. It was significantly smaller than my Trench Maker, and not much of a gun at all. It had a handle, ergonomic and rubbery, with a trigger, but that was about where it ended. The entire thing just looked like a box with a pair of lenses on the end and a recessed tube on the bottom. There was a knob next to where my thumb naturally fit.

It was surprisingly heavy, though.

My augs connected to it, and I noticed a new reticule appearing on the ground where the not-gun was aimed. It had a depth meter next to it. It didn't take a genius to figure out that turning the knob up and down changed the depth.

"Neat," I said. "Let's find something to blend real fast."

I found a crack in the wall around the next bend, a hole that looked like it had been melted out of the stone, with large, obvious claw marks scrabbling at the stone.

"Think they're down there?" I asked.

The hole is rather small.

I eyed it up. It was a bit of a squeeze. If I went in there, I'd have a bitch of a time moving around. And if some alien came down the other way . . .

That, and it was smaller than some of the models Gomorrah and I had cooked. They couldn't have come from here.

"Bomb," I said.

Chlorine trifluoride?

"Yeah."

The canister was roughly energy-drink-sized, made of some silvery metal and with little legs at its base. I set it down, then pressed the one button atop it.

The bomb synced up with my augmentations a moment later, labeled as "bomb one." So, I could activate it at range? Made sense.

I continued down the main tunnel, trying to shake off distracting thoughts and focus on the path ahead. Couldn't help but imagine that Gomorrah was bored back where I'd left her, but she was a big girl, she'd figure it out.

Something shuffled ahead, and I stopped midstep.

There were lumps, here and there on the ground, unmoving. I couldn't see them, not well. I figured they were rocks or something, but then one shuffled forward, pulling itself along on one leg.

An Antithesis? One that was obviously very much injured.

The streaks across the ground, barely visible as more darkness against the dark, had to have been from dragged aliens.

I didn't know they could retreat.

Raising my Claw up, I shifted it around until the reticule sat atop the alien, and then I adjusted the depth. Five centimeters seemed to be the max.

I fired.

The not-gun shifted a bit, losing some weight a moment before it sort of just . . . inhaled.

The Antithesis slumped.

"Well," I muttered. "I guess it is a stealth weapon."

CHAPTER SEVENTY-TWO

MODEL THIRTEEN

The amount of footage we have of an active hive is, even after all these years, very limited. Ten years, and nearly forty incursions, and this is all the video captured of the breeding ground of the enemy.

—*What to Expect When You're Not Expecting Aliens*, 2031

"Myalis, what the fuck is *that*?" I hissed after ducking down.

That was a giant squid-thing. It wasn't that big, but it took up a lot of space. I couldn't count the number of tentacles on it. There were at least nine big ones, but dozens of smaller, whippier ones, like the little stems on lilies. Narrow and green, with a lump at the end. Only these were twice as long as I was tall.

The problem was that this squid-thing had three bodies, each of them about as big as I was, and connected together by some of those bigger tentacles. I was pretty sure each body had wings too, like a cockroach's.

It looked like something a drunk god created midhangover.

That is a Model Thirteen. It's a hive-defense model. You must be close to the hive.

"The number's nice," I said. "But I need more than just that."

Model Thirteens are midsized close-quarters combat units. They are, essentially, flowers connected to the hive itself. Once deployed, they will die naturally after twelve to fourteen hours, or faster if they exert themselves. They have no mouth with which to feed.

I nodded, encouraging her to go on.

They are generally the last line of defense for a hive. Not tough, but difficult to kill. They can't quite fly, but they can leap very high and glide a little. It's worth noting that all three brains must be destroyed to fully kill a Model Thirteen. Their primary appendages, the thicker ones, end in hardened blades. These are essentially just chitin plates with sharpened edges. The smaller appendages have blocks of waste material at the ends, usually quite heavy. They can whip these at speeds approaching supersonic.

I took a moment to process that. Tough to kill, super-mobile, and they had big chunks of fuck-you at the end of their big tentacles. Also, the little ones could whip out probably faster than I could react.

"Waste material?"

Materials an Antithesis hive can't find a use for. Some heavy metals, radioactive elements, certain gases like ozone. Calcium nitrate. Anything the hive can't find an immediate use for but that it doesn't wish to part with too easily. Storing it with a Model Thirteen keeps it close to the main hive and if a segment of the hive needs a small amount of a rare element, the Model Thirteen can detach and cross a great distance at high speeds to deliver it.

I was maybe some three hundred meters deeper into the mine, two forks away from where Gomorrah was likely waiting for me. I didn't think the hive was right around the corner, but I was certainly getting closer.

Leaning forward, I snuck my head around again. Maybe I could catch a glimpse of the Model Thirteen again and plug a few holes into it with my shiny new gun?

It wasn't there.

That had to be half a ton of tentacles and freaky squid bodies that was missing.

I swallowed, then looked up.

There it was, hanging on to the ceiling like some sort of spider. Its three heads were all turning this way and that, the many eyes on them scanning across the darkened tunnels.

I held still, the deer caught in the headlights. Could I take it? Probably. A couple of grenades with short fuses. My Icarus if I could get it out in time. For all that it had a bunch of tentacles, I was sure a few rounds of HE would do a number on it. Myalis didn't say it was tough, just that it had a lot of . . . redundant biology.

The Model Thirteen moved, shooting down the tunnel behind me with a tick-tick-tick from its tentacles tapping the stone. It was ridiculously fast. "Tell Gomorrah that she's going to have company," I whispered.

Message sent.

At least I knew I was in the right direction. I asked Myalis for another chlorine trifluoride dispenser, which I carefully set in a nook where a few rocks had fallen out of the otherwise smooth wall.

Myalis said the dispersal range for the aerosolized gas was going to be about a hundred meters, or fifty in both directions from the can. Being in a tunnel helped a lot. Still, the last dozen meters of that would only be lightly sprayed in the few seconds after the canister opened up, so I was setting a new bomb every twenty or thirty meters or so.

So I wasn't being very accurate with my no-doubt-war-crime-level bomb placement, sue me.

I continued down the tunnel, now paying a whole lot more attention to the ceiling above in case another Model Thirteen decided to show up. The big bastards freaked me out. They were . . . wrong. Not just the tentacle-ness of them. That was not too unexpected. Model Fours had a lot of those and they weren't too weird.

Ugly, but not too weird.

It took a moment to twig onto what was wrong with the Model Thirteens. They had three faces. Or at least three sets of eyes with noses and all that. Three heads on one creature was just . . . entirely wrong.

I paused a ways down, set another bomb out behind a little stone, then continued on my way.

There was another rock ahead; it looked like a good spot for another bomb. I slowed, eyes narrowing in the dark. I couldn't see well, just from my cybernetic eye, and with absolutely no light to work with, even that wasn't great.

Still, I was pretty sure that rock had just twitched; my sonar told me that much. Rocks weren't supposed to move.

I pulled up my Claw, aimed right at the rock, and fired a shot. If I was wrong, then maybe I'd make a bit of noise. If I wasn't . . .

The rock twitched, stood up, and took two steps before flopping down.

Target Eliminated!

Reward: 25 points

New Total: 2,416 points

I lowered my Claw. "Goddamned Model Nines," I muttered as I continued down the mine. I left a bomb on the end of the tunnel opposite the Model Nine's corpse.

A little later I paused again. There was something very much alien out ahead. Big leafy things, each one about as big as I was, pressed against the walls and set so close together they nearly touched.

"What the hell are those?" I whispered even as I moved to be opposite them.

Those are fin leaves. They serve as both heat dispersal and energy generation. A very interesting form of kinetic-energy generation. It's common with hives that are not able to collect sunlight or that are situated underground. The leaves are entirely harmless . . . unless you eat them. Do not eat them."

"I wasn't planning on it," I muttered.

Approaching the leaves, I could actually feel the heat in the air. They were hot. Not oven-hot or anything, but definitely a few degrees warmer than the ambient temperature.

I placed a bomb next to them. Maybe that would warm them up even more.

"We're close," I said.

Very. Be cautious.

"Keep me informed about . . . you know, alien shit. I don't like not knowing."

I moved away from the leaves, still keeping a wary eye on them. I'd have blown them up, but the noise would have been a problem.

The passage bent again ahead of us, and strangely enough, it seemed to open up too. A larger section?

It sorta made sense. The mine was designed to go after specific spots in the ground, where whatever they were mining for was most common. That meant when they reached a deposit they'd mine it all out. A bit sloppy, maybe, but I was hardly complaining.

The bigger room was filled.

Roots, or something like roots, clung to the walls, with big, bulbous sacks hanging from them like grapes in a fancy wine commercial. The ground was covered in foliage, and in that mess were hundreds of aliens. Model Threes moving in packs, Model Fours in small units, a few Model Fives. There were others too, some of those giant worms moving in and out of narrow holes in the walls, and treelike stalks across the room with big gourds on them had flowers that I recognized as Model Thirteens.

There had to be a few hundred aliens. Maybe a thousand. And that wasn't including the tons of plant life. The center of the room looked like a jungle in miniature.

I was going to need a whole lot of bombs.

CHAPTER SEVENTY-THREE

A WALKABOUT

It was actually something of a blessing. Botany as a science was taken seriously, but it was always treated as . . . dare I say, inferior. The less intelligent cousin of biology. Who cares about people concerned over stuff like plants?

And then aliens invaded. Plant aliens.

I never saw so much grant money being flung around in my life. Suddenly, everyone wanted to know more about how plants worked, and we realized that for all that we knew, it was only really enough to know how little we had dug into it.

Let me tell you, having the president ask you where a tree has its brain is a trip.

—Excerpt from *Leafy Me: A Memoir,* 2028

I hesitated for a while as I considered what to do. There was a lot of hive, and there were a lot of aliens moving around it. Though I guess pointing out a difference between the two was kind of useless.

The big egg sacs . . . seeds? The big things, in which the aliens I was familiar with spawned, grew fast. I could tell that some of them had grown in the ten or so minutes since I arrived. How long did it take the hive to grow a Model Three?

It didn't matter, I guess. In the end, they'd all need to be burned down one way or another. I eyed some models that were jumping around from branch to branch, often stopping by a sac that looked ready to be harvested and helping it down.

A couple of them gathered around each fresh alien murder machine and lowered it down, and then they tore off the wrapping, as it were, and quickly brushed down the fur or whatever of the Antithesis.

"What are those?" I asked. My helmet kept my voice from escaping.

Model Tens. Though they should by all rights be called Model Ones. They are one of the original Antithesis models, with very little by means of changes even across centuries of evolution. They are mostly harmless, and will only attack if something threatens the hive directly, and even then, it will usually be an attempt to distract and win time for other combat models to be born. The back of their palms has a small bill that is sharp; it is their only natural weapon other than their grip.

They looked like weird monkeys. Headless, six-limbed monkeys. Their face was where anything else's neck and clavicle would be, and their limbs all ended in strange hands. Three fingers, and two thumbs on either end. They moved by springing and bouncing forward and swinging along on the many vines and branches sticking out of the hive.

"Neat," I said. It was, in a sort of academic way, I guess. "Where's the hive's brain?"

An Antithesis hive has no brain.

"How does it think?" I asked.

The same way any other plant does. It grows, expands, and evolves to suit its environment. It is not intelligent in any traditional sense, but it is infinitely persistent. You will never see an Antithesis surrendering, or tiring in the face of adversity.

That somehow made it worse.

"So I burn the whole thing down, got it."

I wasn't going to just fling canisters onto the Hive and hope none of the models crawling on it noticed me. Looking past the main, forestlike body of it revealed some other mineshafts, three of them. The hive had grown that way too, at least from what little I could see with the bioluminescent light coming off some of the stalks.

If I wanted to burn the whole thing out in one go, I'd need to cut off all the paths around it, not just this one big lump.

Which meant actually going there.

I started walking near the edge of the room, moving slowly, and keeping an eye on all the models moving around in little packs. They seemed to be gathering in little groups, mostly by size.

A few flowers had blossomed here and there, with some sort of liquid sitting in them. The Antithesis models came to those flowers and would drink up some of that juice before moving on. I guessed that was how they fed?

I stopped when a big worm slithered out of a wall and started moving across the room. It halted some half-dozen meters ahead, then started to contract and expand while making a deep, disgusting retching noise.

I almost gagged when the worm vomited on a bed of large, lily-pad-like leaves. Blood and gore, some sort of mulch, and the recognizable remains of something meaty. Not a human, some sort of . . . deer, maybe? It had hoofed feet, at least. I noticed a dog in there, or maybe it was some poor fox.

Some Model Tens rushed over and started grabbing chunks out of the mess, then leapt away; others formed up and lifted the heavier bits, three to a side.

"What are they doing with that?"

The parts will be brought to a digestion chamber where they will be broken down for nutrients, with some of the smaller pieces being broken down further and absorbed into the Antithesis' genetic banks. Given enough resources, it may try to re-create whatever creature that was, or modify a current model.

"Like cloning?"

No. It's far, far less efficient. It will essentially create hundreds of models with random mutations made from splicing re-created genes into the original model seed. Most of these will be entirely nonfunctional. On occasion, with one chance in several hundred thousand, a model will be born with a useful new trait or adaptation, and that model will be consumed so that future models can mimic this new change. You have encountered new Model Threes already, the larger, more tigerlike ones.

"Yeah," I muttered. "One in a hundred thousand sounds like bad odds. Even if they're eating the failures and starting over."

The Antithesis thrive in magnitude above all else. This hive is about as small as a hive can be while still being fully functional. It can likely produce some hundred Model Threes an hour. One thousand hours at its current size to produce one useful mutation. Most hives can produce thousands to tens of thousands of Model Threes an hour. That is assuming there are beneficial mutations in the local wildlife.

I nodded and moved on. I didn't plan on letting this place stand for a thousand more hours.

Walking a bit faster, I moved past the giant worm as it headed back out, only slowing down enough to get another bomb and tuck it next to the hole it had come out of. I'd need a dozen bombs all around the room if I wanted to burn it all, I figured, and with the current diameter of it, just having some on the edges might not be enough.

I had no idea how flammable the hive itself was.

Stop!

I froze, one foot raised. Then I looked down and noticed the little vines across the ground. Was that it? I'd been stepping on roots and stuff already.

That's a vine from a Model Thirteen. It would alert it.

It didn't take much to notice the huge, flowerlike body nearby, still clinging onto the side of a treelike pillar.

"Thanks," I whispered.

This place wasn't safe. For some reason, it was hard to keep that in mind. Maybe it was because I wasn't actively fighting anything.

If the hive goes on alert, you will have a much harder time moving across it.

I nodded and kept low, only pausing to kneel down over a spot where two roots met and order another bomb to tuck away. I noticed some leafy plants wavering in the air at my passing. Was the hive sensing something?

I chose not to find out.

The first passage wasn't very profound. It ended some hundred meters in, a huge machine wedged into the tunnel, with some lights on around it and plenty of signs that the hive had been poking at the device.

"They can't use tech, right?" I asked.

No. Though they can, on rare occasions, observe and replicate the effects of technology, especially the more mechanical parts.

"Great, that's all we need. Aliens pedaling bikes around."

They don't do wheels very well.

I left a bomb next to the mining machine. It was huge and probably cost more money than someone like me—someone like I used to be would see in ten lifetimes.

Sucked for the company whose asset I'd be burning down.

The next passage was a lot more interesting. More of those fin leaves, hundreds of them, all lined up against the walls. The tunnel here seemed to be moving upward a little bit too. It was hot, hot and humid.

"Think there might be an exit down this way," I said. It was just a gut feeling, but when Gomorrah and I came back down to investigate, this was the path we'd take.

I knelt down and placed a canister next to some of the leaves, then another some thirty or so meters deeper into the mine.

I got up, patted my pants down, then turned right into the waiting tentacles of a monster.

CHAPTER SEVENTY-FOUR

SPRINT

Being on comms means providing the information that will keep people alive.

[. . .]

You can generally tell when something has gone wrong when the people at the other end start swearing incoherently.

—Excerpt from *A Guide to Wartime Communications*, 2045

I think the only reason I didn't get myself killed was that the monster was expecting me as much as I was expecting it.

The Model Thirteen was hovering close to the ground, a few of its tentacles holding it up while its much smaller tentacles were reaching out ahead of it. At a guess, it felt as if it was searching for something, like looking for something by touch when the lights are off.

Had it noticed me before? Or maybe it was just suspicious.

It didn't matter. The alien was definitely staring at me with all three of its faces.

I pulled my Claw up and fired, barely even making sure that the reticule was lined up with one of its bodies.

A whip-crack sounded out, and I felt as if someone had just punched me right in the chest.

I'd gotten into trouble once. A bunch of middle-class-looking assholes had been visiting the ground level, and they started to annoy Lucy and a couple of the other kids. They probably wouldn't do anything, just some older teens being assholes.

Of course, I was filled with more nerves than sense back then, and I wanted to impress Lucy, so I started a fight with them.

The sensation of all the air in my lungs being rammed out of them was hard to forget.

I saw a glimmer in the air as my coat's shield-thing stopped a few more tendrils whipping out at me, but it was only a glimpse before I crashed down a few meters back and rolled.

"Guns," I gasped.

My shoulder-mounted weapons deployed and immediately fired.

A railgun shot tore a hole through one of the Model Thirteen's bodies, but that barely made it hitch before it drove itself forward.

"Shit!"

I rolled back.

With my cloaks still on, it would—I hoped—have a better chance dodging the whips, and rolling would get me farther back.

Problem was, while rolling I wasn't firing back. My plasma caster took some potshots, but it kept folding back in not to stop my roll.

The Model Thirteen loomed large above me, the hardened ends of its larger tentacles crashing into the ground.

I gasped as one of them rammed me in the side. It didn't pierce through my coat, and my undersuit hardened, stopping it from crushing me.

Still hurt like a bitch, and it had effectively pinned me in place.

I placed my Claw against the limb and fired, and then I fired again and again. I imagined that having a tentacle filled with a few spinning blenders wasn't great for the Model Thirteen.

I tugged my coat out from under it with one arm, while aiming up with my Claw.

My railgun fired into one of its bodies, so I aimed at the one next to it and fired my Claw until a warning filled my vision.

OUT OF AMMO

"Fuck!"

My plasma caster painted a line of burning fire into the Model Thirteen's other body, even as the Antithesis leapt away from me and clung to the ceiling. It began to scurry around, avoiding bullets with a speed and agility that was really starting to piss me off.

I dropped my Claw, tore my Trench Maker from my coat, and started to stand.

Its tentacles bunched up under it and the alien launched itself at me, smaller whips already cracking as they shot at me.

I had time to plant two shots into one of its bodies before it crashed into me and we both crashed back.

Fighting it off, I wiggled and struggled and cursed until I realized that it wasn't fighting back.

Target Eliminated!
Reward: 100 points
New Total: 2,516 points
I panted for a bit, then squeezed out from under the Model Thirteen's corpse.
You might want to hurry. The hive is now aware of you.
"Yeah," I said.
I stumbled to my feet. A bit sore, but not dead, and not injured as far as I could tell.
That might not stay the case. The hive was . . . changing. The trees were shifting; the egg sacs were nearly all falling down, regardless of how ready the models within were; and all of those other models looked agitated as hell, with a whole load of them heading my way.
I tucked my Trench Maker away, ran over to pick up my Claw, then tugged my Icarus out. "Fragmentation," I said.
I fired, again and again, with a high arc that had my shots landing right in the meat of the hive and near some packs of Model Threes. Then I let my big gun slip back down so that it hung by its strap, and I started running.
Not away from the aliens, but toward them.
I was still stealthed, and my augs said that my cloak and coat and suit were all still at one hundred percent. I trusted them.
The moment I was back in the main room of the hive I turned a sharp right and continued running. A few Model Threes, those nearest the tunnel mouth, shot into the mineshaft I'd just left. Good.
The Model Thirteens detaching themselves from their trees with loud squelches didn't inspire confidence. If one could find me . . .
I ran past the last side tunnel I hadn't explored. "Bomb," I hissed before underhanding the canister into the passage. That would have to do for whatever was down there.
I dropped another beside me, then flung one at the center of the hive and winced as about four different sorts of aliens jumped on it and started scrambling at the canister.
I was breathing hard as I shot past aliens, moving just a few meters past them and hoping they wouldn't notice.
If they did, then I had to hope that there was enough chaos around to keep them busy.
"Myalis," I hissed. "Cats. Three of them. Not in a box!"
Certainly!
The thumps sounded out, one after each step I took. A glance back revealed three mecha-cats unfolding to their full height. Then it was two as a Model Thirteen's whip smashed one of them apart.
The other two jumped back, plasma claws burning and back-mounted

guns unfolding to spray bullets all over the place. They didn't even need to aim to hit an alien, there were so many scrambling after me.

The hive's attention turned on them, and I pressed myself to move faster.

Maybe cardio really was a good idea.

I flicked another canister to the side. The more fire, the better, I figured.

A Model Thirteen dropped from the ceiling ahead of me and I cursed as I whipped out my Trench Maker.

I emptied the magazine into its centermost body, and my railgun unfolded to punch a hole into the leftmost. My plasma gun spat fire at the third, blinding it for long enough that I was able to duck under one of its tentacles and could continue running.

I wasn't the only one running. All the little models were rushing about, and the sacs on the side were being torn open from the inside.

Model Tens were zipping around all over, and I swore as one of them jumped at me, all six limbs trying to grab me at the same time.

I punched it, but it caught my hand.

So I finally got to use the plasma claws in my cybernetic hand, the inch-long burning nails melting into the model before I flung its corpse aside.

One of them jumped onto my back, and I swiped it off with my tail, the plasma thagomizer on the end of my tail batting it aside.

I was losing the advantage I had from my stealth.

"I need grenades. Garrotes! Just keep giving me more!"

I caught the first to appear and flung it over my shoulder after thumbing the trigger on it. It started to blend the models behind me.

Three more tossed back the same way helped, and I started to under-hand some ahead of me, trying to place them around the entrance of the tunnel I'd come into the hive from. My railgun was spinning and firing, my plasma gun hissing as a rejoinder.

The garrote grenades, with their wildly spinning mess of whippy wires, created a narrow passage, one that I squeezed through before turning around and tugging my Trench Maker out again.

I planted a few rounds into the first aliens through the crack, at least until I clicked empty. Another box popped up in the edge of my vision, confirming that I was out of bullets.

I cursed, spun on a heel, and bolted down the center of the tunnel.

The garrotes wouldn't last forever, and the passage between was big enough for plenty of models to pass through.

I had to get out of the AOE of my gas bombs so I could burn this entire place to the ground.

Totally starting to empathize with Gomorrah's love of burning shit.

CHAPTER SEVENTY-FIVE

TRIGGERING, BUT THE FUN SORT WHERE THINGS EXPLODE

People go on and on about what can turn a lady on. Nice men, nicer women, fat stacks of cash. Power.

They're right about the last one. We do love power, especially when it's nice and packaged and easily weaponized.

Some folks think that the purest form of that is the cannon, and it's true: bitches love cannons.

But a lady?

A lady likes explosives.

—Salamander Storm, 2041

I wasn't an endurance runner. Or any other sort of runner.

I was more of a "sit with Lucy on my lap" kind of girl.

My breaths came hot and fast, my heartbeat all crooked, and my thighs and calves burned. Still, I didn't have the option to stop and take a breather.

"My-Myalis, ammo," I huffed, my Icarus raised in one hand. A magazine appeared before me and I caught it out of the air and slapped it into place.

I barely aimed as I ran sideways for a bit and held the trigger down. Most of the aliens behind me were Model Threes, but there were others, Model Tens riding along, and farther back—but catching up—were Model Thirteens.

I'd be swarmed soon.

I needed a moment to think and act. "Garrote!" I caught the grenade, jammed my thumb over its trigger, then flicked it behind me underhand.

That wouldn't do jack to stop them, but it might mulch a couple before they caught up to me.

I needed something bigger, something that didn't explode. "Gas!"

Another grenade, this one a canister. I flipped the top off and dropped it by my feet a second before it started to hiss and spit. A glance behind me showed that the gas was expanding and climbing to the ceiling. It would mess with the Model Thirteen then.

I was pretty sure it wouldn't kill it, but maybe injuring it would be enough. The others might live too, but every bit of damage was good in my book.

I spun around a corner, the same one where Gomorrah and I had encountered the first aliens in this mine. And right there, like some sort of angel, was the woman in question.

"Go left," she said, her head nodding to her left.

I ran past her, then sighed as I felt a powerful wash of warmth at my back.

My run slowed down, and I veered off toward the wall. Slumping against it while I sucked in air. My railgun and plasma caster were both out of ammo. My Claw and Trench Maker too, though those hadn't been terribly useful. All I did was take potshots at the aliens. My Icarus had . . . six HE rounds left.

I wondered if I had time to reload. At least, until I looked over and saw the wall of fire ahead of Gomorrah. It was bright and thick enough that the only things making it through were the half-melted remains of some of the faster models, their momentum enough to carry them past the fire.

My mecha-cats were stationed around Gomorrah, one on each side while the third came over and stood near me. "Thanks," I said as soon as I turned on our comms.

"No problem," Gomorrah replied. "That Model Thirteen that came this way was something."

"Nasty, huh?" I asked.

"It kept avoiding my fire. Your cats ended up doing a lot of the damage. I need to invest in faster-firing weapons."

"Yeah, cool," I said. "Can you cover me for two minutes? I need to reload everything." Gomorrah nodded. I trusted her to keep me alive for a couple of minutes. "Myalis, I need a reload on everything."

I raised my Icarus, switched to HE, and fired the last shots remaining down the tunnel the aliens had followed me from. Figured I might hit one of them if I was lucky.

Reloading my shoulder-mounted guns was a bit of a pain. The rest wasn't too bad. Myalis was giving everything to me one at a time, so I was moving at my own pace, more or less.

"I think we're clear," Gomorrah said. She lowered her flamethrower and let the wall of fire die down a little. If I squinted, I could make out the darkened forms of burning aliens slumped over here and there.

There weren't as many as I imagined, but maybe I hadn't had a good look at them.

"Good work," I said as I slid the last magazine into my Claw, then tucked it away. "That was stressful."

I'd need a good shower after this. My coat might have been cool, but it was still warm, and all the fire and running for my life didn't help.

"Did you find the hive?" she asked.

"Yeah. Nasty place. A hundred or so more models over there. I don't know if they'll stay put or not."

Gomorrah nodded. "I'd like to see the footage later."

"Uh, sure," I said. My cybernetic eye had probably recorded all of that. I bet Myalis had, at the very least. "There's a tunnel past the hive that I didn't get to inspect, otherwise I think I covered it all."

"Did you plant any bombs?"

"Yup. Canisters full of chlorine trifluoride." I was pretty proud that I didn't stumble on that one.

Gomorrah turned her head my way. "Canisters of *what*?"

Did I mispronounce it?

"How many did you place?" she asked.

"About . . . I don't know, twenty?"

Twenty-two canisters.

"Twenty-two, according to Myalis," I said. "They're pretty big. Thermos-sized, you know."

"How much of the stuff is in each?"

Ten liters, liquid and hypercompressed.

"Ten liters," I repeated with entirely unearned confidence.

Gomorrah hesitated. "We . . . should probably not be so close to them, in that case."

I'd lost a few of my nine lives to bombs already, so a bit of caution wouldn't be amiss. "Sure. I'll call up Cause Player at the same time. Want to back out of that entrance hole?"

"Sure," Gomorrah said.

I stretched my back out as I dialed up Cause Player. It felt like I'd had a weight lifted off my back, just from being so close to Gomorrah and out of tentacle range of so many aliens.

"Stray Cat," Cause Player said. "Are you all right?"

"I'm fine. We're both fine. But you might not be. Gomorrah and I are about to set off the mother of all firebombs, and I wanted to make sure you weren't in the burn radius."

"Uh, thanks. I'll send you my coordinates. I've been mostly exploring the offshoot tunnels near the entrance. Not much more than some lower-level models here."

"Good. The hive's not that big, I don't think. It's also covered in explosives. We're clearing out of the blast radius ourselves."

"Right, can you send me the projected area of effect?"

Sending now!

"Got it . . . Looks like I'm way out of it, should be fine. But thanks for calling."

Myalis had been kind enough to let me see that same map, with Cause Player's location blinking away on it, and Gomorrah and me represented by two blinking lights. The center of the blast zone was blue, turning to purple, then red, then orange all the way to green.

We were still in the yellow, but it looked like that was about to end soon.

"Here," Gomorrah said a hundred or so meters later. Right on the edge of the yellow zone, according to Myalis's map. Seemed safe enough.

"Okay," I said. I had twenty-one canisters marked as functional, with one of the lot marked as damaged but operational. The UI to link them all together was as simple as checking the "select all" box. "Do you want to do the honors?" I asked.

"You set them up," Gomorrah said. "Blow away."

". . . Was that innuen—"

"Just set them off," she said.

I grinned and pressed the metaphorical red button.

A whole lot of nothing happened.

"Uh," I said. The "Trigger" button was grayed out. I couldn't even jab it a few extra times.

The canisters are spraying their load out into the air. The aerosolized chemical needs time to disperse and travel. It will trigger the actual burn when ideal saturation is reached. That is, when there's a good amount of chlorine trifluoride in the air without it being either too thick or thin. Which should be happening . . . now.

I turned, my ears picking up a sharp "tack" sound from down the tunnel.

It meant that I could see the wave of dust rushing toward me. Not that I could react.

My coat flapped, and I took a step back as a blast of air shot past.

"Whoa!" I said.

"Was that it?" Gomorrah asked a moment later.

Then the air turned and was sucked back down the mineshaft, and in the end, like some sort of vision of hell itself, came a wall of fire. The floor started to tremble, slowly, then with growing ferocity.

"Maybe we should run?" I asked.

CHAPTER SEVENTY-SIX

FIGHT FIRE WITH FIRE

One way to take care of uncontrolled fire is to use more fire.

At least, I think that's how it works.

I don't know. I kill things, I'm not a smart person!

—US Army, flamethrower tank operator, 2037

I took a deep breath, then another when that one didn't feel so good. There was air in the . . . air, but it was thin, like breathing around some of the vents near street-level factories.

"Think it's safe?" I asked Gomorrah.

The tunnel was pretty much cleared, the charred remains of Antithesis slumped here and there, and the walls ever so slightly blackened by the wash of fire that had burst past. I could feel a stirring in the air, wind coming in from the opening into the mines and pushing in toward the hive.

Had the bombs going off created a sort of vacuum? I didn't know enough to say, really, but that sounded likely.

"I don't think anything about this was safe," Gomorrah said. "But I figure it was a lot less safe for the aliens."

I nodded, then shuffled a bit before tucking my launcher to my shoulder. "Let's move in, then?"

Gomorrah hefted up her flamethrower, the tip of the nozzle burping with a lick of flame. "Take the lead?"

"Yeah, because being in front of the pyro nun is where everyone wants to be," I said. She gave me a look before I chuckled and jogged ahead a bit. My mecha-cats moved up around us, forming up in a wedge with me at its point and Gomorrah in its center.

We started walking down the mineshaft, at first with easy confidence, but when I started noticing the smoke pooling by the ceiling I slowed down a little.

"Let's take it easy, yeah?" I asked.

"Certainly," Gomorrah said.

I flicked my augs around and found Cause Player's contact. I sent him a quick text.

S.Cat: *You ok?*

It didn't take long for him to reply.

CP: *Yes.*

CP: *Thanks for the explosion. It made for a cool scene!*

If he was happy about that, then he was fine. At least, that was what I figured.

We came around a bend, and I slowed down as I noticed light ahead. A lot of light. Oranges and reds and yellows splashing against the gray stone walls. "That's concerning," I said.

"It's a fire, way out ahead," Gomorrah said. "Do you have oxygen?"

"Just a filter," I said.

"Do you have a catalog with that kind of thing?"

I shook my head. "Not that I know of. Nothing specialized for it."

"Give me a second, then," Gomorrah said. "I have a catalog for modular headgear."

"Nah, it's okay," I said. "My helmet's cheap, anyway; it's due for an upgrade. Besides, you'd get me something uncool."

"Uncool?" Gomorrah repeated. She sounded a little insulted.

"Probably all nunlike and appropriate," I said. "Myalis, are there any really cool helmets in my Sun Watcher catalog? Something that'll let me breathe?"

Gomorrah scoffed. "You'll probably go for something ridiculous and over the top. With cat ears again."

"Lucy thinks the ears are cute," I said.

I have something you might like for three hundred points. It has a full communications suite, thermal and night vision, is armored and lined with impact-resistant gel, and has a filtration system that refills a tank, which in turn feeds you an appropriate amount of air. It's of course fully sealed. Also, the eyes glow.

"That sounds good," I said.

New Purchase: Leopard Mark IV Survival System

Points Reduced from . . . 7,854 to . . . 7,554

"Holy shit, I have how many points?" I asked, ignoring the box that appeared by my side.

Was that rhetorical?

I shook my head to clear it. There *were* a lot of aliens around, and a lot of them got crisped. It made sense. Had I fought and killed more last time? I couldn't quite compare the two incursions.

Kneeling down, I opened the box to reveal a face made of some sleek black metal, recessed lenses over the eyes that glowed a faint pink, and a catlike mouth with two long protrusions below acting as fangs.

It's in two parts. Press the front to your face, then press the rear section to the back of your head.

Gomorrah stepped closer and looked into the box too. "Damn, that does look kind of cool," she muttered.

I tugged my helmet off and regretted not holding my breath when I tried to inhale. The air was thinner than I had thought, and it immediately started to scratch at my throat and lungs. Probably not great for my health.

I tried not to cough as I pulled my new helmet out, flipped it over, and pressed it over my face. The other section fit on the back, and everything closed up with a hiss. Some sort of padding grabbed me around the neck, and if I wasn't mistaken, it clasped onto my suit too.

The inside was snug, but soft. Also, really dark, at least until the screens just before my eyes came on and gave me a clear image of the mines around me. I could finally see.

"Nice," I said. I tossed my old helmet to one of the cats, who caught it from the air in its jaws. "Keep that around. We'll give it to Lucy."

"Better?" Gomorrah asked.

I took a deep breath, then coughed a bit. The air from the mask tasted fresh, like the air inside one of those enclosed gardens, only better. "Much," I said. "Say, I just killed a lot of aliens, but you helped, how does the split work? Is there one?"

"*There is,*" Myalis said, not in my head, but out loud. Or at least, through my coms. I had the impression it was to share with Gomorrah as well. "*Points gained by Vanguards working together are split among all Vanguards based on the amount they accomplish.*"

"I assume that the split is fair?" Gomorrah asked.

"*Of course. Most splits are even, 55–55, but in some situations the split will favor one Vanguard over another, if they did more to contribute.*"

"I'm not good at math," I said. "But I'm about a hundred and ten percent sure that that doesn't add up," I said.

"*In order to avoid penalizing Vanguards who wish to work together, the amount of points gained when there is more than one Vanguard is increased. It means that even if a Vanguard working on their own would gain more points, the amount isn't as significant.*"

"Huh," I said. "That's pretty neat."

"*Gomorrah gained some points from your bombing just now, on account of having helped you, and by providing cover fire when you returned. Not as many points as you made, but still a significant number.*"

Gomorrah nodded. "I'm satisfied with it. Should we keep moving? The fire looks like it's calming down. It's burning itself out."

"Right," I said. I took the lead again, enjoying the ability to breathe easily despite the warmth in the air. Still had a bit of an itch in my throat, though. Figured I'd have to ask Myalis for super-lozenges later.

As we moved down and deeper into the mines, I felt the temperature rising. There was a good reason for that.

"Well, shit," I said.

We stood next to the edge of a fire. Not a big roaring thing, but still a steadily burning fire that stretched out across the floor and onto the walls, and onto the ceiling, the stone lit up in a way that stone usually didn't.

The fire went on for a while, deeper into the mine than I could see. The air was thick, warm enough that it almost felt physical.

"The air is acidic. Your equipment should be able to resist most of it. It is settling down, though. Given a few more minutes the area should be merely impossibly hot."

"Nice," Gomorrah said.

I looked at her, then back at the fire. "Is this what you get off on?"

"Oh, shut up, you know my love for fire isn't sexual or anything. I just like fire. The way someone might like a good meal."

"Uh-huh," I said. I wasn't going to poke at that . . . not right then. Definitely later, though. It was good teasing material. "So how do we get past all that?"

"I can manage," Gomorrah said. "At least we know that the Antithesis are going to have a hard time with it. Though I'm sure they could adapt to it eventually."

"Let's get to killing them before that happens, yeah?"

She nodded, then raised her flamethrower and fired a wave of white flames ahead of us that clung to the ground and somehow pushed away the other fire before burning off with whitish smoke. Where the flames cleared, the floor was left smoking, but fireless.

"Ladies first," she said.

I eyed the ground, then poked it with the tip of my boot. "This all seems like it's really, needlessly, dangerous."

"So it should be right up your alley. Now come on." She stepped by me and fired her flamethrower at more of the ground. "Let's finish this."

CHAPTER SEVENTY-SEVEN

DEEPER

The Cleaners are a group of samurai that show up after the main thrust of an incursion is done, and after the hive is declared dead. Some of them are somewhat popular, but never as much as the more famous "main-line" samurai.

Their work is out of the limelight, cleaning up after the bigger, louder samurai, and ensuring that an incursion is well and truly dead.

—Excerpt from *The Cleaners*, a documentary, 2037

Gomorrah continued to clear the way, even though the fires were finally starting to die down. I think the lack of stuff to burn was finally calming things down.

It was still swelteringly hot, though, and I could feel myself sweating like mad in my suit. I kinda hoped that it was going to cool off soon, but the patches of ground that were still glowing-hot after the fire finally went out hinted that it wouldn't cool down that quickly.

"I think we're nearly there," Gomorrah said.

I looked around and vaguely recognized the area. It wasn't like there were road signs to follow, but I did have a mini-map of sorts and the passages seemed familiar. We were at an intersection away from the hive. "How do you figure?" I asked.

"I was looking at your progress on the map earlier; this is about where you stopped. In the next section, I mean," she said.

Made sense. "Aww, were you watching out for me?"

"More points if you leave to join the Lord."

I laughed. "Nice. Yeah, the next spot is where the hive was."

"Was? You sure it's entirely gone?"

"I hope it is," I said.

The room had been pretty large, and I wasn't sure if I'd put enough canister bombs to fully cover it. On our trek down, I could spot the places where the bombs' range didn't overlap—there wasn't usually much damage in those spots. A few Antithesis had tried to hide in there, but it looked like they'd been cooked anyway.

We reached the hive, and I cursed and brought my Icarus up.

Some of the trees remained, burning merrily and tossing up brackish smoke to the ceiling. Roots still covered the ground, oozing pus and whatever passed for blood in an Antithesis hive. The outer layer of the roots had been burned off, but the fire hadn't turned the whole place to ash.

The wrecked remains of one of my cat mecha lay nearby, crushed and broken into scrap.

"Nothing moving," Gomorrah said as she swept her gaze around. "This place is big, though."

"Not as cooked as I'd like," I said.

"I can fix that," she said. "Give me ten minutes or so."

"Yeah, actually, that's not a terrible idea." I pointed across the room. "That tunnel's the one I didn't explore. Some Model Thirteen spotted me when I was going down it. I tossed a bomb in, but I don't think it'll have burned too deep into it."

"Maybe we can head over that way, then burn the hive behind us," Gomorrah said.

I started to nod, then swore and jumped onto Gomorrah.

She gasped as I collided into her and sent both of us sprawling.

Then a Model Thirteen, or a third of one, crashed into the ground where we'd been standing. Its tentacles, mostly cut short and burned to nubs, whipped around and crashed into my back. Shields appeared and burst apart under the impact, and I was shoved down harder onto Gomorrah.

Then my cats opened fire, all three of them shooting at the Model Thirteen from three directions and gouging out the Antithesis' flesh.

I rolled off Gomorrah and scrambled for my gun, but it was already done, the alien slumped down, properly dead.

"Christ," Gomorrah said.

"Yeah," I agreed. I climbed to my feet, then stepped over to the Model Thirteen. It was riddled with holes, some of them bleeding quite a bit. It looked a little charred on the edges, but I guess it had slipped to somewhere safe . . . ish.

I kicked it with the tip of my boot, just to make sure.

"Where did that come from?" Gomorrah asked.

I looked up. "They can cling to ceilings, and there's smoke," I said. "Spooky fuckers."

Gomorrah grunted as she got to her feet. Her back-mounted flamethrowers deployed and started scanning the ceiling. "Good way of knowing that the hive isn't entirely dead. I don't envy the samurai that do cleanup work."

"Isn't that what we're doing?" I asked.

"Not quite. There are some that come in only once the hive is confirmed to be dead, just to root out pockets of Antithesis and burn any remains so they don't start growing again. It's not a job that pays very well, pointwise, but it's lower-risk and someone needs to do it."

"Let's make their jobs easier, then," I said. "Myalis, resonators, I need . . . eh, about six of them?"

The sound-based bombs acted pretty slowly, but they lasted a while. I tossed the first one across the room, then saw Gomorrah shaking her head.

"You okay?" I asked.

"Those things are noisy."

I paused, five more grenades tucked into the crook of my arm. "Want me to put these aside?

She shook her head. "Go ahead. I'm burning this place down either way."

I shrugged and tossed the last grenades around. They made the roots shiver, and I liked seeing all the trees start melting on the edges, turning into so much slush. Hopefully it would slush any still-living Antithesis, though it didn't seem to work as well on the trees and thicker roots.

"Let's keep moving," Gomorrah said.

I pointed to one of my cats, then ahead of us, letting it leap forward to take the lead.

"You brought cats here?" Gomorrah asked as she looked at the wreck of a cat mecha.

"Distraction," I said. "I made it out alive, so I guess it worked."

"I guess so. I'm starting to realize that we are woefully undertrained for this."

"Did you get any training at all?"

"No."

I nodded. "So we're not *under*trained, are we?"

"I don't think that's how it works."

Gomorrah and I crossed the hive, being careful as we stepped over roots and the charred husks of dead Antithesis. I had one scare when a Model Ten flopped out of a tree, looking halfway melted, but mostly unburned.

When we reached the entrance to that one tunnel I hadn't explored, Gomorrah turned and brought her flamethrower up. She fiddled with the controls, doing something with them for a moment before aiming up and at the far end of the room.

A stream of burning liquid came pouring out of the flamethrower, the spray widening and splashing the floor and bits of hive with whatever fire-juice Gomorrah was using.

The nun started moving her gun left and right, coating the far end of the room before she started to lower her aim to spread the joy around a little more. Like buttering a piece of toast, but not.

"Nice work," I said.

She nodded. "That'll do."

The room was a burning inferno, flames taller than I was hissing and spitting even as the remaining trees crumbled apart and the roots and plants clinging to the ceiling crashed down, sending waves of embers into the air.

Gomorrah's flamethrower used some weird shit to burn stuff. I wasn't going to poke at it, it was her area of expertise, and it certainly seemed to be working just fine.

I patted her on the shoulder and nodded deeper into the tunnel. "Let's go?"

"Certainly. Let's just hope this isn't a dead end."

"Uh," I said. "I didn't think of that."

"You're a bit of an idiot, you know?"

"I've been told as much, yeah," I said.

The nun sighed. "The maps say that this tunnel links back up to another; we should be able to loop back around closer to the entrance. That's if the mine didn't collapse anywhere."

We started down the shaft. After a dozen meters or so, the signs of there being a massive fire died down, the floor only streaked by fire here and there. A few bodies were left slumped on the ground—Antithesis that had tried to run?

I almost felt bad for them. It was a hell of a way to go.

The first sign that the hive might not be entirely dead were some small roots, with the start of those sacs that the models grew out of, sprouting all along their length. I traced the root down into the depths of the shaft and around a corner. "Fresh, or was that there before the hive went up?" I asked.

"Either way, it's trouble."

"Well, it's a good thing we're around."

"Because we can do our job?"

I grinned. "Nah, because I figure we're good at making trouble, especially to things that are already troublesome."

Gomorrah chuckled. "I don't think that's how any of that works, but sure. Let's finish all of this; I want a bath."

CHAPTER SEVENTY-EIGHT

M21

Now that we've seen everything these aliens can throw at us, I'm certain our brave soldiers can handle them!

—General Legstronger, USMC, 2026

"Wait, there's another bunch of them here," Gomorrah said.

I sighted down the length of my Icarus, then nodded. "Burn away."

We were some hundred meters down that last tunnel, and I was beginning to suspect that the hive was bigger than I'd thought. Sure, there were plenty of dead plants in that last big room, but the tunnel had dozens of roots crossing the floor, some of them splitting off and rejoining others seemingly at random.

We kept finding dead bodies at first, burnt Antithesis, but that stopped after a while.

The marks across the floor, as if bodies had been dragged off, weren't reassuring at all.

Gomorrah stepped up to a crack in the wall, one the roots were using to hang on and where a bunch of small seed pods were starting to grow. The aliens within weren't any bigger than a fetus and they wouldn't get any bigger as Gomorrah sprayed them with a shower of liquid fire. "That's that," she said.

I nodded. "Let's keep moving," I said.

A couple of my mecha-cats leapt ahead, scouting out the mine before we reached it, in case some Model Nine was pretending to be a rock or some piece of root or something.

"The roots are getting thicker," Gomorrah said.

I looked at them, then nodded. They'd started off no thicker than my wrist. Now they were around thigh-sized. "Yeah. I think maybe that hive I burned wasn't the main thing after all."

"If it wasn't, then the Antithesis learned how to excavate. The maps show that most of the rest of the mine is all tight passages. Though . . . there is an intersection coming up—should be a bit wider."

"Great," I said.

"It looks like Cause Player is down one of the other tunnels; a good distance away, but still coming closer. If he's killing everything there, then we'll only have a very short mineshaft left to explore, and it ends after about fifty meters."

So that was it. If we cleared out this last bit of tunnel, assuming we didn't miss anything, then everything in the mine would be cleared.

One of the mecha-cats rumbled, a low growl that had my hackles rising and my breath catching. I squinted ahead, and my sight zoomed in on . . . something.

The last intersection was wide enough to let one of the mining trucks turn without too much trouble, and they were big trucks.

Something was filling the intersection almost entirely, and it wasn't until we were a little closer that I realized that it was another hive, but one that was different.

Instead of a sort of sparse jungle with dozens of wide trees rising up and holding on to seed pods, this one was more like a massive lump on the ground. One covered in flowers, with a few thicker roots poking out of it that seemed to be gestating new models even as we approached, but still, just a big lump.

"Funky," I said.

"Should we burn it?" Gomorrah asked.

"What kind of question is that?" I asked.

"Well, not burning it might make it easier to check out the last tunnel."

That was a fair point. We hadn't stopped walking and were within a dozen meters of the edge of the room when our conversation was interrupted.

"Careful."

I stopped dead, hands tightening over my Icarus and eyes scanning everything, ceiling included. "What is it?" I asked. Myalis rarely warned me about stuff. She was more of a "let her figure it out when it hurts her" kind of person.

"That's the egg incubator for a Model Twenty-One."

It felt as if my mouth went dry all of a sudden. "The bigger the number, the more fucky the alien, right?"

"As a general rule, yes. Model Twenty-Ones are a stealth model."

"How big are we talking about here?" I asked. I was scanning the rocks and ground, looking for anything that stood out, anything that could be a Model Nine but worse.

Approximately two meters long, one tall. Six-legged, with each limb having a gripping hand. They have segmented plates over their body that are made of a heavy iron-rich compound. Six hearts, two brains. Relatively heavy, but also very fast. Favors close-quarters combat."

"Cat," Gomorrah said. Something in her tone had me looking out the same way she was.

I couldn't see it at first. It was just a small haze in the air, barely visible against the rest. Maybe in full daylight, when I wasn't looking through the color-shifted night vision of my mask.

As it was, I only saw the thing when it started charging at us. "Shit!" I screamed as I raised my Icarus. I fired at it, then cursed again when the first shots went wide and exploded in the plants and muck behind what had to be the Model Twenty-One.

Gomorrah set her legs and sprayed a jet of fire ahead of us, only to have to juke it to the side as the alien jumped to the wall, and then it faded from there and we both stopped firing.

"Where is it?" I asked.

I had seen it hit the wall; there were some marks left from the impact, and then, nothing. "Teleport?"

"Model Twenty-Ones cannot teleport."

"That's some worrying fucking phrasing there, Myalis," I hissed.

"Neither of you are ready to face off against any Antithesis model above Twenty. I would suggest a retreat, but the Model Twenty-One is aware of you. It seems small, recently birthed. It will be relatively weak."

"Can they bur—"

I felt something shift behind me, and I spun just in time to see Gomorrah being flung back, bending almost double in midair as she flew. Her flamethrower hovered in the air for a moment, partially distorted before something crushed it as if it were little more than a soda can.

I spun while firing and backed up.

I only just saw the blur of a large limb swiping out at me and batting my gun aside. A claw scraped across my cybernetic arm.

Stumbling back, I tried to make room to bring my launcher up. Being in the AOE be damned, I wanted the fucker dead. He'd hurt Gomorrah!

Another swipe, and this time my Icarus was launched across the tunnel.

I saw dark eyes. Bored, placid eyes, like a cow in one of those anti-vegan commercials, not the eyes of a predator trying to kill me—not that it mattered at all.

It launched itself at me, mouth wide and filled with serrated teeth.

Then one of my mecha-cats chomped down over its neck and dragged it aside, enough that I was only tossed aside when it struck out with one of its rear limbs.

I landed in a roll and got back to my feet. All three mecha-cats were on it, two of them chomping and clawing at the monster even as they fired into it, point-blank. The third was farther back, guns rattling and poking little holes into the Model Twenty-One's sides that didn't seem to be nearly as deep as I wanted.

Climbing to one knee, I let my back-mounted guns deploy even as I turned my invisibility back on. Leaving it off to make Gomorrah comfortable had been something of a mistake.

My railgun fired.

I stared, flummoxed, as the ceiling exploded. There was a vague slice cut into the air, tracing the path the round had taken. It struck the alien on one of its broad shoulder plates, then went up and hit the ceiling where stone was crumbling down.

The fucker was tough enough to make railgun rounds bounce?

The Model Twenty-One grabbed one of my mecha from off of its shoulder and threw it to the ground, then pinned the mecha down with a clawed hand, grabbed it by the middle with its jaw, and pulled.

I winced as the mecha was torn in half. Its guns never stopped firing into the monster, not until it stomped them down.

Two sputtering hoses of fire hissed through the air and covered the Model Twenty-One from top to bottom. "That . . . that hurt," Gomorrah said.

I laughed, relieved, but I had to focus.

The Model turned toward Gomorrah, evidently pissed, and its muscles bunched to jump.

I yanked my Claw out, aimed at its rear leg, and fired.

The Model Twenty-One launched itself at Gomorrah, but it was a weak, abortive jump, and the nun rolled aside.

It was starting to look worse for wear, and I was more than pleased to help it along, firing every last round from my Claw into its flank.

Its skin peeled off, and it shook itself, molting in the space of a few seconds and revealing skin so dark it was hard to tell where the monster ended and the tunnel behind it started.

I swore.

I didn't know what kind of bullshit this monster in particular was up to, but in my book, anything that had been shot that much should have lain down and died already.

"Myalis, I need a bomb."

CHAPTER SEVENTY-NINE

BOSS FIGHT

Do not underestimate the Antithesis. Just because a model's number is twice as high doesn't mean it will only be twice as likely to kill you.
—Tiny, in a street interview, 2049

The trick was picking the right sort of bomb. Nothing that would kill Gomorrah and me, that was a given, and something that would still put the Model Twenty-One down.

It was injured. The mecha-cats had peppered it with little holes, none that seemed too deep, but in spots where their fire had been concentrated, the alien's skin looked like it had been assaulted by a cheese grater. Gomorrah's fire blackened some of its skin, and I was sure that emptying every round from my Claw into its flank had done nasty things to its musculature.

I'm afraid there's nothing I can give you that will kill the Model Twenty-One instantly without risking yourself or Vanguard Gomorrah.

"Shit," I swore. "Noise grenades."

A grenade appeared in the air next to me and I snapped it out of the air. I didn't have to look to pull the tab on it and fling it under the Model Twenty-One. Almost as soon as the grenade landed it started to make its keening howl.

The Model Twenty-One shook its overly large head, its focus moving away from Gomorrah, who was busy backing up, and to the ground.

A leg stomped down on the grenade, crushing it and killing its noise with a squawk.

I didn't know if the resonator had actually done anything in those few seconds, but if it crushed it, then it didn't like it.

"Another," I muttered as I started to run. I wanted to keep behind the monster. Hopefully it wouldn't notice me tossing the grenades by its feet.

The Model Twenty-One was even faster to destroy the next one.

"Another," I said. "And then give me something that'll blow up in its face."

I tossed the next resonator behind it, and the alien spun and crushed it faster than I could blink. The next grenade clattered by its feet, much quieter.

It stomped on it all the same.

I flung an arm over my face as an explosive blast roared past me.

The Model Twenty-One stumbled to the side, its front looking even worse, with its skin blackened and an entire leg missing from the joint down. Blackish blood was sloping down onto the ground in a rapid pitter-patter beat.

It raised its head, one eye partially shut, and looked right at me.

"Ah, shit," I said.

I tucked my Claw away and grabbed my Trench Maker even as I started running again. My back-mounted guns swiveled around and started to fire at it. The plasma caster didn't seem to do much at all, only leaving glowing welts in its thick hide, but my railgun's next round didn't bounce. It burrowed into the monster's chest, leaving a finger-sized hole of glowing flesh where it had passed.

It still wasn't dead, though.

A wash of fire shoved the Model Twenty-One to the side, its claws scraping against the ground for purchase.

"Thanks!" I shouted as I tried to run faster. I'd seen it wreck one of my mecha, and I was pretty sure they were tougher than I was.

"It's refusing to burn," Gomorrah said. She sounded very insulted about it.

I looked over my shoulder and choked on a curse. The Model Twenty-One was very much on fire now. Gomorrah kept adding to it so that its entire body was covered in flames. It only made it scarier, though. What kind of monster could ignore being set on fire so easily?

My remaining mecha-cat kept its distance, still firing in bursts at where I suspected the alien was weaker.

It skidded past me and bumped into one of the walls.

I turned and aimed my Trench Maker at it, then fired over and over again until I clicked empty.

The bastard barely seemed to notice.

Another railgun round, and another hole punched into it, but there was no explosion in the wall behind it. The round had stayed lodged somewhere in all of its plant-meat. Real tough plant-meat.

"Cat, get down!"

I glanced over to Gomorrah, then stared for all of a moment before jumping as far the fuck away as I could.

Gomorrah had bought herself a new gun.

It was a cumbersome-looking thing, all angular and flat-sided, with cross-shaped cutouts and golden trim over flat black plates. She held it on her shoulder, the barrel—wider than my fist—currently pointing at the Model Twenty-One.

"May God have mercy on you, because I'm fresh out."

I didn't have time to tell her that she sounded cheesy as fuck before she fired, and a gray blur shot out of the launcher and struck the Model Twenty-One.

I was expecting heat.

I wasn't disappointed.

For a moment, all I could focus on was putting more room between myself and whatever the fuck Gomorrah had just fired at that alien.

It wasn't heat, it was something beyond that. My augs started to flicker, warning about my armor being strained, my coat being unable to function at the current temperatures, and that my mask was switching to tanked oxygen because it couldn't filter anything from the air.

I stumbled ahead, and then when I had my feet under me I ran until the heat only felt like a bonfire at my back.

Slowing down, I turned and winced until my mask's visor occluded the part of the tunnel the Model Twenty-One was in.

Gomorrah was walking over to me, her launcher lowered even as the mineshaft behind her glowed like an inferno.

The Model Twenty-One was still moving.

Oh, it wasn't going to move for long, but the thing was crawling its way toward us, even as its sides melted and its limbs came apart one by one.

"What was that?" I asked as Gomorrah came closer.

"That was a very expensive thermate warhead," Gomorrah said. "Three thousand degrees Celsius on the edges, a whole lot hotter in the middle."

She sounded very, very smug.

"Well, it worked," I said.

The Model Twenty-One was still struggling, but it was weak, its remaining limbs barely able to pull it forward.

"Damn, that thing is tough," I said.

Gomorrah lowered her launcher. "Yeah. I knew the higher-numbered models were going to be a challenge, but this is more than I thought."

"That Model Twenty-One was approximately twenty percent smaller than average, and its reaction times were slower than usual. It's very likely that it was born before the end of its incubation period because of the strain on the hive."

So the real thing would be tougher. "And it's a stealth model," I said.

"It's a unit that usually fights as a pack."

I tilted my head left and right, to crack my neck. "Well, then. That's just plain terrifying."

"Agreed," Gomorrah said.

The heat had faded some, and the glowing ball of fire was starting to break up, sending showers of sparks hissing through the air around it with firecracker pops. Then it gradually sank into the stone around it.

"Damn," I repeated.

"We should move on, burn the rest of the hive out and get out of here," Gomorrah said.

"I could use a break. Maybe a nice nap. Something to drink . . ." I considered what else to add to my list. "A hug from Lucy?"

"I think we could both use that," Gomorrah agreed absently.

I shot her a look.

"Shall we get going?" she asked before heading out.

"Hey, wait! Lucy's hugs are mine! I'm not sharing!"

"What are you on about, Cat? Can't you take anything seriously for a minute or two?"

We went the long way around the Model Twenty-One. It wasn't moving anymore, but that didn't stop me from reloading my Claw and then emptying it into the bigger chunks of its body, just in case. If there was ever anything that deserved to be double-tapped, it was that heap of trouble.

"I didn't think the models past Twenty would be that, uh, insane," I said. "Is it dead?"

"We got the points for it," Gomorrah confirmed.

"Models above Twenty make up nearly half of all Antithesis forces. If you were to graph the distribution of models out, it would appear as a near-exponential decrease, with the median of models being between the Model Twenties and Thirties."

"And they get worse as they get bigger numbers?" I asked.

Generally speaking, yes. Though there are of course utility models across the scale. Most models past Thirty aren't necessarily terrestrial.

"Okay," I said. I could have an existential crisis about that later.

I found my Icarus, the gun scuffed and battered, but still functional-looking, and I saw that Gomorrah paused to mourn over her Archangel's Kiss. Figured we'd made enough points to buy another, but I didn't begrudge her taking some time for that.

I had one mecha-cat left, the one that held on to my old helmet still. "Tough one, aren't you?" I said. "Let's hope we won't be putting that toughness to the test anymore."

CHAPTER EIGHTY

BURNING AWAY

The Model Twenty-One is a fast-moving, ground-locked Antithesis unit commonly found on the fringes of the territory of an incursion that has been entrenched for any period over seventy-two hours. They are usually found in packs of three to five, often accompanied by groups of Model Threes.

They are, by nature, ambush predators and scouts for bigger, stronger units, but do not underestimate them on account of their relatively small size. They earn their position in the Twenty-ranks.

—*The Family's Guide to the Enemy*—Ver. 4.8496, 2057

"I think that's it," I said as I took a last look around.

The tunnel leading off that last hive-infested intersection didn't have much to it except some stone walls and another one of those big mining rigs. A few roots were reaching into the room, but they didn't get too far down. Gomorrah made a point of burning them on the way past, leaving the corridor behind us to fill with noxious fumes and smoke.

"Looks like it," Gomorrah said.

I nodded. "Well, I'm ready to get the fuck out of these tunnels," I said. "Maybe see some sky, a few clouds. You know, outside stuff?"

"Breathe in the smog and stretch under the radiation-heavy sunlight?" Gomorrah asked. She looked around at the mineshaft we were in. "Yeah, I think that would be nice."

I couldn't help but glance up at the ceiling. It was easy to ignore that there were several hundred thousand tons of earth above that could come crashing down at any moment. All the bombs and such we'd been using probably didn't do anything to help the local geological stability.

"Let's," I said before I took off back toward the intersection.

Gomorrah had emptied both of her shoulder-mounted launchers at the big egg sac that had produced the Model Twenty-One. It meant that I had to let her carve out a path from the tunnel we were in back to the other passage we hadn't taken over, but that wasn't a big deal.

I was pretty happy with seeing the hive chunk on fire.

Once we were past that, it was straight down a long tunnel where a few roots had gone questing along the floor, but none of them reached all that far.

"One moment," Gomorrah said.

I looked around, making sure there wasn't anything but Gomorrah, myself, and my remaining cat mecha around. Unless there was something else and it was invisible.

Invisible enemies were entirely unfair.

"What are you doing?" I asked when I saw her head bowed for a moment. "Is it prayer time?"

"If it were, your interrupting would be rude," she said. Her hand opened by her side, and a container appeared just above it. "Firebomb. Nothing too spectacular."

She pulled her rocket launcher from her shoulder and shoved the container into an opening in its side.

"I'll be down that way," I said with a vague gesture in the direction opposite the one she was going to burn.

Gomorrah sniffed and raised the launcher to her shoulder just as I started to jog away.

The wash of heat was nothing like the one with her plasma ball nightmare thing, but I still felt it, and it did a number on what was left of the hive, even though it had been on fire already.

No such thing as too much fire in the eyes of my favorite nun.

"That's better," she said as she rejoined me. "I'm liking the range of this thing."

"Not standing right next to the hot death fire is . . . a good idea?" I asked, trying to sound as innocent as possible.

The nun shook her head. "It's not as . . . good when you can't see the impact of your fire on your enemies."

"Wow," I said. "I know this is super-hypocritical, but have you considered therapy? Your . . . pyrophilia can't be healthy."

"Did you just make up a new word for a sexual orientation?" she asked.

"A new word for *your* sexual orientation. I'm clever. I've heard a few words in Latin before."

"Both 'pyro' and 'philia' are Greek, you . . . God wasn't generous when handing out your portion of intelligence."

I laughed. "First time I've been called stupid that way."

"But certainly not the first time in general."

"Nah, I had my first time a long while ago."

She sighed. "And we're back to innuendo."

I couldn't help but grin. I hadn't noticed all the tension from running around and being sneaky piling up on my shoulders, but now that it was all over—or at least, I hoped it was—the tension was drifting off. It probably made things feel funnier than they really were.

"Heat signature out ahead," Gomorrah said.

I pulled my launcher up and flicked my coat's invisibility back on at the same moment. The coat had plenty of time to cool down.

We waited for a moment, and then Gomorrah shook her head. "It's Cause Player. I'm texting him, I don't need to be shot today."

I lowered my gun. Maybe it was a bit too soon to let all of the tension go.

"All right, command, it seems that we have some allies up ahead," I heard Cause Player say. His steps were surprisingly soft. I'd barely heard them. Or maybe I was just bad at paying attention to that kind of thing.

I tugged my cloak's hood up and tucked my launcher between my cloak and coat, where it wouldn't be visible. If Lucy was watching, I didn't need her thinking I was putting myself at any sort of undue risk.

"Hello, Cause Player!" Gomorrah called out.

"I think, Chat, that we're going to be breaking character for a moment," Cause Player said. He walked around a slight curve in the tunnel ahead, still in his green armor, and with a huge, very glowy gun in hand. "Hello, Gomorrah," he said.

Gomorrah nodded. "How did the clearing go? And are you still live?"

I started walking around the two, keeping close to the walls and walking at an angle so that Cause Player wouldn't notice the few bits of me not covered with my cloak. I wasn't going too far with it—I was sure he would see me if he was paying attention.

But he wasn't.

"We are! I hope you don't mind."

"I don't," Gomorrah said.

I saw Cause Player glancing around before spotting me, likely through his augs.

By then, I was already behind him, right where his little livestream camera was floating.

I snapped it out of the air, the little device buzzing and humming in place, its little wings beating against my grip until I brought it around and had it face me. I turned visible again.

"Hi, Lucy!" I said with a wave.

Behind me, Cause Player jumped about three feet into the air and spun around.

Did I spook him?

"Yo!" I said before pointing to his camera. "Hope you don't mind? I was just saying hi to my girl."

"I didn't see you there," he said.

"You should be more careful, then. We've got Model Nines, and we met a Model Twenty-One. Mean bastard. Broke some of my cat mecha." I let go of the camera and it buzzed away from me, almost as if the little thing was insulted that I'd grabbed it.

"A Model Twenty-One, here?"

"A baby one," I said. "Still nasty, though."

He shook his head. "That's unexpected. The hive here wasn't very old."

"It was specialized, though," Gomorrah said. "A stealth model for a stealth hive."

"Did you clear everything on the way here?" I asked.

Cause Player nodded. "Every shaft and side passage, even a few that weren't on the map. Found a few little groups of Antithesis, but the biggest challenge was a pair of Model Thirteens that came out of nowhere. Made for a nice boss-fight, I think."

"Cool," I said. "Does that mean we're done here?"

"I guess so," Gomorrah said. "What's the fastest way out of here?"

"Don't we need to leave from the same hole we came in? Your car's parked there."

Gomorrah shook her head. "The Fury can pilot itself to wherever I want. I wouldn't drive it down these shafts, but otherwise, any exit would do."

"A profitable afternoon," Cause Player said. "A few points, some B-roll footage. I'll edit everything later to make it more seamless before posting it."

"Aren't you live right now?" I asked.

"Well, yes, but that doesn't compare to a well-edited fight scene and a tighter storyline. The people who watch it live do it because it's fun to see the behind-the-scenes stuff."

"Huh," I said. Not my cup of whatever. "Right, should we get going, then?"

With all that said and done, we finally headed back, retracing Cause Player's steps. He spoke with Gomorrah for a bit. Apparently he knew some of the cleanup samurai who'd come in later to make damned sure that nothing of the hive was left. I had to wonder how much the hive could regrow from the few bits left over in just one night.

The answer was probably too damned much.

But all of that was someone else's problem for now.

"Myalis," I asked, my voice pitched low. "How many points did we manage to make?"

Current Point Total:

12,471

I tripped over nothing.

"Holy crap!"

EPILOGUE

I couldn't help the smug grin as Gomorrah drove the Fury around the Black Bear Mining Corporation's headquarters, then found a spot to land.

There were people in the spot Gomorrah chose. A few soldiers sitting on crates and chatting. At least until they saw the car coming down and started to drag things out of Gomorrah's way.

"The job's not done," Gomorrah said as she pulled on some lever-thing in the middle of the dash with a satisfying clunk. I think that put the car in park or something. I needed to take a bit and learn how to drive one day.

"This is the boring part," Cause Player said from where he was squeezed in the back seat. He opened the door and contorted his way out.

"What bit?" I asked.

"Where we ask the corporation some difficult questions about why their maps didn't match up exactly, and where we debrief the army about what to expect," Gomorrah said.

I felt my grin fading a little. "Can I take the third option?" I asked.

"We also need to do a quick patrol of the town, but I think Cause Player's already trying to be the one to do that," Gomorrah added.

"Can't we just go home and rejoice in our huge winnings?"

"Come on, out of the car, you whiner."

I laughed as I stepped out of the Fury, then stood up and stretched. The day was turning to evening pretty quickly. I wasn't sure how much time we'd spent underground, but I was pretty happy that we weren't under there anymore. Open air felt great.

"Do you want to take care of the army, or the corp?" Gomorrah asked.

"Can't our AI do both?"

The nun shrugged. "They can help, but having someone there does a lot more to help."

"We didn't need to do any of this last time," I said.

"Last time, we were both still just small-fry. There were other, more impo— Wait."

I paused in my stretching and turned around to see that Gomorrah was staring at the ground, a patch that had nothing of interest on it.

"You okay?" I asked.

She raised a hand in a "one moment" gesture.

I waited. "Anything going on?" I muttered, too quiet for Gomorrah to hear.

Nothing noticeable. The army has set up a cordon around the town and have begun inspecting it street by street. A second group is breaking into homes to ensure that they are clear of Antithesis presence. They are being rather polite about it. Senior management have been evacuated from the town, along with the relatives of upper-echelon corporate employees.

"Typical," I muttered.

The Family has sent a message informing every Vanguard in the region that a team of liquidators is going to arrive before sunrise to inspect the mine. A few corporate clearing groups are moving to the region as well.

That was different. I didn't envy anyone dealing with Antithesis without someone like Myalis to bail them out. "How do they make money?" I asked.

They capture models and samples of Antithesis flesh, as well as collecting data for resale. It is not a very profitable endeavor, but there is a slim but noticeable profit margin. Mostly, those they hire are indentured to the company in one way or another.

"Ah," I said. If you didn't need to pay people to do work, then you could make a nice profit on that work, I imagined.

"God damn it," Gomorrah swore.

I turned to her in time to see her move to the back of the Fury and pop open the trunk. She practically threw my surviving mecha-cat out, then my Whisper and my climbing gear. "You okay?" I asked.

"I need to go," she said as she slid into her car.

"Uh, in a hurry?" I guessed while leaning into the passenger side of the Fury.

She was already flicking switches on the dash. "Yes."

"This isn't just some way of getting out of doing work, is it?" I asked.

She looked at me, expressionless mask locked in place and staring at me for a few long seconds. "No, Cat, this isn't that. I need to go—something's come up. I . . . I don't think I need help, all right?"

"All right," I said. "But if you do need help, I'm here, okay? You've helped me plenty; the least I can do is return the favor."

"Yeah . . . thanks."

I backed up as Fury lifted off, aimed up, then shot into the sky with enough force that I had to take a step back or be bowled over by all the wind.

Something was definitely up.

I wanted to get back home, maybe relax with Lucy as a reward for a job well done, but I had a feeling in the pit of my stomach that things wouldn't be that simple.

Also, she'd just left me stranded in Black Bear.

"Crap, I'm actually going to have to work."

ABOUT THE AUTHOR

RavensDagger is a Canadian writer who wants to make people smile. The best way to do that, he has found, is by pecking away at the keyboard and hoping for the best.

Podium
DISCOVER
STORIES UNBOUND
PodiumAudio.com